THE MAVERICK & MISS MILLER

MATCHMAKER MISCHIEF

MARIE PATRICK

The Maverick & Mrs. Miller 2024 © Marie Patrick

Cover art by Dar Albert, Wicked Smart Designs

Published by Oliver-Heber Books

0 9 8 7 6 5 4 3 2 1

CHAPTER 1

What a mess!

Everleigh Miller drew in a deep breath and let it out slowly as her gaze swept the patio, the garden, and expanse of lush green lawn, her pride and joy. It was quiet now, the dozens of tables set up on the freshly mowed grass empty, the wedding guests having gone home, or in the case of the ranch hands, gone back to work, which never ceased on a successful ranch like Montaña del Trueno. Lucy, the bride—the youngest of her sister's children and the only girl—and groom were on their way to Serenity to start their new life together.

"It was a lovely wedding. Lucy looked so beautiful." Hilde picked up a platter of leftover ribs from the table and looked at her.

"Yes, it was and yes, she did," Evie agreed, as her focus switched from the mess to Hilde, who had accompanied her to the ranch twenty years ago when she'd been given the honor of raising Regina's children. She cringed a little bit inside, aware this was just the beginning of their conversation, knowing almost exactly the argument Hilde would give, since she had no issue with expressing her opinions, which she did quite often, as unwelcome as they might be.

"You have fulfilled your obligation to your sister," she insisted. "Her children are all grown and married now. It's your turn, I think, ja?" Funny how this particular subject always made Hilde's accent become stronger, despite the fact she'd left her native Germany over forty years ago.

"My turn? For what?" Evie licked a bit of frosting off her finger, then picked up the plate holding the remains of one of the four wedding cakes; she'd send it out to the bunkhouse later for the ranch hands to enjoy, though she knew each and every one of her *vaqueros* had eaten well at the party. She'd heard the groans of over-stuffed bellies and sighs of satisfaction.

Hilde chuckled in her deep guttural way. "Romance. Love. Someone of your own," Hilde called after her.

Evie scoffed as she strode under the awning that shaded this part of the patio and headed toward the kitchen door. "I had that once. It didn't work."

"Ja, you did, but the good Marshal has been gone a long time and you've been alone since he passed." Hilde marched past her, her skirts twitching as she did so. Evie hid her grin. Hilde wouldn't give up, which was one of the reasons she loved her so much.

She laid the cake platter on the table in the big kitchen and just stood there for a moment, surveying the mess she and her companions would spend the next few hours cleaning. Still, despite the chaos and disorder, this room was her favorite. She'd spent many happy hours here, learning to cook, sharing meals with the children, holding hands with Marshal Tom Gray and planning their future. They were to be married until the Good Lord took him home by way of a bullet.

They would have had a good life if he had lived. Instead, she had concentrated on raising Regina's children and building

Montaña del Trueno into one of the most successful ranches in New Mexico.

She pushed thoughts of Tom and what might have been away, and focused on the here and now. Glancing toward the sink, she saw Hilde leaning against the porcelain tub, her graying hair braided into its usual coronet atop her head. The expression on her face was one she knew well—mouth set in a grim line, hazel eyes, more green than brown, steady on her. There would be no reprieve. Their conversation was far from over.

"I'm only looking out for you, *liebchen*."

Evie squelched a groan. Hilde would say what she had to say, whether or not Evie wanted to hear it.

"I think it's time you were happy."

She held up her hand to stop the conversation, then turned on her heel and fled outside to her sanctuary of growing things, ignoring the looks on her friends Felicity and Marisol's faces as she passed them, their arms full of more dishes needing to be washed. She let out a sigh as her hand gripped the lattice arbor that had served as the altar for the wedding ceremony. Roses, in full bloom, their fragrance scenting the air, clung to the wooden frame, the red, pink, and yellow blossoms and verdant green leaves a sharp contrast to the pristine white bunting woven between the slats.

She was happy, wasn't she? She didn't need a man for that. She'd done quite well without one all these years. It would have been a different story if Tom had lived, but he hadn't.

She turned away from the arbor to continue cleaning and came face-to-face with "Uncle" Charley, a dear friend of her late mother and her unofficial uncle. He and his wife, Felicity, would be staying at the ranch for as long as they wanted, now that he had decided to retire. His last official act as a judge had been presiding over Lucy's marriage to Ben Hart. "It was a fine wedding and a heck of a party," Charley said.

"Yes, it was." She smiled at the man she'd known all her life as she walked to one of the nearby tables set up on the lawn. "Thank you for officiating."

"My pleasure. I wouldn't have missed it for the world." He followed her, then started gathering plates from the table, but his focus was on her.

She could tell just from the expression on his face he had more to say. "What?"

"I'm sorry he didn't show up."

Evie stiffened, her muscles tensing as she grabbed a plate, adding it to the stack in his hands. "Who? My father?"

He nodded, sadness and understanding in his eyes.

She shrugged, as if it didn't matter, though it did. The Honorable Reginald Miller hadn't come, though she had invited him. She hadn't expected he would—he hadn't showed up for the weddings of his grandsons—but she still had to try. It would have been nice for him to acknowledge his grandchildren for once. Or her, for that matter, though he had disowned her when she left San Francisco and came to Montaña del Trueno to raise Regina's sons and daughter, just as he had disowned Regina when she married Javier Silva against his demands all those years ago.

"I saw him before Felicity and I came here. Tried to convince him to come, but…" A flush stole over his face and his grip tightened on the stack of plates in his hand. "He's a hard man, Evie. Still angry with you after all these years."

"I know. He'll never forgive me. I disobeyed him. I went against his dictates, choosing to honor Regina's request instead of his." She remembered like it was yesterday, that awful day Uncle Charley had delivered the news her sister had died and she had been named guardian for Regina's children, remembered the terrible things her father had yelled at her, disparaging both her and Regina. "But it's all right. He doesn't have to forgive me. I made my decision and it was the right one. I wouldn't change a thing. It's just a shame he missed out on—" She spread her arms wide, encompassing everything. "—all this and the fine people his grandchildren have become."

He shook his head, his eyes glowing with affection. "You're a good woman, Evie. Not everyone would have walked away from their life and home and done what you did, and I, for one, am proud of you." He gestured with the plates in his hands. "I'll just bring these into the house."

And with those words, he turned away and strode toward the kitchen. She watched him go, noticing the heaviness in his step, realizing how much she loved him—like the father she wished she had. He and Felicity had stood behind her decision, for good or bad. She grabbed a handful of silverware, but her thoughts weren't on her task. She'd spoken the truth. She wouldn't have changed a thing. Though it had been difficult at times, especially in the beginning, she had enjoyed every moment of raising her sister's children and turning Montaña del Trueno into a profitable ranch anyone would be proud to own. Still, after all this time, she wished circumstances had been different, wished Regina and Javier were here to share all this with her. "Ah, Gina, why did you have to die?"

"*Tia* Evie? Who are you talking to?"

Recognizing the voice of her niece, she schooled her features to hide her emotions, and turned away from the table, silverware clutched in her hand. Lucy stood before her, resplendent in her traveling ensemble of green and gold, her long, deep-brown hair pulled away from her face in an intricate style, reminding her so much of her mother when Regina was young.

"What are you doing back here, *mi corazón*? I thought you'd left already."

She came forward and grasped Evie's hand, happiness glowing on her face. And why wouldn't she be happy? Just a few hours ago she'd married the man she loved since she was a child.

"We did," Lucy said, "but we turned around. I couldn't leave without thanking you."

"Thanking me? For what?"

Lucy grinned, though there was something a little odd about her smile—like she had a secret she couldn't wait to tell. "For the beautiful wedding and your generous gift. Ben and I are thrilled with the house in Serenity." She paused, her mocha brown eyes shiny with tears. "But mostly, I thank you for loving me. I don't remember Mama. I was so very young when she died, but you… you have always been there for me, loved me even when I was unlovable…you loved all of us, and I just wanted you to know how grateful I am. We all are. You're the best mother a woman could ever have." She wrapped her arms around her. "I love you, *Tia* Evie."

Evie sniffed back the sudden onslaught of tears, though the truth was those tears hadn't been very far away and hugged her. "I love you, too, *mi dulce angel*." She released her and coughed to hide the tightness in her throat. "Now, go, before I make a complete fool of myself."

Lucy kissed her cheek, then turned quickly and ran toward her husband waiting at the edge of the garden, near the gate. She waved once, then called out, words Evie couldn't quite make out, something about enjoying a gift and then she laughed. There was no denying the happiness on Lucy's face as she linked her arm through Ben's, and they disappeared around the side of the house.

Evie stood there, emotion tightening her throat, her gaze focused on the spot she'd last seen them, then turned her attention back to the mess that wouldn't clean itself. She dropped the silverware on the table, pulled a handkerchief from the sleeve of her dress where it met her wrist, and dabbed at her eyes, but she still smiled. Lucy was proof she'd done a good job after all, despite her doubts. The children had been so young when she'd first come to the ranch. They'd all grown to be responsible, intelligent adults. They knew they'd been loved. She couldn't ask for more.

She piled more plates into a stack, added a handful of silverware, and brought everything into the house. She scraped the remnants of food into the slop bucket for the pigs before placing the dishes into the sink full of soapy water.

Hilde, elbows deep in that soapy water, turned to glance at her and opened her mouth. "I meant what I said, Evie. You should find someone of your own."

"I'm done talking about it, Hilde."

"But—"

"No. I am fine as I am. I'm happy. In truth, I'm not interested in finding a husband, but if it's fated for me to marry, then I will. In the meantime, I'd appreciate it if you'd stop pestering me about it." She leaned over and kissed the woman on the cheek. "I know you're looking out for me. I know you want me to be as happy as you and Antonio are. And I love you for it, but I've accepted the fact that what you have may not be in the cards for me. And I'm not willing to gamble my heart again."

Before Hilde could say another word, Evie fled the kitchen and headed back outside, where there was still more to be done. Feeding the nearly one hundred people had taken days to prepare and necessitated borrowing glasses, silverware, and the like from her friends.

She piled more plates one on top of the other, turned to head back into the house, and stopped.

A man—a complete stranger—stood not twenty feet from her, hat in hand—the most handsome man she'd ever seen. Black hair, though there was gray at his temples, which looked like reflected hints of polished silver beneath the sun's glare. He was tall, too, much taller than her five-foot seven-inch frame. And for a moment, she forgot how to breathe. Indeed, she couldn't even blink. Afraid she might drop the stack of dishes, she clenched her hands, gripping the plates tightly.

Her mouth opened, but no words issued forth, like they were stuck in her throat—her suddenly dry throat.

He walked toward her. Well, not walked, but sort of sauntered, like he hadn't a care in the world, his long legs eating up the ground between them in short order. Startling amber eyes captured her attention. And then he smiled.

Her lungs figured out how to function as she drew in air. His smile was, in no uncertain terms, devastating.

"I rang the bell at the front door, but no one answered." His voice, deep and rich, rumbled through her like thunder in the distance. "I'm looking for Everleigh Miller."

She swallowed—hard—and finally found her voice. "I'm Evie Miller. How can I help you?"

He tilted his head as his gaze roamed over her face. She felt the heat of that gaze all the way to her toes. It warmed her from the inside out, making her fingers tingle with the urge to touch his handsome features. No one had looked at her that way in an awfully long time.

For as much as she denied it and didn't think it would happen for her, she did want romance. And passion. Someone to spend the rest of her life with.

The man's gaze drifted to the rose arbor and the festive bunting fluttering in the breeze, then down at the wedding cake still on the table, that devastating smile never leaving his face. "Well, for starters, you can tell me that I didn't miss our wedding."

She blinked, confusion running rampant in her brain. "I'm afraid I don't understand. Who are you?"

"Jake. Jake Hannigan."

His warm amber gaze met hers and locked. She couldn't turn away. She'd never heard the name before, she was sure of it. And she'd never met him. She would have remembered. How could one forget a smile like that? "Forgive me, please, but I'm confused. Did you say 'our' wedding?"

"I did."

Evie opened her mouth, but before she could say a word, he asked, "You are Everleigh Miller, correct?"

"I am."

"And you were not expecting me?"

"No, I'm afraid not."

Bewilderment clouded his handsome face and those eyes that seemed to see into her soul. He let out a sigh and then he smiled, a bit impishly. "Well, this is awkward."

"Yes, it is." She put the plates on the table to stop the cramping in her fingers from holding them so tightly. "Perhaps, you can tell me why you think I would be expecting you. And why you think we are to be married."

"The advertisement in the newspaper?"

She shook her head, still thoroughly baffled. "I didn't place any advertisements in the newspaper. And the only reason I would place one is to hire ranch hands, but I'm not looking for any at the moment." He didn't seem like a man who liked getting dirty, not in the fancy duds he was wearing—blackest black trousers and suit jacket, gold brocade vest, and pristine white shirt. Evie knew excellent quality clothing when she saw it, and what he wore did not belong to a *vaquero*.

He flashed a self-confident grin and her insides turned to mush. "Not a ranch hand. A husband."

"A husband?" she repeated, taken aback by the statement. "There must be some mistake. I would never do something like that."

"But you did." He reached out and gently rubbed his thumb against her cheek, causing an immediate reaction she hadn't expected, nor experienced before. Her stomach quivered and her knees grew weak even as blood rushed to her face.

Humor twinkled in his eyes. "You had frosting on your face."

Startled by the gentleness of his touch and the rush of pleasure as well as embarrassment coursing through her, it took Evie a moment or two to gain her composure. "You must be looking for a different Everliegh Miller. I have never, or would I ever, advertise for a husband."

"And why is that?"

She shrugged. "I don't need one."

He laughed. "From what I understand from the wives of my limited acquaintance, no woman really needs a husband, but they can be quite handy to have around."

Evie just stared at him. "How can you find this amusing? It isn't."

He sobered but a sparkle remained in his eyes. "Think about it, Miss Miller. It is sort of funny."

"I don't think so." Her gaze roamed over his face. It was a handsome face, with laugh lines extending from the corners of his eyes and a charming smile. "Would you mind waiting here for a moment? Please, help yourself to a cup of coffee and a piece of cake. I need to find out what's going on, who brought you here, and why."

"Of course."

With as much decorum as she could muster, she walked away and let herself into the kitchen, her mind a whirlwind of questions. Her gaze went to her friend Marisol standing beside the sink, dish towel in her hand as she dried the dishes Hilde washed, then to Felicity, Charley's wife, sitting at the table, sorting clean silverware into their respective boxes. "There is a strange man in my garden," she said.

"A strange man? Here? In your garden?" Hilde repeated the statement, rather stupidly, in Evie's opinion, then turned back to the sink, but not before Evie saw a hint of a smile. Suspicion made her stiffen as she stared at Hilde's back then eyed each of her friends in turn—Marisol, the one who never forgot a detail, and Felicity, Miss Manners herself. They, one at a time, met her stare for a moment before dropping their gazes.

"Would someone explain why there is a man standing in my garden, claiming to be my future husband?" She waited, arms folded across her chest and waited a little longer. No one, it seemed, was willing to answer. She tapped her foot on the Saltillo tile, the sound loud in the suddenly silent room. "Well? Is anyone going to answer me?"

"It was Lucy's idea," Felicity blurted out, her face turning pink. "She wrote an advertisement for a husband and put it in the newspaper."

"Lucy did what?"

"At the time, we all agreed it was a good idea," Marisol added. "You've been taking care of everyone for so long, Evie, you've forgotten how to live for yourself. And Lucy didn't want you to be lonely now that she's married and going to live in town."

Evie paused to calm her thoughts before she asked, "You all thought it would be a good idea to arrange for a…a mail order husband for me?"

"What does he look like? " Felicity rose from the table and peeked out the window of the kitchen door. "Ooh, look! He's handsome!"

Marisol and Hilde joined her.

"So, what am I supposed to do with him?" Evie asked.

All three looked at each other, then answered in unison, "Marry him."

Heat rose to her face at the knowledge her friends—and her niece—would do something so underhanded, so—she couldn't even think of the word—but if it weren't happening to her, the situation would be humorous. These women, her closest companions, more like sisters than friends, were only looking out for her best interest. So was Lucy—dear, sweet, conniving Lucy.

"I don't need a husband, and even if I did, don't you all think I couldn't find one on my own?" She looked at all of them gathered at the back door, staring at the handsome stranger in her yard. "This is so embarrassing."

"Not at all," Marisol said. "There are a lot of people who meet and marry this way. It's perfectly acceptable."

She looked at her closest friend, then at the women beside her. "You are all out of your minds!"

"You always said you'd look for your own happiness once all the children were married," Marisol argued. "You said—"

She cut Marisol off in mid-sentence. "I know what I said, but I didn't mean on the same day as Lucy's wedding. That's just ridiculous! And it should be my decision. I should be the one to choose instead of having a strange man, whom I know nothing about, just show up on my doorstep and tell me we are to be married." She threw up her hands in frustration. "I don't know who any of you are!"

Lucy! The instigator in this whole mess! No wonder she had laughed as she and Ben disappeared around the corner of the house. Now her words made sense. He was her gift.

"What are you going to do?" Marisol asked without looking at her—her focus still on the handsome stranger.

Evie had an idea. If this man was truly serious about marrying her then he would have to prove himself, show her what kind of man he was. "I'm going to invite him to stay," she said. "Now move away from the door and stop ogling the man."

Once they did as she asked, she left the kitchen, closing the door with a bang behind her.

He—her mail order husband—sat at one of the tables, long legs stretched out before him. A calico cat, the one Lucy had named Flower, sat on his lap. He smoothed his hand over her fur in long, steady caresses. He had helped himself to a cup of coffee and a piece of cake, but they sat on the table, untouched while he stroked the cat, who seemed to be enjoying the attention, which was unusual. Flower didn't normally take to strangers and never —ever—sat on someone's lap and allowed herself to be petted like this. They all, at one time or another, bore the scars of her reluctance to be touched.

Evie slowed her pace and just watched for a moment, listening to his voice rumble as he spoke to Flower in hushed tones.

"My apologies, Mr.—what did you say your name was?"

He removed the cat from his lap and stood as she approached him, rising from his chair in one fluid motion, grabbing his hat as he did so, charming smile firmly in place. Oh, what that smile did to her! If she let herself, she could fall under its spell.

"Jake. Jake Hannigan."

The rich baritone resonated through her. "I am sorry, Mr. Hannigan, but it seems that you were brought here under false pretenses, by people I thought I knew. I did not place that ad. I am not in the mind to marry anyone." She glanced at the rose arbor and let out a sigh.

"I see." His fingers worried the brim of his hat. "I came here in good faith, Miss Miller, in order to marry you, as we agreed in our letters."

She held up her hand to stop him. "I never agreed to anything. I did not place the advertisement in the newspaper, nor did I write any letters. However, you can stay here at the ranch. We can always use another hand."

His eyes widened as if the thought of actually working was something he never considered. "A ranch hand?"

"Yes." She glanced at his hands. Not a callous to be seen. Nails perfectly trimmed. Certainly not the hands of a working man. Indeed, he didn't look like the kind of man who picked up anything heavier than a pen. Looks could be deceiving, though. She glanced at his broad shoulders and the sleeves of his suit jacket, noticing the muscles beneath the fabric. "You can stay in the bunkhouse. Antonio will get you settled."

"You want me to stay in the bunkhouse?"

"I do."

"Why can't I stay in the main house? It's certainly big enough." That grin appeared on his face again, doing funny things to her insides. He could probably charm the rattle from a rattlesnake with that smile. "It would be a way for us to get to know each other."

"Which is precisely why I want you to stay in the bunkhouse. We don't know each other at all. And as far as marriage is concerned, I am not promising anything."

"This letter says differently." He reached into his pocket and withdrew a letter, the envelope nearly pristine. He slid the pages from within and unfolded them before handing them to her.

Her hand shook a little, the pages rustling. She recognized the letterhead in an instant, as well as the handwriting. He took a step forward, leaned toward her until his mouth was only inches from her ear and spoke in a voice that was both knowing and sensual. "From this letter, I know many things about you, Miss Everleigh Miller, but I'd like to know more."

Gooseflesh broke out on her skin in an instant, and a flood of emotions cascaded through her. If the circumstances were different, she could have melted into his arms.

But she had never melted in anyone's arms, not even Tom's. She'd never allowed herself to lose control in that way and she wasn't about to start now, with a stranger she knew nothing about. Everything she had done—or not done—had been centered around the children and what was best for their future.

The children were grown now. Teddy and Esteban even had children of their own, though Heath did not, and Lucy was just beginning her married life.

She took a careful step back and raised her gaze to his face. She closed her eyes for a moment, searching for some semblance of dignity. "Mr. Hannigan, I've already told you that I did not write this letter, nor did I place any advertisements in any newspaper. Unbeknownst to me, my well-meaning niece placed the ad and wrote this letter. So these are your choices—you may stay and work the ranch as I've offered, or you may leave."

He carefully plucked the letter from her hand, folded it, and slipped it back into its envelope, his gaze never once leaving hers. "I'll stay."

15

CHAPTER 2

She told him she was going to get someone named Antonio to get him settled in. He watched her walk away, her backside swaying gently beneath yards of pale blue silk. Oh, he liked her already. She had spirit. And gumption. Quite pleasant to look at, too, with her long light-brown hair, kissed by the moon with strands of silver, pulled away from her face to fall down her back in a riot of curls, and blue-gray eyes the color of storm-laden clouds. Her mouth—full and soft—seemed quite kissable. And the way color bloomed on her cheeks? Well, he liked that, too.

Why would a woman who looked like her need to advertise for a husband? It just didn't seem plausible, but then she'd stated, quite clearly, that she hadn't. It had been her niece working on her behalf.

And it didn't matter. None of it.

Miss Everleigh Miller didn't know it, but she—and this ranch hidden in a valley not far from the little town of Serenity—would be his salvation...for now. No one would dream of looking for him here.

He took his seat and finished the piece of cake, which was

delicious but did little to fill the empty hole in his stomach. He'd been traveling for days, first by train, then by stagecoach, until finally hiring someone in Santa Fe to bring him here. That ride used up quite a bit of his available cash. The windfall he'd won at the gambling table from kingpin Erik King was safely stashed in a black valise with Father O'Malley, the only man Jake trusted.

Still, all the travel had been worth it. He was in a safe place, far from Erik King and San Francisco. He had told her he'd stay, yet he knew nothing about horses or cattle and had an idea this job meant getting up at the crack of dawn. The only time he usually saw the sun rise was when he'd stayed out all night because the cards had been in his favor.

A cat, a pretty little calico, jumped into his lap again and settled herself, her purrs rumbling from deep in her throat. He stroked her soft fur, eliciting louder purrs, which made him smile. He liked cats, and they seemed to like him. There had been one at the home for boys where he grew up, a big orange tabby that prowled into the dorm room on a nightly basis and chose a child to sleep with, which had usually been him. Strange thing, that cat didn't belong to anyone at St. Anselm's. Like them, she was a stray. How she got into the orphanage after Father O'Malley locked the doors, no one seemed to know. Or care.

He was a gambler by trade for the past five years, and he'd been luckier than most, winning enough to buy a beautiful home in San Francisco for cash and live the life he wanted—good food, good clothing, fine wine, beautiful women—a far cry from the boys' home where he spent his youth. But even with all that, something was missing.

How quickly that life of leisure, that pursuit of pleasure, had disappeared, not by a loss, but strangely, by a win. He should never have played poker with Erik King. He'd known of the man's reputation long before he'd dealt the cards, though he had never met him. It was said among his fellow gamblers that King hated to lose, that he was ruthless, easily offended, and persistent in his single-minded pursuit to get any perceived loss returned, by fair means or foul. More than one man had lost his life to King when they'd won against him.

The rumors about King were true, as he'd quickly learned, after a series of unfortunate, life-threatening events.

Something had to change. And that change had come in the form of a newspaper advertisement Father O'Malley conveniently left beside his coffee cup one morning. It was time, the good Father told him, most emphatically, to stop gambling and become respectable. He'd responded to the advertisement to appease the old man, mostly, which is how he ended up here, waiting for the delightful Miss Miller to return. Besides, what was one last gamble, perhaps the biggest one of his life?

"It's not funny, Antonio." He heard her say, then male laughter, and looked up to see her walking toward him. Once again, he couldn't help noticing how beautiful she was—for someone who had been described in the advertisement as a mature, older woman. He pegged her at around the same age as he was, which was thirty-five, though it was often difficult to tell.

An older man accompanied her, one who carried himself proudly, like he was accustomed to giving orders and having them obeyed. Tall and brawny, he walked with a slight limp...no, that wasn't a limp. The man was quite bowlegged. From years spent in a saddle? Lines crinkled from his deep-brown eyes, as if he'd spent his entire life outside, squinting into the sun. Hair, not silver or gray, but pure white, surrounded his head and repeated in the impressive horseshoe mustache that covered his upper lip and extended down the sides of his mouth to flow, unimpeded, past his chin.

Jake removed the cat from his lap and rose to his feet.

There was no smile on the man's lips now, but amusement remained in his eyes and on his face. Despite that, Jake got the distinct impression that this man brooked no disobedience, no shenanigans, as Father O'Malley called them. He'd hate to see him sitting across the poker table, cards in hand, money in a pile. He'd be the type to smile as he laid down an ace-high flush.

Everleigh Miller stopped in front of him. "Mr. Hannigan, this is Antonio Lucero, my good friend and former ranch foreman. He'll get you settled."

Jake found his hand engulfed in the man's, felt the calluses of hard work on his palm and the strength in his fingers.

"Hannigan," the man said, his mustache moving as he spoke. Was that humor dancing in the older man's eyes as he glanced at her? Did he find the situation amusing? If he had to guess, he'd say yes.

"I'll leave you in Antonio's capable hands." When she walked away, Jake watched her until she entered the house and closed the door behind her.

Antonio cleared his throat, drawing his attention. "Let's grab your gear."

Confused, Jake stared at him. "My gear?"

"Your saddle. Your horse."

"I don't have a saddle but my bags are on the front porch." He didn't ride, had only been on a horse once in his life—when he was five—and it was not a good experience. His backside, after all these years, still remembered the pain of being thrown. "I don't have a horse, either."

"Fine. We'll fix you up." He cast a questioning glance his way, mustache twitching. "Do you ride, Hannigan?"

"No, sir."

The man heaved a sigh, his shoulders slumping as he turned toward the house, as if trying to see the woman who had given him this problem. "Guess we'll have to teach you, then. Teach you how to rope, too, 'cause I don't suppose you know how to do that either."

"No, sir, I don't." Jake looked around him. Exactly what had he gotten himself into?

"We'll start you off doing just basic things around the ranch until we can teach you how to ride and you're comfortable in the saddle." The man quirked a bushy white eyebrow. "Ever muck out a barn?

"No, sir, I don't believe I have."

"Chop wood?"

Jake shook his head. "I lived in the city. If I needed wood, I bought it."

"Milk a cow?"

"No, sir." Milk came in glasses in the fine restaurants he used to dine in.

Antonio rubbed the back of his neck. "I don't suppose you have ever fed chickens?"

Again, Jake shook his head. There had been some chickens at the boys' home, but collecting eggs and tossing grain to the birds hadn't been one of his chores, for which he remained thankful. For as much as he liked cats and dogs, chickens, especially roosters, made him extremely uncomfortable. He much preferred to see them on his plate, fried to golden perfection. "But I can learn anything you want to teach me."

The man stared at him, a slow smile lifting his mustache. The twinkle of amusement was back in his eyes. "Let's get your gear."

A few minutes later, bags in hand, he followed behind Antonio toward a long, low building.

"This is the bunkhouse. You'll be sharing it with six other men." Antonio opened the door wide, revealing the interior. Jake had nothing to compare it with, as he'd never been in a bunkhouse, but it seemed nice enough. Clean. There were ten sets of bunk beds, several sofas and chairs, and a big table. There was also a sink, stove, ice box, and glass-fronted wall cabinets filled with dishes. Nice rug on the floor. Red-and-white checked gingham curtains on the window. A bookshelf crammed with hard-covered books and dime novels, some of the covers torn and tattered, obviously well-read.

"There are rules here, Hannigan, the biggest one being that

you will respect your bunkmates. I don't tolerate stealing, and neither does anyone else. No women in the bunkhouse. No fighting. No gambling. Miss Evie doesn't approve. Is that understood?"

No gambling? Jake nodded even though his stomach plummeted. Still, it was for the best. If he hadn't gambled in the first place, King wouldn't be looking for him now. And he had promised Father O'Malley he would never place another bet.

"You can take that single bunk in the corner." Antonio pointed to the bed on the far side of the room, near one of the windows. "There's a trunk for your belongings." He grabbed a key from a small box hanging on the wall and handed it to him. "Breakfast is at five sharp. If you miss it, you won't have anything until lunch. Trust me, you'll want breakfast. Supper is at seven. Payday is every other Saturday. You're more than welcome to join the others and head into town. There are a couple saloons, if you're a drinkin' man, and a bawdy house or two, but I'm thinkin', since you're here to maybe marry Miss Evie, you'll be passing those by.

"Later, when everyone comes in from the field, I'll introduce you to the rest of the men, but you'll be reporting to Teddy eventually. He's the one you'll have to impress with whatever knowledge you have." His eyes roamed over Jake, taking in his clothing. "This should be interesting." He paused. "One last thing, Hannigan." Any humor that had once been in his eyes disappeared. Indeed, he seemed down-right intimidating. "I'm very fond of Miss Evie. She's like the daughter I never had. If you hurt her or treat her with disrespect in any way, you'll answer to me. And after me, you'll answer to the boys. Teddy, Esteban, and Heath won't take it too kindly if their aunt is unhappy. Do I make myself clear?"

Jake stiffened. This wasn't the first time he'd been threatened, but it was the first time he knew the man would follow through. He rather liked his face the way it was. His nose had already been broken once. He didn't fancy it being broken again. "I would never hurt Miss Evie. You have my word."

The big man gave one final word of warning. "And don't ever lie to her, son. Lying would be a big mistake."

Too late. He'd already lied to her. Granted, it was a lie of omission, but still, it counted. Jake shifted his weight from one leg to the other beneath the man's unwavering perusal and gave a nod.

"Good enough. Make yourself comfortable, put your gear away, and I'll be back shortly to show you around." Antonio stepped out of the bunkhouse, closing the door behind him.

Jake walked over to his bunk, dropped two small suitcases on the mattress, and began to empty them into the trunk. It didn't take long. There wasn't much—after his house burned to the ground, he assumed by one of King's henchmen though he couldn't prove it, he only had some clothing and a photograph in a silver frame.

That silver-framed picture was the only thing left of his mother, Skye Hannigan. It had been with his belongings when he arrived at St. Anselm's after she passed away. Apparently, there had been no one who could take him in. Certainly not a father, who wasn't around. Hell, he didn't even know the man's name. He had been only three when his mother died.

He let out his breath. It wasn't good to dwell on the past. He locked the trunk, shoved the key in his pocket, and stood at the window, where he could clearly see the patio at the main house, the garden and yard—and the lovely Miss Miller as she scurried back and forth from the tables set up on the lush, green grass. She was a rather enjoyable sight, much better than the dark thoughts from his past.

The sound of the door opening made him turn. Expecting Antonio, instead an older man, probably about the same age as Antonio, though not nearly as big and certainly not as bow-legged, made a beeline for the big stove. He mumbled to himself as he pulled an apron from a hook on the wall and tied it around his waist. Apron in place, he flipped down one of the hatches on the stove, filled the space with kindling and twists of paper, then struck a match against the sole of his boot. He held the flame to the paper until it was fully engulfed then added larger pieces of wood and snapped the hatch in place with a bang.

Was he singing? Cussing? Jake couldn't tell, but the man's muttering was constant. He turned and stopped, stiffening as his gaze fell upon Jake. His eyes narrowed with suspicion and maybe a little surprise. "Who're you?"

"Jake. Jake Hannigan."

"Cleaston Jones, but most folks call me Grub. I'm the cook." He didn't approach him or offer to shake hands. Instead, he opened the ice box and pulled out a platter filled with ribs and steaks, already cooked. Probably leftover from the party earlier. "The boys'll be coming in from the field soon, hungrier 'an bears that ain't eaten in months, even though most of 'em ate their fill at the party." He placed the platter on the table, his gaze roaming over Jake, much like Antonio had done. "You cowboyin' for Miss Evie?"

"I suppose so."

Grub didn't say anything more, but the expression on his face spoke volumes. It said, quite clearly, what he thought of Jake cowboying, but then he shrugged and went back to pulling food from the ice box, still muttering.

The door opened again, bringing in late afternoon sunshine, which was blocked momentarily by Antonio. "Ah, I see you've met Grub. Best cook this side of the Mississippi. We're lucky to have him."

The man blushed, his face turning a shade of red Jake rarely saw on a man. It highlighted the grizzled white whiskers on his chin, making them seem even whiter. He didn't say a word, but Jake could see he was pleased by the compliment as he shuffled back and forth from the ice box to the table.

"You ready?" Antonio asked, as he moved out of the doorway, once more allowing sunshine to slice into the room.

Jake shrugged. "Ready as I'll ever be."

The barn was nice if one could say that about a barn. Big. Clean, though there was still the smell of animals and hay and other aromas he didn't want to identify. Stalls, empty now, lined the walls on either side of a central corridor. Birds twittered from the rafters, and another cat, this one black with a splotch of white on its head, ambled along the top of the wooden plank between stalls, then jumped to the ground, sure-footed and agile. In moments, he was winding his way around Jake's feet, purring.

Still, he had nothing to judge by. He wouldn't know a good barn from a bad one. His experience was more toward saloons and gaming halls, where tables covered in green or red felt had been the norm, rooms filled with cigar and cigarette smoke, the triumphant shouts of men winning a hand or groaning with disappointment when they lost, and the occasional report of gunfire when there was doubt between the two. "For right now, until you learn to ride and go out with the boys, you'll be mucking out the stalls and making sure everything in the tack room is orderly and in good repair. I'll show you how."

They exited the barn and stopped at one of four paddocks. Several horses were in one of the corrals, gathered in the shade of the building, two of them much larger than the others. Draft horses, he assumed, the kind that pulled wagons or plows. They rushed to greet Antonio, who indulged them with quick scratches on their noses or behind their ears. "In the morning, after the boys have left, you'll bring the remaining horses here. Make sure there is hay and plenty of water." He pointed to the trough and the water pump. "The hay is in the barn, up top."

In the other enclosure was a cow. "You don't have to milk the cow. That particular chore belongs to Savannah and Miguel, Teddy's children, with me supervising. We'll just keep it that way...for now."

Jake didn't know how to milk cows, although, as with everything else, he could learn. He was just glad he didn't have to.

They walked a few steps across the barnyard toward the chicken coop, where behind the fence chickens pecked the ground. A rooster was perched on the roof of the coop, surveying his domain. He crowed, obviously unaware that it wasn't morning, but late afternoon, almost evening, then set his eyes on Jake. Even from this distance, Jake sensed malevolence in the beady-eyed stare. It was enough to make him take a step back.

Antonio, obviously having witnessed him stepping back, snorted. "That's Lucifer. Meanest rooster I ever knew," he explained, giving Jake proof of what he already suspected. "There's a shed behind the coop where we keep the grain. You won't have to collect the eggs, but you will have to feed them every morning, just watch yourself with him. Lucifer has a habit of sneaking up behind you. Ain't so nice when he starts pecking at your legs."

A group of men rode into the barnyard, kicking up dust. Three separated themselves from the rest and slid from their saddles, then began walking their horses toward the barn, conversing with each other.

"Ah, the boys are back. Wait here."

Jake watched the big man amble over to the three. Hats were removed as Antonio approached and he was struck by the similarities between the men. There was no denying they were brothers. All of them had dark hair, nearly pitch-black, and all were tall, almost as tall as he was. He suspected they were Miss Evie's previously mentioned nephews, Teddy, Esteban, and Heath, simply by the deference and respect Antonio showed them.

He observed as they gathered around Antonio. There was a lot of hand gesturing, accompanied by some of the older man's deep, rich laughter.

"Her *what*!" The tallest of the three brothers exploded, and shot a glare in his direction while Antonio continued to talk. Unlike the rooster who had stared him down, there was no malevolence in that look, but there was enough suspicion in this young man's expression to make Jake question the wisdom of his choice to stay. And he knew, without being told, the man was the eldest, simply by the weight of his stare and the explosion of his voice. "Lucy! That little scamp!"

"Now, don't go losin' your temper, Teddy. Nothing's been done that can't be undone," one of the other men spoke in a calm and soothing tone. He appeared to accept the situation with humor, if the huge grin on his face was any indication. Jake pegged him as Heath, though he had no way of knowing for certain. He was obviously the peace-maker, and someone who might, one day, become a friend. The third must be Esteban, who said nothing. There was no suspicion in his direct perusal, but there was a frank assessment, and somehow, Jake thought he came up lacking, as if Esteban knew the truth of his past and why he was there. He had faced that expression across a card table before. The man could be won over. Maybe.

"Wasn't plannin' to, Heath, but if you think, for one moment, I'm going to allow—"

Antonio cut him off. "It's done, boys. Your aunt is allowing him to stay. She'll decide whatever it is she'll decide. Who knows, there could be another wedding here. Or maybe it won't work out, but it's her decision. Just remember, she's spent all her life raising you boys without a thought for herself."

"There was Marshal Tom," Heath added. "*Tia* Evie wasn't the same after he died."

"No, she wasn't, but I still don't like him here. We don't know anything about him, except he ain't no cowboy. Look at the way he's dressed." Again, this coming from Teddy, accompanied by another expression of distrust as he placed his hands on his hips and stared him down.

Jake held his ground. He'd never been one to be bullied —

something he learned early on in the boys' home—but he did know how to fall back and regroup.

"You don't have to like it," Antonio stated.

There was definite tension as the four men approached him and Antonio performed the introductions. Teddy, the most vocal of the three, extended his hand, and said, "I'll be watching you, Hannigan. You do anything to hurt my aunt, even the smallest thing, and you'll be answering to me."

Jake simply nodded, taking the threat for what it was. He had no doubt the man would be as good as his word.

"I'm Heath." The youngest of the three held out his hand with a wide smile. "You ready to work?"

Though he wasn't, Jake said, "I am.".

The last man, Esteban, hadn't spoken and still didn't speak, but he nodded and held out his hand. Teddy might be the boss and the most outspoken, but this was the man he'd have to win over…that is, if he intended to actually marry Miss Everleigh Miller.

Evie watched from the kitchen window, dish towel in hand while Jake was introduced to her nephews. There were no punches thrown, no open hostility, but she could see there was tension. It was almost palpable through the open window.

"Esteban isn't happy. Neither is Teddy. Only Heath seems to be alright with Mr. Hannigan being here."

Hilde handed her a pot to dry. "Did you expect anything different from Heath? Out of all of Gina's boys, he is always the easiest going. The happiest." She pulled the plug from the sink and allowed the water to drain then wiped her hands on her apron, but her focus never left the window or the spectacle outside. "Uh oh, here they come." Without another word, she scurried out of the kitchen, leaving Evie alone to face her nephews.

She draped the dish towel over the back of a chair, poured herself a cup of coffee, sat down at the table and waited. It wasn't long before the door flew open, and Teddy stood on the threshold, his brothers behind him.

There was no greeting as Teddy came further into the room and got right to the point. "You gonna marry that...that...city boy?"

Oh, he was upset. There was a twitch at the corner of his left eye and his jaw was clenched. Even when he'd been a little boy, she'd always known exactly how upset he was just by looking at that twitch. The faster the muscle moved, the more displeased he was. "I haven't decided what I'm going to do."

He began to pace, striding from the sink to the ice box to the other side of the room, passing in front of his brothers then her at the table, his bootheels heavy on the tile, his hands tightening into fists then relaxing. "I'm gonna wring Lucy's neck!"

"You'll leave Lucy alone," she said.

"I don't like it."

"You don't have to like it." She took a careful sip of her coffee, but her gaze never left his. "I'm a grown woman. I can make my own decisions, and right now, you're acting like my father instead of my nephew. I will not have it, do I make myself clear, Teodoro Augustus?"

He stopped moving and just looked at her, obviously recognizing the tone and the fact she used his full name. He'd heard it often enough over the years. It didn't matter that he was a twenty-eight-year-old man and not the angry little boy he'd once been. He huffed, but still responded with the respect he'd been taught. "Yes, ma'am."

"I have not agreed to anything. Not at this moment, at least. He is a stranger. But maybe I want to get to know him since he's—"

He didn't let her finish. "You're too old to be thinking about getting romantically involved with someone."

Too old? Not only did his words catch her off guard, but they hurt her. She never considered herself old. "Is that what you think, Teddy? That I'm too old for romance? Too old to fall in love?"

He didn't answer, but his face began to take on a reddish hue. His mouth opened and closed several times, but no words came out.

"I have some news for you. I may be forty, but that doesn't make me old. Being afraid to experience life with all its good and bad makes one old. Being so set in your ways you won't try anything new makes one old, but falling in love, no matter what a person's age, makes one young." She rose from her chair, forcing him to take a step back. "This is my decision and mine alone."

"I don't think you're too old, *Tia* Evie. I think it's about time," Heath said, his eyes, so much like hers and his mother's, twinkling with amusement. Yes, Heath would find this amusing. He always did have an odd sense of humor.

As usual, Esteban said nothing, but there was suspicion in his dark eyes. Whereas Teddy had always been verbal expressing his anger—or happiness—and Heath had always taken whatever life threw him with aplomb, her middle nephew had always been the quiet one, leaving her to wonder what was on his mind, even when he was young. She held his gaze with her own. "Do you think I'm too old?"

He shook his head but did not speak.

"Good, because I just might marry him." She gave them all one final glare, then, head held high, she left the room. As the swinging door closed behind her, she heard the explosion of voices, which made her smile.

Too old, my foot! We'll just see who's too old!

CHAPTER 3

"*O*h my!"

Evie laid aside the garment she'd been mending and watched Marisol fan herself as she watched the shirtless man chopping wood in the barnyard, just beyond the garden, and where three cats sat perfectly still in the shade of the bunkhouse, watching him just as intently as the women on the patio were. Even Smoky the dog was watching him.

"Marisol! I'm surprised at you! You're a married woman!" Evie followed her gaze though it wasn't the first time she'd looked at him. One would only have to check the crooked stitching on her grandnephew's shirt to see that her mind wasn't on mending. Indeed, from the moment Jake stepped into her sights, her attention had been on him as he swung the axe over and over, his skin glistening in the sun, muscles, previously hidden by his clothing, rippling with every movement.

Marisol laughed as she took a sip of her lemonade. "I might be married, but that doesn't mean I can't appreciate the sight of a fine-looking man."

"And does your husband know you look at other men?"

"Sergio says the day I stop looking is the day he'll start to worry."

Evie laughed. She couldn't help it. The comment was not out of character for Marisol. Neither was watching Jake chop wood. From the moment they'd met all those years ago when Evie first came to the ranch from San Francisco to take care of Regina's children, Marisol had been outspoken, almost brazen, but always kind, loving, and generous. A good friend. The best friend she'd ever had, aside from Hilde and Aunt Felicity. There were no lies or secrets between them. Never had been. Never would be.

Marisol continued to gaze at Jake. "What do you know about your mystery man?"

Evie picked up her mending and tried hard to make the stitches even, but it wasn't working, not when the distraction at hand was the enigmatic, too charming, too handsome by far Jake Hannigan. "Not very much. He seems like a nice enough man. He hasn't balked at any of the chores Antonio has given him. And he's learning very quickly. The boys are not happy he's here, though, especially Teddy."

"Bah! Teddy! He's an old woman!" Marisol said. "So…what are you going to do? Are you going to marry him?"

Evie glanced down at the shirt in her hand, avoiding Marisol's curious expression. She shrugged, feeling the tension in her shoulders. "He's only been here a few days. I don't know him, and I will not commit to spending the rest of my life with someone I don't know."

"I understand, but that situation is not going to fix itself with you just watching him from afar. You have to talk to him, too, Evie. Get to know him." Marisol paused, mischief in her light-brown eyes. "I don't have to ask if you find him attractive, the way you keep looking at him."

She hesitated, then told the truth, as she'd always done with Marisol. "He's got the most amazing smile. And the nicest eyes. Kind. Soulful. Yet I have the feeling he doesn't miss anything."

"Then what's holding you back? You talk to everyone, Evie. That was the first thing I noticed about you when we met. You were a regular little chatterbox, so why are you avoiding him? What makes him so different?"

She didn't know how to even begin getting to know him, but before she could admit that, Ana, the young woman she was training to be a housekeeper, came out to the yard, carrying a fresh pitcher of lemonade. Ice tinkled as she refilled their glasses. "You have a visitor, Miss Evie."

"Who is it?"

"He said his name is Oscar Peña. He said you were expecting him."

His name was not familiar, and she wasn't expecting anyone, but it wasn't unusual for someone to call without an invitation. Montaña del Trueno had a reputation for some of the finest horseflesh in the area. It wouldn't have been the first time someone just stopped by to purchase one of their horses. "Where is he?"

"In the parlor."

"Thank you, Ana. I'll be there in a moment. Please offer him some coffee or lemonade."

"I already have. He declined both." Ana lifted her head just a fraction and smiled, pleased she'd done what was appropriate, then went back in the house.

Evie placed her mending in the basket beside her, then slowly rose to her feet.

She turned toward Marisol, who had gone back to watching Jake.

"Come with me, Marisol. Meet Mr. Peña with me."

"And miss this wonderful view?" She gestured toward Jake swinging the axe high, sweat glistening on his skin, his biceps prominent. "I don't think so."

"Fine, you stay, but don't blame me when you get a crick in your neck."

Marisol laughed. "The pain would be well worth it, I think."

Evie headed across the lawn, following the path Ana had taken just a moment before, and let herself into the kitchen. Hilde stood at the counter, kneading dough, an apron tied around her ample waist. A smudge of flour stood out against the redness of her cheek. "You have company."

"I know." She pushed through the swinging door and strode down the hallway.

She met her Aunt Felicity coming down the stairs. "I hear you have another gentleman caller," she remarked, as she tugged on her gloves.

"Perhaps. I don't know who he is, but I'm about to find out."

"Charley and I are heading into town. I thought we might stop by and see Lucy. Do you need anything?"

"No, thank you, but give Lucy my love."

Felicity buttoned her gloves. "Of course." She took another step down the risers until they were eye level, Felicity being the shorter of the two of them. Kindness showed in the older woman's light-green eyes as they roamed over Evie's face. She reached out and gently laid her hand on her cheek. "You're a beautiful, vibrant woman, Everleigh. You deserve every happiness. I'd like to see you find it."

And with those words, she stepped off the stairs and headed down the hall.

Evie frowned as she watched Felicity stroll toward the kitchen—probably to conspire with Hilde before she and Uncle Charley drove into town. She patted her hair to make sure every strand was in place, then stepped into the parlor to see her guest standing at the window, hands on his hips, his gaze focused on the view outside. She stood for a moment, silently comparing him to Jake. He wasn't as tall, or as muscular. He did have dark hair, though not quite as black as Jake's. And there were no strands of silver. "Hello. I'm Everleigh Miller. May I help you?"

He turned quickly, bumping into the potted plant beside him.

The heavy brass stand wobbled, but before it could fall to the floor, he caught it and set it right. He mumbled an apology then rushed forward, tripping over the edge of the rug in his haste. He took a few awkward steps, but managed to keep his balance, then grabbed her hand. For a moment, she thought he was going to drop a kiss on her knuckles, but he simply shook her hand instead. "Oscar Peña. How nice to meet you in person." He smiled, showing a full complement of pearly white teeth in his young, much younger than her, face. His smile did not make her heart flutter the way Jake's had done, but it was charming, nonetheless. Friendly. Full of confidence.

And his eyes? No, they didn't make her want to melt, either.

"Please, have a seat." She gestured to an overstuffed chair beside a small table holding one of the photographs Lucy had taken with the camera she'd received as a gift, this one of Miguel, Teddy's son, when he was just a baby. The entire table jiggled as he bumped into it in his haste to sit. The frame holding Miguel's photograph rocked. She caught it before it could fall and possibly break the glass. "How may I help you, Mr. Peña?"

A flush colored his face even as he flashed a sheepish smile. "I...uh...I'm here in...response to your letter."

That little minx! Lucy *had* corresponded to two men!

"I see. May I see the letter?" She had briefly looked at the letter Jake had handed her long enough to recognize Lucy's handwriting and the letterhead, but hadn't read anything except the first few lines.

If Oscar thought it odd she would request to see the letter she'd written, he didn't say so. He didn't even blink as he pulled the envelope from his suit jacket and handed it to her. As he did so though, he knocked over the picture of Miguel. The silver frame clattered against the table. Thankfully, the glass did not break. She righted the picture then smiled at the man sitting beside her. He returned her smile, his expression one of definite interest and expectation as well as curiosity, but only for a moment before his gaze fell to the table between them.

She glanced at the envelope and instantly recognized Lucy's penmanship. Her stomach twisting with anxiety, she pulled the letter from the envelope and began to read. After a moment, relief rushed through her. The knot in her stomach started to unravel.

It wasn't a proposal of marriage at all. Instead, it was an invitation to visit the ranch for an opportunity to get to know one another. The prospect of marriage was sometime in the future if all parties agreed; however, there was no promise of such. The words in the letter did not say "come to Montaña del Trueno to be married." It was simply an invitation to meet.

Evie folded the letter and placed it back in the envelope. As she did so, she studied his face. It was a nice face, younger than she originally thought, and right now, his expression was full of hope. "I'm afraid you've been misinformed, Mr. Peña. My niece placed the advertisement in the newspaper unbeknownst to me. She was the one who also wrote this letter. I'm not looking for a husband."

"Oh."

It was the smallest word, but it held such regret.

"I'm sorry." Her gaze roamed his face, and she noticed the emotion in his voice was reflected in his expression. She hated to be the cause of someone else's unhappiness, and since he had come all this way, the least she could do was extend an offer of work, like she'd done for Jake—she just wondered how many others there would be. The ranch could handle quite a few ranch hands, but the bunkhouse could not. "I can offer you a job as one of my ranch hands, providing you want to stay. Do you have experience?"

"Yes, ma'am." His face brightened, the disappointment nearly gone. "I grew up on a ranch. I know how to ride, how to rope, how to brand. Anything you need me to do."

A stark departure from Jake, who couldn't do any of those things. "Excellent." She handed him the letter, which he stuffed in his suit jacket pocket. "I can have Antonio show you to the bunkhouse and get you settled." She rose from her seat, her gaze on him as he did the same. "Just out of curiosity, why did you answer the advertisement?"

He shrugged, a reddish hue suffusing his face. "There weren't too many eligible ladies where I'm from and I was competing with my older brothers," he blurted out, though she wasn't sure he meant to say it. His face seemed to turn even redder, and sweat beaded on his forehead as if he realized his faux pas.

At least, he was honest. "No need to apologize, Mr. Peña. I value honesty." She smiled at him, trying to put him at ease. "You have brothers. How many?"

"I have seven brothers," he said, the redness on his cheeks beginning to fade. "And six sisters. I'm the youngest."

"Being the youngest of so many children can be hard."

"It can be. There's a lot to be said about being part of a big family. You're never lonely," he chuckled. "How could you be with so many people around all the time?" He let out a sigh. "I've always wanted a spread of my own, though, not something I had to share with my brothers and sisters and their children."

She filled in the words he didn't say—that by marrying her, he thought he would get that spread of his own—that what she owned would become his with the marriage certificate. She should disabuse him of that right now but didn't see the need. She'd already told him she wasn't looking for a husband.

"And how old are you, Mr. Peña?"

"I'll be twenty-nine on my next birthday."

Twenty-nine! She knew he was young, but more than ten years younger than herself? That would be a scandal. Or would it? It wasn't for a man. They could marry someone twenty or even thirty years younger than themselves and no one batted an eyelash. Well, some did, but the rules just weren't the same for a woman. Never had been.

"If you'll wait here, I'll get Antonio so he can show you around."

"Thank you, ma'am."

She left the room, leaving him to wait, hoping he wouldn't break anything in the meantime. She found Antonio in short order, explained the situation, which was difficult because he kept laughing, then she joined Marisol in the garden once more.

Evie sat down and said, "It was another man answering Lucy's advertisement."

Marisol laughed. "And?"

"And nothing. I've offered him a job, but nothing more. He accepted."

"You might not find a husband from Lucy's ad, but you are hiring plenty of ranch hands, *amiga*."

She laughed and picked up Miguel's shirt from the basket. "I'm not looking for a husband. What was Lucy thinking?"

"Well, if you're not looking for a husband then what about… oh never mind. You'd never."

"I'd never what?"

"Take a lover."

"Marisol! I couldn't!" She jabbed her finger with the needle, shocked by her friend's suggestion, though she shouldn't have been because of who said it. A drop of bright red blood blossomed on her finger. She brought her finger to her mouth and sucked at it, leaving a metallic taste on her tongue.

"Why not?"

She added pressure to her finger to stop the bleeding. "Because that's not who I am. You know Teddy thinks I'm too old for that sort of thing."

Marisol laughed. "As I said before, Teddy is an old woman!" She turned serious eyes toward her but before she spoke, her attention was drawn to the barnyard. "Is that him?"

Evie turned her head, following Marisol's line of vision to see Antonio and Oscar walking toward the bunkhouse, a big black stallion with a fancy saddle inlaid with silver and turquoise following behind. "Yes. Antonio is showing him around."

"He's attractive." Marisol sounded amused. "Nice-looking horse, too. And that saddle!"

"Yes, I suppose he is, but he's so young. More than ten years younger than me."

"So what? A younger man would be…energetic." Marisol winked.

Evie shook her head as her face warmed. "I just…couldn't."

"What about the other one? Mr. Hannigan?" She suggested. "You've been drooling over him all afternoon. Don't think I didn't notice."

"I don't know what you're talking about," Evie said, even though she *had* been admiring him. It was difficult not to. She was attracted to him—and more than just a little. Indeed, watching him as he did his chores left her stomach quivering and feeling flushed all over.

Marisol looked at her. "I think you do." She finished the lemonade in her glass and rose to her feet. "What's more, I heard you sigh a couple of times as you were watching him." She picked up her basket of mending, which she hadn't touched all afternoon. "Why not, Evie? Tom passed away a long time ago and you've concentrated all your energies on raising the children and running Montaña del Trueno. The children are grown and married now. The boys run the ranch. It's your turn." She laid her hand on Evie's shoulder in a gesture of sympathy. She'd been there when Tom had passed. She'd been there every step of the way since. "And with that thought stuck in your head, I shall take my leave." She bent down, dropped a kiss on Evie's cheek. "I'll see you next Tuesday. I'll bring my mending, just in case."

Evie rose as well. "I'll see you out."

"No need. You just stay and watch your mystery man and

think about what I said." Basket in hand, she strolled over the grass toward the garden gate, waved one last time, and disappeared around the corner of the house to head home to her own ranch.

Evie took her seat, her gaze immediately drawn to Jake once more. He finished chopping the wood, and with one last thwack, buried the head of the axe in the stump then slipped into his shirt, hiding his perfectly sculpted back from her sight.

She watched him stroll toward the barn, sunlight reflecting off his black hair, highlighting the strands of silver. He moved with innate grace, his long legs eating up the short distance to the barn, the cats and dog following closely behind him. "Why not, indeed?" she asked quietly.

But that left more questions than answers. Like how to even approach him. Would he consider an arrangement instead of marriage? And what about her? The only man she'd ever been with had been Tom, and that was only after they'd become engaged. There had been no one since, but she wasn't the type of woman who gave herself freely. She'd been in love with Tom, loved him deeply and without reservation. The physical side of their relationship had been an expression of that love.

Could she consider the physical side without the emotion?

No answers presented themselves as Jake disappeared into the barn. Evie let out a sigh and continued working on Miguel's shirt, but it was no use. The stitches were more lopsided than before and the reason for her inability to concentrate wasn't even in sight. She put the mending away, picked up her basket, and strolled into the house, but that didn't stop the thoughts running through her head nor the flush that seemed to encompass her entire being.

CHAPTER 4

*L*ightning flashed behind the window, illuminating the interior of the bunkhouse for a split second. Jake opened his eyes and silently counted the seconds before thunder rumbled in the distance, something Father O'Malley had taught him many, many years ago to judge how far away a storm was. At that point in time, he'd been very young and afraid of the fury of a storm, most especially the crashing boom of thunder. As he grew older, he came to love it—the thunder, and the lightning, the smell of the earth after a good soaking, the electricity in the air. It made him feel alive.

He lay still in his bunk, listening to the sounds around him, feeling the weight of Flower the calico, who nestled against his leg. Cesar, one of his bunkmates, snored like a broken concertina, high pitched and wheezy. And the new man, Oscar, talked in his sleep, though for the most part, the words were mumbled and undistinguishable, except for the occasional shout. His night-time talking competed with Grub's. Sometimes, listening to the both of them made his head hurt, but for the most part, he could ignore it. There were other noises, too. Grunts and groans and other, less savory bodily functions, the rustle of bedcovers as the men shifted position, the occasional sigh—the sounds one heard when several people shared close quarters.

Thunder rumbled, becoming louder as the storm moved closer. He didn't hear rain patter on the roof, but that was only a matter of time. He settled himself deeper into the mattress and just listened, mentally counting the seconds between flashes of lightning and the deep rumble of thunder. He closed his eyes, letting the sounds ease him into sleep.

His eyes flew open. The horses! He might love the sound of a storm, but he would bet the horses did not. He sprang up in his bed, dislodging Flower from her sleeping position. The cat blinked her wide eyes, which seemed to glow with an unnatural light.

He grabbed his trousers from the top of the lock box at the end of his bunk and slipped them on, careful not to make noise, though he doubted anything he did would wake his bunkmates—they slept like the dead—then grabbed his shirt and his boots. The cat stretched, then leapt to the floor, following him as he walked quietly across the room, avoiding the floorboard that squeaked, and let himself out of the bunkhouse, closing the door carefully behind him. The wind buffeted him immediately, bringing with it the smell of impending rain and making the limbs of the trees around him bend and groan. Lightning flashed, illuminating the barnyard. He glanced at the house and saw the glow of a lantern behind one of the windows on the second floor, though he didn't know whose room that window belonged to. Had the storm awakened someone else?

He sat on the edge of the stump where he chopped wood and slipped on his shirt, not bothering to button it up, then pulled on the boots Antonio had given him. He started walking toward the barn, the cat right behind him, and noticed weak beams of light leaking from beneath the edge of the doors. Was someone in the barn? Thieves intent on stealing the horses under the sound of the storm?

He retraced his steps and picked up the axe from the stump. If there were horse thieves, he'd have a weapon. He'd always depended upon his fighting skills in the past. A well-placed punch was all he'd ever needed against those that would do him harm, but this was different. He wasn't in San Francisco anymore.

He sidled up to the big double doors and listened, but couldn't hear much against the whooshing of the wind. He opened one of the doors, just a little, and slipped into the building.

Two lanterns were lit against the darkness inside, the source of the light he'd seen. He heard the noises he expected to hear—hooves against straw as the horses moved about, their chuffs and nickers and snorts. There was no noise from the milk cow in her stall. She lay on a matt of fresh straw, asleep.

He strolled down the central aisle, checking each horse as he passed. And then he heard something he shouldn't have, not at this hour of the morning. A voice—*her* voice—soft and soothing. A moment later, he saw her. Evie. She was in the last stall, calmly brushing her horse and singing to her like she'd sing to a frightened child. He recognized the melody of an old lullaby, though she sang it in Spanish. It had the desired effect. The horse stood still except for occasionally turning her head to look at Evie.

He should leave before she noticed him, but he couldn't. He was held, enthralled, her voice touching a part of his soul, soothing him just as it soothed her horse, despite the fact he didn't understand the words. "Well, don't just stand there. Come and help me." She said it in the same singsong way she sang, and turned to face him.

Startled, he dropped the axe, nearly hitting the cat, who had stopped right beside him. The dull thud seemed overly loud in the stillness of the barn, as did the startled yowl from Flower, who took off for a quiet, safe corner.

She laughed then sang, "You won't be needing that."

He picked it up and just looked at it then smiled as he hefted it in his hands, feeling a little foolish.

"What are you doing out here, Mr. Hannigan, with that?" She nodded toward the axe in his hands.

"I came to check on the horses. Make sure the storm wasn't disturbing them, and then when I saw the light from under the door, well, I—" The explanation deserted him, and his face warmed with embarrassment.

"Did you think someone was trying to steal my horses?" she asked, as she continued brushing Spitfire.

"The thought had crossed my mind." He leaned the axe against one of the posts that separated the stalls.

"Thank you, Mr. Hannigan. I appreciate your concern."

She was still calling him Mr. Hannigan though he had asked her several times already to call him Jake. Perhaps, she just needed reminding one more time. "Jake, please."

She nodded in his direction. "As you can see, Jake, they're all fine. All except Spitfire here. She doesn't like thunder." She continued brushing, her movements slow and methodical, and once again, all he could do was watch her. She was dressed in one of the suede split skirts she favored and a simple blouse. Her light-brown hair fell over her shoulders like she'd just rolled from bed, which she probably had. The lantern cast its warm glow over her, and she was, in that moment, so beautiful, it made his heart beat a little harder. "And no one would dare to steal my horses. That simply doesn't happen on Montaña del Trueno." She gestured toward the tack room behind her. "Grab a brush."

He quickly did as she asked, then joined her in the stall. Spitfire shuffled slightly, her skin twitching as he began to stroke the brush over her coat.

"What does it mean?" he asked after several moments of silence.

"What does what mean?"

"Montaña del Trueno."

"Thunder Mountain." She smiled and his heart thumped harder still. "When it storms, like now, thunder echoes against the mountains and it feels like the sound goes on forever. It's quite magnificent. At least in my opinion." She continued brushing but looked at him over the horse's back. "This ranch has been here for three generations. Regina's children, my niece and nephews, are the fourth. They'll carry it forward for generations to come." Her smile widened, her pride evident. "Already, Toughie—excuse me, young Tomas, Esteban's son—is learning to sit a horse, when we can get him to be still for more than a minute, despite the fact he's only thirteen months old, and Miguel is quite accomplished already, though he's only four. Savannah rides like the wind. It's never too early to teach children. And they're so smart, eating up every bit of wisdom from everyone, learning every day."

"You love this place."

"I do. I can't think of anywhere else I'd rather be." She gave a small sigh and the sound, for a moment, seemed louder than the thunder rumbling outside. "What about you, Jake?"

He never told people about his past. It was just not something he did. No one, aside from Father O'Malley and the good Sisters at the home, knew about his life, but this wasn't San Francisco. And she wasn't just anyone. She was different. Special. And the words seemed to tumble out of his mouth without censure. "Father O'Malley and the good Sisters at St. Anselm's Home for Boys raised me until I was sixteen. After that, I was on my own."

It was the first time he'd mentioned where he'd come from to anyone and the admission seemed to sadden her. She stopped brushing Spitfire and looked at him over the horse's back, her eyes full of sympathy. "I'm sorry."

"Don't be." He shrugged. "It wasn't a bad life. I had a roof over my head, three meals a day, and an education anyone would be proud to have, thanks to Sister Agnes. She was a taskmaster when it came to learning, whether we wanted to learn or not." He grinned as he continued brushing Spitfire, surprising himself that he'd told her so much. Perhaps it was the expression of interest on her face and the curiosity dancing in her eyes. Whatever the reason for his lack of verbal control, he found himself wanting to tell her more.

"From Sister Theresa, I learned to appreciate good food. She was an excellent cook. It was simple fare, but filling and tasty. Helping her in the kitchen was one of my chores."

"So you can cook."

He nodded. "And then there was Father O'Malley. He was a good man. Still is. He still runs the home, iron-fisted, yet kind. He did his best for us, and we knew it. For a long time, I thought I would become a priest like him."

"Apparently, you didn't." She stopped brushing Spitfire, and stared at him, one eyebrow rising. "Or did you?"

He laughed. "No, I didn't. Too many restrictions. Father O'Malley always called me a maverick because I didn't like following the rules. I still don't."

She smiled, as if she could see that about him. "Where is St. Anselm's?"

"San Francisco."

"I've never heard of it, and I was raised in San Francisco. Spent my first twenty years in a house on the Hill."

She didn't seem like someone who would come from Nob Hill. He'd met many across a poker table, those who were fortunate to be born to wealth and didn't mind losing it, but she didn't act like that. There were no airs, as if she were better than anyone else. Indeed, as far as he could see, she worked just as hard as the men she employed. And if there was wealth behind her, she didn't flaunt it.

"Well, that's why you never heard of it. Most folks, especially those who lived on the Hill, wouldn't know of St. Anselm's. It's a far cry from those that live in the big houses. The orphanage was small and located on the outskirts of the city."

"How did you end up at St. Anselm's?"

He shrugged, though his heart still hurt from the loss, even after all these years. "My mother died."

"What about your father?" Once again, sympathy flashed in her eyes, turning them more gray than blue. "Could he not have raised you?"

"I never knew him. He wasn't part of my life."

"I am sorry, Jake."

"As I said, there's no need to be sorry. I had a decent life."

She couldn't imagine not having a family. Even though her father had disowned her for leaving home to raise Regina's children and run Montaña del Trueno, she still had the memories of her mother's love. Victoria Miller had been a wonderful mother, full of wisdom and fun, though her life ended much too soon trying to give her husband the son he wanted. Neither she nor the baby boy survived childbirth.

"Are you all right?"

Evie blinked, startled, and forced her attention back to Jake. "Yes, I'm fine."

"For a minute there, you looked like you were far away."

There was concern in his voice and in his expression, and she smiled a little. "I was. Lost in memories, I suppose."

"Good ones, I hope."

"Some."

He went back to brushing Spitfire, his slow movements mimicking hers.

His shirt was unbuttoned, allowing her to see the dark hair glistening on his chest. She stared at it, until she caught herself. *What is wrong with me? I go from thinking about my mother to staring at his chest.* She struggled to get control of her thoughts. "What did you do after you left St. Anselm's? How did you support yourself?"

"Oh, a number of odd jobs. For a little while, I worked on a steamer, delivering supplies up and down the coast. The captain was a good man, but I'm not a sailor, that much was clear. I never got used to the constant movement of the ship. Or rather, I should say, my stomach never did."

"I worked for a tailor for a number of years." He glanced down at his shirt and his face took on a reddish hue, as if just now noticing that his shirt was open, the edges gaping wide. He quickly buttoned a few, enough to cover up his chest. "That's where I developed an appreciation for fine clothes." He started brushing Spitfire again, his movements causing the buttons to strain against the fabric, and it was all she could do to try to ignore the sight. In that moment, she wanted to smooth her fingers through that mat of fine hair still exposed at the collar of his shirt. Never before had such a thought come to her, not with a man who was still a stranger in so many ways, but the urge persisted. She blamed it on Marisol, who put the idea in her head to take this man as her lover.

In her life before Mr. Jake Hannigan's appearance on her ranch, it never would have occurred to her to invite someone to her bed, not without being in love, like she had been with Tom. Now? The notion occurred to her too often for her own comfort.

"I cooked, bused tables and washed dishes in some of the finest restaurants in San Francisco, too. And for a time, I managed a small hotel." He smiled, showing a dimple in his cheek. "I also joined the Army, but it wasn't a good fit for me. Father O'Malley was right. I was too much of a maverick. I spent more time being reprimanded for not following orders than anything else."

Evie forced her attention away from hair peeking through the collar of his shirt so she could listen to his words. She could just picture him, a much younger version of the man he was now, eking a living out of odd jobs, probably making just enough to cover his rent. She doubted he owned a home. Perhaps, he didn't need to own one. Growing up as he had, perhaps that hadn't been a priority. He didn't seem to regret any of it.

"You never worked on a ranch?"

He shook his head. "Horses, if you want to know the truth, always made me a bit nervous. They're powerful beasts. We had one at St. Anselm's, but he wasn't very friendly. The only one Redeemer seemed to like was Father O'Malley."

"And yet, you're so good with them." And he was, which surprised, yet pleased her. Like Teddy, he seemed to be a natural when it came to the horses. "They seem to like you."

"I've learned, in my short time here, so many things, but mostly that horses are fine, majestic creatures, deserving of our attention and gratitude. They no longer make me nervous. Spitfire here, despite her name, is very gentle, as is Clementine. Even Horatio is gentle, though I will admit to bribing him a bit with apples. In truth, I've grown quite fond of all of them, even the cowboys' horses. Respect and gentleness go a long way when it comes to them." He stopped speaking and glanced upward toward the ceiling, listening to the gentle patter of raindrops falling on the roof. "Ah, it's raining. I love it when it rains."

"I do, too. There's something so cleansing about rain. Like a fresh start, a new beginning."

"Exactly." He stopped brushing and stared at her, his warm amber eyes intense. "You said you grew up in San Francisco. How did you come to be here at Montaña del Trueno?"

"Regina."

"Your sister, correct?"

"Yes." She willed the lump in her throat to go away. Even after all these years, it was still difficult to talk about. The pain and circumstances of Gina's passing still had the power to hurt her heart. She missed her every day. "She was ten years older than me and as kind and loving as you can imagine. I adored her."

"What happened to her?"

"She…was killed." She inhaled sharply, the pain in her heart ever present, but more so when she remembered the senseless loss. "She and Javier, her husband, both. They were in town one afternoon, picking up supplies, and simply walking by the Silver Spur Saloon, when shots rang out. Apparently, a gambler, upset that he lost, decided to start shooting." Her throat tightened to the point she could hear the difference in her own voice. She cleared her throat, trying to dislodge the lump, but it remained, almost choking her.

"From what I was told, the man who won defended himself and chased the other out of the saloon, but they continued shooting at each other right there in the middle of the street, neither one caring where their bullets landed. Six people died that day, not only one of the gamblers—the other got away—but innocent people like Regina and Javier…just because someone lost a card game. It was all…so pointless and devastating." She blinked to clear her eyes of the tears that blurred her vision.

"Uncle Charley was contacted by the Silva family lawyer. I was named guardian for the children. I think Serafina, the children's grandmother, was relieved. She wasn't a well woman, never had been. Raising four children and running Montaña del Trueno would have been a hardship for her."

"I'm sorry about your sister and her husband." His voice was soft and full of empathy. "I'm sorry for you, too. You were so young to suddenly find yourself in those circumstances."

"I was." She stopped brushing Spitfire while she gathered her composure. "I was only twenty. And I knew nothing about raising children. Or running a ranch, but I wasn't about to let Gina down. She trusted me to raise her children, although she probably realized that our father would disown me like he had her."

"And did he?"

"Yes. I wasn't surprised. My father is not a loving man." She started brushing Spitfire again, the simple act soothing while her memories were anything but. "We argued, as I expected we would. He wasn't happy with the choice Gina had made when she married Javier against his wishes, wasn't happy with the decision I was making. He said the most horrible things about us, called us names no father should ever call his daughters." Her face heated, still indignant after all these years that a father should treat his flesh and blood like he had.

"And the children! The things he'd said about his own grandchildren! At that moment, I was ashamed of him. And embarrassed. I almost pitied him." She looked at him over Spitfire's back, searching his face, wondering what he thought. There was nothing but sympathy in his expression. "Defying my father was the hardest, yet easiest thing I've ever done. When I walked out of the house on the Hill that day—Hilde beside me—it was for the last time. I never looked back, though I've written him letters, letting him know how his grandchildren had fared over the years. He never responded and yes, that hurts a little, but after all this time, I realize it was probably better that he wasn't part of our lives."

"Were you scared?"

She gave a quick nod. "Terrified, but determined not to lose what Regina and Javier had entrusted to me. More importantly, I wanted the children to know how much they were loved, not only by their parents, but by me."

She laughed, remembering the first time she'd walked into the house, though at the time, it wasn't such a happy experience. "Hilde and I arrived here in the middle of a thunderstorm, much worse than this one tonight. We were soaked to the bone, tired, and still reeling from the news that Regina was gone. The children were crying as was Serafina. She'd lost her only son and was as inconsolable as the boys. The house was in turmoil, and there was Antonio, trying to help. He took one look at me—he didn't even ask my name, though I suppose he knew who I was—and shoved Lucy into my arms. I don't know who was more startled, her or me." She remembered holding the squirming bundle that was her niece, the both of them in tears.

"I was lucky though. I had a tremendous amount of help. Antonio taught me what I needed to know about ranching. Serafina taught me to cook, as did Grub. Hilde bakes like a dream and makes a fine cup of coffee, but she can't make anything other than toast without burning it."

"The love part. That was easy, I'm sure."

There was something in his voice that drew her attention, a certain sadness in his tone. Was he envious he hadn't had that? Growing up as he had, without a mother or father or siblings, surely he felt he'd missed out, though he did seem to hold Father O'Malley and the Sisters at the boys' home in high esteem. That wasn't the same as love, though.

She studied his expression, but there was nothing except genuine interest in his tawny, nearly golden, eyes so she continued. "I loved the children long before I met them. Regina and I had exchanged letters for many years, though it was forbidden by my father. Uncle Charley was our go-between, passing our letters back and forth. She'd told me so much about them, I felt I knew them. Still, it didn't prepare me for what was to come. Teddy was so angry. At everything. I understood. I was angry, too."

She glanced up at the ceiling, listening to the rain hitting the roof, trying to keep her emotions in check. Those early days of coming to the ranch and the circumstances of why still made her eyes burn with unshed tears. "Esteban didn't speak to me for months. He still doesn't speak much. And Heath, though he was only four at the time, became my helper. Perhaps he was too young to truly understand, but he had a sense that everything would be all right. Has that sense to this day. Heath seems to handle problems with a smile and a shrug and a 'get down to business of fixing that problem' attitude."

"I've noticed that about him." He chuckled as he drew the

brush through Spitfire's mane. "He's got quite an odd sense of humor."

"That he does. And Lucy! She doesn't remember her mother or father at all. She was just over a year old when Regina and Javier were killed. I didn't even know how to change a diaper! I learned rather quickly! I really had no choice, but those first attempts…they were laughable."

"But you persevered." His mouth curved with admiration. "And look what you've accomplished. I don't know anything about ranching, but even I can see Montaña del Trueno is prosperous and well-run."

She acknowledged the compliment with a slight nod. "It was, and still is, a labor of love. Like I said, I was determined not to lose what Regina and Javier had entrusted to me, and I wanted—no, needed—to make the ranch better than how I found it." She glanced at him and smiled. "I've been told I can be a little stubborn. Tell me I can't do something, and I'll have to do it, just to prove you wrong."

He laughed, not just a chuckle, but a full-bodied burst that came from deep in his chest. Humor danced in his warm amber eyes as they swept over her. "Yes, I can see that about you."

"Don't laugh. Being stubborn has helped in ways you can't even begin to imagine."

"I suppose it would, given certain circumstances." He looked up at the ceiling. "Listen, it's not raining anymore."

"The thunder has stopped, too."

The barn door flew open, not driven by the wind, which had died down, but by Teddy, who stood on the threshold, holding a lantern. Evie jumped. So did Jake as Teddy stomped up the aisle, his stride long and angry, his hair furrowed, as if he ran his fingers through it repeatedly. He probably had. Teddy had always been her worrier, which made him quick to anger.

"What is going on in here?" he demanded, suspicion making his dark eyes snap.

Evie laughed, seeing the expression on his face. He looked like he could take on the world with one hand tied behind his back. "We were just keeping Spitfire calm. You know she doesn't like thunder."

He came to a standstill on the other side of the stall, the expression on his face one of distrust and censure—and yes, even anger—as his eyes darted back and forth between them. "Well, it's stopped thundering. I don't think—"

"I'd like a word, Teddy. Outside, please." Evie laid the brush on top of the railing and left the stall. She headed down the central aisle at a quick pace, fully expecting her nephew to follow. She left the barn, closing the door which Teddy had left wide open. He slipped through a moment later.

She started to ask him why he was so upset, but he didn't give her the chance.

"What are you doing, *Tia* Evie? Out here in the barn, just the two of you! It's three o'clock in the morning!"

"Now, Teddy, it was all perfectly innocent."

"Perfectly innocent!" he scoffed. "He's standing there with half his shirt open. It's indecent. And you know nothing about him!"

"That's not true, Teddy. I know plenty about him. He seems to be a genuinely nice person."

"I don't trust him. There's something…not right."

Evie laughed. "Marisol is right. You *are* an old woman." She sobered immediately. "I'm an adult, Teddy. I can take care of myself."

That didn't appease him at all. She knew Teddy was determined to protect her, perhaps because he was the oldest and felt responsible for her. Right now, he was worked up, thinking the worst seeing them together, thinking she needed protection from Jake.

"You need to stay away from Hannigan. Especially at three in the morning alone in a barn."

"I don't need you to look after me. I'm a grown woman."

"But what do you know about men like him, Tia? You have no experience with men. You—"

She cut him off. "Excuse me? When did you become my keeper? When were you put in charge of making decisions for me?"

"When I find you alone in the barn with a stranger. Someone has to protect you."

Facing Teddy's anger with her own had never been the way to deal with him. She knew that, had known it from when he was younger. Teddy needed calmness and logic, not emotional outbursts, but still, it infuriated her that he should issue such an order. "Go back to bed, Teddy. We'll discuss this in the morning."

He didn't move, not one inch. In the glow of the lantern, his expression left no room for doubt, his dark eyes shined with determination, his mouth set in a grim line. "I'm not going back in the house without you. I'm not leaving you out here...with him...alone."

"Go back to bed," she repeated, forcing her voice to stay calm when she felt anything but.

He still didn't move, holding his ground in front of the barn door, almost blocking her from going back inside.

She hadn't lied when she told Jake she was stubborn. Regina had been stubborn, too. It ran in the family. Teddy seemed to have received a double dose, and at this moment, it was quite clear he would not be leaving her alone with Jake.

Which left her three options. She could simply ignore him, go around him and back into the barn, though she had no doubt he would follow her and act as her chaperone. She could stand here and argue with him, at three in the morning, which would only succeed in angering them both further, something she didn't want to do. Or she could go in the house.

When the sun rose on a brand-new day, there would be time to sit down and have a serious discussion. Just the two of them. She could gently explain, when he wasn't so angry, her point of view. Perhaps, he would actually hear her words then because he definitely wasn't hearing them now.

But she couldn't bring herself to do it. This was one time she wasn't about to back down. She folded her arms across her chest and just glared at him.

He shifted his weight from one leg to the other, clearly uncomfortable, yet unwilling to give an inch.

"As I said, we *will* discuss this in the morning. For right now, I'm going back into the barn and continue my conversation with Jake. You can stay or you can go. The choice is yours."

He seemed startled, his expression now one of puzzlement. "What? You are going back in there with him?"

"I think I made myself perfectly clear but I'll say it again. I am a grown woman. I am more than capable of making my own decisions, which I've been doing for a lot longer than you. I am not stupid. I'm not some starry-eyed young girl sneaking off to see the boy her parents have forbidden her to see, Teddy. And I will not be told what I can or can't do."

He said nothing. Had she shocked him? Perhaps so.

For a moment, it didn't seem like he would move out of her way, but then he did with an exaggerated bow. He opened the door for her, leaving it wide open once more. Jake was still in the stall with Spitfire, but he wasn't brushing the horse. He leaned against the railing, his gaze on her as she strode down the central aisle. His eyes flicked to Teddy, who remained by the door, then back to her. There was no smile on his face now, just deep concern as she drew closer.

"I'm sorry. Did I get you in trouble with your nephew?"

She shook her head and smiled. "Don't worry about Teddy. He's just being…well, himself. I guess, over the years, he's gotten it into his head that it's his job to protect me. I just needed to remind him that I can take care of myself." She took a step closer and looked into his warm amber eyes and the desire to melt into his arms rushed through her, but now was not the time or the place. "I just wanted to say goodnight and thank you."

"Thank me? For what?"

"For caring so much about the horses...and for the conversation. I'm going to head in now. The storm has passed." She glanced toward Teddy still standing in the doorway, although now he was inside the building and not outside. In another moment or two, she was certain he'd be striding up the aisle toward them, find a convenient bale of hay and sit there, making his unhappiness known. She looked back to Jake. "At least one of the storms has."

They exchanged smiles.

"Good night, Jake."

He gave a slight bow. "Good night, Miss Evie."

She should turn away but for a moment, she couldn't move. Didn't want to. Damn! She was a grown woman. If she wanted to stay in the barn all night, getting to know Jake, she could. And if she wanted to melt into his arms and kiss him, she could do that, too.

Teddy cleared his throat, rather loudly. With a slight nod toward Jake, she finally turned and headed toward Teddy, who had come a few more feet into the barn. He opened his mouth, but she held her hand up, stopping him from saying anything. "As I said, we will discuss this more in the morning. Good night."

She strode past him and across the barnyard at a quick pace, gaining the house in short order. She wanted to slam the kitchen door but didn't. It wouldn't do to wake the entire household. She thought about sitting at the kitchen table and waiting for him, but decided against that, too. Morning would be soon enough to let Teddy know exactly what she thought.

CHAPTER 5

*E*vie patted her hair one last time, pulled on her work gloves, grabbed her favorite sun hat, old and battered as it was, and left her room. A ride out to the summer pasture, where the horses and cattle were, sounded like a fine idea when Teddy had mentioned it at breakfast. He'd said he wanted her advice on which of the two-year-old horses to train next, but she knew it was just a ruse. Teddy was perfectly capable of choosing which horses were ready. He'd been doing it a long time, though he now left the actual training up to her and Antonio unless he thought it necessary to step in. She wasn't needed in the daily work on the ranch, not like the old days when she'd been out every day.

No, she suspected that his invitation had more to do with making sure she and Jake kept their distance.

Teddy was taking his self-imposed role of protector much too seriously. She'd had the discussion with him the morning after the storm, once again made it clear that if she wanted to get to know Jake Hannigan better, she would. He hadn't been happy about that, but in the bright light of day he had accepted her arguments. At least he seemed to.

Whatever the reason for the invitation today, she felt that rush of anticipation she always felt when planning to ride out to the summer pasture. It had been a few days and she missed riding as much as she used to. Funny to think when she first arrived at the ranch, she couldn't ride at all. Her father hadn't thought it was a seemly pursuit for a young lady. Her first experience had been unnerving, but Antonio, bless his heart, had helped, guiding her, teaching her, until she became an accomplished horsewoman. Now, if she couldn't ride every couple of days, she felt antsy, like she had too much energy and no way to expend it.

The sounds of the house in full swing of the morning routine made her smile. She could clearly hear Hilde's voice coming from the kitchen, admonishing little Miguel for stealing a *lebkuchen* she'd just made, and that child's infectious giggle. There was no such thing as quiet in the *casa*, not with four little ones in residence, but it was music to her ears, reminding her of days long past.

As much as she loved it, perhaps it was time to move into *Pequeña Casa*, the original homestead, just a short walk through the cottonwoods and walnut trees west of the barn, and give this one over to the next generation. Teddy and his wife already had three children, a girl and two boys—Savannah, Miguel, and the baby, Ramón.

Esteban had one, a rough-and-tumble son affectionately called Toughie. At thirteen months, he was a handful. He never walked, really. He just stood up one day and started running… and he hadn't stopped. Catalina, Esteban's wife, had recently announced that another child was on the way. She was hoping for a girl, one who didn't run as fast as Toughie.

And Heath, the youngest of Gina's boys, only married a year, was, as he said, trying to keep up with his older brothers, though as yet, all the fun was in the practicing, much to the embarrassment of his former schoolteacher wife, Jenny.

The big house was bursting at the seams, filled, as it had

always been, with love and laughter. Antonio and Hilde had their own little house on the ranch and loved their quiet time. When the children were running and screaming through the house, as they were wont to do, Antonio and Hilde could escape to their sanctuary of peace and quiet, where they sat on the porch in rocking chairs, he whittling, and she either reading or knitting, her favorite forms of relaxation.

Uncle Charley and Aunt Felicity were currently staying in one of the guest rooms down the hall, but were debating on whether to stay and build a small house on the ranch or one in Serenity. Either decision would be fine with her. As long as they didn't go back to San Francisco. She rather liked having them close.

She'd miss this house, though, the familiar creaks and groans, the smell of lemon oil rubbed into the paneling over the years, the third tread from the bottom of the staircase that squeaked when one stepped on it. She'd been happy here. The thought of leaving filled her with anxiety, but maybe it *was* time.

The alternative was to arrange for the children, though they were hardly children, and their spouses to build their own homes, the way they wanted, on the property. There was more than enough land to do so. Montaña del Trueno was a small town unto itself with so many outbuildings. Two or three more wouldn't make much of a difference.

She ran her hand along the polished banister as she made her way downstairs. Ana met her at the bottom.

"Miss Evie, you have a visitor. He's waiting in the parlor."

"Who is it, Ana?"

The woman shrugged. "He did not give his name, but he said you were expecting him."

Dear Lord, another potential suitor? Hopefully not. "Thank you, Ana. I'll be there in a moment. Would you please bring us some coffee? And some of the *lebkuchen* Hilde made, if there are any left."

Ana stopped. "I put some aside just for you, before the children ate them all."

"Thank you." She pulled off her gloves and shoved them in her pocket as she continued down the hall, trying, unsuccessfully, to tame the uneasiness growing in her stomach.

She left her hat on the small table beside the door and entered the formal parlor. Her gaze settled on an older man, his hands folded behind his back as he studied the family photographs in their silver frames crowded onto every available space on a long table in front of the windows.

He was a big man, much bigger than both Jake and Oscar, but not necessarily in a good way. The suit jacket he wore, while in good condition, was old, and seemed to be stretched too tight across his shoulders and back, obviously too small for his frame. There was a tear at the shoulder, which had been mended, but repaired in such a way she knew it had not been professionally done. His hair hadn't been professionally cut either. Wild and bushy, and much too long, she guessed this man did not visit the barber on a regular basis, and took scissors to his locks himself, as evidenced by the unevenness. "Hello. May I help you?"

He turned quickly and her attention was drawn to the big, bushy mustache on his upper lip, reminding her very much of the pictures she'd seen of walruses. His eyebrows matched that mustache. They, too, were big and bushy, like woolly caterpillars had settled on his forehead above his small, round eyes. Both brows and mustache were dark threaded with silver. A lot of silver. The hair on his head, too, held more silver than dark brown. "Are you Miss Everleigh Miller?"

"Yes."

"Horace Quinn. A pleasure to meet you," he announced in a booming voice too big for the small room as he lumbered across the carpet and grabbed her hand. Instead of shaking it, he dropped a kiss on her knuckles, leaving wetness on her skin. It was all she could do not to pull her hand from his grasp and wipe it on her skirt. She expected wet, slobbery kisses from the children, not from a grown man.

"Please, have a seat, and tell me why you're here." As if she didn't already know. Her stomach clenched.

He squeezed himself into the chair, the same one Oscar had occupied just a few days ago. He, at least, did not jostle the table or knock over Miguel's picture. "Come now, Miss Miller. You know why I'm here. Your letter stated you were looking for a husband." He was blunt, she'd give him that. No beating around the bush, no attempt to even pretty up his words. "I'm here in answer to that request."

"Ah, the letter. I should probably explain about that, Mr. Quinn. I actually didn't write that letter or the advertisement that prompted your correspondence. It was my niece, Lucy, on my behalf. I had no idea she'd done such a thing. I'm not—"

"I have a successful hardware store in Santa Fe with several employees. And a big house, fully paid for, in the nicest section of town." He spoke over her, as if he hadn't heard her at all. "Of course, once we're married, we can work in the store together. Why pay someone, right?" He laughed and leaned a little closer, as close as he could get with the table between them. She caught a whiff of his breath and pulled away from the offensive smell.

"Mr. Quinn, I—"

"I'm assuming you know how to cook, yes? And keep house?"

"Mr. Quinn—"

He kept right on talking, didn't bother to sugar-coat his intentions at all, and the only thing she could see was that bushy mustache and his wet lips. She shuddered, barely able to keep her composure.

"Mr. Quinn!"

"We can be married right away. I took the liberty of making arrangements with the Justice of the Peace in Santa Fe. He's waiting for us." He stood abruptly, as if by saying the words, it would be done. "We should leave now. If we do, we can be back at the store before my employees steal me blind."

As well as being blunt, he was forceful, too. And assumed much too much. He didn't want a wife. He was looking for cheap labor to work in his store, instead of employees who he thought would steal from him. He wanted someone to keep his house, without having to pay for it. And warm his bed, too.

He couldn't have been more wrong—about everything—and while other women may have jumped at his offer, such as it was, she wasn't one of them. She'd never leave Montaña del Trueno.

She was about to try to tell him that she wasn't interested in marriage when Toughie ran into the room with a high squeal, completely naked, Hilde's *lebkuchen* in both hands.

"Share!" he shouted, as he jumped in her lap and shoved the cookie at her face. Evie pretended to take a small bite of the soggy cookie, much to the boy's delight, then kissed his forehead, the only place on his face that didn't have cookie crumbs.

She glanced over Toughie's head. The expression of horror on Mr. Quinn's face was almost too much. He sank heavily in the chair as if in shock, the thin spindly chair legs creaking under his weight.

"Is he...yours?" he whispered, terror in his voice.

"In a manner of speaking. He's my grandnephew, Tomas, but we all call him Toughie."

There was obvious relief on Mr. Quinn's face. What was even more obvious, to her at least, was that he didn't like children. In fact, they seemed to scare him more than a rattlesnake ready to strike. She smiled sweetly, kissed the top of Toughie's head, and looked directly at him. "But I love children. I'd like to have a few of my own. At least half a dozen."

And again, the terror in Mr. Quinn's expression was back as quickly as it had been gone. Worse, Toughie chose that moment to slide from her lap and toddle over to him, cookie crumb hands and all.

"Share!" The boy shouted, and offered one of the treats to Mr. Quinn. The big man actually recoiled, trying, unsuccessfully, to pull away from the boy and the soggy cookie. His small eyes were now huge in his face, caterpillar eyebrows rising up to his hairline.

"We're teaching him how to share. Pretend to take a bite," she suggested, as the big man's face paled, making his mustache and eyebrows stand out in stark relief. .

Catalina, Toughie's mother came rushing into the room, and stopped. "Oh, I'm so sorry, *Tia* Evie! I didn't know you had company." She made a beeline for her son and scooped him up. "He escaped me. Again. I turned my back for one minute and he was gone."

"He is fast, I'll give him that, but it's all right. No harm done." She laughed and rose to her feet, tweaking the boy's cheek with all the affection she had for him. "He was sharing."

"He was?" Catalina asked, a little surprised, then kissed the boy's cheek. "You were sharing?" The boy nodded eagerly and offered her a bite of the cookie.

Mr. Quinn sprang up from his chair, an expression of horror on his face. "Madam, I'm afraid we won't suit. Good day!" He gave a slight bow, then rushed from the room like his hair was on fire. She was certain the man had never moved so fast in his life.

"Who was that man?"

Evie laughed. "That was Mr. Horace Quinn, another potential husband Lucy chose for me."

Her eyes, framed by thick black lashes, widened. "You're joking, right?"

"No, I'm afraid I'm not." Evie led the way out of the parlor, Catalina following closely behind. Evie grabbed her hat from the table and placed it on her head.

"What was she thinking?" Catalina shook her head, her lips pursing together for a moment. "That man is not who I would have chosen for you."

Evie squelched a groan, suspicion rising in her mind, as she voiced her question. "Were you in on the husband hunt, too?"

"Well, not exactly. Lucy had mentioned it." Toughie squirmed in her arms and tried to escape, but she held him tightly, which didn't please him at all. "But I told her she shouldn't do it."

"Just for curiosity's sake, what kind of man would you have chosen for me?"

The smile disappeared from Catalina's face as she considered the question. "He'd have to be kind. And love children and animals." She thought for a moment longer, and said, "He should be handsome, but that's not the most important thing. He'd have to have a sense of humor."

Funny, Catalina described Jake Hannigan. He was kind. And he did like children. More importantly, they seemed to like him. She'd seen Miguel and Savannah sitting on bales of hay and pestering him with questions as he mucked out the barn, and she was impressed with the way he interacted with them. He answered all their questions patiently, which said a lot. One could easily get frustrated with Savannah, for whom every answer had three more questions. To say the girl was inquisitive would be an understatement.

Animals liked him as well, as evidenced by Flower, who jumped into his lap every time the man sat down. Apparently, the cat also slept with him, settling at the foot of Jake's bunk, or so Grub had told her, and the other cats and the dog followed him as he went about his chores, hoping for a bit of affection, which he supplied without hesitation. Even the horses liked him, quickly running up to the side of the corral as he passed by.

And he was handsome, with his black hair liberally streaked with silver and startling tawny eyes. His smile still did funny things to her insides. The only thing she didn't know about yet was his sense of humor.

"Let's go take that nap, young man." Catalina gave her son an affectionate squeeze but didn't dare let him down. He'd be off in a shot, faster than a bullet leaving the barrel. "You know, *Tia* Evie, if I'm not mistaken, I believe there's someone here who has all those qualities."

"And who would that be?"

"Why, Mr. Hannigan, of course." And with that, she walked down the hall to her room, leaving Evie to stare at her departing back in wonder, as if the woman had read her mind. Toughie waved a cookie at her before he took a big bite, his grin spreading as crumbs floated to the floor. She'd have to sweep them up before they became imbedded in the carpet runner.

After cleaning up the crumbs, Evie headed into the kitchen. Hilde had the coffee service spread out on its silver tray on the butcher block worktable and was just finishing pouring the brew into the server. Steam rose, scenting the air with her wonderful coffee.

Aunt Felicity sat at the table, the latest issue of the *Ladies' Home Journal and Practical Housekeeper* spread out before her. Her hat and a pair of gloves were within easy reach, as if she was just waiting to head out. She smiled and offered her cheek. Evie obliged and planted a light kiss on her pale skin, though it was obvious, she had interrupted their conversation. It was also apparent, by the pinkish glow on Felicity's cheek, that she—and her recent visitor—were the subjects of that discussion.

"I was just going to have Ana bring in the coffee." Hilde glanced in her direction. Her cheeks, too, held a slightly pink hue, confirming Evie's suspicions.

"No need. Mr. Quinn has left."

Hilde stilled, the coffee pot still in her hand. "So you chased off another one?"

"Another one? How can you say that? Mr. Hannigan and Mr. Peña are still here. Besides, I didn't chase Mr. Quinn off at all. He left of his own accord. Rather quickly, I might add."

"Oh? And you had nothing to do with that?"

Evie laughed. "Actually, I didn't. It was Toughie."

"Toughie?" The woman's hazel eyes narrowed, and she could just see the wheels of her mind turning.

"Yes, Toughie. It appears Mr. Quinn doesn't like children. I think they scare him. At least, that's the impression I got. He wanted me to leave Montaña del Trueno—today, I might add—and work in his store. He even had the audacity to arrange for a Justice of the Peace to marry us in Santa Fe this afternoon." She shuddered, thinking about his wet lips on her hand. "Thankfully, Toughie saved me. And just in time, too." She picked up one of the *lebkucken* Hilde had arranged on a plate and took a bite. "I think I'll go for that ride now and meet up with Teddy."

Hilde gave a non-committal grunt, then poured herself a cup of coffee. She joined Aunt Felicity at the table, but didn't say anything, which was unusual—Hilde always seemed to have an opinion.

"You two can go back to talking about me."

"We weren't talking about you, dear," Aunt Felicity said, but the blush on her cheek deepened.

Evie didn't believe her, but that was neither here nor there. If her oldest friends wanted to talk about her, well, that was fine. She imagined they had a good laugh at her expense considering the circumstances. She'd find it amusing too—if it wasn't happening to her—but she would have a talk with Lucy, find out why she'd done this thing, and how many more prospective husbands would show up.

She walked across the lawn toward the barn. None of the cats were wandering around, neither was the dog. Jake wasn't there either. In fact, the barnyard was completely empty. The barn doors, as well as all the windows, were wide open to let in fresh air. Her horse Spitfire, along with Clementine, Horatio, and the draft horses, were in the corral next to the barn. Petunia, the milk cow, was in her own little paddock, munching on some fresh hay.

Spitfire saw her coming and raced to the fence. "Are you

ready for a ride?" she asked, as she ran her fingers lightly over Spitfire's long nose.

The horse chuffed in answer, blowing hot air through her nostrils, then pawed the ground with her right hoof, sending puffs of dust into the air. Evie removed the rope that held the gate in place and swung it open. "Come on, then." The horse stepped through the open gate, then stayed, as she'd been trained, for Evie to close it, then took a few steps toward the barn. While Spitfire waited, Evie headed down the central aisle toward the tack room at the back of the barn. She grabbed a blanket and slung it over her shoulder, then looped the bridle and reins around her arm and hefted the saddle off the sawhorse, lugging it back outside.

"Let me help you with that."

Evie turned quickly to face Jake as he took the saddle from her. She took a step back. "Oh, Mr. Hannigan!" She paused. Was it possible he was more handsome now than the night in the barn? She particularly liked the way the sunlight brought out the strands of silver in his dark hair.

"Jake, please," he reminded her once again. "I wanted to apologize again if my being in the barn with you caused an argument between you and Teddy."

"Did he say something to you?"

"No, but there was this look in his eyes this morning. It was the same look as yesterday morning. And the morning before that." He chuckled. "Actually, it's no different than the look I've been getting since I got here."

"A look? You mean his lips pressed together, eyes narrowed and shooting daggers, the muscle near his eye twitching? I've been on the receiving end of *that* look before."

"Oh, he wasn't happy. That much was clear, but at the same time, I definitely saw some humor in his expression as well." He placed the saddle on Spitfire.

"Humor? That doesn't sound right. I'll talk to him again."

"No need. He is protecting you…from me. I understand. I just wish I could make him see that I would never hurt you, Evie." His gaze swept over her face. It was almost as if he touched her. "I would protect you, just like he would. I imagine everyone here would do the same."

He tightened the cinches, then bent over and laced his hands, providing a step for her. Evie placed her foot into his hands and her hand on his shoulder, the muscles beneath his skin hard and unyielding and so warm, and lifted herself into the saddle. He adjusted the stirrups, making sure her feet were positioned correctly. Was it just her imagination or did she actually feel the heat of his hand through her boot?

She looked down from the saddle, focusing on his mouth as he smiled up at her and her heart melted a little. He said he would protect her. "Thank you."

"My pleasure, ma'am." He grinned that devastating grin, his amber eyes crinkling at the corners, and for an insane moment, she wanted to slide from the saddle and into his arms. She wanted to press her lips to his and kiss him. Instead, she turned away, nudged Spitfire, and rode out of the barnyard to meet up with Teddy, but that didn't stop her from feeling the heat of his gaze. Or imagining what could be.

Jake stood in the barnyard, his attention focused on the horizon, long after Evie disappeared from view.

"How are you getting along here, son?"

He turned to see Charley leaning against one of the fence posts. How long had he been standing there?

"Fine, sir."

The older man moved away from the fence and walked toward him, hands on his hips, eyes squinted against the sun. "She is something, isn't she?"

"Who?"

Charley stopped beside him, a grin that said 'you know exactly who I'm talking about' hovering about his mouth. "Evie. I've known her from the moment she was born. Her sister Regina, too. Their mother, Victoria, was a dear friend. The girls' father, too, by extension, though he and I didn't see eye to eye very often. I hated how he disowned both his daughters, but there was no changing his mind, and believe me, I argued." He pulled his hat a little lower, blocking out the glaring rays of the sun. "She's a good woman, Evie. Not many would have given up what she did for her sister."

"No, sir. They would not."

"Even fewer would have put their lives on hold to raise the children." He gave him a direct look. "Felicity and I love her like a daughter."

Ah, there it was. Not a threat, like Antonio and Teddy had given him, but a warning just the same. Clear and unmistakable. Jake glanced at the older gentleman, only to find himself on the receiving end of a very thorough scrutiny, almost as methodical and complete as any he'd received from Teddy and Esteban.

Charley's intent was apparent—don't hurt Evie.

Warning noted. "I just want you to know that I would never hurt Miss Evie."

"You'd better not."

Jake acknowledged the statement with a nod.

"Felicity and I are heading into town."

"I'll get the buggy." Jake said, before the man even asked.

"Thank you. I appreciate that, son."

Jake walked into the corral and retrieved Winston, one of the draft horses, from its confines. The man's eyes remained on him as he led the horse toward the building behind the barn.

It didn't take long to harness Winston to the buggy, nor wipe down the seats with an old rag. He brought the buggy around to the rose arbor at the end of the garden path where Charley waited for his wife.

Felicity came out of the house and approached them with a wide smile. "Good afternoon, Mr. Hannigan."

"Good morning, Miss Felicity. Don't you look lovely."

The woman blushed, the redness spreading over her cheeks as she reached up to adjust the ribbon holding her hat in place. "Thank you, Mr. Hannigan."

"Are you ready, dear?"

She gave her husband a slight nod and a smile. A *loving* smile. There was no other word for it. No one had ever smiled at him that way.

He started to assist Felicity into the buggy, but Charley took his wife's hand first and helped her, then made sure she was settled comfortably before he trotted around to the other side of the buggy and climbed in.

As Charley flicked the reins and started the vehicle moving, Felicity faced him. "Have a lovely afternoon, Mr. Hannigan."

"Thank you, Miss Felicity. You as well."

He watched the buggy until it disappeared from view, his hands on his hips, his lips pressed together in thought. There had been such love in Felicity's smile for her husband and such devotion on Charley's face when he looked at his wife.

Is that what a loving relationship looked like? He had no experience to draw from. That wasn't to say he wasn't fond of women. He was. Tremendously. And there were some in his past, former lovers whom he now considered friends, but not one of them had ever looked at him like that.

Charley and Felicity weren't the only ones, either. He'd seen that expression of love and devotion on the faces of all the couples around him. Antonio and Hilde. Heath and his Jenny. Teddy and Esmeralda. Even Esteban, who spoke very little, more than made up for his lack of speech when he gazed upon

Catalina…and she returned his expression, as if words were unnecessary.

Is that what I want?

The plain, honest truth was…he didn't know. One does not miss what one has never had, but one could definitely *want*. Could Evie be the woman he'd been waiting for all his life, though he hadn't known it? Could she be what had been missing, even though he had everything he thought he wanted. He wasn't sure, had never really thought about it until Father O'Malley reprimanded him for his way of life, convincing him that it was time to put away the cards and become respectable. Was he worthy of her? Could he offer her more than what she already had? He had no family except for Father O'Malley and the good Sisters. And he had a past, one he knew Evie wouldn't approve of. She despised gambling after losing her sister the way she had.

Shaking his head as if that would help his thoughts roll into the right place, he strolled back toward the barn.

CHAPTER 6

$\mathcal{E}$vie came in from the garden with a sigh. She couldn't put it off any longer. With the children and their mothers down for their naps, and everyone else busy elsewhere, it was the perfect time to work on payroll.

In truth, it was not a chore she enjoyed. Lucy had been doing it for the past few years, but Lucy was married now and living in Serenity with her new husband, so the task once more belonged to her.

She strolled down the hall and stopped short in the doorway to the study. The desk chair was already occupied, the payroll ledger, neat piles of coins, packets of greenbacks, and little envelopes spread out on the desk's shiny surface. Steam rose from a coffee cup. The door to the safe in the corner stood wide open. Pleasure swept over her in an instant. She'd recognize the back of her niece's head anywhere—there was no mistaking those ringlets of dark brown, nor the pencil shoved into those glossy locks. "Lucy! What are you doing here? I thought you'd still be setting up the house." She entered the room with quick footsteps, her paralysis broken.

"Hello, *Tia* Evie." The young woman smiled at her as she

swiveled the chair around to face her and leaned back into the soft leather, a smudge of ink on her chin. "The house is set up, everything put away exactly how I like it. We're just waiting for a few more pieces of furniture that Ben is having made, and it'll be done. He decided to leave his medical office where it is for now, because all his patients know where it is, but eventually, he'll move his practice to the house. It's certainly big enough." Undeniable happiness shone from her eyes, obviously proud of her accomplishments over the past two weeks. "Thank you for our home. The house is perfect."

"Thank your brothers, too. It was their decision as well. They wanted you and Ben to have a good beginning."

Lucy stood as Evie gave her a hug and kiss on the cheek, then flounced back into her chair.

"I'm glad you're here." Evie took a seat on the sofa and studied her niece. "I have some questions for you, young lady."

Lucy settled herself more deeply into the chair and leaned forward a little, giving Evie her undivided attention. Her eyes were wide and twinkled with mischief. "I'm sure you do."

"I find myself in the strangest of circumstances and it's all, as I understand it, because of you." There didn't seem to be a bit of remorse on Lucy's face. In fact, it seemed that she was trying hard not to laugh. "You think this is funny?"

The young woman nodded. "Yes, I do."

"Well, I don't." She stared at her niece. "Would you mind explaining to me why you put an advertisement in the newspapers for a…a…mail order husband? Exactly how many newspapers did you put it in?"

"Oh, a few." She giggled, her exuberance almost contagious. Almost. "You'd be surprised how many men responded to my advertisement. Apparently, you're quite the catch, *Tia* Evie!"

"Lucy!" She very rarely raised her voice, but this time, she did. "Please be serious. How many advertisements did you place? And where?"

"Seven." She counted off the cities. "Santa Fe. San Francisco. Denver. Phoenix. Sacramento. New Orleans. Even Atlanta."

Seven! Evie groaned. "And how many men are going to show up here claiming that they are my future husband?"

"Well, I corresponded with several men, but only chose the best five, in my opinion, based on their letters. I wanted you to have a choice."

Her stomach clenched with the information. *Five! Oh, dear Lord!* On the heels of that, another thought occurred to her. How had Lucy managed all this without her knowing? The answer was simple. Lucy often rode into Serenity to see Ben, and picked up the mail before returning home. That's how she kept all this secret. Until now.

"How many have shown up so far?"

Evie stiffened. "Three."

Another giggle escaped her. "Three is good. For a start."

"No, it's not." Evie glared at her. "This isn't funny, Lucy!"

"Oh, yes, it is. You've played matchmaker for my brothers, but you don't like it when someone plays matchmaker for you."

Lucy was correct. She had played matchmaker for Teddy, Esteban, and Heath.

"Yes, I did help your brothers choose the right wife," she admitted, "but this is different. I didn't interfere. I didn't...place advertisements in newspapers, for heaven's sake. I didn't correspond with them and invite them to show up on my doorstep. I am not happy with this entire situation, my girl." She rose from her seat and walked toward the desk where Lucy sat, her hands on her hips. "I want it to stop. Right now."

"Yes, ma'am." Lucy's smile disappeared, so did the humor that had been dancing in her eyes, as if the realization struck her that nothing about this was funny. "You're angry with me."

"Yes, I am." Evie paused, determined not to let her emotions get the better of her, but it wasn't working. "Why did you do it? Why did you advertise for a husband for me?"

Lucy looked down at her hands then back up at her, wide eyes suddenly brimming with tears. "I didn't want you to be lonely."

"When have I ever been lonely? This ranch is filled with people. There isn't a chance to be lonely."

The girl dropped her gaze. "I wanted you to be happy," she whispered.

Evie threw up her hands, frustration getting the better of her. "Why does everyone assume I'm not happy? I am. I have everything I need or want. Stop interfering in my life. I will decide when or if I want to meet someone. I don't need help. I don't want it."

Still fighting with her emotions, Evie lowered her voice and knelt down in front of her niece. She reached for Lucy's hand and held it within her own. "It could have been dangerous, too, Lucy, which Teddy has brought up a few times. I'm sure you didn't consider that, did you?" She didn't give her a chance to answer. "I don't know these men and neither do you. Who knows what kind of man could show up here? He could be an outlaw. Or a thief. Or a murderer. People aren't always what they seem, especially on paper. It's very easy to write lies just as easily as it is to lie to one's face."

The tears filling Lucy's eyes spilled over and rolled down her cheeks as the full implication of her actions hit her. She gulped in air. "I'm so sorry, *Tia*. I hadn't thought of that." She swiped away the wetness. "I never intended to hurt anyone."

"I don't want your apologies, Lucy. I want you to fix this. No more prospective husbands. I mean it."

"Yes, ma'am." Lucy nodded, sniffing away the tears. "Do you forgive me?"

Evie raised her hand and cupped Lucy's cheek. "Yes, I will forgive you but only as long as you promise never to do something like this again. It isn't fair. Not to me or any of the gentlemen coming here looking for a wife, especially since I have no desire to marry." She dropped her hand then stood but maintained eye contact. "Since you're so good at correspondence, I want you to write to those men who haven't shown up yet and rescind any offers you may have made."

Lucy nodded, swiped at her eyes once more. "Yes, ma'am."

"Today."

"I will." She picked up a fancy fountain pen from the desktop and grabbed a sheet of paper from the drawer. "Just tell me who you've met."

Evie closed her eyes for a moment and paused before she said something she'd regret then answered once she had full control of her thoughts. "Horace Quinn arrived yesterday, but, as he stated to me before he left here like someone put a burr under his saddle, 'we won't suit'." She began to pace but her gaze never left Lucy's. "Did you know he expected me to leave here and live with him in Santa Fe where he has a hardware store? He even had the audacity to arrange for a Justice of the Peace for the very afternoon he came here! Like I would ever leave Montaña del Trueno."

She shuddered, remembering her revulsion when he kissed her hand, his lips soft and wet, like a child's. Or a fish. "And another thing—he doesn't like children. Did you know that? Did he tell you that in his letter? The look on his face when Toughie interrupted our conversation and offered him a cookie was one of pure disgust. And fear. I got the distinct impression that he just wanted a wife to take care of him and work for him in his store."

"I am sorry, *Tia* Evie. He did not mention in his letter that he didn't like children. Or that he expected you to leave the ranch and move to Santa Fe." She made a note on the paper. "Mr. Quinn wasn't what you would consider a good husband. What about Mr. Peña? Did you meet him?"

"I did. He seems like a nice enough man, I suppose. Attractive. I've offered him a job, so he'll be staying. For a while, at least. It wouldn't surprise me if he didn't stay long."

"What aren't you telling me about him?"

Evie continued to pace, going from one end of the room to the other, stopping only to pick up a picture in a frame, this one of Toughie, who, surprisingly, sat still long enough to have his photograph taken. "He's...too young.

"Too young? How young is too young?"

"He's more than ten years younger than I am, Lucy." She put the picture back where it belonged and turned slightly to see Lucy studying her intently.

"A younger man could be...interesting."

"That may be so, but he only responded to your advertisement because he wants a ranch of his own and assumed, incorrectly, that Montaña del Trueno would be his if we married."

"I'm sorry. That wasn't anything he mentioned in his letter." She frowned and some of the teasing light that had been in her eyes dimmed. "I'm crossing Mr. Peña off the list as well. A potential husband he is not." She wrote another note. "Mr. Robicheaux? Have you met him?"

Evie just looked at Lucy then shook her head at the audacity of her niece. "No, Mr. Robicheaux has not arrived at the ranch yet."

"What about Mr. Ambrose?"

"My God, Lucy, what have you done? Sending all these men here? What am I supposed to do with them?"

"Marry one of them," she said, rather flippantly in Evie's opinion, which didn't help the situation at all. "If you want. Did Mr. Hannigan come?"

"On your wedding day, in fact." Her face warmed at the mere mention of his name. She averted her eyes and studied the photograph sitting on the desk of Serafina, the children's grandmother, Savannah in her arms. "He strolled into the yard just after you and Ben left for Serenity. He was quite the surprise."

"Did you send him packing like you did Mr. Quinn?"

"I didn't send Mr. Quinn packing. He left of his own accord.

Rather quickly, I might add," she defended herself. "As for Mr. Hannigan, I offered him a job, even though he doesn't know how to ride, doesn't have his own horse or saddle. In fact, he didn't seem to know anything about ranching at all." She felt Lucy's intent stare and focused on her once again, even though her heartbeat seemed to pick up its pace. "I will admit that he's learning and picking things up rather quickly though he hasn't learned how to ride yet."

"What did you think of him?"

Evie stiffened. It was one thing to harbor thoughts about Jake in her head. It was another thing to admit to her niece—or anyone else for that matter—that Jake Hannigan made her knees go weak when he smiled. Or that sometimes the look in his eyes made her want to melt into his arms. Or admit that she watched him as he went about his chores and admired his physique. Or that she thought about kissing him and running her fingers through the crisp hair on his chest. Or that—

"*Tia* Evie?"

Startled out of her thoughts of the man, she wrestled control of her wayward emotions. "What?"

"You were going to tell me what you thought of Mr. Hannigan."

Instead of answering her niece, she asked again. "Why did you do this, Lucy?"

"I thought it was time."

Evie sat heavily on the sofa and stared at her niece.

"You've spent the last twenty years taking care of us, sacrificing for us," Lucy confessed, the light in her luminous dark eyes showing her love. "It's your turn to live a little, and you always said that once we were all settled, you'd look for your own happiness." She smiled, trying to look innocent. "I thought I was helping you."

"I didn't need this kind of help, *mi corazón*." Evie frowned, crossing her arms over her chest, as if trying to ward off any more help. "I'm perfectly capable of finding a husband if I so choose."

A dark eyebrow rose on Lucy's forehead and the expression on her face clearly said she didn't believe her. "Oh? Is that why you've been alone all these years? Is that why you pushed Marshal Corwin away? I know he asked you to marry him. I know you said no."

Evie wasn't aware anyone had known that Travis had asked her to marry him—or that she had turned him down. It had happened last year, long before Lucy had gotten it her head that she needed to be married. As a result, Evie had lost a good friend. She felt the need to defend herself. "I've never been alone, Lucy. I have all of you. And Marshal Corwin is a wonderful man."

"But he wasn't the man for you. I understand." Sympathy crept into her eyes. "It was his profession, wasn't it? You'll never fall in love with another lawman."

"Let me make myself clear, *mi amor*," Evie told her. "I'm not interested in marrying just to be married. There's much more to a marriage. You should know that. You've been in love with Ben since you first set eyes on him, and you were what? Six? Seven? And he felt the same, even though he was a few years older. I see the way you look at each other. I feel the love between you. And when he went off to school to get his medical degree, that love didn't diminish. It grew and flourished, despite the separation. He was always the one for you."

"Even Hilde found love with Antonio, though she swore up and down and three ways from Sunday that she wasn't in love with him. Look at them now. Eighteen years later and they still look at each other like there is no one else in the world for them."

She stopped speaking, stunned. That's what she wanted—someone to look at her like she was the reason they got up every day, the reason they put one foot in front of the other. "So no, I'm not going to marry someone just to be married."

"You want someone to sweep you off your feet."

She shook her head. "No, I don't want someone to sweep me off my feet. I don't need flowers or candies. I don't need someone to fill my head with sweet words. Those things aren't important to me." That was the truth. She was too practical for that, and yet, that very feeling of being 'swept off her feet' seemed to be happening every time she caught sight of Jake Hannigan. No, there were no flowers or candies or whispered words of professed love, but her heart seemed to beat a little faster whenever she caught sight of him, and her stomach felt like it was filled with butterflies.

"If that's not it, then what do you want? The truth, *Tia* Evie." Lucy leaned forward in her seat, the fountain pen in her hand finally still.

"The truth? I want someone to grow old with. Someone to sit on the patio with me and watch the sun set. I want late night conversations about nothing and everything. I want laughter and tears." She gazed at her niece, her eyes roaming over her lovely face. "I want someone who loves you all like I do. Someone who knows that family comes first. Someone as committed to Montaña del Trueno as I am."

Lucy nodded, seeming to absorb the information. Looking at her, one would think she was mentally marking off a checklist in her head. She probably was. "Lucy!" she raised her voice again. "Just stop and listen to me. Love doesn't happen with lists and agendas. It just happens. And sometimes, it doesn't happen at all, no matter how much a person wants it to."

"That is true, but it doesn't have to be." Still, Lucy put down the pen, properly chastised, but only for a moment. "Sometimes it helps to know what you want." She eyed her aunt. "What do you want?"

Evie didn't answer. Lucy pressed the issue. "Passion? Companionship?"

Evie sighed and stared at her niece. She didn't want to be

talking about this with her, and it took a long time before she admitted, "Yes, I suppose."

"Can none of these men fulfill what you want?"

Evie leaned forward a little. "Aside from that Horace person, Jake and Oscar seem like…nice men, although I'm hardly in a position to know them. And there are still those men I haven't yet met."

Her stomach knotted just a little more, and suspicion, entirely warranted, raised its ugly head. "What aren't you telling me?"

Lucy tilted her head and smiled. "There might be one more. I just met him. His name is Ryland Parrish. He's a widower and seems very sweet. He's renovating the old Serenity Hotel."

That little bit of information was the one that pushed Evie beyond her limits and irritation swept through her. "One more? Another complete stranger will be showing up at my door?"

"I'd like you to give these men a chance," Lucy argued in that way she had. She never raised her voice, but she always got her point across. "Get to know them. You don't have to marry any of them, *Tia* Evie, but you do owe it to yourself to at least consider the possibilities. What have you got to lose?"

"You're not listening to me, Lucy. I am not interested in having a parade of men waltzing in front of me like they're auditioning for the role of 'husband.' This is my life. You have no right to interfere in it." She rose from the sofa and strode to the door, then turned and pinned her niece with a look Teddy would recognize. "This is the end of it. Write to those men who haven't shown up yet and tell them you were mistaken. There will be no weddings in their future. Or mine." She stepped through the door and closed it behind her, willing her frustration away. She started walking down the hall, then slowed when she distinctly heard Lucy comment about stubbornness through the closed door.

Her lips pressed together in annoyance. What gave Lucy the right to think she knew what was best? Who gave her the authority to interfere in her life, like Teddy was trying to do? And it *was* her life. She was perfectly capable of making her own decisions. She'd been making them for a long time, and the majority of those were usually right.

She understood Lucy's motivation though, and her exasperation faded a bit. Lucy was happy, therefore she wanted everyone else to be happy. It's just the way she was. Still, she didn't appreciate the fact that her niece had advertised for a husband for her and invited strange men to Montaña del Trueno. That was just taking it a step too far, and her choices, so far, seemed to fall far short of ideal.

Except for Jake.

She rushed through the kitchen, opened the door, and ran smack into the man she'd been thinking about. A muffled "oof" escaped them both as her nose smashed into his hard chest and her body pressed up against the rest of him. The clean scent of soap filled her senses as his strong arms came around her, perhaps to steady her. Or maybe, just to hold her. At this moment, she didn't care which. If he let go, she just might fall.

He was a solid wall of muscle, and she fit so comfortably against him. His hands splayed across her back, the heat of his palms seeping through the sheer fabric of her blouse. "Are you all right, Miss Evie?"

She looked up into his face, his amber eyes warm and filled with concern. For once, no smile spread his lips, which, for reasons she couldn't explain, devastated her more than his smile usually did.

If she wanted to kiss him, now would be the time. Right now, while he held her. Right now, when she was off balance, and not just physically. He really was the most handsome man she'd ever met. She pushed back. "Yes, I'm fine. I'm sorry. I wasn't paying attention to where I was going."

He released her then and took a step back, the smile she adored coming to his face, and all at once, in addition to feeling off balance, her heartbeat picked up its pace.

"No harm done."

His voice struck at her very core, but her chance to kiss him, to touch her lips to his, disappeared, mostly from her own cowardice, which struck her as strange. She was no coward—never had been—so why was she now? With him? Wasn't this what she wanted? Hadn't she wondered what kissing him would be like?

"Where are you going in such a hurry? Is there something I can do for you?"

Evie shook her head, her tongue as twisted as the ropes filling the tack room. She took a moment—an eternity, it seemed—as her gaze roamed his face. Her focus fell to his mouth, the upper lip a little fuller than the bottom, and she noticed the beginnings of a mustache. "You can kiss me."

A strange expression came over his face and something warm and exciting sparkled in his beautiful amber eyes.

Heat infused her, from her toenails all the way to the top of her head. Had she said the words out loud? Apparently, she had, but before she could even begin trying to explain, his grin widened. He tipped his hat back and moved closer, filling the small gap between them. Once more, his arms wrapped around her, pulling her even closer.

"Yes, ma'am, you're the boss." There was humor in his voice as his head dipped and his lips touched hers, gently at first then with more pressure as his arms tightened around her.

The world ceased to exist the moment his lips touched hers. The kitchen disappeared in a flash as his clean scent of soap surrounded her, the warmth of his mouth on hers and his strong arms the only things she could feel. Perhaps she was out of practice—after all, Tom had passed away a long time ago and no one had kissed her since, but this? This was a full-on assault of her senses!

He broke the kiss but didn't release her.

Evie blinked, crashing back to reality. Her face was on fire.

Indeed, her entire body thrummed with both embarrassment as well as excitement. She had never been so bold and yet, he didn't seem to mind. Not one bit.

She pulled out of his arms and took a wobbly step back, her gaze focused on him and the warmth emanating from his eyes. "I'm sorry. This was a mistake. I have to go." She squeezed past him in the doorway, her body brushing up against his, and escaped, running across the lawn and out to the paddock, where Spitfire met her at the fence. She didn't bother with a saddle or bridle, simply opened the gate then climbed up on the fence and settled herself on Spitfire's back and raced out of the barnyard.

CHAPTER 7

"I'm going to marry her." Oscar pulled himself away from the window, where he'd been standing for the last twenty minutes, his focus on the garden, and wandered over to the table in the middle of the room.

Jake knew what he'd been staring at. Miss Evie Miller. And he knew that because he'd been watching her, too—when Oscar's big head wasn't in the way. From his bunk, if he positioned himself exactly right, he had a clear view of the garden. She'd come outside to clip roses and arrange them in a crystal vase, then took a seat in one of the cushioned chairs on the patio, her gaze on the last glow of light as the sun set in the horizon. She seemed wistful, dreamy. He couldn't see her expression from here, but he could certainly see the way she sat. From years of watching people across a poker table, he could tell a lot about them. And her posture definitely told him she was deep in thought.

What was she thinking about? The kiss they shared in the kitchen doorway? He had been just as surprised as she had apparently been, but the taste of her, the feel of her soft lips pressed to his, the warmth of her body seeping into him lingered.

He glanced down at the sketch pad he'd found among the collection of dime novels and classic literature on the bookshelf and the picture he was drawing of Evie clipping the roses. This was the latest sketch and he flipped through the pages before it, not completely pleased with the images.

He paused on one of her hanging laundry on the clothesline to dry. Her movements that afternoon were so graceful that he'd had to try to capture them. He flipped through a few more pages before stopping on the one he'd drawn of her playing with the children. Her laughter had alerted him to the scene, and he couldn't resist recreating it on paper. He closed the sketch pad, his favorite still the one he'd done of her brushing Spitfire the night of the thunderstorm. It probably had nothing to do with the quality of his work and more to do with the memory.

He slipped the sketch book under his pillow and glanced at the table in the bunkhouse. Oscar had finally taken his seat, joining his bunkmates who were gathered around for their after-supper coffee and a piece of Hilde's lemon cake before hitting the sack. Morning came quickly on a ranch.

"I don't think so, Oscar. Miss Evie ain't innerested in getting' hitched. Heard her say so m'self. 'Sides, you're too young." That came from Marcus Bryant, whom everyone called Mayhem.

Oscar puffed out his chest. "Am not."

"What makes you think she'd marry a cocky sumbitch like you? Miss Evie's a lady." That came from Slick. No one knew his real name. And no one seemed to care. He was a good ranch hand and had a fine sense of humor and that's all that mattered.

Face turning red, Oscar boasted, "I got a letter. That's what."

Jake sat up, his interest fully captured. Oscar must have responded to her niece's advertisement. He wondered how many other men got letters.

He told himself it didn't matter how many men showed up. Then the old familiar feeling of being "not good enough" for a respectable woman such as Evie Miller surged through him, especially considering his past life and how she felt about gamblers in general.

Still, what would she say when she learned of his past? More than likely she would ask him to leave.

The thought depressed him more than he cared to admit. In all honesty, he liked it on the ranch—the slow rhythm of the days and the camaraderie of these men—with the exception of Oscar, whose arrogance annoyed him—so different than those he'd known in his other life. And then, there was the opportunity to gaze upon Evie…and the prospect of kissing her again. That, more than anything, made him want to stay and wonder what could be.

Besides, he had nothing to go back to San Francisco for. His home was gone, burned all the way to the ground, nothing left but ashes and memories. The life he'd known was gone, too, which wasn't exactly a bad thing. And Erik King was probably still looking for him—the man never gave up—but the odds of him looking here were minimal.

"A letter?" Cesar stuck his pipe in his mouth and spoke around the stem to the other men gathered around the table. "Oh, I heard 'bout that. Miss Lucy placed an advertisement in a couple o' newspapers, lookin' for a husband for Miss Evie. I heard she ain't real happy 'bout that." He struck a match against the table and brought the flame to the bowl. In moments, the fragrant aroma of tobacco wafted toward the ceiling. "So why ain't ya out there courtin' her? From what I seen, you just stand at the window and stare at her."

"I'm waiting for the right time."

"Uh huh." Cesar grunted. "Yer chicken, that's why."

One of the other men began making clucking noises, very low, but still quite audible. Someone else hummed the Wedding March. Jake thought it was Mayhem, but he couldn't be sure. Still, it made him smile. Oscar was in for a good old-fashioned razzing by his fellow bunkmates. He couldn't think of anyone who deserved it more.

"Am not!" The man bounded up from his seat so quickly, the chair toppled over. His hands were drawn into fists and his eyes narrowed. It wasn't the first time Oscar had shown his temper and it wouldn't be the last. The man had a problem in that regard, in addition to his usual attitude of superiority. Jake knew it was only a matter of time before a fight broke out.

"Ain't no fightin' in the bunkhouse." That reminder came from Emilio, who sat back in his chair and raised a coffee cup to his lips. After he took a sip, he stared at Oscar. "If you wanna fight, ya gotta go outside. Them's the rules. 'Sides, we're just teasin'. You ain't the first man to fall in love with Miss Evie." He grabbed an empty cup and poured coffee, then slid the cup across the table toward Oscar with a nod. "At one time or 'nother, we all fell in love with her. Hell, I did. Hard." The calmness of his tone and his understanding words seemed to be enough to still Oscar's temper. The man's fists uncurled. He picked up his chair and sat then stared at Emilio.

"You? You fell in love with her?"

"Yes, sir." Emilio smiled, but his eyes took on a faraway quality. "Fell in love with her the very first time I saw her. Love her still, but not in that romantic kinda way."

"Why not?"

The man shrugged and took another sip of his coffee. "She never looked at me *that* way an' you know how I mean."

Though the comment wasn't directed at him, Jake knew exactly the look Emilio meant. He'd seen it before, most recently when Felicity smiled at Charley. There was love in that look.

"She was too busy trying to raise Miss Regina's kids and running Montaña del Trueno." Emilio paused then let out a sigh. "An' then there was Marshal Tom."

It was on the tip of his tongue to ask about Marshal Tom, but Slick saved him from speaking.

"Marshal Tom?"

"Hmm, Marshal Tom Gray. Good man. The kinda man you'd trust with your life." Emilio glanced at Slick then turned his attention back to Oscar. "You know that look I was talkin' 'bout?"

The young man nodded.

"She had that look for Marshal Tom. This was way back. 'Bout three years after she came here. She was in love with him and he her. They were goin' to get married."

"So how come they didn't?"

"Marshal Tom died 'bout a week before the wedding. Killed by the same gambler that took Miss Regina and Mr. Javier. Miss Evie weren't the same after he died. That's why we ain't allowed to gamble in the bunkhouse."

Jake sucked in his breath upon hearing how Marshal Tom had died. Losing him to the same gambler's gun that had taken her sister must have been devastating and his sympathy for Evie rose. It also made him feel even less worthy of her than before. Did he even have the barest whisper of a chance with her? Considering what he now knew, he doubted it. And yet, there was something about her that drew him, something he couldn't deny, something that made him want to try.

"An' it's jes a damn shame," Cesar remarked, as he shook his head.

Emilio nodded in agreement, and it was obvious to Jake that he did, indeed, still love Miss Evie. "She's a fine-lookin' woman, especially when her hair is down and blowin' in the wind an' her eyes are smilin'."

Jake had to agree, though he didn't say so out loud. That was the image he had of her in his mind and the one he should try to sketch. He slipped out of his bunk and headed toward the door.

Cesar watched his progress, a smile hiding beneath the mustache on his face. "Where you goin'?"

Jake could almost hear 'city boy' after the question, even though the words were not said. He'd heard them before, mostly from Oscar, but chose to ignore them. After all, he did come from a city. He knew the unspoken words were meant as an insult. If that's the worst they could come up with, he'd take it. "Take a piss."

"Sure you are." Cesar scoffed and grinned. "So what's your story, Jake? You been here almost two weeks, showin' up just before Oscar here," he gave a nod toward the other man, "and we don't know nothin' 'bout you, 'ceptin' you don't ride. Hell, you don't even own a horse or a saddle." He narrowed his eyes as his gaze rested on Jake. "You get a letter, too?"

"No, sir," he lied, not willing to let these men know he did. He wasn't in the mood for a razzing. "And my story is that I gotta go take a piss."

He left the bunkhouse, though that didn't stop the sound of laughter his departure brought nor the comments he could clearly hear.

Evie was still sitting on the patio. She'd lit a lantern against the growing darkness. The warm glow settled on her skin and reflected off her hair.

He walked toward her. "May I join you?"

She glanced up at him. In the light cast by the lantern, he could see color blossoming on her face. "Oh, Mr. Hannigan, of course."

He took a seat then leaned back against the cushion and crossed his legs at the ankle. From inside the house, he heard quiet conversation coming through the open windows, as supper dishes were washed. Apparently, that was a chore the older two children participated in, as he could clearly hear their young voices and the gentle encouragement from an older woman. There were other voices, too. He recognized Antonio's deep tone as well as Heath's. "It's a lovely evening," he finally said.

"Yes, yes, it is." She didn't look at him, her gaze trained on her lap. "I'm sorry," she blurted out.

"Sorry? For what?"

"For asking you to kiss me." She glanced at him, then returned her focus to her hands folded in her lap. "I shouldn't have."

His gaze roamed over her face, settling on her rosy cheeks and a dark curl that fell over her shoulder. He was struck by the urge to reach out and caress that curl. Actually, he wanted to pull the pins from the loose bun at the back of her head and let the rest of her hair flow free, like it was the night of the storm, when it looked like she had just rolled out of bed. "I didn't mind. Honestly."

"I'm glad you didn't mind, but still, I shouldn't have." She gave a rueful laugh. "I don't know what possessed me. I've never done anything like that before."

"What? Kissed someone?"

She laughed again as she shook her head, that curl bouncing against her shoulder. "Be that bold."

"Why not? I'm a firm believer in asking for what you want."

"And what do you want, Mr. Hannigan?"

"For starters, I wish you would call me Jake. I thought we agreed you would."

She tilted her head to the side, and it was the most adorable thing he'd ever seen. "I'll try to remember that."

That cocking of her head made her too irresistible. He stood then and walked around to her side of the table. He hid his smile as she watched his every move, her brow furrowed in puzzlement, her eyes full of curiosity. He stopped in front of her, placed his hands on the chair's armrests on either side of her, his gaze roaming her face, seeing the anticipation in her expression. "For another thing," he whispered just before he lowered his head. He captured her mouth in the sweetest of kisses, molding his lips to hers.

Her surprised intake of breath was followed by a sigh as she responded to his kiss. Her hands rose to rest upon his on the arms of the chair, then moved to his upper arms and finally around his neck. He'd only intended to have a taste, but realized in an instant, one taste was not enough. She was intoxicating. Innocent, yet knowing, making him want more. Without taking his lips from hers, he slowly brought her to her feet.

She came willingly, pressing her body close to his, sharing her warmth as his arms wrapped around her, pulling her closer still. He deepened the kiss as he slid his tongue between her lips and explored the warm recesses of her mouth. He tasted mint mixed with her sweetness.

As much as he wanted to kiss her until dawn streaked the sky with its brilliant colors, he couldn't. Ending the kiss, he took a step back. "Good night, Miss Evie."

He walked away, while he still could, knowing that if he stayed there, holding her, tasting her mouth, he'd never be able to stop. Not that he wanted to stop. He didn't. There was something more, something he couldn't explain even if he tried. He'd noticed it earlier. This only confirmed the notion.

He let himself into the bunkhouse and headed straight to his bunk, aware that Emilio and Cesar watched him intently. The other men were asleep or on their way to dreamland, Grub's mumbling in competition with Oscar's. He waited for one of them to say something, but neither did as he stretched out on his bunk, folded his hands behind his head and purposely closed his eyes. As soon as he did, a kaleidoscope of images flashed before his eyelids: Evie riding out to the summer pasture, looking magnificent on horseback; Evie gardening, a big floppy hat protecting her from the sun; Evie walking toward him, a beautiful smile on her face.

The images weren't going to stop, and he accepted the inevitable. He smiled to himself and let the visions in his head lull him into sleep.

~

Evie stood right where Jake left her and watched him walk away until the door to the bunkhouse closed. Well, he didn't actually walk. He swaggered. Yes, that's the only word she could think of. Swagger. She admitted, as he disappeared from view, that he had the nicest backside of any man she knew.

She brought her fingertips to her lips. That kiss, so tender, so gentle, was more devastating than the one earlier today. She could still feel the touch of his lips as well as the heat of his embrace, his strong arms surrounding her, pulling her against the hard muscles of his chest, the clean scent of soap in her nostrils.

A light went out in the bunkhouse, then another, until nothing but darkness spilled from the windows, and still, she didn't move. She pictured him stretched out on his bunk, his hands folded behind his head, long legs crossed at the ankles. Or maybe his arms were crossed over his chest. "Oh, I am in trouble," she whispered to the empty garden.

"Are you all right, *liebchen?*"

"Yes, yes, I'm fine, Hilde."

"Why are you in trouble?"

"I'm not."

The older woman grunted then tugged on her earlobe. "Then my hearing must be going because I distinctly heard you say you were in trouble." She chuckled as she moved a little closer. "It's that Jake Hannigan, isn't it?"

"What makes you say that?"

"I saw him kiss you and then I saw you just standing here, not moving, staring at the bunkhouse. If looks could burn a house down, this whole ranch would go up in flames."

"I don't know what you're talking about." Embarrassed, her face on fire, Evie denied the truth, the second or third time she lied when it came to Jake Hannigan, which wasn't like her at all. She never lied and here, she'd done it again.

"You can lie to yourself all you want, *liebchen*, but I have eyes in my head, and I know what I see. You're attracted to him. You can admit it."

Evie shook her head. "I will admit no such thing." She stared at her companion. "And I don't want to talk about it."

"Of course you don't want to talk about it, but in my opinion—"

"For once, Hilde, I can do without your opinion. Good night." She let herself into the kitchen before Hilde could respond and closed the door firmly, though she didn't slam it. She headed up to her lonely bed with the thought that it didn't need to be lonely.

CHAPTER 8

$\mathcal{J}$ake stepped out of the barn to see the ranch hands riding into the barnyard with whoops and hollers. It was early, too early, for the men to be coming in from the summer pasture. He pulled his pocket watch out and snapped open the cover. Only four o'clock. "What's going on?" He caught Slick slipping from his saddle, puffs of barnyard dust billowing around his feet.

The man grinned. "It's pay day. Come on over to the bunkhouse. Antonio will be handing out our envelopes in about an hour." He wrapped his horse's reins around the post. "If'n you're plannin' to head into town, now would be the time to get cleaned up. You don't want those pretty ladies at the Spur to be wrinklin' their noses 'cause you smell like a horse."

Cesar rode up beside them and dismounted, joining the conversation before his feet even hit the ground. "Come down to the river."

"The river?"

"That's where we go to get ourselves all spit shined and polished before we head into town. Helluva lot better than washing up at the barrel." He nodded toward the barrel of rainwater at the edge of the bunkhouse porch, then rubbed his hands together with obvious glee. "I got me a brand-new deck o' cards and I'm feeling lucky!"

"No, thanks."

"Suit yourself," he said as he wrapped his horse's reins around the post in front of the barn, hitched up his trousers and headed toward the bunkhouse. He came out a few minutes later with a bundle of clean clothes—at least, Jake thought they were clean—and headed behind the barn.

The rest of the men followed, laughing, and pushing at each other, all carrying a clean set of clothing, and the barnyard grew quiet, but the quiet didn't last. Teddy, who still managed to give him *that* look at least once a day, if not more often, rode in, followed by his brothers. He dismounted in front of him and tossed him his horse's reins. "Jake."

"Teddy."

"You heading into town with the boys?"

"No, sir. Not this time."

Teddy looked at him as if trying to read his thoughts but failed. That look was in his eyes though and there was no mistaking it. The warning was clear. Stay away from Evie. It hadn't changed since that night he found them in the barn. He was thankful Teddy knew nothing about their kiss or he doubted he would still be upright and his nose not broken.

After a few moments of intense scrutiny, Teddy tipped his hat back. "Hitch up the carriage when you have a minute."

"Of course."

"Hey, Jake." Heath gave him a big smile. "Give ol' Goldie extra oats tonight. He had a rough day." He patted his horse's side before giving him the reins.

"Will do."

Esteban handed him his horse's reins as well. "Don't bother

removing his saddle. Catalina and I will be heading back out again, but if you could saddle up Horatio, I'd appreciate it."

Surprised the man uttered more words than Jake had heard before, he smiled. "Of course."

Esteban gave him a quick nod, his quota of words apparently spent, then headed toward the house, following after his brothers.

Jake took care of the horses, putting them in the corral to cool down before he brushed them, then saddled Horatio. When he was done, he headed toward the building behind the barn where the fancy carriage was housed. He wiped it down with a cloth, swiping at the seats to make sure no spiders or other critters were hiding among the cracks then hitched up the draft horses. He guided the horses to where the flagstone ended and the barn-yard began, unsure if he should bring them to the front of the house or not. He hadn't been instructed.

Dusting his hands off on his trousers, he headed back to the corral. The horses he put in there should be cool enough to brush down. He didn't make it very far as the sound of laughter and crude jokes drifted toward him. In a moment, he saw his bunk-mates troop back to the bunkhouse, all 'spit shined and polished,' as Cesar called it, hair still wet, slicked back, faces clear of the dust and dirt they seemed to wear as part of their everyday attire. His bunkmates weren't normally the cleanest bunch of men. Aside from splashing cold water on their faces in the morning to help them wake up, hygiene didn't seem to be high on their list of priorities, though Grub made them wash their hands before they were allowed to sit at the supper table, which Jake found amusing.

He knew they sometimes looked at him strangely because he was the opposite, washing up as best he could from the barrel outside the bunkhouse every night. He may not be living in the lap of luxury like he had at one time, but that didn't mean he couldn't be clean. Nor did it mean his clothes couldn't be clean, either, and he rinsed his socks and undergarments every night and hung them out to dry on the fence behind the barn, which made his bunkmates laugh.

Apparently, that was something that never came to their minds. Laundry was done once a week, on Wednesday, but the men handed over their clothing to Ana begrudgingly when she came to collect them. Even Oscar, who spent a great deal of time combing and waxing his mustache, which was rather impressive, didn't extend the practice to the rest of himself.

Antonio sidled up beside him, carrying a small wooden tray with raised sides. "Come on inside, Jake. It's payday and you earned every penny." He picked out one of the envelopes and shook it, making the coins inside slide back and forth. "I had my doubts when we first met, but you've done well."

The unexpected compliment pleased him, and he followed the man into the bunkhouse. The other men were already lined up at the table, waiting for their pay, the atmosphere full of expectation. Antonio pulled out a chair, made himself comfortable, picked up an envelope and called out the first name. His name was called last, and he wondered if the big man had done that on purpose.

"Here ya go, Jake."

Jake ripped open the little envelope and glanced inside. Crisp new bills and several shiny coins met his eyes. "Thank you."

"Don't spend it all in one place." Antonio picked up his empty box, then addressed the rest of the men. "Have fun tonight, *amigos*, but not too much fun. I don't want to see any broken bones or busted heads tomorrow morning. And I'm not bailing any of you out of jail either. Just keep that in mind." He left amid crude comments, though they were said in jest, followed by Cesar, Emilio, Mayhem, and Oscar. Even Grub, apparently, intended to join his bunkmates for a night on the town.

"You're not heading into town with us?" Slick asked, as he stepped up beside him, his own envelope in hand.

Jake shook his head. "No, I promised Antonio I would finish cleaning up the tack room." It wasn't the truth. There would be gambling at the saloon, he was sure of it, and he might not be able to resist. He hadn't touched a playing card since he left San Francisco. He hadn't broken his promise to Father O'Malley, but he didn't want to tempt fate. "Is there a post office in town?"

"Sure is. Miss Gemma at Goldwater's handles the mail."

"Would you drop off a letter for me?"

"I can do that."

"I'll have it ready for you before you leave."

"That's fine, but ya better hurry." Slick grinned as he removed his pay from the envelope and stuffed everything in his pocket. He didn't even count it. "I got me a pretty little miss at the Silver Spur. Don't wanna keep her waitin'." He tipped his hat and walked outside, leaving the door wide open.

Jake retrieved the letter he'd been writing to Father O'Malley from his trunk as soon as Slick exited the bunkhouse. He finished it quickly, folded it around several of the new crisp bills he'd been given and stuck it in an envelope. He wrote out the address that had been part of his life for as long as he could remember, included a return address in the upper corner, and headed outside. All the men were on their horses, anxious to be off for a night of carousing and gambling and whatever other entertainment there was to be found. He handed the envelope to Slick along with a few coins to pay for postage.

The man glanced at the envelope, then looked at him, his eyes widening with surprise. "Father Ryan O'Malley?"

"An old family friend," he said, not wishing to share any more than that.

Slick shrugged and slipped the letter in his shirt pocket, then let out a whoop and kicked his horse. The other men followed suit, racing out of the barnyard, leaving a cloud of dust in their wake.

It wasn't long after that Teddy and Heath, along with their wives and Ana, came out of the big house, all dressed in their town finery, and climbed into the waiting carriage. Apparently they enjoyed a night on the town as well as the men, though he assumed their celebration would be a bit more subdued. Instead of a noisy saloon, he supposed they'd dine at a nice restaurant, perhaps take in a play or listen to music, if Serenity had an opera house. Or they might be going to visit Lucy. He doubted very much that they would sit at a felt-covered table and gamble.

Antonio and Hilde, he noticed, did not join them. Neither did Charley and Felicity. He didn't see Evie, either, which was a good thing. She wasn't heading into town. He supposed she was inside with the children, but maybe she'd come out later, sit on the patio and watch the sun set. And just maybe, she'd like some company when she did.

He saw Esteban and Catalina come out of the house a few moments later and head straight for the corral. They each carried saddle bags as well as burlap sacks. They mounted up and rode out in the opposite direction.

The barnyard grew quiet, except for an occasional meow from the cats wanting some attention, the clucking of the chickens with an occasional crow from Lucifer, who still didn't know what time it was, and the soft sounds of the horses in the corral. He wandered toward the paddock and opened the gate. One at a time, he brought the horses into the barn, brushed them down, gave them their share of oats—a little extra for Goldie, as Heath requested—and settled them for the night.

Once that chore was done, he took a seat on the stump he used to chop wood. Flower jumped in his lap, her purrs quite loud as she rubbed her face against his. The dog wasn't far either, lying in a patch of sunlight. The evening stretched out before him. He could go back into the barn and keep company with the horses. He hadn't lied when he said he'd grown fond of them. Or he could settle in and finish reading one of the books he'd chosen from the bookshelf in the bunkhouse. Or he could pick up the sketch pad once more and try to capture Evie's face just before he kissed her last night.

The object of his thoughts came out of the house, a tray in her hand, covered with a checkered napkin, and walked through her garden toward him. He stood as she drew closer, once again admiring her beauty, which wasn't hard to do…he found himself doing that more often than not. She wore one of her favored split skirts, this one a light tan suede, pairing it with shiny black boots that reached the hem of the skirt and a plain white blouse. Her hair had been left loose—no bun at the back of her head or horse's tail that swung back and forth as she walked—to curl in wild abandon around her shoulders. She looked very much like she had the night of the storm. His pulse quickened and warmth flooded him as blood rushed through his veins.

Color flamed on her cheeks as she handed him the tray. "I noticed everyone went into town, including Grub, which means you have no supper."

"There's enough in the ice box to cook something up, but I appreciate it." Holding the tray from beneath with one hand, he removed the napkin and his mouth watered. A bowl brimming with a hearty beef stew and a thick slice of bread, already buttered, met his eyes. There was even a piece of chocolate cake and a tall glass of milk. "Thank you."

He gestured to the makeshift chair he'd been sitting on. "Please."

"Oh, no." She leaned against the wall, her hands behind her back. "You sit. You need to eat."

He studied her for a moment, then laid the tray on the stump and disappeared into the bunkhouse. He returned in a moment, bringing one of the kitchen chairs with him. He placed it beside the stump.

Evie gave him a quick smile, then sank into the chair, her gaze moving to the horizon.

He did the same, though his focus was more on her than the sunset. Still, the vibrant colors of the setting sun seemed to glow on her face. "The sunsets here are beautiful," he said, before he took a big bite of the bread. The sweet creamy butter and the tartness of the sourdough hit his taste buds all at once and he nearly groaned at the combination.

"What?"

With bread in hand, he gestured toward the horizon and the myriad of colors streaking across the sky, a deep magenta being the predominant shade. "The sunsets. Are they always this beautiful?"

"Yes, I like to think so. This is my favorite time of day."

"Mine as well."

"Why didn't you go into town?"

"Why didn't you go into town?" They asked the question at the same time, which amused him.

"You first," he said, watching the blush spread across her cheeks and loving the sight.

"There's nothing in town I needed. Besides, I thought it was important that Ana go. She hasn't been to see her family in a couple of weeks. You?"

"Didn't see a reason." He smiled at her, then said, "And I'd hoped, maybe, that you and I could spend some time together, get to know each other a little more. I learned a lot about you that night in the barn, but there's still so much I don't know."

"But there are entertainments. A few saloons, where there's music, the whiskey and beer flow freely, and a poker game or a fight is always ready to happen." She lowered her voice to almost a whisper and tilted her head to the side, peering at him sideways. "A bawdy house or two."

"Not interested."

"Why aren't you already married?" she blurted out.

The question caught him off guard. He wasn't quite sure how to answer, so he took a spoonful of the stew and mulled it over as he chewed. Finally, he said, "I could ask the same of you."

She smiled. "I asked you first."

His gaze roamed her face, settling first on her eyes then on her mouth—her utterly kissable mouth—and the memory of the taste of her lips made responding almost impossible. He pulled in a breath, trying to control his thoughts. Finally, he shrugged. "Never found anyone willing to put up with my faults."

"Your faults? Surely you don't have that many."

He laughed at the serious expression on her face. "Oh, I can list them out for you, if you'd like, but I have to warn you, we could be here for days."

She chuckled at that. "I don't think that will be necessary." Her gaze was still on him, a fine web of wrinkles, though he thought of them as laugh lines, radiating from the corners of her eyes. There were laugh lines around her mouth, too, but they didn't detract from her beauty—not at all. They only enhanced her loveliness and told him that this woman laughed. A lot. "Have you ever been in love?"

He shook his head. "No."

The answer seemed to surprise her. "Never?"

"Is that so hard to believe?"

"Yes, I find that hard to believe. Everyone has fallen in love at some point in their lives, even if it was unrequited."

He didn't agree, but then again, what did he know of love? Absolutely nothing. There were people who were fond of him, like Father O'Malley and Sister Agnes, and he was fond of them in return, but love? No, that was something he hadn't experienced. "What about you?" he asked, even though he knew about Marshal Tom. "Were you ever in love?"

"Once," she admitted with a sigh. "A long time ago." She stared at her hands folded in her lap. The fading sunlight, filled with shades of red and pink and gold, reflected on her, making the strands of silver in her hair turn a pale golden red.

"What was his name?"

"Tom Gray."

"Tell me about him."

She glanced at him then turned back toward the sunset though he didn't miss the flash of sadness in her eyes. "He was the Marshal here in Serenity," she said softly. "He was a good man."

"How did you meet?"

"He rode out to the ranch one morning to warn me about horse thieves in the area, wanting to make sure we were aware of the danger, wanting to make sure I was safe. He was like that. Caring. Sweet. Protective, very much like Teddy. The boys adored him. So did Hilde and almost everyone who knew him. I adored him." Her voice grew hoarse and she cleared her throat.

"After the horse thieves were arrested, he kept coming around, a couple times a week, on his 'rounds,' as he called his visits. He started staying for a cup of coffee and we'd talk. Coffee turned into dinners here at the house and in town." She laughed. "It didn't take long for me to fall in love with him or for him to feel the same way. When he asked me to marry him, I said yes. What else could I say? I loved him. Still do." She drew in her breath and didn't say anything for the longest time. When she finally spoke again, her voice was stronger, but he could still hear the sadness in her tone.

"We spent weeks planning our wedding, making lists of who we should invite, what we should have to eat. He wanted a big wedding. He said it was the only one he'd ever have. We were going to have it right here in the garden. My friend Marisol made my wedding dress. Hilde was going to make my wedding cake."

She grew quiet then, her face in profile as the sun dipped lower in the horizon, perhaps remembering Tom, or perhaps, trying to forget him, though one never truly forgets.

"Then a week before the wedding, Owen Pierce came out to see me. He was Tom's deputy and a good friend. I knew before he opened his mouth that it was bad news. And it was. It broke his heart to tell me that Tom…died. It broke mine, too."

"I'm sorry." What else could he say? He *was* sorry, not only for asking the question, but for making her remember the pain of Tom's loss.

After a moment, she turned to face him, and her eyes were shimmering with tears. "It was a long time ago. I've learned to live with his decision to go after the man who killed my sister and her husband, even after he promised me he wouldn't. Deep in my heart, I know he had to do what he had to do. I just wish he hadn't lied to me. I wish I could have at least said goodbye."

His gut tightened as sympathy flared in his heart for her. He should change the subject to relieve her pain and his, make her laugh. Say something, anything to get rid of the sorrow on her face, in her voice.

Before he could open his mouth and follow through on his thought, she gave a slight nod then swiped at her eyes. She drew in her breath, her chest moving with the effort, drawing his attention to the ivory buttons on her blouse before he focused on her face once again. The sadness in her eyes seemed to be dimming.

She looked at him. "Why did you respond to Lucy's advertisement?" A slight smile tugged at the corners of her mouth. "You're a handsome man. I'm certain you wouldn't have any problem finding a wife without resorting to an advertisement. In fact, I daresay you would have to chase them away."

"I've never had to—as you say—chase women away."

"I'm serious, Jake. Why would a man like you answer an advertisement for a husband and come to a ranch, when it's quite obvious you know nothing about ranching?"

Should he be truthful as Tom hadn't been? Obviously, honesty was especially important to her, but one look at her face, and he knew he couldn't blurt out the fact that he'd been a gambler for the past five years, or that a ruthless, persistent man was looking for him for the money he'd won from him. He couldn't say he was afraid he'd end up dead in San Francisco Bay. He hated that he had to lie to her, so he kept to the truth he could tell her. "Honestly, I was looking for a change, something more to my life, something I've been missing."

She nodded, as if the answer he gave was acceptable, but then her head tilted just a bit and she gazed at him. He noticed that she could give the same look as Teddy. Unflinching, as if it could see into one's soul. Perhaps that's where Teddy got it. She didn't blink, which was a bit intimidating, but there was something else, too, in her beautiful blue-gray eyes. A wish, perhaps. A spark of hope. "I'm sure you know that Oscar responded to Lucy's advertisement."

"Yes, I know." He finished the stew, then took a bite of the chocolate cake, which melted on his tongue, but he never admitted how the knowledge that Oscar was here for the same reason he was made him feel. Whereas he'd never felt love, he had, most certainly, experienced jealousy and any number of other emotions.

"I've read the letter Oscar received from Lucy," she said, when he didn't comment further. "If the letter you received from her was the same as his, it was merely an invitation to meet, perhaps get to know each other better, so why did you say that you hoped you hadn't missed our wedding when we first met?" she asked.

He'd known, eventually, she would ask, but still, he wasn't prepared. If he lied, she would see right through it. Truthfully, he didn't want to do that to her. She didn't deserve it and he already had one lie under his belt, though it was a lie of omission…he didn't want more. His gaze swept over her face. "I saw all the tables set up and the banner on the rose arbor with the words "Forever as one" written in gold, and I knew there had been a wedding, and then…I saw you. I thought—I'm not even sure what

I thought at that moment or if I even had a thought at all." He laughed. "All I knew was how lovely you are and that perhaps I'd missed my chance. That perhaps you had married someone else." His gaze drank in all the beauty she possessed. "Have I? Missed my chance."

She shrugged before she stood abruptly and took the tray, then looked at him and smiled, but didn't answer his question. "Good night." And that was it. She walked away, her backside swaying gently, causing her skirt to swing against the top of her boots.

He watched her go and wondered what it might be like to see that sight for the rest of his life.

Evie closed the door and just stood there for a moment, fighting for her equilibrium. The whole time they'd been talking, all she could think about was kissing him again. She felt off-kilter, unsure. And yes, a bit cowardly, which was so unlike her. Why did this man, this stranger, make her feel this way?

"You just going to stand there or are you going to give me that tray?"

Evie faced Hilde. "Yes, yes, of course." But instead of moving toward Hilde at the sink, she strode across the kitchen to the swinging door, the tray firmly in her hands.

"Evie!" Hilde's strident voice cut into the fog in her brain, a fog that seemed thicker than anything she'd ever experienced in San Francisco.

Evie looked down at the tray still in her hands. The heat of embarrassment rushed to her face.

"What is the matter with you?"

"Nothing," she said, as she headed toward the sink, where Hilde waited patiently, her hands on her ample hips.

"Hmmm, nothing *my foot.*" Hilde clicked her tongue as she

took the tray. "Your head is in the clouds, *liebchen*. I have never seen you act like this…except once." The older woman's hazel eyes twinkled with humor as she started taking plates and silverware off the tray and putting them in the sink.

"When? I don't recall that at all."

"A long time ago. I remember a certain young man, a certain Marshal, who turned your head. So much so, you were going to marry him," Hilde said, sympathy flashing in her eyes. "I know how much you loved Tom, but he's gone, *liebchen*. It's time to open yourself to new possibilities."

Evie nodded and gave her a gentle smile. "Perhaps you're right, Hilde. Perhaps it is time."

Surprised, Hilde stopped wiping off the tray with a washcloth and just looked at her. "Well, that wasn't what I expected."

Evie laughed, equally surprised. "It wasn't what I expected to say, either." She reached out and touched Hilde's arm gently. "Now, if you'll excuse me, I'm going to check on the children." She started for the door, then stopped when she saw it opening.

"Ah, Evie, you're here." Antonio entered the kitchen, followed by Uncle Charley and Aunt Felicity. "I think Jake's ready for riding lessons," Antonio announced, as he settled himself at the table and reached for the pot of coffee.

Uncle Charley and Aunt Felicity sat as well. It wasn't long before Hilde joined them.

"That would be fine," she said, her mind still on Hilde's words and the possibilities for a future different than the one she had imagined.

"I'd like for you to do it."

"Of course." She snapped herself to attention, realizing what she'd just agreed to. "Wait, you want *me* to teach him?"

He exchanged glances with Charley and Felicity, then one with his wife. "I can't think of anyone better."

Evie nodded and let out a sigh, but didn't argue. "I'm going to bed," she said instead, then pushed through the swinging door, grateful to escape Antonio's intense stare and smiling countenance as well as the smothered laughter from Hilde and Uncle Charley.

She grabbed one of the lamps from the table in the hall, struck a match and lit it, then climbed the stairs.

She checked on the children, all sleeping in their beds. Ramón clutched his stuffed lamb, thumb in his mouth, sleeping like an angel. She crept into the room and picked up the light blanket from the floor; he'd kicked it off again. He didn't really need it. This June had been unusually warm, the temperatures higher than normal. Or maybe it was just her. She'd never been particularly bothered by the heat, but the last two weeks, she seemed to be warm all the time. And that wasn't the only thing unusual. When had she become so scatterbrained, unable to complete a thought in her head?

She laid the blanket over the rail of the crib, then headed toward her room. She set the lamp on the dressing table, pushing several ribbons out of the way, then removed some of her clothing. Still in her corset, chemisette, and drawers, she washed her face from the bowl and pitcher on her bureau, dried her skin, then sat at the dressing table. Opening a jar of cream that was supposed to prevent wrinkles, she smoothed it on her face.

She stopped and stared at her reflection. *Is that a new wrinkle on my forehead?* She ceased frowning and it went away, but of course, it would come back. She put the lid back on the jar and dropped it in the wastebasket. Whatever claim the cream made was a lie. There were still fine lines on her face, especially around her eyes and mouth.

There seemed to be more strands of gray in her hair, too. She'd found her first gray hair when she was thirty and immediately, despite Hilde's warnings, plucked it from her scalp. It hadn't helped. Oh, she didn't have a head full of silver hair, like Antonio, but there was enough to be noticeable. Too noticeable?

Does Jake see an old woman when he looks at me? He is younger than me, maybe not by much, but still? And yet, he kissed me, not once but twice. Granted, the first time was because I asked him, but the second time, he'd done it on his own.

She let out a sigh. All the creams in the world and all the plucking of gray hair wouldn't change the fact that she was, indeed, as Teddy put it, too old. She rose from her seat, tugged on the corset strings, and removed the garment, then slipped out of her chemisette and drawers. Nude, she turned in front of the mirror. She was still slim and trim, muscles defined from riding and working the ranch, belly rounded but not overly so, breasts not quite as perky as when she was young, but not bad for a forty-year-old woman.

She put on a clean cotton nightgown, propped the pillows against the headboard, and slid between the sheets. Grabbing the book from the nightstand, she opened it at the bookmark. She wouldn't sleep until her nephews and their wives were back home and safe, but she could relax with a good story.

After reading the same paragraph for the fourth time and still not comprehending what it said, she put the bookmark back in place and laid the book aside.

She rose from the bed and went to the open French doors that led to a small balcony. From here, she could see all the outbuildings and far off into the distance. Moonlight illuminated the barnyard, casting its glow on everything. She saw Hilde and Antonio walk across the yard to their little house. A flash of light flared in the window before the door closed. Tomorrow Hilde would be back in the kitchen before the sun rose, sometimes before Lucifer even crowed, and soon the aroma of her fine coffee would be wafting through the house. Evie awoke to that smell every morning.

A few minutes later, she heard Uncle Charley and Aunt Felicity come up the stairs and head toward their room at the opposite end of the hall.

Life on the ranch was all about routine and yet, her routine had been shaken.

She looked toward the bunkhouse. What was Jake doing now? Trying to get to sleep? Thinking of her like she was thinking of him? Feeling restless and too warm?

A moment later, the door to the bunkhouse opened and Jake came outside, lanterns in each hand. He set them on the railing of the porch, where they cast a warm glow against the side of the barn. He took off his shirt and tossed it over the stump, then bouncing on the balls of his feet, started throwing punches like he was fighting someone, although there was nothing there except his shadow.

What was he doing?

It didn't matter. She was enthralled by his actions, the grace he exhibited as he pretended to evade punches thrown his way. He moved like a dancer, light on his feet, his hands in constant motion—a jab here, a jab there. It was like watching a carefully choreographed ballet. If he knew she was watching him, he didn't let on. Not once did he look in her direction, which made watching him thrilling, perhaps because it was a little intrusive. She shouldn't be doing it and yet, she rested her hands on the balcony railing and continued to watch him dance and dart and jab. How long she stood there, she had no clue.

And then he stopped and moved toward the barrel that captured the rain from the bunkhouse roof. He dipped his head into the barrel and came up sputtering, flinging water everywhere. Droplets sparkled in the light cast by both the moon and the lanterns shining on him. He washed up, grabbed his shirt, and used it to dry himself off then carefully laid the garment over the porch railing to dry.

He picked up the lanterns, then went inside the bunkhouse and closed the door. Evie let out a sigh as she saw the warm glow from the lantern extinguish, and the bunkhouse windows grow dark. Now she'd never be able to get to sleep and it would be her own fault.

She didn't move from her spot, her hands still gripping the brass railing surrounding the balcony. Was she willing him to come back outside?

Whether she willed it or not, the door to the bunkhouse opened and Jake walked out to the porch. He sat on the chair he'd brought out earlier, leaned back, crossed his legs at the ankles and his arms over his chest…and looked at the house…as if he knew she was there, knew that she'd been watching him the whole time.

She fled inside her room, her entire body flushed with both excitement and embarrassment, hoping he hadn't seen her, but that was impossible. Wasn't it?

Just one more kiss. That's all she wanted. She was a strong, confident woman, had raised her niece and nephews into fine adults. She had built up this ranch, making it one of the most successful in the area when it hadn't been before. Why couldn't she just walk across the barnyard and straight into Jake's arms? What was stopping her?

Nothing. Not a damned thing.

She grabbed her robe and slipped it on then took several steps across the room. She paused with her hand on the doorknob.

Just do it, Evie.

Anticipation racing through her, she opened the door then crept down the stairs, heading through the empty kitchen and outside…

Just in time to hear the rattle of the harness, the steady clip-clop of the horses' hooves, and the voices of her nephews and their wives as they drove into the barnyard and stopped at the at the edge of the garden. Evie stood in the doorway, thoroughly disappointed, and turned around. Instead of racing across the barnyard to collect her kiss from Jake, she lit several lanterns, grabbed a bottle of brandy and several snifters from the cabinet, then took a seat at the kitchen table to wait for her nephew's wives to give her the latest news of Lucy and her new house.

It didn't take long before Esmeralda breezed in through the door, followed closely by Jenny and Ana. "Oh, *Tia* Evie, I'm glad you're still up. The boys are putting the carriage away, but they'll be in in a minute," she announced, as she slid into a chair and dropped her drawstring purse on the table. "We had such a lovely visit with Lucy and Ben!"

"The house looks amazing," Jenny added as she followed suit. "Lucy has it all fixed up so nice. Even Ben's office is taking shape. It won't be long before he can move his practice there. Lucy's very excited about that. So is Ben." She poured a little brandy into the glasses, then passed them around the table.

"And she made the most excellent dinner," Esmeralda said, as she removed her gloves and adjusted the cuffs of her black-and-white town dress. She stuffed the gloves in her drawstring bag. "She cooks almost as well as you, *Tia* Evie." Her grin widened. "She did burn the rolls though."

"That was our fault," Jenny chuckled, then took a sip of her brandy. "We just kept talking and talking and the next thing we knew, smoke started to billow into the dining room. Well, by that time, the rolls were beyond saving."

"Dinner was lovely without them." Esmeralda said. "Left more room for dessert, which was a chocolate cake so light and fluffy, Hilde would have been jealous."

That surprised Evie. Lucy didn't bake. It's not that she couldn't, she just never had time. She always had other things to do, like take photographs and keep the books. "Lucy baked a cake?"

"No, she bought it from the bakery that just opened up. It's called Sweet Somethings, and the cake was to die for!"

Evie looked around the room and noticed that Ana wasn't with them. "Where did Ana go?"

Jenny frowned. "Probably to her room. She's upset. Her visit with her folks didn't go so well. Her mother is ill and has been for quite some time."

The news both surprised and saddened Evie. "I wasn't aware Mrs. Castillo was ill."

"I don't think it's common knowledge," Esmeralda admitted with a small sigh. "Ana certainly didn't know. She was devastated when she found out. We tried to get her to stay, letting her know you would understand, but she wanted to come back here. Her sisters are there, as well as Mr. Castillo, so Mrs. Castillo isn't alone, but I get the feeling there's more to it than that. Ana didn't want to talk about it, but I could tell she'd been crying when we picked her up."

Sympathetic to Ana's situation, Evie made a mental note to talk to her in the morning. "Tell me more about your visit."

"We met a lovely widower," Esmeralda changed the subject. "Lucy invited him to dinner as well. His name is Ryland Parrish. He's renovating the old Serenity Hotel."

"He's a very nice man." That came from Jenny, who it seemed was all in favor of helping Lucy in her scheme to find a husband for Evie, whether Evie wanted that or not.

"I thought so as well." Esmeralda took a sip of her brandy and peered at Evie over her glass. One of her dark eyebrows rose, as if to imply Mr. Parrish might be considered excellent husband material. "Funny, too, and quite handsome."

Evie said nothing, though she recognized Mr. Parrish's name. Lucy had mentioned it. Considering that this Mr. Parrish had been invited to Lucy's 'family' dinner, Evie was more than relieved that she hadn't gone. Of course, her niece wasn't above a little more matchmaking, aside from the mail-order husbands she'd already arranged for and been warned to never do again. She was just surprised that it was only one gentleman and not more. There were a number of single men in Serenity she could have invited.

"I hope the children were good for you." Esmeralda reached

across the table and laid her hand atop Evie's, startling her out of her thoughts.

Evie smiled. "They're always good for me." She looked up at the clock as she heard the voices of her nephews coming closer to the house, then rose from her seat. If she was going to make an escape before the boys came in and added their opinion about Mr. Parrish, now would be the time. She finished the little bit of brandy left in her glass. "I'm glad you're all home and safe, but I'm going to bed. Good night, ladies."

She left the kitchen just as the back door opened and her boisterous nephews came in, making her escape just in time.

CHAPTER 9

Finished spreading fresh straw in the stalls, Jake stepped out of the barn just in time to see Evie come out of the house. She spoke a few words to Jenny, who sat on the patio with Savannah and Miguel, teaching them their morning lessons. He heard her laughter, and his heart took notice. Indeed, his entire body took notice, and he ached to take her in his arms and kiss her sweet mouth once again.

She strode across the lawn with purpose, the hem of her split skirt swirling around the tops of her black boots, her hat, apparently her favorite, shading her eyes. He watched her come closer, admiring her figure and the way she moved as she cut through the space between rose bushes, then finally came to stand before him. "Good morning, Jake."

"Good morning, Miss Evie." He smiled at her. She really was the most extraordinary woman. Out of all the women he'd known throughout his life, he'd never met anyone quite like her. She was sweet and kind, yet she could be tough when she had to be. And she loved. Hard. He saw it with her nephews, their wives and their children, and every member of her extended family.

"You heading out to the summer pasture? Can I saddle Spitfire for you?"

"Not today. No, today, we're going to do something different." She smiled at him and once again, his heart seemed to stop, then start beating again—almost painfully.

"And what would that be?"

She tilted her head as she looked at him. He loved it when she did that. "I think it's time."

Jake leaned his shovel against the side of the barn and pushed his hat back so he could wipe the sweat from his brow. Why was she being so mysterious? "For what, Miss Evie?"

"Your first riding lesson."

His stomach clenched. He'd been avoiding this. Yes, he was coming to know the horses, and he had to admit he'd become attached to them, but the thought of climbing into the saddle filled him with dread. Guess he couldn't put it off any longer. "If you say so."

She gestured toward the shovel. "Unless, of course, you'd rather shovel manure."

He laughed. "No, ma'am."

"I thought you'd say that. If you'll saddle Clementine and bring her to the ring, we'll get started."

"Yes, ma'am." He watched her walk toward the riding ring, the subtle sway of her backside mesmerizing. He turned away, grabbed the shovel, strode down the center aisle of the barn, and entered the tack room in the back.

At least the horse she chose for him was a good one. Clementine was gentle, and if horses could have a sense of humor, she had one. She liked to steal his hat off the top of his head if he wandered too close to the paddock fence. And then she'd run with it, as if daring him to chase her. Out of all the horses he took care of, she was his favorite.

He leaned the rake against the wall, then retrieved a blanket and saddle, reins and bridle, and wandered toward the paddock.

Clementine raced to the fence, he assumed for an opportunity to steal his hat once again, but he took a step back just in time. He laid the equipment over the fence then opened the gate and stepped inside. Clementine gave him a big horsy smile and tried to grab his hat. "Not today, sweet girl. Today, I'm going to ride you. Are you all right with that?"

She gave a slight nod and chuffed, as if answering his question. Leading Clementine by her leather halter, he brought her outside the gate, and closed it.

"I'm a little nervous, Clem," he admitted, as he spread the blanket over her back. Clementine blew air from her nostrils and gazed at him with her big soulful eyes. "The last time I was on a horse, it didn't end well for me."

The horse stood silently and didn't move as he put the saddle on her and made sure it was secure.

"I suppose that was my fault. I had no business trying to ride Redeemer. Father O'Malley made it very clear no one was to ride him, but one of the older boys dared me." He laughed as he adjusted the cinch, then moved in front of her to fit her with the bridle. "Even at five, I couldn't resist a dare."

He rubbed his hand over her nose before slipping the bridle into place, making sure it, too, was fitted properly as Antonio had shown him.

He glanced toward the riding ring, where Evie waited, her arms resting on the top slat of the fence, but her head was turned in his direction. He looked at the horse. "All right, Clementine, I'm ready. How about you?"

Of course, the horse couldn't answer, but she did dip her head just a bit. He grabbed the reins and led her to the riding ring.

Evie opened the gate and escorted them through, stopping them at a wooden step she had pulled into the ring. "Don't be nervous, Jake. It'll be fine. Clementine will take excellent care of you. She's very patient and forgiving. Both Savannah and Miguel learned to ride on her. I did as well." She gave him an assuring smile. Too bad he didn't feel assured. "Do you know how to mount a horse properly?"

"Not really. But I've watched all of you" He glanced at the step by his feet. "There was no step when I tried to ride Redeemer all those years ago. There wasn't a saddle either. I climbed to the top plank of the stall like the older boys at the home told me to and jumped on his back."

"And Redeemer bucked you off immediately, didn't he?"

"Yes, ma'am." He tipped his hat back and laughed, though the remembered pain wasn't funny at all.

"Well, it's no wonder. If I was Redeemer, I'd have thrown you off, too." Her smile widened. "That's not going to happen here. We'll start from the beginning. We will be using this step today, but eventually, you'll be able to do this without one." She nudged Clementine into the proper position. "One of the most important things is that you never want to hurt your horse by being clumsy or inconsiderate. Your horse is your friend, your companion. He or she has feelings and emotions, just like we do. They feel love and jealousy, happiness and sadness. They can feel pain, too, just like us. Treat them well—always—because out here, your horse can be the difference between life and death."

"I've never looked at it that way."

"I'll demonstrate proper mounting while I explain the steps." She glanced up at him, her beautiful blue-gray eyes a little bluer than normal, her smile firmly in place before she reached for the reins in his hands and climbed the wooden steps. "Start with the reins. You want to hold them just so." She slid the reins between her fingers until they were at the proper length, close to the horse's mane. "You'll be holding the reins in such a way that you can also rest your hand on Clementine's mane." Her movements matched her words. "Place your right hand in the middle of the saddle." She performed the action then lifted her left foot into the stirrup. "Always point your toe toward her nose. Raise yourself up and swing your leg over. It should be a smooth motion." The leather creaked as she settled herself in the saddle then looked at him. "That's it. Do you want me to show you again? Or do you think you're ready to try?"

She made it look so easy, but he had doubts. Besides, it was such a pleasure to watch her. He could do that all day long. He pressed his lips together so he wouldn't smile. "Show me again."

"All right." She dismounted, her actions the direct opposite, and showed him again...then once more. "Now you try."

He did exactly as she showed him. Clementine, bless her, didn't move, but she did look at him, her big eyes round. He could swear she was smiling at him. She probably was.

Once he was settled in the saddle she continued, "Sit up straight and keep your back relaxed."

How could he sit up straight and be relaxed at the same time?

"This should be enjoyable for both of you. You can't be as stiff as a fireplace poker. Relax your arms. Rest the reins gently in your hands."

Her instructions seemed to be such a contradiction. He tried, though. He wasn't comfortable at all. He was waiting for Clementine to buck him off. But it didn't happen. Clementine didn't move.

"To get Clementine to move forward, nudge her a little by squeezing your knees against her sides. It shouldn't take much. To get her to stop, pull the reins toward yourself. It doesn't have to be hard. Actually, I prefer that it not be hard. If your horse is well trained, you don't have to use much force. I've seen how others do it and I can't say I agree with it. There should be no reason to pull that hard." She rubbed her hand against the horse's side, and he wished that she was touching him that way. "Are you comfortable?"

"No," he admitted.

She laughed. "You'll be fine. Why don't you take a couple turns around the ring? See how it feels."

He waited until she moved toward the fence, taking the step

with her. She climbed up to the top plank of the fence and made herself comfortable, her focus on him. Now, if that didn't make him more nervous, he didn't know what would. He looked down at the horse, and whispered a silent prayer he wouldn't make a complete and utter fool of himself. He nudged Clementine like he'd been told.

Clementine didn't move. Instead, she turned her head and just looked at him. After a moment, she showed her big yellow teeth. A thought came to him. "Are you laughing at me?"

The horse blew air from her nostrils, giving a little grunt at the same time.

"Well, stop it. You're embarrassing me in front of Miss Evie."

The horse continued to stare at him, then turned her head and looked toward Evie sitting on the fence. He tried again, squeezing his legs against Clementine's sides. And still, she didn't move.

"Don't do this to me." He tried one more time. Either he wasn't doing it right or the horse just didn't want to obey his signal. He assumed it was the latter. Clementine did have a sense of humor. Perhaps, she thought this was amusing. "Please."

She took one step then stopped, once more turning her head to look at him. Yes, she was doing this on purpose. He glanced toward the fence to see Evie jump down from her perch and approach him.

"What's the matter?" She peered up at him beneath the shade of her hat, curiosity making her brows dip a little.

Jake let out a sigh of frustration. "She doesn't seem to want to move. I've squeezed my knees against her sides, like you said, but she only takes a step then stops."

"I have an idea. Give me the reins."

He did as he was told, silently handing her the reins, his face flushing with embarrassment. Indeed, his entire body felt as if it was on fire. He hated the thought that he'd failed, especially in front of her.

She clicked her tongue and tugged lightly on the reins, leading Clementine toward the step she'd placed by the fence.

"Scoot forward in the saddle a little."

He did, then stared at her, puzzled. "What are you going to do?"

"This is how I taught Savannah and Miguel." She climbed the step then mounted Clementine behind him, settling herself in the saddle, her body pressed against his, so close, he could feel the warmth of her through her clothing and his. She wrapped her arms around him then placed her hands over his on the reins gently.

Jake stiffened. The act of reaching around him pushed her body more firmly against his back. He imagined he could even feel the buttons of her blouse pressing into his flesh.

Evie chuckled. "Relax, Jake."

Now how am I supposed to relax with you pressed up against me like this? Or concentrate on what I'm doing?

"You ready?"

"As I'll ever be." His voice came out more like a groan, even to his own ears, which embarrassed him a little more.

She squeezed the muscles of her legs while at the same time, pulled the reins gently toward the right. "Can you feel that?" she asked, as the horse started to move.

How could he *not* feel that? He stiffened as his body reacted. Blood surged through him, pounding in his ears, rushing to places it should, but not right now, making it almost uncomfortable to sit. "Yes."

They went around the ring a few times, slowly at first, then a little faster, her thighs and knees communicating her wishes to the horse and Jake felt every slight squeeze, every release. He'd have dreams of this…even when he was awake.

"I'll admit, this was much easier with the children. At least, I can see where I'm going over their heads. Are you comfortable taking the reins by yourself?"

No. He wasn't. He rather liked having her hands over his, but that wouldn't help him in the long run. "I think so."

She let go of the reins and just wrapped her arms around his waist, which was somehow worse. Now he could feel her breasts pressed against his back—tight. And if he wasn't mistaken, she turned her head to the side and rested her cheek against him. He paused for a moment then squeezed Clementine's sides, and guided her around the ring several times, though it was more difficult than he would have thought possible. Not the riding part. *That* he was beginning to get the hang of. No, it was Evie, and the way the heat of her body seemed to sear him from the outside in.

And suddenly, she moved her head and sat up straight, her grip around his waist lessening. "I think that's enough for today. Bring Clementine toward the step."

Was it his imagination or did her voice seem a little strained? And was she a little stiff, too, not so relaxed anymore? Did sitting so close to him, her body pressed against his, make her feel and think things she didn't think she should? It certainly had for him.

He led the horse to the step. She dismounted, then took the reins from his hands so he could do the same. "You did well, Jake." Her voice was still tight, and if he wasn't mistaken, her cheeks seemed a little redder than usual. It was her eyes though that told the whole story. No longer more blue, now they were the color of storm-filled clouds, and in their depths, he saw... what did he see? Longing? Desire?

He forced his attention away from the silent message in her eyes—mostly so he wouldn't pull her into his arms and kiss her until she couldn't breathe...until they both couldn't breathe. It's what he wanted to do. He smoothed his hand over Clementine's shoulder instead, oddly pleased by her compliment.

"We'll do it again tomorrow. And the day after that. Before long, you'll ride as well as I do...and every other person on this ranch."

"Yes, ma'am."

"Now, brush her down and give her some extra oats. She worked hard today." With those instructions given, she left the riding ring.

He watched her walk away, admiring the graceful way she moved. His focus shifted to her legs. The split skirt she wore didn't show a hint of muscle, but he'd certainly felt them when she squeezed Clementine's sides, and he couldn't help wondering what that would feel like wrapped around his hips.

He shook himself from his thoughts, improper as they were, and turned his attention to the horse. He rubbed her nose, then reached up and scratched between her ears. "You're a smart horse."

She showed her teeth and flapped her lips, as if agreeing with him.

∼

Evie let out a sigh as she crossed the lawn. She could feel his eyes on her and turned her head toward the riding ring. Jake hadn't moved. Not one inch. He still stood by the fence, Clementine's reins in his hands, the directness of his stare making her feel a little warm…no, not a little, but a lot.

Sitting behind him, pressed against him as she'd been, she'd felt every muscle, every sinew of his body.

When Antonio reminded her earlier this morning of the promise she'd made to teach Jake how to ride, she knew it was a mistake. How could she do that when all she wanted was to be in his arms?

Now, she wouldn't be able to forget how it felt to be sitting so close to him, her body pressed against his. It left her wanting more—so much more. She took a deep breath to still her rampaging thoughts, and let it out in a huff when another idea popped in her head. Had Antonio tricked her into working closely with Jake?

Jenny sat at the small table on the patio, gathering up the materials Savannah and Miguel had used while she taught them their lessons. She looked up at Evie and simply grinned—a big, Cheshire-cat grin. She didn't say a word though, as Evie passed her and entered the kitchen.

And there they were—Antonio, Hilde, Charley, and Felicity. Lucy's conspirators. It was obvious to her that they'd been watching from the window and had only just scrambled to their seats. Bright spots of color painted Hilde's cheeks, and the playing cards in Felicity's hand were backward, the colorful face cards in clear view. Evie saw the queen of hearts and the ace of spades. So could everyone else around the table.

"How'd he do?" Antonio asked, his face full of innocence, though his mustache twitched as if he tried not to smile.

"He did well, as if you didn't know."

He shook his head. "I don't know what you're talking about."

"Hmm, I don't believe that for a moment. I know you were watching. You all were."

"How can you say that?" Antonio asked. "We've been sitting here playing cards."

Evie cocked an eyebrow and looked directly at Felicity. Unable to bear the direct stare, Felicity lowered her head, though her face glowed pink.

"It would probably be easier to play if Aunt Felicity could actually see the cards in her hand."

Felicity turned a brighter shade of pink as she quickly flipped the cards so she could see them. A master of intrigue Felicity was not. She wore her emotions on her face for the world to see. She raised her eyes then shrugged her shoulders, her lips moving into a shy smile. "Are you angry, dear?"

"No, I'm not angry." And that was the truth. She found it to be amusing that her trusted friends had fallen so easily into Lucy's plan, were so willing to help it along. "I'm surprised you actually stayed inside. Just think how much easier it would have been to watch us if you were outside." And with those words, she pushed through the swinging kitchen door, smothering the chuckle that built in her chest, and rushed up to her room to splash some cold water on her face.

CHAPTER 10

ake removed his hat and wiped the sweat from his
brow, put his hat back in place and picked up the
pitchfork. Out of all the chores he performed, this
one was by far the worst. Mucking out the barn was only the first
step in this particular job…after loading up the wheelbarrow, he
had been instructed to add the straw mixed with manure to the
growing compost heap on the other side of the house. It was
honest work, but the odor was sometimes unbearable. Even tying
a handkerchief around the bottom half of his face didn't help.
The smell didn't seem to bother the cats—all three of them—and
the dog, who sat lined up, just watching him.

He'd much rather be in the riding ring, having his daily
lesson. He was enjoying those hours spent in the saddle under
Evie's tutelage. She was patient and kind, her smile lovely as he
progressed. He thought he was doing well—he certainly felt more
comfortable —and she agreed, though Clementine still made a
habit of ignoring his commands every now and then so she could
wander over to Evie, watching from the fence.

He scraped the last of the manure from the wheelbarrow and
added it to the top of the heap. That part wasn't so bad. It was the

next part that made his stomach roil—mixing the new with the old. Sweat made his shirt stick to his back and frankly, his arms hurt, the muscles screaming in protest. One of the men he bunked with said the pain would go away…it was just that he'd never used those muscles in that particular way before. Shoveling manure was much different than boxing.

Still, he could see the rewards. The compost fed the vegetable garden. Neat rows of corn, beans, potatoes, melons, bright red tomatoes, and other edibles he couldn't identify with just a glance extended into the near distance, the leaves and stalks vibrant green against the darkness of the soil. It was the same with the flowers Evie carefully cultivated. The compost did good things for the roses. He'd never seen blooms so bright, or so many, but then, he had little experience with flowers aside from picking out a bouquet from the little stand on the corner near his home in San Francisco.

Done with the smelly task, Jake wiped the sweat from his brow again, then grabbed the empty wheelbarrow by the handles and began pushing it toward the barn on the other side of the house. The animals followed, as they always seemed to do, though the dog moved a bit slowly.

A wonderful aroma wafted by from the open window, tantalizing him. Something was baking in the kitchen. Bread? Pie? He couldn't tell. His stomach growled. Maybe Grub had something in the ice box, leftovers from supper the night before he could munch on. Supper seemed a long way away at this point.

As he passed by the garden, he heard Evie's voice—low and throaty—sultry, like a siren's call. Answering that call, he stopped and glanced over the row of waist-high rose bushes that formed the border between the garden and the barnyard. He smiled as he took in the sight before his eyes.

Evie sat in one of the chairs on the lawn, shaded at this time of day by the awning over the patio. The children—all of them— were spread out on a blanket at her feet, even the youngest, a baby he'd seen before, but didn't know. She had their complete attention as she read to them. The children didn't move at all, not even Toughie, who never seemed to sit still. On more than one occasion, he'd caught the toddler running away from his mother, naked as the day he was born, his giggles filling the air, his chubby little legs carrying him much farther than one would think possible.

He didn't recognize the story, but that didn't matter. It wasn't so much the words that enthralled him, as it obviously did the youngsters, but her voice. He took a step closer, slipping through the rose bushes to stand there, listening. The cats and dog followed but didn't go farther, as if waiting for him, although Flower butted her head against his leg.

She closed the book at what he assumed was the end of the chapter. "All right, upstairs with you. Time for a nap."

The only girl in the group, Savannah, pouted. He expected nothing less of her. She knew exactly what she wanted, as she'd told him several times. Inquisitive and bright, she had quite a lot of opinions—and even more questions—for a six-year-old. And she adored her *Tia* Evie. "I'm too old for naps," she huffed, obviously displeased.

Evie laughed, that low sultry voice filling his head, making his body respond as much as his heart and soul. "One day you'll wish you had time to take a nap, *mi amor*. Take them while you can." She handed the book to the girl. "Now, bring this inside with you, please."

"Yes, ma'am." The girl huffed again, but took the book, and scrambled to her feet. The other children followed suit, leaving only the baby still on the blanket. "I'm still too old for naps!" she called out as she led the boys—Toughie by the hand—into the house and slammed the door behind her.

Evie shook her head then stood and reached down to pick up the baby, holding him close. The boy gurgled and the tone of her voice changed as she almost sang to him, like she'd sung for Spitfire not so long ago. "She's stubborn like her *Tia* Lucy, isn't she, Ramón?"

The baby laughed, obviously as captivated with her voice as he was. Ramón reached for the gold hoop hanging from her ear. She grabbed his hand and brought it to her mouth, then proceeded to make *num num* noises against his fat fingers. The baby giggled.

The action, as well as the baby's reaction, made Jake burst out in laughter. He'd never seen anyone do that before, but then, he had no experience with babies. Was that normal? Had his own mother done that so long ago?

Evie swiveled her head in his direction, her face taking on a becoming blush. "Oh, Jake, you startled me."

"My apologies. That was not my intention." He took a few steps closer and caught the scent of her perfume. Or was it the roses he smelled? Sometimes, it was difficult to tell. "What were you reading to the children?"

"*Around the World in 80 Days* by Jules Verne."

His attention was diverted by the sight of the baby tugging on the buttons of her blouse, trying hard to manipulate the round pieces of ivory with his pudgy fingers. He snapped his attention back to her face. "I haven't read that one."

"If you like to read, you should take advantage of the books in the bunkhouse."

"I have been. It's quite a collection. I'm currently reacquainting myself with Mary Shelley's *Frankenstein*." He took a step closer until he was looking down at her face. And such a lovely face it was, too, especially right now with her cheeks stained pink. "It's always been one of my favorites, though I will admit I'm enjoying the dime novels as well."

"Mine, too." Her voice was almost breathless now, and so much sultrier than before if that were possible. Like the expression in her eyes, it was filled with...what? Anticipation? Longing?

He couldn't tell, but he could listen to her all day long…and longer.

"Do you read to the children often?"

"Not as often as I'd like. This was my first opportunity in a long while." She smiled up at him, her eyes glowing with the love she had for the children. "They seem to enjoy it. I do as well."

And why wouldn't they enjoy it? He certainly did, and for a moment, he was a little jealous of the children and the time she spent with them. He wanted to spend more time with her, too. Their mornings in the riding ring didn't seem to be enough. He planned to remedy that. "Do you have any plans for the afternoon?"

"You mean what am I planning to do now?" Once again, she removed the baby's fingers from her earring, pressed her lips against his palm and blew out, making a funny noise that produced giggles from the boy.

Jake watched with fascination, a chuckle building in his chest. He tamped it down as his gaze swept over her. "Well, yes."

"Work on the ranch never stops, as you know." She smiled, and his heart gave a quick lurch, then started pounding again—hard. That had never happened to him before either, and he took a small step back, his mind concentrating on his reaction, instead of her words.

"I have plenty of mending to do. Or I could help Hilde in the kitchen. She's making her famous *lebkuchen* today."

"*Lebkuchen*? Is that what I smell? What is it?"

"It's a honey-sweetened cookie with spices and nuts. Hilde made them for me when I was young, and now she makes them for the children. They love them and she loves making them."

"I'd like to try one." He picked up the blanket from the ground, shook it a bit, then folded it, but didn't know what to do with it, so he just held onto it.

"I'll make sure to send some out to the bunkhouse when they're done." She looked at him, her eyes wide in her face, full of hope and promise, and for a second—a lifetime—he couldn't think of anything else he'd rather see. And then his gaze dropped to her smile, and he changed his mind. He wouldn't mind seeing that smile for the rest of his life.

"What about you? Are you finished with your chores?"

"As it happens, I am. At least, until everyone comes in for the night. I thought I'd take a walk."

"Where to?"

"I heard there's a nice spot where the river bends. My bunkmates tell me it's a good place to fish or just sit beneath the trees and while away an hour or two." He looked down at his sweaty state. "Or wash up."

"I know the place well. It's where *Pequeña Casa* is."

He didn't know much Spanish, but he was picking up a word or two here and there. "The little house?"

"Yes. It's the original homestead. When the Silva family first came to this valley, that was the house they built. After time, and as the family grew, they built this house." She gestured to the two-story structure beside them. "As long as you're heading that way, you could pick some blackberries for pies."

Flower rubbed up against his legs, her purrs loud, as if she was trying to tell him something—like here is your opportunity to spend a little time with Evie outside of the riding ring. The fanciful thought pleased him. He glanced at the cat then at her. "Would you like to come with me? I don't really know the way."

She drew in her breath and that smile, the one he was so enchanted by, appeared. "That would be lovely."

"I'll meet you back here in fifteen minutes?"

She nodded. "Yes. Fifteen minutes." She hefted the child more securely in her arms then took the blanket from him and headed toward the house. He could hear her talking to the baby as she laid the blanket on the small table on the patio. She had reverted back to that husky sing-song voice, and it filled his head.

Jake waited until the door closed, then left the garden. Grabbing the wheelbarrow, he headed toward the shed behind the barn, the cats and dog following behind him. As he raised his arms to hang the pitchfork on the hook, he caught a whiff of himself. And here, he'd been thinking it was the compost pile that stunk.

It wasn't.

He had fifteen minutes to make himself presentable and remove the stench. He left the tool shed, removed his shirt, and headed toward the bunkhouse and the barrel of water. He dunked his head and came up sputtering then used his discarded shirt to wash himself off, rubbing extra hard under his arms. Too bad he didn't have time to take a proper bath.

"No, you can't come with me," he said quite clearly to the animals as he let himself into the bunkhouse. It was empty at this time of day—his bunkmates, including Grub, were out in the summer pasture with the horses and cattle, though Grub would be returning soon to start supper. He grabbed a clean shirt from his trunk and slipped it on, ran a brush through his wet hair and left the bunkhouse to wait for Evie, anticipation singing through his veins. He smiled as the parade of cats and one old dog followed him to the garden.

"You go to sleep now." The baby reached for her earring as she put him in his crib, babbling to himself as he did so, words he was just beginning to learn. Mama was quite clear. So was Papa and horse. There were other words and phrases he used for what he wanted. At eleven months old, he was learning to speak much sooner than the other children, but that didn't surprise her.

"No, you can't have that," she whispered, as she removed his hand from her earring, then covered him with a light blanket. She handed him a stuffed animal in the shape of a lamb, his favorite. He clutched the fuzzy toy, kicked off the blanket then turned on his side, stuck his thumb in his mouth, and closed his eyes. In moments, he was asleep.

She glanced around the room and smiled. For a girl who'd said she was too old for a nap, Savannah was fast asleep. So was Miguel. She was certain Toughie, in his mother's room on the first floor, was sleeping as well, cuddled up on the big bed.

She quietly crept from the room, closing the door softly behind her. The house, usually a whirlwind of activity with the sound of children laughing and running from room to room, had grown quiet. Nap time was a good thing. She loved the quiet of this time of day, almost as much as she loved the end of the day, when the sun set, and the world breathed a deep sigh.

She walked down the hall to her room and grabbed her hat, then headed downstairs.

She paused with her hand on the banister. Anticipation bubbled through her. Such a small thing—to take a walk—and yet, she looked forward to it. Much more than she probably should. Perhaps it was just because she enjoyed Jake's company. Or maybe it was the opportunity to steal a kiss or two—or ten— from him.

She continued down the hall, picking up one of Miguel's carved horses as she did so and placing it on a side table before entering the kitchen.

Hilde sat at the kitchen table, a cup of coffee in front of her. Steam rose from the brew, lending its fragrance to the air to mix with the batch of *lebkuchen* baking in the oven. "And where are you going?"

"I thought I'd pick some blackberries." She opened the pantry door and glanced inside but didn't see the basket she looked for. Closing the door, she headed to the cabinets beside the sink and looked in there. Still no basket.

"Alone?"

"Well, no." She closed the cabinet door and stood next to the sink, then pushed the curtain aside and looked behind it. "Where is the basket?"

"In the hall closet." Hilde took a sip of her coffee. "Who are you picking berries with? The children are all napping."

"Jake."

Hilde smiled. "Good. He seems like a nice man. And *muy guapo*," she said, using the Spanish words for 'very handsome,' which sounded funny with her German accent.

"I've watched him with the children. He's very good with them. Kind. Patient, even with Savannah and her million and one questions." Hilde chuckled. "He's good with the animals, too. That menace of a cat seems to adore him. And his riding lessons seem to be coming along very well. It hasn't gone unnoticed. I heard Antonio and Teddy talking about it."

Evie couldn't deny what she was saying. She'd seen these things with her own eyes, including Flower's behavior. "What are you trying to tell me without telling me?"

"I'm not trying to tell you anything."

"Oh yes, you are. Just spit it out." She grabbed one of the *lebkuchen* from the plate where they were cooling, wrapped it in a napkin then turned. "You've never been known for your subtlety, Hilde, nor have you ever been afraid to express your opinion."

Hilde cocked an eyebrow as her gaze dropped to the napkin in Evie's hand, then rose to her face. "Like I said, I think he's a good man." She didn't blink, but she did smile. Broadly. Like she had a secret—or was about to suggest something just a tiny bit wicked. "There could be wedding bells in your future. Or not. It's really your choice, Evie. You don't have to marry him."

"Why are you pushing me at him?"

"I think you finally deserve to be happy, *liebchen*, even if it's just for a little while. But you'll do what you want, as you always do."

She took the comments for what they were worth, acknowledging that Hilde was doing what she'd always done, which was look out for her. "I love you, Hilde, but why do you think I'm not happy? Why does everyone assume that?"

"You've been alone for so long, taking care of everyone else, raising Gina's children into fine adults, building this ranch to what it is." Hilde waved her hand to encompass the room. "But there's more to life than this ranch. You have a big heart. A good heart. You should share that with someone special."

"Thank you, Hilde." She pushed through the door, grabbed the basket from the hall closet, and left the house through the front door instead of facing the woman again.

She walked around the side of the house and her heart picked up its pace when she caught sight of Jake. He stood by the chair she'd occupied earlier, hat in hand, and talked to the cats and dog who sat patiently. She couldn't hear what he was saying, but the animals didn't move, obviously listening to every word he said. He patted the dog on the head, then rubbed one of his silky ears. Smokey leaned against his leg, obviously loving the attention.

"They like you," she said, as she approached him.

"I think they do. They're great companions, though they don't say much." He laughed and his soulful amber eyes crinkled at the corners. "I've always liked cats. Their independence speaks to something in me. I've never had much experience with dogs, though." Smoky leaned harder against his leg as Jake continued to rub the dog's ear. "Why doesn't he go out with the men when they leave in the morning? I notice he whines and just sits there, watching. It's obvious he wants to go with them."

"We retired him. He's getting too old to chase cattle, though he wants to." She reached down and scratched the dog's ear, too, then ran her fingers through his soft fur. "The desire is there, and will remain for the rest of his life, I'm sure, but he pays for it. One day out in the summer pasture and he limps for a week. For now, he gets to stay at the homestead and play with the children. Or follow you around."

"Are you ready?" he asked, as he held out his arm.

She held up the basket, slipped her free hand into the crook of his elbow, then glanced at the animals at their feet. "Stay," she commanded, though she knew giving the cats a command like that only worked one out of a hundred times. The dog obeyed, and stretched out on the grass, his muzzle resting on his paws. He whined as they walked away, but never moved from his spot. The cats weren't so obedient and followed for a short distance...until their attention was captured by something moving in the shadows of the barn and they went to investigate.

She and Jake wandered between the bunkhouse and the barn, coming to the gate in the fence that separated the homestead from the grove of tall trees and the river a short distance away. He held the gate open for her.

Once on the path, Evie reached into the basket, pulled out the napkin-wrapped cookie, and handed it to him. "I brought you this."

"Is it that cookie you were telling me about?"

"*Lebkuchen.* It's still warm."

She watched him take a careful bite, then another, and another. She didn't have to ask if he liked it. That much was obvious by the expression on his face, which was one of pure pleasure.

"That's the best thing I've had in a long time. Thank you."

She liked walking beside him like this. He matched his stride to hers as they ambled along, the basket swinging from her arm. He didn't speak, but then, neither did she. For the moment, there didn't seem to be a need for words, the silence between them comfortable as they traversed the meandering path.

"Do you miss San Francisco?" he asked, breaking the silence.

No."

"Not even a little?"

"Actually, not at all. My life here is so much different, so much better."

"How is it different?" Curiosity danced in his beautiful amber eyes.

"If I had stayed in San Francisco, I would have married the man my father chose for me, whether I wanted to or not. It wouldn't have been for love, but rather standing and accumulated wealth. That's what wealthy young women did. They married to advance their standing in society or to please their fathers."

She paused then looked up at him. "I never wanted that. Even before I was given this—" she searched for the word, "opportunity to come here and take care of my sister's children, I wanted to be free to choose my own…path."

She spread her arm, the one holding the basket, wide to encompass the path and the trees surrounding them. "There's freedom here. Don't you feel it?"

"I do." He nodded in agreement.

"I would never have been able to accomplish there what I have here. This ranch is thriving. Successful. People come from all around to buy our horses, drawn by our reputation." She glanced at him again, loving the attention she clearly saw on his face, knowing that he listened to every word.

"Something else I never found in San Francisco." She gestured to the trees, then raised her hand to the sky above them, seen between the leaves of the trees. "Have you ever seen anything more beautiful?"

"Yes, I have," he said.

There was something in his voice that made her take her attention from the sky and bring it back to him. "Tell me."

He shrugged as if embarrassed, then uttered, "You."

Pleasure at his compliment rushed through her, making her warm all over.

"When you're talking about this ranch, your eyes light up. You become…*animated*, I guess would be the word, and the love you have for this place shows on your face and in your voice."

"You're right. I do love this ranch. And I'm grateful that I've had a part in making it what it is."

"You have plenty of reason to be proud."

They left the shade of the trees and came into the sunlight in a clearing; blackberry bushes, cultivated over the years, now lined the path. Evie stopped, as she always did in this spot, to gaze upon the little house nestled there, the sound of birdsong and the river rushing filling her ears. "And this is *Pequeña Casa*. Isn't it beautiful?"

"It is."

She loved this little house. It wasn't abandoned, but it wasn't really used much. No one lived in it anymore. It wasn't very big, but it was sturdy and comfortable. From the front porch, one could sit and listen to the river, which was peaceful and calming. Someday, she might live here. She'd toyed with the idea before, but lately, it seemed to be in her mind more and more often. Perhaps it was time to give the big house over to her nephews' growing families.

She removed her hand from the crook of Jake's elbow as her gaze fell on the blackberry bushes lining the path. "Look at all those blackberries. There's a good crop this year." She moved closer to a bush loaded with ripe, purple fruit, plucked one, and popped it into her mouth, the sweet flavor exploding on her tongue. "These will make an excellent pies." She nodded in another direction. "Over there are apple and walnut trees. A few peach trees. Some pear trees. The apples and pears won't be ripe for another month or so, but there should be some peaches left we can pick if you want." She ate another blackberry, then glanced at him.

She had his full attention, his gaze filled with undisguised warmth. And his smile! Oh, that smile made butterflies dance in her stomach. It looked like he wanted to kiss her. She wished he would. He took a step closer, and she almost closed her eyes in anticipation, but instead of pressing his lips to hers, he simply reached behind her, pulled a blackberry from the bush, and ate it.

"Sweet," he murmured, but she couldn't be sure from his look if he was talking about the fruit. Or her. His gaze never left hers. Her stomach did flips.

Evie cleared her throat and forced herself to stop looking at his mouth. Only then was she able to remember what she'd been saying. "The Silvas, when they first settled here, did everything they could to make this ranch self-sufficient. For flour and sugar and other necessities, of course, they could go into Santa Fe or Serenity, but my understanding is that the Silvas preferred to stay on Montaña del Trueno as much as possible, though I would hardly know if that's true. They were long gone by the time I came here. The only one left was Serafina, the children's grandmother."

"Come." She led him closer to the house. "Toward the end of her life, her memories had faded quite a bit and she couldn't remember much of anything. There were times when she didn't know who we were. Or thought we were someone else." She let out a sigh of regret. "She passed last year."

"I'm sorry." His voice held sincere sympathy.

"She was a good woman." And as she said the words her throat constricted a little. "I miss her."

"I'm sure you do."

"There's a photograph of her with Savannah in the study. Lucy took it just after Savannah was born." She paused, then added, "I will admit, sometimes I still talk to her."

"Nothing wrong with that."

At the front of the house, she stopped and stepped up to the porch. "Would you like some water? I think there might be a bottle of whiskey if you'd prefer that."

"Don't put yourself to any trouble. Water will be fine, thanks."

"Make yourself comfortable." She gestured to one of the rocking chairs, then let herself into the house. Someone had been there recently. There wasn't any dust on the furnishings and the floor had been swept clean. There were two glasses on the counter beside the sink, washed and left to dry on the drainboard. One of the boys, perhaps, looking for a moment alone with their wives?

She filled two glasses with water from the pump and brought them outside. "I saw you outside the bunkhouse the other night," she said, as she handed him his.

He accepted the glass and frowned as she took her seat next to him and slowly rocked back and forth.

"You were…well, it looked like you were fighting."

"You saw that?" He laughed.

"I did."

"Father O'Malley, at the home, loved boxing, which one would find unusual, I'm sure, given that he's a priest. He loved the mechanics of it, the elegance, the discipline, and yes, even the brutality, though he'd never admit that part to anyone. He taught boxing to all of us boys."

He'd spoken of the priest before, and she loved the way his feelings for the man animated his features. "Clearly you were quite fond of Father O'Malley."

"I was. Still am. In many respects, he was the only father figure I had in my life."

She took a sip of water, watching him over the rim of the glass. "What would you have said if, when we first met, I wanted to get married? If I had written to you? Would you have gone through with it?"

A look passed over his face and his warm amber eyes seemed to be full of secrets. But then he smiled and said, "Yes."

She watched him, wondering if he told the truth or not. "When I asked you why you responded to Lucy's letter, you said you were looking for change, looking for something more. Have you found it?"

He looked out at the river, and for a moment, she didn't think he would answer, and then he spoke, his voice rather hoarse. "I think I have." He cleared his throat. "Perhaps it was fate that Father O'Malley placed the newspaper with Lucy's advertisement in front of my face and told me, in no uncertain terms, that it was time I grew up, became responsible. Respectable. Fall in love, marry, and settle down. Make a life for myself other than what I'd known."

"Oh."

"He was angry at the time, but he was right." He paused, then looked at her. His eyes were bright. "It was time. I was lost, Evie. In so many ways. A man without commitment to anyone or anything aside from myself. And I had been looking for…something. I just didn't know what. Purpose? A reason to keep going? A special person who would be an answer to the prayers I hadn't known I'd been praying? At that point in time, I seemed to have failed at every turn." He smiled a sweet smile, then reached out for her hand.

"Plus I was amused by the advertisement." He recited the beginning of the notice Lucy had placed in the newspaper. "Wanted: Gentleman interested in marriage to a mature, older woman."

She laughed even as her face flamed. "Is that what it said? That's awful!"

He laughed as well. "But effective. The advertisement listed some of the benefits of such an arrangement. I admit, I found it charming and funny. It struck something in me. I wanted to meet the person who wrote such a sweet advertisement, so I responded. I didn't think anything would come of it, but then I got your—I mean Lucy's—letter, inviting me to come here to meet." He rubbed his thumb against her fingers. "I couldn't pass up the opportunity. I took that leap of faith, as Father O'Malley would say."

"Are you sorry?"

He shook his head. "No, not at all. I've learned so much since coming here. A lot about myself. Things I never knew."

"Like what?"

He laughed. "Well, I like the hard work, believe it or not. There's a certain dignity to getting your hands dirty and putting your back into a task for the good of everyone, not just myself. I learned that I love the horses. Their beauty and intelligence speak to something in me." His voice gentled and became serious. "And I met you and your family. That alone was worth the trip."

She hadn't expected such a response and her throat constricted. "Are you happy here?"

"I am. Very. More so than I thought I would ever be. You are right about this place. There is a freedom here, and a chance to be the best person I can be. Thank you for letting me stay."

She cleared her throat. "I'm glad you did." She tore her gaze away from him and looked out at the sunlight playing upon the river's surface. "We should pick those berries if we want pie for dessert tonight. Are you ready?"

"Sure." He handed her the empty glass and rose to his feet. Evie brought the glasses in the house and washed them, leaving them on the drain board to dry. Outside, she grabbed the basket and slipped the handle over her arm.

He gave an exaggerated bow. "After you."

They spent the next half hour picking blackberries…well, she picked. He grinned as he put one berry in his big hand and one in his mouth, repeating the process until he had a handful.

"You're supposed to be putting them in the basket, not eating them."

"But they're delicious." He laughed. He dumped his handful into the basket, then plucked another berry from the bush and ate it. He swallowed, his Adam's apple bobbing, drawing her attention, and she wanted to place a kiss right there.

He dumped another handful into the basket, but his gaze was on her. She could feel the heat of it all the way to her toes.

He looked in the basket. "What do you think? Do we have enough?"

"I think we have enough for two pies."

He switched his gaze to her. "So that means we have to head back."

"We should."

A look of disappointment passed over his face.

"It has been a lovely afternoon...but there are chores to do. Pies to make."

His expression said he didn't want the afternoon to end. "I suppose if we must." He popped a last blackberry in his mouth, took the basket from her, then extended an arm to her. Evie placed her hand in the crook of his elbow, feeling the warmth of his flesh through his thin shirt and the muscles tightening beneath her fingers. They walked without speaking, though the silence was comfortable. The homestead was just ahead. She didn't want to step through the gate and go back to the chores that awaited her on the other side. She stopped in the middle of the path and blurted out, "You haven't tried to kiss me."

He stopped as well and faced her, warmth making his amber eyes glow. "Well, I can fix that."

Anticipation rushed through her, making every nerve in her body zing. Her heartbeat increased in speed until she could hear it as he slowly placed the basket on the ground then drew her close, wrapping his arms around her, holding her tight.

Evie pressed her hands to his hard, muscled chest as his head dipped and his mouth captured hers. His lips were warm and firm as they pressed against hers, provoking a response, promising so much more. She opened her mouth, allowing his tongue entry, unable and unwilling to resist giving into that promise.

If a kiss could make one burst into flames, she'd be incinerated on the spot.

"I'll thank you to take your hands off my aunt!"

Evie jumped, startled, and stepped out of Jake's arms. Blood rushed to her face as she turned and faced Teddy. Her entire body felt flushed.

Teddy sat atop his horse on the other side of the fence, the expression on his face a mixture of anger...and something else, something she couldn't identify. She turned to Jake, who stood beside her, his body tense, his hands balled into fists.

The last thing she wanted was a fight between them.

She'd seen Teddy go after a former ranch hand who had been inappropriate toward Ana, and there were the normal scrapes between him and his brothers, but she'd also watched Jake when he was boxing his shadowy opponent. The way he moved, the way he maintained complete control, she had no doubts who would come out the victor should they resort to blows.. "I should go."

"Should you?" Jake asked, his voice close to her ear, low and seductive.

"Yes, I should." But she didn't want to. It was time Teddy stopped this ridiculous notion that he was her protector. She thought she had already made that clear.

"Why?"

"I don't want any trouble between you,"

"If that's what you want." He stepped back but he took her hand and brushed his lips against her knuckles. It was a gallant, romantic thing to do. And right in front of Teddy. His eyes held hers for a moment, then he released her hand.

She pulled her gaze away from his. "Thank you for a lovely afternoon." She picked up the basket then passed through the gate, where Teddy still sat on his horse a few feet away. She turned once. Jake was still watching her, his intense gaze making her feel warm and tingly. She gave him a slight nod, then walked over and turned her attention to her nephew. "Were you spying on me?"

"No, but someone has to watch out for you, *Tia* Evie." He

looked down at her, but only briefly as his unrelenting glare returned once more to Jake. The warning was silent, but clear.

"We've had this discussion before," she all but hissed at him. "I am a grown woman. I am perfectly capable of making my own decisions. Up to now, you have agreed with many of them, so what's different?"

"He's a maverick, *Tia* Evie." Again, another quick glance in her direction and then his intense focus went back to Jake, who started walking toward them in that loose-hipped swagger he had. "I've seen his kind before. Follows his own rules without regard for honor. A man, I suspect, who breaks hearts wherever he goes. I don't want your heart to be among the many."

"You don't know Jake at all. He isn't like that."

"I see he has you fooled." The sarcasm in his voice was thick.

"Teodoro Augustus, you have no right to speak to me that way. I am no fool. Apologize."

"I'm sorry." Even though he said the words, it was obvious to her that he didn't mean them. The expression on his face hadn't changed. There was still anger there.

She paused for a moment to still her own ire. "Why are you here?"

"I was looking for you. I didn't expect to see you…kissing him."

She ignored his comment. "Why were you looking for me?" A sudden thought had apprehension racing through her. "Is someone hurt? Is it one of the children?"

"No one is hurt. You just have a visitor. He's been waiting for quite some time."

Another kind of anxiety rippled through her. "Who is it?"

He shrugged. "Don't know. I was riding up to the house when Antonio flagged me down and asked me to fetch you."

Evie really didn't want to meet whoever had come to see her, probably another 'husband,' not after the lovely afternoon she'd spent with Jake. Not for the first time, she asked herself why

Lucy had started all this 'mail-order husband' business. She repressed a sigh then focused on her nephew. "This conversation is far from over, Teddy. Go back to the house. I'll be there in a minute."

"Actually, I'd like a word or two with Jake." He tugged on the reins before she could respond, and made his way through the gate, coming up on Jake in a slow walk. Evie watched him, her heart in her throat, waiting for that first punch to be thrown or a kick from his position in the saddle. Neither happened.

Instead, Teddy slipped from the saddle to stand beside Jake, and started talking, their voices low, surprising her. She couldn't hear what they were discussing, but it didn't matter. There were no punches thrown, no sharp angry words. Relieved, she continued toward the house, determined to send her visitor on his way, then tell Teddy exactly what she thought once they could have a moment alone.

CHAPTER 11

$\mathcal{E}$vie entered the house to the sound of laughter. Hilde, Antonio, Uncle Charley, and Aunt Felicity were sitting at the kitchen table, enjoying glasses of lemonade with a man she'd never seen before. A handsome man—almost as handsome as Jake. Strands of silver were woven into his thick sheaf of wheat-colored hair, concentrating mostly at his temples, and fine lines radiated from the corners of his startling cobalt-blue eyes.

"Ah, here she is." Uncle Charley rose from his seat and took the basket of blackberries from her. "Miss Everleigh Miller, please meet Mr. Ryland Parrish." He performed the introduction, then placed the basket on the kitchen counter near the sink.

Her guest rose from his seat as well and offered his hand. His grip was warm and firm, but not overly so. "Please pardon my unexpected visit. Your charming niece suggested we meet."

Evie smiled. "Knowing Lucy, it was more than a suggestion."

"That is true. She has a forceful way about her, but she seems like a delightful young woman. Strong-willed and determined. Qualities I admire." He smiled and it was a lovely smile, but it didn't make her stomach do flips. He laughed. "And might I add, rather persistent."

"She is all those things and more." She glanced at her loved ones around the table, all watching her with anticipation. Hilde cocked an eyebrow, her expression full of hope as if to say *he might be the one*. "Would you like to sit outside on the patio? It's a lovely afternoon."

"I would." He grabbed his hat and glass from the table then gave a slight bow to Hilde and Aunt Felicity. "Ladies, it's been a pleasure." He then turned to Uncle Charley and Antonio, who had resumed their seats. "Gentlemen, if you will excuse us." He looked at her, and flashed a smile, then held out his hand. "Lead the way."

Evie held open the kitchen door for him to pass through, but in fine gentlemanly fashion he insisted she go first, which she did, but not before giving Hilde, Aunt Felicity, Antonio, and Uncle Charley a warning look. She knew they'd be at the window in no time at all, watching and listening.

As they stepped outside, Mr. Parrish paused. "What a lovely garden."

"Thank you. It's my pride and joy."

"I see you like roses. My late wife, Fanny, loved roses as well, particularly the yellow ones. It's a shame, in a way, we never stayed in one place long enough for her to grow her own."

He made the statement matter-of-factly, though there was no hiding the deep regret she heard in his voice. She'd known loss, knew the hold it could keep in one's mind. Saying 'I'm sorry' just seemed so inadequate, but she murmured the words anyway, then she gestured to one of the chairs in the shade of the awning. "Lucy told me you're renovating the old Serenity Hotel."

"Yes, ma'am, I am." He put his glass on the table, followed by his hat, but didn't sit until she did. "It's a lot of work, but I'm enjoying it immensely."

"Is this the first hotel you've renovated?"

"Oh no," he laughed as he made himself comfortable. "I can't even remember what number this one is. Fanny and I renovated many over the years. In fact, we have been to nearly every state and territory in the country, except for Alaska, fixing up old hotels and inns. There were a few taverns and a saloon or two as well, but Fanny didn't like renovating those as much. It's what we enjoyed doing, and as our reputation grew, the more opportunities seemed to come our way. Fanny had such an eye for decorating—subtle, understated. And she was always up for a new adventure."

"You didn't have children?"

"We were not blessed in that way. Besides, it would have been difficult uprooting any children we might have had, traveling all around the country the way we did."

She wouldn't be able to do that. Just the thought of ever leaving Montaña del Trueno made her heart hurt.

"But we were happy, me and Fanny."

It was quite clear that he missed his late wife. How long ago she had passed? She wouldn't ask. If he volunteered the information, that would be a different story. Instead, she asked, "How long were you married?"

He smiled and the love he had for his Fanny reflected in his eyes. "Twenty-five of the best years of my life." He let out a sigh then said, "Lucy tells me you never married."

"No, I never did, but I was engaged to be."

"What happened? Why didn't you?"

Evie glanced at him, then down at the table. "He died. He was a Marshal here in town."

"I'm sorry."

"I am, too. He was a good man."

"And now? Lucy mentioned something about looking for a husband. Are you?"

She laughed and shook her head. "No, I'm not. The truth is, Lucy is searching for a husband for me, even though I never asked her to."

"Good." His smile widened. "Then you and I can be friends."

"Perfect."

Hilde came out of the house carrying a pitcher of lemonade and a glass on a tray, a big, conspiratorial smile on her face. She said nothing as she poured, but she did wink before she went back into the house, leaving the tray on the table.

"Are you staying at the hotel while you renovate?"

"I am. It's quite comfortable, if one doesn't mind sawdust and the sound of hammering, not to mention the number of people traipsing in and out. Fortunately, I love all that. Fanny did as well."

Evie didn't miss the sound of longing in his voice, nor did she miss the expression on his face. It was quite clear to her that Ryland Parrish was still very much in love with his late wife. "Fanny sounds like a lovely woman. You must miss her a great deal."

Sadness reflected in his bright blue eyes, but only for a moment or two. "She was, and I do. She would have loved this hotel. She—"

A noise from the barn had her glancing that way, just in time to see Jake coming out of the building, carrying several lead ropes as he strode toward one of the smaller paddocks, where a young horse, a beautiful sorrel, waited, a supple leather halter around her face. Teddy leaned against the paddock fence, his foot resting on the lower plank.

Ah, this was the filly Teddy had pointed out to her not too long ago, chosen from the herd for her beauty, stamina, and temperament. He always selected wisely, and now, he was going to teach Jake how to build a bond, the first step in training. She considered it a compliment toward Jake. This was a task that Teddy didn't relinquish to anyone aside from herself and Antonio, and it lightened her heart.

She blinked and brought her attention back to Mr. Parrish, but it was hard. In less than a minute, her gaze wandered again, alighting on Jake as he let himself into the paddock and slowly approached the horse.

"Is this a bad time, Miss Miller?"

"What?" Startled, Evie swiveled her head to look at her guest, embarrassed she should be so rude. Her cheeks heated. Indeed, her entire body felt flushed. "I'm sorry."

"You seem to be…a little distracted?" His eyes, filled with curiosity, crinkled at the corners when he smiled.

"My apologies." She nodded at the paddock. "I'm usually involved in training a new horse. And please call me Evie. You were telling me about your plans for the hotel."

He gave her an understanding smile. "I'll save that for another time." He rose from his seat and grabbed his hat. "I should be heading back. I'm expecting a shipment of lumber and I don't want to miss it. My foreman is a good man and knows what to do, but…" He glanced at the corral. "I think you understand."

Evie smiled at him, relieved that he accepted her excuse. She walked him to the gate that separated the garden from the front of the house.

He turned toward her. "Would you care to take a ride with me? Perhaps on Saturday? I've only been in Serenity for a short time and haven't quite found my way around. I thought perhaps you could show me the sights. I'm told there's a spectacular lake not too far from here."

"There is. Do you fish?"

"When I have the time, I do enjoy it." He gave her a questioning look, his brows rising just a bit. "What do you say? Should I stop by around eleven? I could show you what I've done with the hotel so far, and then, perhaps we could have a picnic by the lake."

Why not? He seemed like a nice man and he already said they should be friends. She'd like that. "Yes, of course. Saturday morning. That would be lovely."

"Excellent! Until Saturday then." He gave her a slight bow, put on his hat, and walked to where a nice buggy waited in the drive —high-end, and brand-new, by the looks of it. The horse pulling the buggy was also superior quality horseflesh. He climbed in, tipped his hat in her direction and left.

Evie strode across the grass, her attention once more on Jake in the corral with the young horse. She stopped and just stood there, watching. Despite his lack of knowledge, the horse seemed to be responding well to him. Perhaps, like Teddy, Antonio, and herself, he had a natural ability.

Forcing her attention away from him, she retrieved the glasses and the pitcher of lemonade from the patio table and headed for the kitchen.

"Well?" Hilde demanded as she looked up from the blackberries she was rinsing.

"Well what?" Evie placed the glasses and pitcher on the counter beside the sink.

Aunt Felicity stopped peeling potatoes to gesture with the paring knife. "I thought he was rather charming."

Hilde glanced at Felicity and winked. "Handsome."

"I agree." Felicity said. "Such a gentleman."

"Would you two just *stop*?" Evie rolled her eyes. "Yes, he is handsome and charming, and I enjoyed his visit very much."

"I sense a 'but', *liebchen*."

"I am not interested in finding a husband, as I've told you before. And I don't think he's interested in getting married again. From the way he talked about his late wife, he's still in love with her." She tucked her hair behind her ear, her movements jerky from frustration. "I wish Lucy had never started this…this…I don't even know what to call it." She turned on her heel and left the room.

"You still need to make the pie crust," Hilde called out.

Evie stopped and turned around, then pushed through the

door. "I'll make the pie crust, but I don't want to hear one more word about Mr. Parrish."

Hilde laughed. "That's fine. We can always talk about Mr. Hannigan."

"Or Mr. Peña," Felicity chimed in, as she scraped the paring knife over a potato, though why she should mention Mr. Peña remained a mystery. They hadn't so much as spoken two words aside from 'good morning' or 'good evening' since she hired him.

"We're not talking about them, either." But even as she said the words, she glanced out the window and saw Jake gently smooth his hands over the horse's withers, and an involuntary sigh escaped her. What would it be like to have his hands caress her that way?

She shook her head, then forced her attention away from the window and concentrated on gathering the ingredients to make the pie dough, but her mind just wasn't on her task, and she almost dropped the canister of flour. Setting the canister on the table, she began measuring out the flour, but try as she might, her attention kept going to the sight beyond the window. Jake was in deep conversation with the sorrel—the filly kept looking at him as he smoothed his hand over her flanks. She imagined she could hear his voice and another involuntary sigh escaped her.

Suddenly aware she was being watched, Evie turned back to the women in the room with her. "What?"

Hilde hid a smile. "Nothing, except how many pies do you think we'll be making?" She nodded toward the bowl on the table.

Evie looked down and stifled a groan. It was a valid question. The bowl was overflowing, and flour spilled over the sides to sprinkle on the table. "Sorry. I guess my mind wasn't on my task."

"Hmmm, I never would have known." Hilde laughed in that deep, guttural way she had, and nudged her out of the way. "I'll finish this. Why don't you go out and talk to Jake? It's what you want to do anyway. And don't bother trying to deny it, neither."

"You're right. I would." She handed her the measuring cup, removed her apron, slung it over the back of a chair, and made a quick exit out of the kitchen. As soon as the door closed, she heard Felicity's giggle. "She's got it bad."

"That she does!"

Evie stepped off the patio, her feet sinking into the thick grass, and headed toward Jake. He just stood in the barnyard, hands on his hips, his gaze not on her, but on the horizon. After a moment, he tilted his hat back then turned in her direction, as if he'd felt her watching him, and he smiled.

Evie stopped in her tracks. Oh, what that smile did to her! Her stomach quivered and her mouth went dry, as excitement, and something else she couldn't—wouldn't—define rippled through her. Even her knees were a little weak, like butter on a sweltering day.

A moment later, she heard the sound of horses, their hooves pounding the earth, and her *vaqueros* came in from the summer pasture.

So much for a moment alone with him.

The riders dismounted, laughing, and carrying on as they were wont to do, and started handing the reins to him. Evie threw up her hands in disappointment and disgust.

There are too many people here!

She turned on her heel and headed back into the house, closing the door a little more forcefully than she should have. Hilde looked up from the now half-empty bowl of flour, full measuring cup in hand. "I thought you were going to talk to Jake."

Evie glared at her, just a little beyond frustrated. "I don't always listen to what you tell me, Hilde. I'm a grown woman!"

She stalked through the kitchen and pushed through the swinging door, a flush heating her face as she heard both Hilde and Felicity burst into startled laughter. She continued up to her room, looking for a little peace and quiet, hoping she wouldn't run into anyone on the way.

Who would have thought he'd love this?

Or ever be given the opportunity to train a horse, especially coming from Teodoro Silva. Honestly, he thought Teddy just didn't like him. Obviously, he'd been wrong. He'd thought, after catching him kissing his aunt, the man wouldn't have been so…gracious, but here they were, for the fifth day in a row—he in the corral, and Teddy giving orders and encouragement from the fence where he sat.

"You're a natural, Jake. I've seen you with the other horses and how they respond to you." He laughed, as Jake led the filly past him. "Are you sure you've never done this before?"

"Never." He was pleased with the compliment, even more so that it came from Teddy.

For the first few days, he'd gotten the sorrel filly used to being touched, bathed, and groomed. Today, he was walking Cinnamon, as she'd been named, around the corral with a lead rope. According to Teddy, all this was required to earn the horse's trust, and while he was enjoying this, he found his thoughts wandering.

Because of Evie. She'd come outside with a basket, and now hung clean sheets on the clothesline to dry, while Savannah and Miguel played around her feet, their school lessons, taught by Jenny, finished for the day. He couldn't help watching her or smiling when he heard her laughter in response to something one of the children had said.

"Jake?"

Startled, he brought his attention back to Teddy. "What?"

"Something on your mind?"

There was humor in Teddy's voice, which he didn't quite

expect, and his face warmed. Did he know he'd been watching Evie instead of paying attention to what he was doing? He shook his head as he led the horse once more around the corral.

"You need to keep your mind on what you're doing. Building trust is important to training…much more so than other things."

"Yes, sir."

Despite his best intentions, Jake couldn't help himself. He glanced in Evie's direction on the next circuit he and Cinnamon took around the ring. She pulled a pillowcase out of the basket and shook it then pinned it to the clothesline. On his next trip around, his interest was piqued as he saw Antonio step into view and stop to talk to her. The big man had his hands on his hips and kept nodding toward the corral. Evie turned in his direction then returned her attention back to Antonio. She nodded to whatever it was he said, then glanced in his direction again.

After a moment, Antonio walked over to the corral and rested his forearms on the fence. "How's he doing?" he asked, loud enough to be heard, probably all the way to San Francisco. The man did have a booming voice.

"Excellent," Teddy said, and gave Jake a confident nod as he passed by, leading Cinnamon by the lead rope. "Did you know he was this good?"

"It's a complete surprise to me. Thought he didn't know anything about horses. He admitted that when he first arrived."

Jake continued around the corral, no longer able to hear what was said; however, what he'd heard was enough. Pride made him stand a bit taller. No one had ever complimented him on a job well done before. He didn't quite know how to react, although that didn't stop his grin from widening on his face and making his cheeks hurt. After a few more moments of conversation he couldn't hear, Antonio walked away in his bow-legged strut, leaving Teddy alone at the fence.

"I think that's enough for today, Jake." Teddy said, as he passed by him. "Tomorrow, *Tia* Evie will be in the ring with you. I need to head back out to the summer pasture, so *Tia* Evie will continue with the training."

Anxiety and excitement rushed through him with those simple words. He watched Evie pick up the empty basket and head into the house. She was more than a distraction, but he had to admit, seeing Evie at the fence would be a much better sight than seeing Teddy, and his heart beat a little faster.

CHAPTER 12

"You have a visitor, Miss Evie," Ana, who'd come back to the ranch after staying with her folks for more than a week, stated as she stopped at the riding ring's fence. "A Mr. Ambrose. He's waiting in the parlor. He says he's here in regard to the letter he received."

Another one of Lucy's mail-order husbands. At least she was prepared this time. She knew what to expect and what to do. She'd be honest and forthright, but kind when she sent him on his way. "I'll be right in, Ana. Would you please bring us some coffee?"

"Yes, ma'am."

She watched the young woman go back in the house, and let out another sigh, then hopped down from the fence where she'd been perched, watching Jake with Cinnamon. He'd done well, considering he'd never done this before. He was a natural, despite his initial statement revealing he was uncomfortable with horses, but then, his only experience had been years ago, and with a horse who probably didn't like anyone except for Father O'Malley.

Yesterday, they had put the bridle in the horse's mouth.

Cinnamon hadn't liked it much, but Jake managed to handle her just fine. Today, they'd put a saddle on the filly for the first time. Cinnamon hadn't been happy about that, either, but Jake had managed to calm her down…and keep her calm, talking to her. The horse seemed to understand..

"Jake? Will you be all right out here with Cinnamon alone?"

"Cinnamon and I will be fine. She likes me." He stopped and stroked the horse's neck, the reins held loosely in his hands like he'd been doing this all his life.

She was amused and touched by his obvious affection for the filly, as well as his growing confidence. "Yes, she certainly seems to. Take her around the ring a couple more times then let her into the paddock with the other horses. When I come back, we can continue your riding lessons."

He touched the brim of his hat, then smiled at her in such a way that her pulse quickened and flooded her with warmth. "Yes, ma'am."

Evie walked across the barnyard and garden and entered the house. Hilde, Ana, and Felicity were in the kitchen, obviously waiting for her, expectation and humor on their faces.

"Not one word," she warned them, as she gave them each a look, then pushed through the swinging door and walked down the hall. She peeled off her gloves and removed her hat, leaving them on the table beside the parlor door. Pasting a smile on her face, she stopped in the parlor doorway, the greeting on her lips dying.

The tallest, thinnest man—emaciated might have been a better word—she'd ever seen wasn't sitting in one of the chairs waiting for her. No, he was busy rearranging all the photographs on the table in front of one of the windows, using his pristine white handkerchief to wipe the dust from both the surface and frame before placing each picture precisely so. He stepped back and admired his handiwork, adjusted one of the photographs and let out a sigh. She could have sworn she heard him mutter "perfect" before he bent low and picked up a wooden block with the letter A on it from the floor. He started to put the toy on the table among the photographs, seemed to shudder as if doing so would offend his sense of order, then stuffed the block into the pocket of his loose black suit, followed by his handkerchief.

Who does that? Who comes into a complete stranger's home and begins cleaning it?

Granted, she didn't have the cleanest home in the valley. Who would with so many people living in one space, not to mention the children, who were prone to leaving their toys wherever they happened to be playing with them?

He hadn't seen her yet. Maybe she could just slip away and have Ana say she wasn't available, but that wasn't her way. She pasted a smile on her face and walked into the room. "Hello. May I help you?"

He turned quickly and Evie took an involuntary step back. She'd never seen a person so pale before, as if he'd lived in the shadows and never walked in the sunlight. Or perhaps, he'd been ill for a long time…a very long time. The blackness of his suit didn't help at all. The color only served to make his skin even whiter by comparison.

Twin spots of color flared on his high cheekbones, as if he'd taken rouge and drawn red circles on his face. His prominent Adam's apple bobbed as he swallowed. "Miss Miller?" His voice was just as reedy as the rest of him, like it was an effort for him to speak.

"Yes." She couldn't judge how old he was. Certainly older than her, but by how much, she couldn't tell. There wasn't a wrinkle on his gaunt, clean-shaven face, not even smile lines around his mouth. His hair, a dirty dishwater gray, was slicked back with much too much pomade, the comb marks clearly visible…and perfect somehow.

"Barnaby Ambrose." He moved toward her and extended a skeletal hand, his fingers long and bony, the nails surprisingly manicured. For a moment, she thought he might kiss her hand, but he grasped hers instead, his grip weak and so very dry. "A pleasure to meet you in person after our exchange of letters," he said as he pumped her hand up and down, precisely twice then released her. "I hope you don't mind, but I took the chance you would be home this afternoon. I just arrived in Serenity yesterday and I would have liked to have visited you then, but the journey, quite frankly, exhausted me."

Yes, she could believe that. Just the short walk from the window to where she stood had left him breathless and wheezing.

His pale gray eyes swept over her face, then came to rest on her cheek. A small shudder rippled through him as that white handkerchief came out of his pocket once more. "If I may? You have something on your face." His lips pressed together as he raised his hand. "I believe it's…I'm not sure what it is."

Was he going to touch her? She resisted the urge to recoil from the possibility, but she did take a step back and grab the handkerchief from him. "Oh, I was out by the corral. It must be dirt."

"Dirt?" His eyebrows lowered, forming a perfect furrow and his lips pressed together even more, making his cheeks sink in a little. What was that? Disgust? Distaste? Intolerance? A ranch would be the last place he should be if that were the case. Instead of being offended, as he seemed to be, Evie was amused. Montaña del Trueno was not the place for him.

"Well, yes, this is a working ranch. There is dirt and dust everywhere," she said, as she strode to the small mirror beside the door. She inspected her face and noticed a small splotch of dirt on her cheek, hardly enough to be noticeable, and yet he had noticed. She resisted the urge to giggle as she wiped it away and turned away from the mirror and walked across the room. She held out his handkerchief. "Thank you." Mr. Ambrose hesitated before he took it with just forefinger and thumb with an expression of pure horror. Evie stifled the urge to laugh and gestured to one of the chairs. "Please have a seat. Ana is bringing coffee."

He used the handkerchief again, despite the fact that it was now a little dirty, to swipe at the chair before he sat then made a huge production of straightening the crease in his trouser leg and flicking some imaginary lint from the black material. When he finished, his gaze flew to her boots. She followed his line of sight. Her boots were covered in dust, as one would expect them to be, while his shoes were buffed to a high polish. Again, those thin eyebrows furrowed on his pale forehead, and it took everything she had not to laugh out loud. Oh yes, a ranch, especially one with young children, was the wrong place for this man to be. One couldn't walk through the barnyard without kicking up dust.

She got right to the point. "Mr. Ambrose, there has been a misunderstanding. I did not write the advertisement you responded to, nor did I write the letter asking you to come here to meet. It was my niece, doing so on my behalf...without my knowledge I might add, but I must ask—given your obvious... *distaste* for all things dirty and dusty, why would you come here? Surely, you must have expected such, considering that this is a working ranch."

He cleared his throat and those twin spots of color on his cheeks seemed to get brighter. "My doctor suggested a climate drier than Atlanta. For my lungs. And then, I saw your advertisement and I thought, New Mexico has a dry climate. I considered it serendipitous."

So, in reality, he wasn't truly looking to get married, he was just looking for a dry place to live. If a wife came with the location, so much the better.

Ana chose that moment to bring in the coffee service. Given the expression the young woman wore, it was clear that she'd never seen a man such as Mr. Barnaby Ambrose. She bit her lip, but her chocolate-brown eyes twinkled with amusement. She placed the tray on the table between them, nudging the photograph of Miguel out of the way.

"Thank you, Ana."

She dipped a slight curtsey then exited the room as fast as her feet could carry her. Evie was certain she heard a bubble of muffled laughter as she slipped through the door. She could just imagine that Hilde and Felicity were trying to steal peeks at him, too. By supper, the news that another one of Lucy's potential husbands had visited would be all over the ranch—if it took that long—and she could just imagine the description they'd give of this man.

Evie turned her attention back to Mr. Ambrose...and wished she hadn't. He was staring at her in the most peculiar way, his dull gray eyes wide in his gaunt face. She concentrated on keeping any emotion from showing on her face, but there was no way on earth she was willing to contemplate any sort of future with this man.

"Coffee?"

"Yes, please."

"Tell me a little about yourself, Mr. Ambrose," she encouraged while she poured Hilde's fine coffee into thin china cups and offered one to him. "What do you do?"

He accepted it, using the handkerchief so he wouldn't have to touch the saucer. He took a sip of the coffee and made a face, as if the beverage was too strong. "I was a schoolteacher before I became ill."

"I see. How long did you teach?"

"Ten years, first in New York, then Atlanta. It was enjoyable... for the most part. Children, when taught well, are our finest gifts and our best future. I will admit that I am a bit of a taskmaster. When I give an assignment I expect it to be done." His gaze roamed her face. "I believe all children should be well-behaved and speak only when spoken to."

She didn't quite know what to say to that. She didn't believe that philosophy for a moment. Children, in her experience, did better when they were able to express their thoughts.

She happened to look out the window and saw Lucy ride up to the front of the house. How appropriate. Now, not only could she tell her niece what she thought of the men she'd chosen, but she could show her as well and put a stop to this nonsense once and for all.

"As I said, Mr. Ambrose, I did not write either the advertisement or the subsequent letter in response to your reply. Quite frankly, I am not interest in getting married."

"My dear Miss Miller, that is simply not acceptable." He heaved in a breath—a wheezing breath—and let it out slowly, the bright spots of color on his cheeks beginning to dull, but not very much. "I have come a long way, with the express purpose of marrying you."

"I am sorry, Mr. Ambrose, but I believe the letter my niece wrote suggested we meet and get to know each other. There was no promise of marriage, unless, of course, we happen to get along and both agree."

He stared at her and then the corner of his mouth lifted upward in what she assumed was a smile, but it didn't quite meet the definition. "Then I would like the opportunity to do so. Get to know each other, that is."

Just the thought of getting to know this man made her stomach knot, but still, he had come a long way. "You may stay here at Montaña del Trueno if you wish. I can offer you a position as a ranch hand, considering the circumstances. The position includes a bed in the bunkhouse and meals, plus a dollar a day."

If possible, his face paled even more, except for the color on his cheeks, which seemed to be permanent. "Miss Miller, I can assure you that I am no ranch hand." The tone of his voice clearly conveyed his displeasure. Indeed, he seemed offended that she should make such an offer. He put his cup and saucer back on the tray, none too gently. "I do not ride. Nor do I keep company with cattle, filthy beasts that they are."

Evie bit the inside of her bottom lip to keep from smiling. Her plan, such as it was, seemed to be working. "There are other things to be done on a ranch, Mr. Ambrose. One does not need to know how to ride."

That sparked his interest. "Other things? Such as?"

"Well, the barn needs to be mucked out daily, chickens need to be fed, pigs slopped, wood chopped. Things of that nature."

He flinched with every task she mentioned then took a deep, wheezing breath, his thin chest moving with the effort. He opened and closed his mouth several times before he managed to ask, "Are you suggesting that I…clean up…after filthy animals?"

"It's not a suggestion, Mr. Ambrose. It's all part of living and working on a ranch. These are the things that need to be done."

He stood abruptly and stalked across the room, retrieving his hat from the chair beside the table where he'd been rearranging her photographs, and placed it on his head precisely so. "Miss Miller, your proposal is—" Indeed, her offer seemed to be so offensive to him that he couldn't even express it in words, though he did shudder. "Hardly necessary. I have secured a position teaching here and purchased a small house." He glared at her as if she'd done something wrong, which she hadn't. "On further consideration, I would like to rescind my request that we get to know each other better. Good day." He gave a slight nod and left the room in such a hurry, she was afraid he'd collapse, necessitating a stay here, where, she was certain, he expected to be waited on hand and foot.

"Excuse me, miss," she heard him say to someone in the hallway just moments before the front door slammed.

"Who was that?" Lucy entered the parlor, her brow wrinkled.

"That, *mi corazón*, was Mr. Barnaby Ambrose." Evie rose from her seat and walked to the window. "The latest in your mail-order husbands."

Lucy joined her at the window as she watched him climb into the buggy he had rented from the livery in Serenity—she recognized it as well as saw the name emblazoned on the side—and shake the reins. In moments, he was gone, leaving a trail of dust in his wake. The sense of relief rushing through her made her shiver.

She turned toward her niece. "Do you see what I have been dealing with?"

"Oh, *Tia* Evie, I am sorry." She laughed. "I had no idea."

"It isn't funny, Lucy. I thought I told you I wanted this to stop. I don't want any more potential husbands showing up, expecting…whatever it is they're expecting." .

"I sent the letters like you asked me to, Tia, but I think it was too late."

She studied her niece. "Then I suggest you send a telegraph to whoever hasn't shown yet and tell them not to come."

"Yes, *Tia*. I *am* sorry. Truly. I should never have embarked on trying to find you a husband." Her smile dimmed. "I have learned my lesson."

"Have you?"

Lucy backed up a step, and her eyes widened in shock, already beginning to well with tears. "You're still upset with me."

"I am."

"I don't like it when you're upset with me."

"I know, but Lucy, you have to think of the consequences before you do something." Evie raised her hand and reached out to lay a gentle hand on her shoulder. "But I still love you and I will forgive you. Eventually." She dropped her hand. It was the truth. She would forgive her. "I know you did what you thought was…helpful, but Lucy, it really wasn't. We have been lucky that everyone who has come here has been decent, even sweet, if a little strange."

"I know that. Now." Her voice was low and hoarse.

Evie simply stared, unmoved by the sparkle of tears in her eyes. "I hope you do. All this could have turned out so badly."

Lucy walked to the chair recently vacated by Mr. Ambrose and flopped into it. She swiped at her eyes then took a deep breath. Evie could feel her gaze on her back and it grew quiet in the room. The silence didn't last long. "I understand you're going for a drive with Mr. Parrish tomorrow."

"Yes, I am." She stayed at the window, making sure Mr. Ambrose wasn't coming back, then turned back to her niece, utterly frustrated. "Did you not understand what I just said?"

"I did, but you've already met Mr. Parrish. He enjoyed his visit with you."

"Lucy, just stop." She raised her voice. "You are the most stubborn…" She paused, realizing she was describing herself as well, then relented a bit and answered the question. "I have no romantic interest in him."

"Why not? He's a handsome man." Lucy grabbed one of the cookies from the platter and took a bite.

"Ah, Lucy, there's more to it than being handsome, as we've discussed before. Someone could be the handsomest man or the most beautiful woman in the world, but if their heart isn't kind, then it's only half the story. Looks fade. A good heart does not." Evie shook her head and stepped away from the window. "Mr. Parrish seems to be a very nice person and he does seem to have a good heart, but he's still in love with his late wife, which is obvious if you talk to him for more than a moment."

She joined her niece but didn't sit. Instead, she grabbed her coffee, though it had gone cold, and took a sip. "He's not looking for a replacement, as if any woman could ever replace his Fanny. He's just looking for companionship, and I wouldn't mind that at all. Don't make it more than it is."

"Yes, ma'am." Lucy rose from her seat and grabbed the tray with the coffee service. "I should work on the payroll. I'll take the coffee with me."

"I'll bring you a clean cup." She removed the cup Mr. Ambrose had been using and followed her niece from the parlor. They parted ways in the hall, Lucy heading for the study, Evie heading toward the kitchen.

"Is he gone?" Hilde asked, as Evie entered the kitchen.

"Yes, he's gone." She dumped the contents of both cups in the sink then grabbed a clean one from the cabinet for Lucy.

"I'm glad, *liebchen*. He wasn't for you." She shook her head and went back to kneading dough. "Never saw a man so pale in my life. Or so skinny. Like someone took the stuffing out of him and just left skin and bones."

"He's not coming back. Too much dirt." She laughed as she left the kitchen and headed down the hall, Lucy's cup in her hand.

Before she left Lucy, she said, "Come out to the riding ring when you're done with the books."

"Why?"

"I'm teaching Jake Hannigan how to ride."

"On Clementine?"

"Of course, on Clementine. She helped all of you learn how to ride. I wouldn't trust that job to another horse." She paused then added, "For a man who said he didn't know how to ride, he's doing remarkably well. He's learning to train, too."

Lucy smiled. "You like him."

Already feeling the heat rising to her face, Evie gave a slight nod, then escaped the room before her niece could ask more questions, but the thought remained in her head. Yes, she did like him. Very much so. He, at least, seemed to be honest in his intentions, without any other motives such as marrying her to own this ranch or so she could be his workhorse. That in itself was refreshing.

CHAPTER 13

*H*e's here again.

Jake scowled at Evie and her visitor on the patio as he laid the shovel across the wheelbarrow. It was the same man who'd been by last week when Teddy had caught him kissing Evie, then instead of punching him in the nose, told him he'd be learning how to build trust with a horse. This time, the man brought her a box of candy; the fancy rectangular tin on the patio table sat unopened next to a pitcher of lemonade. Based on Evie's reactions, she liked her visitor. He was well dressed. Handsome, even if Jake was loath to admit it.

Evie laughed at something the man said, and his jaw clenched as his scowl deepened.

Who is he? Another suitor, like Oscar?

Jealousy swept through him, and he gritted his teeth. The fact that Oscar had come to the ranch as a possible husband for Evie didn't bother him. Oscar was too immature, and just a tad too hot-headed, not to mention arrogant and just...full of himself. But this man could definitely be trouble.

He pursed his lips with annoyance as he pushed the wheelbarrow full of manure across the barnyard, but his attention remained on Evie and the gentleman—until he hit the rose-covered trellis, causing the whole framework to shake and a few rose petals to float gracefully to the ground.

Neither Evie or her caller seemed to notice, for which he was thankful. He was also grateful that he hadn't damaged the trellis. He wasn't sure how'd he'd explain it.

His gaze swept over her, seeing that instead of her usual uniform of skirt and plain blouse, Evie wore a fancy blue-and-white town dress, as fashionable as any he'd seen in San Francisco, which emphasized her figure and made her seem younger. Or perhaps it wasn't the dress at all that made it seem that way, but rather, the enjoyment on her face. His jaw clenched even tighter.

Her hair was different, too. Instead of being pulled into a bun or tied back with a ribbon, it was done up in an intricate style, the ringlets bouncing as she laughed. She looked entirely too beautiful.

He jerked the wheelbarrow back and maneuvered it away from the rose trellis, all the while cussing under his breath. He looked up and his gaze met that of Evie's gentleman caller. The man smiled at him. It wasn't a smug smile, like Oscar wore. Not at all. It was friendly and confident, as if this man never met a stranger.

A man…whom Evie belonged with. Not a gambler by trade, though Jake hadn't touched a playing card since before he arrived here, not even for a game of solitaire.

Things were changing though. Every day. Despite the demanding work, he liked being here on this ranch. Working with the horses, taking care of them, learning how to ride and train them. It touched something deep inside himself, something he hadn't even known existed. It was honest and humbling and exactly what he'd needed.

Evie laughed, drawing his attention once more, and his jaw clenched even harder. At this rate, he'd break his teeth.

She rose from her seat. Her suitor did as well, a true gentleman. She picked up the tin of chocolates—at least, he assumed they were chocolates…they could have been peppermints or lemon drops—placed it on the tray with the pitcher of lemonade and the glasses they'd used, and brought everything into the house. She came out a moment later, carrying a frilly parasol and a drawstring bag that matched her outfit.

Her gentleman caller extended his arm, that same confident smile on his face. Evie placed her hand in the crook of his elbow, and they walked along the flagstone path, through the garden gate, then disappeared around the corner of the house.

Where is she going with him?

He started pushing the wheelbarrow full of manure toward the other side of the house, but his focus was still on the garden gate, waiting for Evie to come back, knowing full well she wouldn't.

"Better watch where you're going, son."

Startled, he stopped and whipped his head around, finally focusing on something other than the last place he'd seen Evie. He'd come close to hitting Charley with the wheelbarrow. Or Antonio, who stood right beside him. He froze in place, his hands still gripping the wheelbarrow handle as if he couldn't let go.

"My apologies. I didn't see you there."

Charley laughed. "It would probably help if you were looking ahead."

"Yes. Yes, you're right. I was—"

"We know what—or should I say 'who'—you were looking at." The big grin on Antonio's face lifted his mustache.

He could feel heat burning the tips of his ears. He'd been well and truly caught. There was nothing he could do but laugh and admit the truth. "You're right. I was looking at her. Can you blame me?"

Charley shook his head. "No, son. Can't blame you at all."

"Who was that man?" he asked, unable to stop himself.

"Ryland Parrish. He's renovating the old Serenity Hotel. Nice man." That information came from Antonio, humor dancing in his dark eyes.

It was on the tip of his tongue to ask where she was going with him, all dressed up, but he restrained himself. He didn't want to know, though the curiosity was killing him.

"Gentlemen." He gave a slight nod as he lifted the wheelbarrow and maneuvered it around them.

"You know, son, if you'd rather not see her leaving the house with someone else, you need to make your intentions known." Charley's voice came from behind him. "Exactly what *are* your intentions?"

Jake didn't stop his forward momentum, nor did he turn around and look at the man. He had no answer. Instead, he pushed the wheelbarrow toward the other side of the house and the compost heap waiting for him, but that didn't stop Charley's question from careening around his brain like balls on a billiard table.

What are my intentions?

He picked up the shovel lying across the wheelbarrow, scooped up a hefty amount of manure and tossed it on to the heap.

Court her like I would if our circumstances were different, as if I hadn't responded to that stupid advertisement and we'd just met by chance? Would she be heading into town or wherever she was going with me instead of him? Is that what I want?

Another shovelful went on to the heap. Sweat beaded on his forehead and he dropped the shovel, removed his hat, and wiped it away with his shirt sleeve. He studied the horizon for a moment, and there, in the distance, he could have sworn he saw Evie riding toward him, the wind in her hair, a beautiful—and welcoming—smile on her lips, though he knew that wasn't true. The vision faded, leaving him with a feeling of loss so deep, it hurt his heart, but in that same instant, he had his answer.

Yes, that's what I want.

~

"Thank you for a lovely afternoon, Ryland." Evie said as Ryland stopped the buggy near the front door and hopped out of his seat. He walked around to the other side and offered his hand to help her alight. She accepted the assistance with a smile.

"My pleasure, Evie." He dropped a kiss on her hand, then climbed into his seat and picked up the reins. "Don't forget about the concert."

"I won't. Next Saturday."

"I'll swing by to pick you up."

She watched him flick the reins and start the carriage moving. He waved one last time as he left the drive. Evie climbed the porch steps and entered the house. She took off her hat and gloves and left them on the table in the hallway, then turned in time to catch Toughie in mid-run—once again as naked as the day he was born. "Where are you going in such a hurry, little man?" She scooped him up in her arms and planted kisses on his face, despite the mud liberally spread on his cheeks and forehead. There was even mud in his hair.

"Cookie!" he exclaimed, his face wreathed in a grin.

"No, it's almost time for dinner. You can't have a cookie now." She laughed at his expression. "And where did you find mud?"

"Cookie!" he exclaimed again, although his smile was beginning to fade and his eyes squinted, probably in preparation for the big tears he was ready to cry at being told *no*.

Evie shook her head and started walking down the hall toward the bathroom, where she could hear Catalina still talking to the boy—who wasn't there. "No cookie. Bath time."

The boy mimicked her shake and insisted, "Cookie!"

"After dinner." She stopped at the bathroom door and saw Catalina leaning over the bathtub, testing the water with her elbow to make sure it wasn't too hot. Toughie's wet, mud- covered clothes were in a pile on the tile floor. "Did you lose someone, Cat?"

Catalina let out a sigh as she stood. "He escaped me again. I thought I closed the door."

"You probably did." She kissed the boy on the forehead. "He just knows how to open the door now."

She transferred the child to his mother then swiped the dried dirt from her dress. "Looks like he had a great time playing in the mud."

"He did. I fear Savannah and Miguel look the same, and they'll take their baths after him. He was the dirtiest."

She laughed. "Of course, he was."

"Hilde, Aunt Felicity, and I were outside on the patio, talking, and the children were right where we could see them. The next thing we knew, it had grown quiet."

"Oh, no! When children are quiet, it usually means they're up to no good."

"And they were. Up to no good. Found them by the bunkhouse, digging for all they were worth. Hilde isn't pleased they took the good spoons to dig their hole, but she couldn't be upset with them too much. She said she remembered when Heath did the same thing."

"Oh, I remember, too."

"It's an impressive hole, too. Not too deep but very wide. Savannah said they used water from the barrel outside the bunkhouse to 'make it easier to dig'." She wiped some of the mud from Toughie's face. "I don't think this little stink pot did too much digging. Looks more like he rolled in the mud instead."

She laughed again. "He probably did. I'll leave you to it then. And you might want to lock the door this time."

Catalina nodded. "That's a very good idea."

Evie closed the door but didn't move away until she heard the lock slip into place. She glanced down at her dress and sighed. It would have to be laundered, but it wasn't the worst thing to have happen. She wasn't a stranger to mud. Or cookie crumbs. Or any of the other things children could get into, and she wouldn't trade the messiness for anything.

She went upstairs and changed, slipping into her a simple skirt and blouse, then headed to the kitchen by the back stairs.

Felicity and Hilde were there, as she knew they would be—Hilde up to her elbows in flour, punching the dough in the bowl to remove any air bubbles, and Felicity rinsing the vegetables they'd have with dinner. The smell of a roast in the oven—Felicity's favorite recipe and the one she loved to make—filled the air. Since Felicity had come to stay, she'd taken over much of the cooking, something she enjoyed doing. Truthfully, Evie was happy to let her.

Jenny and Esmeralda, who both sometimes helped in the kitchen, were nowhere to be found, but Ramón was in his highchair by the table, happily munching on a carrot. The sight made her smile.

She grabbed an apron from the hook on the pantry door, slipped it over her head, and tied the strings around her waist.

"How was your picnic with Mr. Parrish, dear?" Felicity asked, as she put the clean vegetables in a bowl and brought them to the worktable in the middle of the room, then grabbed a knife from the drawer and handed it to Evie.

Evie took the paring knife and picked one of the potatoes from the bowl. "It was lovely."

Hilde sniffed, then swiped at her nose with her wrist, leaving flour on her face. "That's it? Lovely?"

"What more would you like me to say?" The truth was, she'd spent most of the picnic thinking about Jake instead of Ryland, wishing she was back on the ranch with him. That wasn't to say Ryland was boring, he was anything but. Charming and funny, he'd regaled her all afternoon with stories of the people he'd met and the hotels he'd refurbished, and though she liked Ryland very much, he was just a friend.

"Do you like him?" Felicity asked, as she joined her at the worktable and started arranging pieces of broccoli, cauliflower, and carrots on a baking sheet.

"I do." She finished peeling the potato, quartered it, and tossed it into the pot, then chose another from the bowl. "He's charming. And very funny. I haven't laughed that hard in a long time."

"Will you be seeing him again?" Hilde removed the dough from the bowl, halved it, and arranged the dough into pans for baking, then pushed them aside to allow for the last rising. She covered both pans with dish towels, then turned her attention to Evie, an expectant smile on her face.

Evie nodded. "He invited me to a concert next Saturday. I thought I'd stay with Lucy that night and come home the following morning."

Hilde gave her that look, the one that said if she played her cards right, he could be the man she married.

Evie shook her head, denying what she saw in the woman's eyes. "No, Hilde, he doesn't plan on staying in Serenity. In fact, as soon as the hotel is finished, he'll be moving on. The man doesn't like to stay in one place for very long. He does his work and heads off to his next adventure."

"Oh." Hilde said, with such disappointment in her voice, it was hard to ignore.

"But while he's here, I see no reason why we can't be friends. In fact, I'd like that very much."

"Tia Evie!" Savannah ran into the kitchen, interrupting their conversation. She let the door slam against the wall in her exuberance. Like Toughie, she had mud on her face and clothing, some of it dry, but not all of it. Her hands were clean though, which surprised Evie. "I found this on the table outside under a rock. It's you!"

Evie stopped peeling the potato, wiped her hands on her

apron, and took the sheet of paper from her grandniece. It *was* her, cutting roses. She remembered that evening, remembered what she'd been feeling at that moment, which was mostly guilt with a little bit of wistfulness thrown in for asking Jake to kiss her. Whoever had drawn this had managed to capture that.

She studied the sketch, looking for a signature or initials to tell her who had drawn it. There was none.

"Let me see," Felicity moved around the table to get a closer look.

Evie held up the paper.

"Oh, it's beautiful. Whoever drew this has talent. Raw talent, but quite good just the same."

"Did you see who put it on the table?" Evie asked, as her eyes took in every detail, from the basket hanging from her arm to the lace on the collar of her blouse.

Savannah shook her head, then grabbed a piece of cut broccoli from the tray and popped it into her mouth. "No, ma'am," she mumbled around the food in her mouth. "Me and Miguel and Toughie, we were…playin'.'"

Evie chuckled. "Yes, I heard about the hole you were digging."

"They took my best spoons to do it, too!" Hilde declared as she gave Savannah a look meant to show her disappointment but failed. Savannah simply grinned at her, showing the space where her front tooth had been up until a week ago.

Evie moved to the window, the drawing still in her hand, and looked outside. The horses were in the corral, the milk cow grazed on fresh hay in her little paddock, and the chickens pecked at the ground, except for Lucifer, who perched on top of the chicken coop. Aside from Miguel, still digging in the dirt, she didn't see another human being.

Who could have left this for me?

None of the ranch hands had ever shown a proclivity toward this sort of thing, and she'd known most of them for a long time, which left Jake and Oscar, the two she knew the least about. Had one of them left this for her? Whoever it was, the gift was rather thoughtful. And different. Never before had she received anything like this. She had a fondness for peppermints and received tins of the candy before, but this...this was special, something that would last, not like candy or flowers.

"You should put that in a frame." Felicity sidled up beside her. "Hang it up."

Evie glanced at her and said, "Yes, I think I will."

CHAPTER 14

*B*eing that this was the second Saturday of the month and pay day, the ranch hands swooped into the barnyard earlier than usual with whoops and hollers, making Jake smile. They so looked forward to heading into town and blowing off some steam. And why shouldn't they? Chasing cattle and horses was hot, tiring work.

As he'd done on other occasions, he'd join his bunkmates at the river. He still wouldn't be joining them when they went to town, though he continued to be invited. He just wasn't interested. The allure of a card game didn't appeal to him anymore. Funny, it hadn't since he arrived here, not even when his bunk mates played poker at the table, though gambling was strictly forbidden in the bunkhouse.

His thoughts flew to Erik King.

Is he still looking for me?

He shook his head, forcing the question from his mind. Best not to think about King.

Besides, he'd much rather think about Evie.

He stole a glance toward the house, wondering if the drawing he'd left for her earlier had been found. His stomach knotted just a bit. He'd never shared his artwork with anyone before, other than Father O'Malley. He kept that hidden talent to himself as he did so many other things, though the good Father had encouraged him to develop it, a much more worthy pursuit than gambling.

"Jake." Teddy dismounted and handed him Soldier Boy's reins, then reached up to help Esmeralda, who had ridden Horatio out to the summer pasture today.

"Afternoon, Teddy." Jake touched the brim of his hat, then grabbed Horatio's reins. "Miss Esmeralda."

She greeted him with just a nod, but her eyes glowed with warmth. He wondered if they planned to head into town as well, but didn't ask. If they needed the carriage, they would tell him, but neither said anything as they walked toward the house. He watched them for a moment, admiring the way they held hands, their heads together. Envy whispered through him for what they had. His jaw clenched as he led the horses into the corral to cool off.

Esteban followed closely afterward, but didn't say much, as was his way. He handed over Fuego to his keeping before following his brother.

Heath and Jenny weren't too far behind. Heath gave him a big grin and a jaunty salute as he brought Goldie to a halt beside him. Jake reached up to help Jenny dismount—she didn't ride much, but she did enjoy going out to the summer pasture on occasion.

"Miss Jenny."

She smiled as she removed her hat to reveal her golden tresses, though most of them were flattened against her head from wearing the hat all day. She ran her fingers through her hair, trying to loosen the strands into their natural curls. "Afternoon, Jake."

Heath handed him the reins. "No need to unsaddle or brush Goldie down. We're heading back out again."

"Yes, sir."

He tied Goldie's reins to one of the fence slats then entered the bunkhouse to collect his clothes, just in time to see Oscar standing beside his bunk, the sketchbook he'd forgotten to hide under his pillow in his hand. Three of his drawings were on the floor, one of them crumpled into a ball.

Instantly, his stomach clenched, and his hands balled into fists as the man ripped another page out of the sketchbook and tossed it on the floor.

Jake stomped into the room, anger making his footsteps heavier than usual. "What the hell are you doing?"

Oscar snarled at him as he ripped out another page and held it out. "You after my woman, *pendejo?*"

Jake ignored the taunt and grabbed for the pad of paper, but Oscar snatched it away, hiding it behind his back, and took a step closer. He puffed out his chest and threw his shoulders back to make himself look more intimidating. The impressive mustache on his upper lip quivered with anger. "I saw you with her! Saw you kiss her! She spreading her legs for you, too?" His eyes narrowed and spittle sprayed from his mouth. "Think you could steal her from me, *bastardo?* She's mine!"

Oscar's tone and blatant disrespect, not only for Evie, but for his private property, infuriated him, but he held still, though it was an effort. "She's not your woman. And you will not speak of her in that tone."

"Who's gonna stop me?" Oscar scoffed as he jutted out his chin and very deliberately, brought the sketchbook from behind his back and ripped out another page, crumpling into a ball before throwing it at him. "You?"

It grew silent in the bunkhouse. The other ranch hands had stopped collecting their clean clothes and turned all their attention to them. He felt a trickle of anticipation. Not from himself, but from them. For the most part, they all got along fairly well, though there were one or two who didn't like Oscar's attitude. And weren't afraid to say so. In fact, Oscar had been warned a time or two to shut his mouth and keep his opinions to himself. That didn't stop him and he frequently went on tirades about anything and everything, disparaging the ranch, how it was run, and the men he had to work with. Jake, more often than not, became his target. For the most part, he could ignore the younger man, but not now, not after he spoke of Evie with such disrespect. And not ever again.

Oscar dropped the sketch book on the floor and stepped on it, grinding the heel of his boot into the pages, then struck a classic fighter's pose, fists drawn up to protect his face. A smug smile tilted up the corners of his mouth, his dark eyes filled with determination.

"No fightin' in the bunkhouse." That reminder came from Emilio, always the peacekeeper. "Them's the rules."

Jake inhaled deeply, trying to keep his temper under control. Never before had he wanted to punch someone in the mouth as much as he did this man, not just for this offense, but for all of them. "I don't want to fight you, Oscar."

The man sneered as he twisted his heel on the sketchbook a little more, as if daring him. "Why not? You chicken?"

Jake shook his head but didn't move. He remained alert, warily watching the other man, fully aware that he, too, was being watched by his bunkmates. They were probably wondering if he'd take the bait. He never sought a fight, but he never backed down from one either.

He kept his focus on Oscar, sizing him up, studying him. Oscar seemed like the kind of person who would hit someone when they weren't looking. A dirty fighter. He'd seen—and fought—plenty of them. "Not at all. Just don't want to see you get hurt."

Apparently, those weren't the correct words to diffuse the situation. Oscar's fists tightened, his knuckles turning white, as a smile spread his lips. It wasn't a pleasant smile, not in the least. Perhaps he was just immature, but Jake didn't think so. He was a bully, plain and simple. He'd seen others like him his entire life. "If you want to do this, we'll do it behind the bunkhouse. I don't want Miss Evie or the children to see this."

"Afraid she'll see you for the coward you are?"

Jake shrugged and smiled. The first thing to know about fighting: emotion could make you lose your concentration, and you could end up leaving yourself open for a hit you didn't want to take. "No, sir. I'm thinking of you. I wouldn't want you to be embarrassed when I knock you on your ass."

Oscar spit out a word that would have made Father O'Malley wash his mouth out with soap. That emotion, the one that could make one lose complete control? That was Oscar. Already he could see what his comment had done. The man stiffened, his face reddening, causing his thick black mustache to stand out in stark relief. And his eyes? They were so dark, they appeared almost black. And filled with murderous intent.

Jake gave an exaggerated bow and gestured toward the door. "After you."

Oscar strutted across the floor, full of confidence. He may have held his own in a barroom brawl a time or two, but he didn't know he was no match for Jake.

The other men trooped out after Oscar, except for Slick, who waited at the door for him. "Think you can take him?"

Jake said nothing, just looked at Slick as he walked outside and down the two steps from the porch to the dirt.

Slick followed him. "Do me a favor and hit him once for me. I'm tired of him thinking he knows more than anyone else and trying to tell us all what to do."

"I wouldn't mind if you hit him once for me, too." That comment came from Mayhem, accompanied by a wide grin, as he joined them. "He deserves it more than most. Maybe he'll learn some respect, especially for Miss Evie. Ain't the first time he talked about her like that."

Jake still said nothing as he strode behind the bunkhouse,

where Oscar waited, arrogant smirk spreading his lips, hands on his hips, surrounded by an air of superiority and just plain meanness. The other men—Cesar, Emilio, even Grub—were there as well, murmuring among themselves, the anticipation palpable. He heard bets being placed on who would win as Slick and Mayhem joined them. Surprisingly, the consensus was evenly split, though one and all were looking forward to a good fight.

"You can still walk away, Oscar," Jake said, keeping his tone even, offering the man the opportunity to save himself.

"No chance. I'm gonna teach you not to mess with your betters." He spit out a crude cuss word, then raised his fists, once again protecting his face, and began rocking back and forth on the balls of his feet. It was obvious this wasn't Oscar's first fight. And probably wouldn't be his last, not with his attitude.

"Have it your way." Jake faced his opponent and took his stance, bringing up his fists, focusing all his concentration on his opponent. "Just remember, you asked for this."

Oscar threw a punch, which Jake neatly side-stepped then threw one of his own. His knuckles slammed into Oscar's face.

And that was all it took. Oscar went down, blood spurting from his nose.

The other men grumbled with disappointment. Jake was certain they were expecting a no-holds-barred brawl. They hadn't expected that with one punch, the fight would be over.

"You broke my nose!" Shock and fury filled Oscar's voice. Apparently, such a thing had never happened before.

Jake lowered his hands and stood over the man. "It's over." Though he said the words, he knew it wasn't true. Oscar, like another man he knew, was not the type to accept defeat. Still, he extended his hand to help the man up. Oscar slapped it away with a sneer, though he accepted the help of others.

"It'll never be over, Hannigan. Watch your back."

Though he slowed as he walked away, Jake didn't stop until he entered the bunkhouse and strode over to his bunk. He picked up the sketchpad from the floor as well as the pages Oscar had ripped from the book. Anger flared, but he tamped it down as he looked at the crinkled and torn drawings. Maybe he could salvage a few.

"I never seen anything like that!" Slick exclaimed as he came to stand beside him. "One hit and the man was down." He laughed. "Serves him right. He shouldn't have been touching your things or talkin' about Miss Evie that way. As if she would have him."

Jake said nothing, just stared at his ruined drawings. His knuckles were a little sore, but not nearly as sore as his heart.

"I'm sorry he ruined your book. Your sketches are pretty good." Slick laid a hand on his shoulder awkwardly, obviously trying to offer some comfort. "Come on, let's head down to the river."

Whatever enjoyment he might have found at the river disappeared. "You go on without me." He tossed the sketchbook as well as the pages in the trash can and left the bunkhouse to take care of the horses. He saw the men leave, their clean clothes bundled under their arms, knowing he was the subject of their animated gestures. Oscar brought up the rear by himself, still pressing a handkerchief to his broken nose. He glared, his eyes fairly glowing with hatred. Jake knew exactly what was going through the man's head. And it wasn't good. He'd made an enemy of Oscar, as the man didn't seem to be the type to forgive.

And it didn't matter. He didn't care. He wasn't a violent man, but he'd never backed down from a bully and Oscar definitely had some come-uppance coming to him. Still, he wasn't happy about the situation as he strode to the corral and grabbed Esteban's horse by the reins and led him into the barn. He removed the saddle and reins, slipped a halter over his head then picked up the brush and began smoothing it over the horse's coat, the simple act soothing his soul.

He heard the men come back from the river as he walked

Soldier Boy toward the barn, actually felt Oscar's stare burning a hole into him as they all trooped into the bunkhouse. Antonio showed up a few minutes later with his wooden tray filled with little pay envelopes.

He stayed where he was, not trusting himself to hold back if Oscar should say another word. Next time, he'd do more than just break the man's nose.

He put Soldier Boy in his stall, gave him some oats, and headed back outside to the corral to brush down Horatio, just in time to see his bunkmates head out. Oscar lagged behind and took his time mounting up, his dark-eyed gleam intense, his mouth drawn into a thin line beneath his mustache. He kicked his horse and rode right up to him, coming so close, Jake could see the sweat on the horse's face. He stepped out of the way at the last minute, but never took his eyes from the man.

"We ain't done." Oscar glared down at him, his nose swollen and just a bit crooked.

"Didn't figure we were. Anytime you want your nose broken again, you just let me know."

The man scoffed and called him a word in Spanish Jake didn't know the meaning of, but whatever it was, he was certain it wasn't nice. "It was a lucky punch, and you know it."

Jake shrugged, ignoring the slur as well as the man's attitude. "If that's what you want to think, you go right ahead."

Oscar said nothing more, but his face turned beet red, and his lips pressed together tighter as his hands gripped the reins. His eyes narrowed as he stared at Jake.

Jake wouldn't put it past this man to do something dirty, like kick him in the face from his perch in the saddle. Whatever Oscar planned, he was prepared. He stood his ground, his muscles tense, ready to defend himself and take the man down another notch or two.

A moment passed, then two, then three, and suddenly, Oscar spurred his horse and rode off. Jake watched him go, then continued brushing Horatio, knowing in his heart that Oscar might plan some type of revenge. He would be ready for it.

He finished with Horatio and brought him into the barn, then went outside to grab Clementine.

"Thought I'd find you here." Antonio hooked his boot on the bottom rung of the corral fence, the wooden tray dangling from his hand. "I noticed you didn't come inside to pick up your pay." He held out the envelope, the coins within jingling as he did so.

"Thanks."

As Jake reached for the envelope, Antonio's gaze flew to his knuckles. "Saw Oscar's nose. Knew it was you that busted it."

Jake tucked the envelope into his pocket. He had missed his chance to send Father O'Malley money, but that just meant he'd send double the next time. If there was a next time. "You gonna fire me for fighting?"

"No, son. Slick and Mayhem told me what happened. I don't see how you could have walked away. *I* wouldn't have been able to." He let out a sigh that stirred his mustache. "I'm considering firing him," he said.

"That would be up to you, sir. Just don't do it on my account."

There was more Antonio was going to say—Jake could see that clearly, but whatever it was, the man must have thought better of it. After a moment of silence, he finally did speak. "When you have a minute, hitch up the carriage and bring it around front."

"Sure thing."

Antonio nodded then pushed his hat further back on his head. "You know, any time you want to head into town with the boys, I can take care of the horses. Just let me know."

The offer surprised him, but probably shouldn't have. "I appreciate that, but I'm not interested in going to town."

"Suit yourself, but the offer still stands." Antonio finally walked away, but there seemed to be a bounce to his step that hadn't been there before, almost as if he was proud of what Jake had done. Or maybe it was the fact that he preferred to stay on the ranch instead of raising hell in town. Whatever the reason for Antonio's pride, it made Jake's chest swell just the same.

"Well, that was interesting, don't you think?" He rubbed his hand over Clementine's nose, then reached up and scratched the horse behind the ears. She blew hot air from her nostrils, then tried to bite his hat. He brushed her down, then brought her inside the barn, settling her in her stall. He removed his hat, wiped the sweat from his brow. Two more horses to take care of —Spitfire, who had spent the day in the corral, rolling in the dust, and Cinnamon—and then he could hook up the carriages. Or maybe he should do that now.

Evie was waiting for him at the corral fence as he stepped out of the barn, feeding carrots to Spitfire and Cinnamon. She turned to look at him as he approached, her blue-gray eyes bluer at the moment, a beautiful smile on her face. "Hello, Jake."

He touched the brim of his hat with two fingers as his gaze roamed over her face. She really was the most beautiful woman he'd ever seen. Oh, maybe not in the eyes of some people, but most definitely his. "Evenin', Miss Evie."

"Come to the house and join us for dinner." She slipped another carrot to Spitfire. "After you're done, of course."

"I would like that. Thank you."

"Say in about thirty minutes?"

He thought she would head back to the house, but instead, she just stood there. Her eyes held so much warmth, it was hard to look away.

A blush rose to her cheeks. "I'll see you at the house," she said finally, then walked away. As usual, he watched her go.

"What do you think about that, Cinnamon? I've been invited to the big house for dinner." He laughed as he brought the horse into the barn.

When he came outside again, it was just in time to see Heath and Jenny ride off toward the summer pasture, a burlap sack tied to Goldie's saddle. She waved. Jake waved in return, then collected the big draft horses used to pull the carriage.

It didn't take him long to finish his chores and hitch up the carriage as he'd been asked, though he did regret not heading to the river with the others to bathe. He washed up with water from the rain barrel as best he could, then changed his clothes, brushed his hair, and left the bunkhouse.

Evie plucked the last strawberry from her plate and popped it in her mouth, then sat back and watched Jake interact with the children. He even teased Ramón in his highchair, making funny faces at the boy to make him giggle and for a short time, he sat with Toughie on his lap. It amazed her that the boy sat still for more than five minutes. It was obvious they liked him, and he returned the feeling. It was also obvious that Felicity and Charley, as well as Hilde and Antonio liked him, too, and that made her heart glad.

"That was the best roast I've ever had, Miss Felicity. Just about melted in my mouth." Jake said.

Felicity blushed. Even the tips of her ears turned red. "Well, thank you, Jake. I'm glad you liked it."

"And Miss Hilde, I've never had a more delicious Angel Food cake, not even in San Francisco." He smiled. "Or anywhere else." He paused and his smile grew a little wider. "Have you ever been to Seattle?"

"No, I have not."

"There's a little café on the waterfront that serves the lightest, fluffiest Angel Food cake I have ever had, but it doesn't compare to yours."

Evie smothered a laugh as Hilde turned bright red, almost redder than Felicity.

"When were you in Seattle?" Antonio asked. "I've never been

off the ranch. Never had the bug to travel though." He glanced at his wife, then patted her hand. "I have everything I need right here."

Hilde, her face flushed from the compliments from both men, rose from her seat and clapped her hands. "All right, children, let's get these dishes done."

"Years ago," Jake waved his hand, picking up the conversation, "when I worked on a steamer that delivered supplies and passengers up and down the coast." He sat back in his chair and fiddled with the fork in his hand, but his gaze found her and stayed.

It didn't take long for the butterflies to start dancing in her stomach.

"Where else have you been?" Antonio asked, then turned his attention to Savannah and tugged on one of her long braids as she reached for his dirty plate. He whispered something in her ear. She looked at him and grinned, her smile a little crooked since she'd lost that tooth. She eagerly nodded and left the kitchen at a run. Evie watched her go, then turned to look at Antonio as she, too, rose from her seat to help with the dishes, curious to know what that was all about.

Antonio said nothing as he gestured to Jake to answer the question.

"Too many places to name. Some of them awe-inspiring, like Bridal Veil Falls in Oregon, some not so much. I will tell you, though, out of all the places I've been," he said, his gaze once again finding hers, "I have never seen a place as beautiful as this ranch."

The statement touched her and she was about tell him so when Savannah raced back into the kitchen, making the swinging door bang against the wall, something hidden behind her back.

"This is for you, Mr. Jake." She handed him a sketchpad as well as several pencils sharpened to a precise point. The book wasn't new, but there were plenty of pages left, and the pencils, some short, some longer, still had a lot of life in them.

The look on his face, a combination of confusion as well as gratitude as he accepted the gift, warmed her heart even more. He glanced at her, questions in his beautiful amber eyes. "What is this?"

Evie shook her head. She had no answers, but obviously, Antonio knew. "Antonio?"

"I saw what happened to your old sketchbook. Thought you could use a new one."

Evie closed her eyes for a moment as realization slammed her. It was Jake who had drawn the picture of her. She opened her eyes and simply stared at him.

Color infused Jake's face. "I don't know what to say, except thank you."

"Draw me," Savannah demanded, then plopped in her chair and struck a pose with her elbows on the table, her folded hands supporting her chin.

Jake leaned back in his chair a little and flipped open the cover of the sketch pad to reveal a clean page. He chose a pencil from the handful he'd been given, studied the girl for a moment, then started drawing.

Evie continued to clear the table, but stopped several times to stand behind him and watch with amazement as his pencil flew over the paper. In moments, he captured Savannah's sweet face and charming grin. He ripped the page from the book and handed it to the beaming girl. The expression on her face was priceless.

"I want one, too!" Miguel, not to be outdone by his sister, took a seat next to her and posed as well. Once again, Jake studied the boy and quickly drew him, managing to capture the devilish glint in Miguel's dark eyes.

"That's enough now," Hilde spoke up as she filled the sink with hot water from the kettle and little slivers of soap to make suds. She added cold water from the pump so she could put her hands in the water without scalding herself. "Time to wash the dishes."

"But we were having fun!" Savannah pouted.

"Hilde's right. It's time for dishes." Jake closed the cover on the sketchbook. "Maybe tomorrow, we'll do some more drawings."

Savannah scooted from her chair and rested her hands on the table, her direct gaze on him. "You promise?"

He laughed. "I do."

"Okay." She grabbed a few dishes and brought them to the sink.

Jake rose as well, a slight blush coloring his cheeks. It was the most charming thing Evie had ever seen, and something in her heart shifted.

"I should go. Thank you all." He grabbed the sketchbook and pencils from the table and slipped out the door before she could utter a word.

She followed him outside. "Jake, wait."

Jake stopped and turned to face her.

"It was you who left the drawing for me."

"Yes." His gaze roamed her face, causing those butterflies to flutter in her belly once more. "Do you mind?"

"No, not at all. I was...I am flattered." She studied his handsome face with its boyish charm. "Why did you draw it?"

"I saw you that afternoon and you looked so lovely, I knew I had to capture that moment. I wanted you to see how beautiful you are to me. I'm not sure I fully managed that, but I tried." He reached out with his free hand and smoothed his knuckles along her jawbone then dipped his head and kissed her, his lips warm and inviting. By their own volition, Evie's arms raised and wrapped around his neck, pressing her body close to his as the kiss deepened. She felt the sharp jab of a pencil but ignored it as her toes curled in her boots and a certain excitement rushed through her, making her pulse race and her heartbeat thunder in her ears.

He broke the kiss and smiled down at her as he took a step back, neatly breaking their embrace. Caressing the side of her face with his knuckles once more, he stared into her eyes. "Good night, Evie, and thank you." He left the patio with a swagger in his step.

Evie let out a sigh as she watched him go, suddenly bereft that he wasn't holding her close, though the feeling of his lips on hers remained.

She should follow him, just to steal another kiss.

Be brave, Evie. Take a chance. Not because it would benefit Regina's children or Montaña del Trueno. Do something for you. Just you.

She took a step off the patio—a small step in one way, but a big one in so many others—then stopped as the back door opened behind her, and a little voice interrupted her thoughts. "*Tia* Evie, will you read us a story?"

She glanced down at Miguel and sighed. "Of course, *mi corazón*. After the dishes are done."

"Okay." The boy disappeared into the house. "She said yes!" he exclaimed to his sister, then launched into which story he wanted to hear. She heard Savannah's reply, claiming a different story than the one Miguel wanted amid the clanking of dishes being washed and dried.

Evie watched as light flashed in the bunkhouse window and the door closed. *So much for being brave*, she scoffed, then turned and went into the house.

CHAPTER 15

From the corner of his eye, Jake saw Evie jump from the top railing of the fence where he was riding Clementine and head toward him. He turned the horse in her direction, then squeezed his knees, bringing Clementine to a halt. "Am I doing something wrong?"

"Not at all." She tilted her head as she looked up at him. He loved it when she did that, the sight warming his heart and making him want to pull her into his arms. "I think you're ready."

"For what?"

She rubbed Clementine's nose as she studied him. "We're heading out to the summer pasture today. You should see what we do out there, see all the horses and the cattle. It'll be good for you."

It was one thing to ride Clementine around the riding ring. It was an entirely different story to ride her out to the summer pasture. "If you think so," he said, with a confidence he didn't feel.

"I do. You'll be fine. I wouldn't say it if I didn't think it was true," she assured him. "If you'll saddle Spitfire for me, we can go."

Jake slipped from the saddle, walked Clementine toward the

corral gate, and wrapped the horse's reins around one of the slats in the fence. Evie followed him into the barn. She let Spitfire out of her stall while he headed to the tack room for the saddle, bridle, and reins.

It didn't take long before he was mounted up and following her out of the barnyard and into the field beyond the outbuildings. He had no idea how far they'd gone, but the house was no longer in view when he turned in the saddle. A ribbon of blue off to the left—the river that wound through Montaña del Trueno—supported a multitude of cottonwood trees, their limbs spreading out to provide shade. Other trees—ponderosa and spruce possibly, but he couldn't be certain—formed a line of green against the horizon. Beyond the trees, he saw nothing but mountains rising up to the azure blue sky.

He rode beside Evie, admiring the way she sat in the saddle, her hands on Spitfire's reins sure and competent. And the expression on her face! It was a mixture of pride and love and excitement, making her cheeks flush and her eyes turn more blue than gray. She really did love this ranch, loved everything about it. He'd never felt like that about any place, but he was beginning to. Montaña del Trueno seemed like heaven on earth, but he suspected it was only because *she* was here.

He followed her through the thick stand of pine trees until she broke free and reined in Spitfire, her gaze encompassing what lay before her. She turned toward him, and his heart stopped for a moment then resumed with a hard thud. She had never looked more beautiful, although he admitted—to himself, at least—Evie, with the glow of the setting sun reflecting on her, was a picture he'd keep with him for the rest of his life, and a close second to what he saw now.

She let out a sigh. "This…is the summer pasture."

It was an effort, but he shifted his focus from her to the vista before him.

No wonder she loved this place so much. It was beautiful,

almost as beautiful as her. Grass grew tall here, fed by gentle spring rains and the river, which meandered in twists and turns throughout the field. At least thirty horses, some having been born just a few short months ago, judging by their size, others, a spring or two before, grazed alongside their mothers at the river's edge, and cattle, at least two hundred head, were further in the distance, their constant lowing seeming to echo off the mountains surrounding them.

"I had no idea." Awestruck, he could only stare.

"It's magnificent, isn't it?" She glanced at him, and he could see her pride clearly.

"It is."

She spread her arms wide. "Having the herd in the summer pasture allows us to save on feed. See how tall the grass is? Once winter comes, we'll move them closer, but for right now, we can let them graze to their hearts' content." She smiled at him. "And it's tradition. This is what the Silvas have always done, according to both Serafina and Antonio."

He noticed a tent, a spot of white against all the green in the distance, and finally made the connection as to why not all the ranch hands came in at the end of the day. At least one stayed to protect the herd during the night, except on pay day, when Teddy and his wife, Esteban and Catalina, or Heath and Jenny watched over the herd to allow the cowhands to head into town.

Out in the pasture, Teddy separated from the other horses and rode up to him. "Nice to see you out here, Jake."

"Nice to be here."

Teddy, the man he didn't think would ever become friendly toward him, seemed to be doing just that. Not only had he entrusted him with a young horse to train, but his entire attitude had changed, for which Jake remained thankful. There seemed to be an acceptance in his eyes that hadn't been there before.

"I thought it was time for him to see this." Evie gestured

toward the pasture beyond them. "He's done well with his lessons."

"I agree." Teddy nudged Soldier Boy and rode off. "Keep up the good work," he called over his shoulder.

Pride that Teddy should note his accomplishments brought a feeling of satisfaction deep in his heart.

Oscar rode up beside them then, his big, black stallion coming dangerously close, almost touching Clementine. The mare took a step to the side and snorted, as if warning off the other horse. Oscar maneuvered his mount a little closer, just enough to be intimidating then turned his attention to Evie. He touched the brim of his hat with two fingers. "Good afternoon, Miss Evie."

"Good afternoon, Oscar."

Oscar acknowledged the greeting then turned his attention to him. "Shouldn't you be shoveling shit?" he scoffed, despite the fact such a word should never be said in front of a lady. He glared at Jake, his lips curled into a smirk, before he rode off, no doubt in an effort to show off his skills, skills that Jake was just learning. Horse and rider disappeared from view, and it was just as well.

Jake really didn't want to look at Oscar's smug face or hear his whiny voice. Ever since their fight, Oscar had been continually baiting him, egging him on for a rematch. Jake did his best to ignore the man, but it was becoming increasingly difficult. It was just a matter of time before he'd knock the man on his ass again. The day was coming, and in his opinion, it couldn't come soon enough.

Evie frowned, her shapely brows lowering to form a deep furrow between them as she watched the man ride away then turned back to him. There were questions in her eyes, questions he wasn't sure he wanted to answer. "What was that about?"

"We had a disagreement."

"About what?"

"I'd rather not say."

Her eyes narrowed as her frown deepened, drawing the corners of her mouth down as well. "If something is happening on the ranch, I need to know."

"It's nothing for you to wor—"

Clementine emitted a high-pitched whinny before he could finish his sentence and reared up on her hind legs. Startled, not quite sure what to do except not fall off, Jake gripped the reins and squeezed the horse's sides. Clementine came down hard on her front legs and bolted, like someone had set her tail on fire. Jake bit his tongue as his teeth clicked together from the impact and the coppery taste of blood filled his mouth. The reverberations of her pounding hooves travelled up his spine as the horse headed toward the river at a dead run, jostling him in the saddle.

He couldn't stop her. No amount of squeezing his legs or pulling on the reins slowed her headlong rush. Panic gripped him, causing his throat to constrict. He couldn't yell. Hell, he could hardly breathe. And his heart pounded so hard, he thought it would break through the wall of his chest.

This horse is going to kill me!

Water splashed up as Clementine galloped into the river, blinding him temporarily but somehow, he managed to hang on, squeezing his knees against her sides, praying for her to stop. He could jump, now that he was in the water, but couldn't bring himself to do it, having no idea if there were boulders beneath the surface—boulders that could surely be his doom.

Salvation came in the form of a slim, gloved hand reaching for the reins. Jake took his eyes off the horizon for just a moment and glanced to his left to see Evie right beside him, Spitfire keeping up with Clementine's frantic run.

Strange the things he noticed in that split second before he met his maker. There was no panic on her face, just a grim determination. Her hat flew off her head, revealing a wealth of light brown hair, the sun glinting off the strands of white, making them seem even whiter.

She made a grab for the reins and missed. She tried again and managed to seize the reins from his hands. A moment later, Clementine slowed, her sides heaving as she blew hard. She stopped, finally, up to her belly in the water. The horse turned her head to look at him, like she was apologizing for almost killing him.

Jake drew in a deep breath, the first one in what seemed like hours, but in reality was only a few minutes. His heartbeat returned to normal…or whatever normal was now. He still felt like it was beating too hard, pounding against his ribcage, echoing in his ears.

He turned toward Evie and gratitude filled his thundering heart. "Thank you."

Evie studied him, noticing the paleness of his face, the slight shaking of his body. Fear could do that to a person. Her own hands were trembling, though she gripped both his reins and hers. Clementine's behavior could have seriously injured him. He could have fallen and hit his head on the boulders beneath the surface of the water—some as big as Clementine herself—and wound up with a concussion. He could have broken bones. Hell, he could have broken his neck.

He could have died.

She sucked in her breath as the truth hit home, making her swallow hard over the sudden lump in her throat.

I'm in love with him.

When it happened or how, she didn't know, but she had. "Are you all right?"

Jake gulped in air and let it out in a huff. "I am now. What the hell happened?"

"I don't know, Jake."

His face reddened, his amber eyes almost bronze with fear. "I almost broke my fool neck!"

"But you didn't." Her heart slowed to a steady beat and the constriction in her throat eased. "You didn't fall, either. You managed to stay in the saddle."

"That's only because you grabbed the reins and stopped this four-legged freight train from drowning me."

She laughed. She couldn't help it. Not only was she relieved Jake wasn't hurt, but the expression on his face was amusing—a mix between embarrassment, fear, and gratitude.

"I don't know why she did that. Never saw Clementine act like that before. Almost like she was spooked." She guided Spitfire around Clementine, looking for anything obvious to explain her behavior. She saw nothing out of the ordinary. "Still, you did well, considering you don't have much experience."

"You all right?" The voice came from the riverbank. Evie turned to see Esteban, his face shadowed with concern. Beside him on his big black stallion was Oscar, but there was no concern on the man's face. No, it was more a smirk of arrogance. It was in the way he sat in his saddle, too—shoulders back, chest puffed out. And there was something wrong with his nose. She didn't remember it being so...crooked, like it had been broken and not set right.

"We're fine," she called out as she handed Jake Clementine's reins. "Jake and I are heading back to the house."

Esteban tugged on the Fuego's reins, moving his horse a little closer. "Never saw Clementine act like that."

"Me either, but she seems to be fine now."

"Can we walk?" Jake asked, hope filling his voice.

"It's too far to walk, Jake. Besides, Clementine is calm now. Whatever happened is over, at least in her book." But even as she said the words, she still wasn't sure what *did* happen. What made Clementine act like that? Had a horse fly bitten her? The pain would be enough to make any horse, no matter how serene and well-trained, rear up and gallop off like that.

Had it been something else?

She glanced at Oscar again. His expression hadn't changed. It was still smug. He tapped the brim of his hat with his fingers and rode off.

She watched him go then returned her attention to Jake. "You sure you're all right?"

"Yes. I think so." Jake gave an embarrassed laugh. "Nothing appears to be broken except my pride."

"I don't think your pride is broken. Not in the least. You should be proud you stayed in the saddle. I'm not sure I could have."

"If you say so."

"I do." She smiled at him, then reached up to settle her hat more firmly on her head, only to find it was gone. "Where's my hat?"

"Is that it?" He pointed further down the river, where something brown bobbed in the near distance. She rode that way, splashing through the water, then bent low and scooped it up. It was saturated, but she plopped it on her head anyway and rode back toward him because he hadn't budged.

"Let's go home."

Jake gave her a sheepish smile. "I'm not sure I can move."

"Sure you can," she encouraged him, though she knew exactly how he felt. She'd been on a runaway horse once or twice in her life. It was frightening to say the least. And she hadn't managed to keep her seat, opting to jump from the horse's back at the risk to her own mortality. "One step at a time. I have faith."

She led the way out of the river, checking to make sure he followed. He did, rather slowly, concentration making his brows furrow and his jaw clench. His hands gripped the reins so tightly, his knuckles showed white.

"Don't let her know you're afraid."

"And how am I supposed to do that?" he asked, with a touch of sarcasm in his voice.

"Relax." She slowed Spitfire, allowing him to catch up to her. "Hold the reins loosely and let her just walk. There's no rush to get back to the house. No rush at all. We can take as long as we want. We'll follow the river. There's a nice path beneath the trees."

She set the pace—a slow, gentle walk, but didn't speak, allowing him all the time he needed to get over his fear, though she did understand why he was afraid.

After a while, she glanced at him from beneath the brim of her hat. He was beginning to relax a little, his grip on Clementine's reins not quite as tight, but there was still tension in his face—his eyes were squinted, focused straight ahead.

Her heart ached for him. "How are you doing, Jake?"

"So far, so good." He glanced at her and gave her a half smile. "I will admit that I can't wait to get my feet on the ground."

"We'll be home soon enough."

As she'd promised, *Pequeña Casa* came into view, and she led the way past the little house, staying on the path that would eventually bring them behind the bunkhouse. She kept turning around, making sure he was still with her. His face was still a little pale, but gaining color, and his breathing had returned to normal.

I almost lost him! She shook her head to dislodge the horrible thought and dismounted at the fence behind the ranch's outbuildings. "We can walk from here."

"Thank God!" Jake laughed as he slipped from the saddle. He stomped around for a minute, his boot heels making indentations in the dirt. "Nice and solid. I like it."

She opened the gate, allowing him to lead Clementine through, then followed through herself, making sure the gate was latched properly. "I'm glad you're all right. I'll admit, I was afraid for you." She fell into step beside him.

"I was afraid for me, too." He let out a deep sigh. "Any idea what happened? Why Clementine acted the way she did? She could have killed me."

Evie shook her head, her eyes roaming his face. She started to smile as some of her concern dwindled. She'd fallen in love with his gentle ways, with how he treated her as well as everyone else on the ranch, and that included the horses, dog, and cats. He was, in her book, a good man—an honest man, in both his actions and his words, and honesty was such an important thing for her.

She stopped Spitfire in the middle of the path. Jake stopped beside her, giving her such a quizzical look, she couldn't help smiling at him.

"Why are we stopping? We're almost home."

She said nothing as she dropped Spitfire's reins and approached him. Tilting his hat back a little, she placed her hands on both sides of his face and gazed deeply into his soulful amber eyes. "I'm so glad you're all right." She brought his head down and touched her lips to his.

Jake dropped his reins as well and wrapped his arms around her, pulling her closer, so close she could feel the beating of his heart. Or was that her own heart pounding so erratically?

He broke the kiss but didn't release her. Instead, his embrace tightened, bringing her closer still, pressing her body against the full length of his. "Well, if that's what I'm going to get every time I face death, I'll do it more often."

"Let's just avoid that, shall we? I don't need an excuse to kiss you." And to prove her point, she sought his lips once more.

He let out a long sigh as she pulled away, just a little, his mouth spreading into the smile she'd fallen for the moment she met him.

She touched his face, running her fingers along his jawbone. "Let's go home."

"Yes, ma'am."

She led the way into the barnyard, cutting between the barn

and the bunkhouse, then stopped, surprised to see Heath was already there, standing in the open doorway of the bunkhouse, arms folded across his chest, as he watched whoever was inside. She assumed it was Oscar, because his horse, the big black stallion with the fancy saddle, stood next to Goldie, his reins wrapped around the porch railing, his sides heaving.

Strange that they'd beat Jake and her to the house. She hadn't seen him pass by. Then again, she had taken Jake back to the ranch by way of the river to slow their progress and make the ride easier and more comfortable for him.

"What's going on?" She moved a little closer, then brought Spitfire to a stop.

Heath, her easy-going, no-problem-is-too-big nephew turned his angry eyes on her, which surprised her. Teddy was her angry one, not Heath. "I fired him."

"Who? Oscar?"

He gave a slight nod then went back to watching the man in the bunkhouse. A few colorful words, said in Spanish, which she understood perfectly, came from within the building and met her ears. Her face heated. Some of them, she assumed, were aimed at her—if she was the *puta* of his tirade—but mostly, the expressions Oscar used denigrated Jake. None of it was acceptable. She glanced at Jake. If he understood what Oscar was saying, he didn't show it.

"Why?" she asked, though the way Oscar was speaking right now, the things he was saying about both her and Jake, was reason enough but she wanted to hear what Heath had to say.

"I saw what he did."

Heath's uncharacteristic angry tone shocked her. She'd never heard that from him before. "What did he do?"

Oscar appeared in the doorway, saddlebags slung over his shoulder. His face was crimson with anger, making his thick black mustache and crooked nose stand out, and his eyes...she'd never seen such hatred. She cringed just seeing the depths of his hostility. It seemed to be directed at both her and Jake, though she didn't know why.

"Tell her," Heath demanded as he glared at the man.

Oscar said nothing as he glowered at her, his rage an almost tangible thing. Evie recoiled, moving a few steps away from him. She hadn't noticed that about him when they met, but then again, she really hadn't spent much time with him after that day. She'd told him the truth—she wasn't interested in getting married— and though he seemed to have accepted that, perhaps he hadn't.

Instead of addressing her as he'd been told to do, Oscar glared at Jake. "You got lucky, Hannigan."

Jake tipped his hat further back on his head. A look came into his eyes she'd never seen before, a look that clearly said 'don't mess with me.' "No, I didn't and you know it, but any time you want a rematch..." He left the statement hanging, an invitation if there ever was one.

Her chest tightened with confusion as her focus shifted back and forth between the three men. "A rematch? What are you talking about?"

None of them explained and her frustration rose. She didn't like it when there was dissention on the ranch, which didn't happen very often. For the most part, everyone got along well enough, though in the past she had one or two ranch hands who just didn't seem to fit in with everyone else. They never stayed long. "Isn't anyone going to answer me?"

Oscar ripped his attention from Jake and focused on her, and again, she retreated from the rage on his face. He didn't say a word as he stepped off the porch and strode to his waiting horse, knocking his shoulder into Jake as he did so. Jake, to his credit, stood his ground. She noticed that his hands were balled into fists though and there was an expression on his face that fright- ened her just a bit.

She didn't have time to dwell on it as Oscar mounted up, kicked his stallion, and took off in a hail of dust.

"What did he do?" She focused on both her nephew and Jake.

Heath watched as Oscar disappeared from sight and finally faced her. "He took his slingshot and hit Clementine in the rump with a rock. That's why she reared up and took off like she did. Jake could have broken his neck!"

The answer shocked her. "Well, then, you were right to fire him, Heath." She turned to Jake, her eyes roaming over his face. He was still angry, that much was clear. It was in his stance. Was it just the fact that Oscar had tried to hurt him, or was there more to this story than she knew? "That's not all he did, is it?"

"No, but the rest doesn't matter now. I'll take care of the horses." He said nothing more as he led both Clementine and Spitfire into the paddock. She watched him walk away, his steps a little stiff. There was no jaunty swagger right now.

She turned once again to Heath on the porch, his arms still folded across his chest, though his anger seemed to be fading. "Do you know what happened between them? Why there's so much animosity?"

"No, but I'm sure it had something to do with you."

That surprised her, too. "With me?"

"Yep." He smiled at her. "Or maybe it had something to do with Jake breaking his nose."

"Jake broke his nose?"

"That's what I heard. Slick mentioned something about defending your honor. Apparently, Jake didn't like what Oscar said about you."

She turned toward the corral, where Jake was busy removing Clementine's saddle and reins, and her heart melted. *He defended my honor?*

"You better hang on to that one, *Tia* Evie." He climbed into Goldie's saddle. "I'm heading back out." He was once more back to his usual, happy self. "Glad your man wasn't hurt."

CHAPTER 16

"I'm going to do it." Evie announced, as Marisol pulled a sock from the basket of mending and put it in her lap. She chose a spool of thread that matched the color of the sock then grabbed a needle from the pin cushion and threaded it.

"Do what?"

"I'm going to...ask..." Oh, saying the words aloud was hard. She'd practiced them in her head since she'd made her decision, but actually giving voice to those thoughts proved to be almost impossible, and if she couldn't say them to her best friend, how would she ever say them to Jake? She licked her lips and stared toward the horizon, the shirt she intended to repair bunched on her lap.

"I've decided..." She tried again but couldn't finish, ending her sentence on a sigh.

Marisol stared at her, her smile wide, yet her eyes were full of sympathy and understanding. "What is it you're trying to tell me?"

Evie's gaze roamed over her friend's face. They'd never kept secrets from each other. Ever. She trusted this woman more than she trusted any other person with the exception of Hilde, but this was something she could never say to her companion of thirty years. Nor could she say it to Felicity, whom she trusted as well. Heck, she could hardly say it to herself.

She opened her mouth, but still couldn't bring herself to say the words out loud. "It's hopeless. I'm hopeless. I can't even say the words."

"It's just me and you here, Evie. No one can hear us. You can say anything at all, and it won't go any further. You know that. Just blurt it out like you always do."

She gave a slight nod, took a breath, and said, "I'm going to ask Jake if he…I mean…"

"Oh, for cryin' out loud, Evie. If you can't say the words, I'll say them for you." She grinned. "You're going to ask Jake to become your lover."

"Yes."

"It's about damned time." Marisol laughed. Well, it wasn't quite a laugh. It was more of a surprised cackle. "I've been watching you make calf-eyes at that man for far too long. Good for you, *cariña*. Good for you." She patted Evie's hand then went back to her sewing. "When?"

"I don't know. I don't even know how to begin or what to say or…anything." She stared at the garment in her lap. "See? I told you it was hopeless."

"No, it isn't hopeless. Nothing is hopeless. Do you love him?"

She didn't hesitate. "I do." Happiness bubbled inside her, finally admitting what she knew to be true to someone other than herself. "After Tom, I never thought I would feel this way again, but yes, I do love him."

"Do you want him?"

"Yes." And that was the truth. Ever since that first kiss, she'd thought of nothing else. She did want him. She thought he wanted her as well, but couldn't be certain. He certainly seemed to.

Marisol laid her sock aside, careful with the needle. "Then

this is what you'll do." The woman lowered her voice as she gave detailed directions.

Evie laughed when Marisol finished. "It seems you've been thinking about this for quite some time."

"I have, almost since the moment I laid eyes on him." Marisol chuckled, then grew serious. "Can you do it?"

"I'm not sure. I've never…seduced anyone before."

"It won't be hard. I've seen the way he looks at you. I think all you need to do is set the stage, and what better place than *Pequeña Casa*? It's quiet. It's private. It's comfortable." She grinned her incorrigible grin. "I've used it myself over the years."

"Wait. What are you saying? You've used the little house for secret assignations?" Funny, she wasn't upset about her friend using the house. After all, it was in the perfect location, just on the other side of the river that separated Montaña del Trueno from Hacienda Zepeda, surrounded by tall, shade-giving trees. It wasn't that at all. It was the fact that she'd never known. "I thought we didn't keep secrets."

"We don't. Well, except for that one. Sergio and I have met there a few times, and no one ever knew, not until now." Her smile widened, as if relieved she'd finally shared her secret. "We didn't think you'd mind."

"I don't mind, but I don't understand either." Evie fiddled with the material in her lap, then picked up the shirt and began to sew, her stitches short and precise this time, despite the confusion in her mind. "You and Sergio have a home of your own and a ranch as big as Montaña del Trueno."

"Yes, we do. I also have children and grandchildren running around. My house is full, as yours is. And you know as well as I do that work on the ranch never stops." She sighed, and an expression came over her face that Evie recognized. It was contentment and the love Marisol had for her husband of almost thirty years. "Sergio and I just need to get away by ourselves for a little peace and quiet for a few hours." She cast a glance Evie's way, one dark eyebrow raised into a perfect arch. "Haven't you wondered why it's always clean?"

"I assumed the boys' wives kept it clean." She hadn't been to the little house in a long time until just the other day when she and Jake picked berries.

"As well they should, as they all meet there, too." She actually blushed, something she didn't do very often. "Sergio and I were almost caught by Teddy and Esmeralda one afternoon and by Heath and Jenny another time."

Evie lowered the shirt, finished repairing the small tear. "So you're telling me that everyone uses *Pequeña Casa* for secret trysts except me?"

"That's what I'm telling you," she said. "So maybe you should take a page from our book and invite Jake there." She wiggled her eyebrows, which made Evie laugh.

"Maybe I will."

They continued with their mending and talk turned to Marisol's newest grandchild.

Later, after Marisol went home, Evie climbed the stairs to her room. She sat at the small desk, pulled a piece of stationery from the drawer, grabbed her fancy fountain pen, and jotted a short note. She blew on the ink to make it dry quicker, then folded it and placed it in an envelope. Now to get it to the bunkhouse without being seen.

She rose from her desk, envelope still in hand, and ran downstairs before she lost her nerve. No one was about, either in the kitchen or on the patio as she stepped outside and ran across the lawn. She stood on the porch of the bunkhouse, her heart pounding in her chest, her hands shaking.

Am I insane? This is the stupidest idea.

The thought slammed into her brain, followed by more devastating ones.

What if he doesn't want to meet me? What if...

She pushed all doubts from her mind and knocked lightly. No

one answered, no noise came from inside, although she wasn't sure she'd hear anything the way her heart was thundering in her chest loud enough to drown out the sound of the birds chirping. She pushed the door open. Sunlight flooded the big room, illuminating everything, including the fact that it was empty.

Which bunk was Jake's? She'd hate to leave this note for one of the other ranch hands.

She stood in the doorway, her gaze scanning all the bunks.

Ah, that one. It was the only one that was made, the blanket pulled taut over the mattress, the pillow placed precisely at the top of the bed. So like him. Despite the work he did on the ranch, he was always neat and well groomed.

It only took a moment or so to slip the note under his pillow and make her escape, blessedly unseen by anyone.

Once back in her room, she caught a glimpse of herself in the mirror. Her eyes were bright, and redness stained her cheeks. Exhilaration surged through her, though satisfied with her little bit of intrigue and daring, yet at the same time, anxious that her note wouldn't be received well.

What if he doesn't want me? The little voice in her head whispered again, putting a damper on that excitement. *What if he thinks I'm too old? What if I make a complete fool of myself, waiting for him, and he just doesn't show at all? What if—*

She firmly pushed her doubts aside once again, refusing to allow them to take root in her head as she strode toward the armoire in the corner. If she was going to seduce Jake Hannigan, she wanted to do it right, and that meant dressing the part.

She pushed clothes out of the way, reached toward the very back, and pulled out a satin and lace peignoir in pale lavender, so different from the white cotton nightgowns she usually wore. A sigh whispered between her lips as she hung it up on the armoire door and took a step back. She'd never worn it, hadn't even looked at it since Tom passed. She had planned to wear it on their wedding night...the wedding that never happened.

Did it still fit?

She started to remove the garment from the hanger and stopped. *What am I doing? I can't go to him wearing something meant for another. It isn't right.*

She fingered the lace as she pushed the peignoir back onto the hanger and hung it up on the door again.

Besides, this is not who I am anymore. I'm not some idealistic young woman, naïve and full of dreams. I've lived. I've learned. I've grown. Unable to help herself, she admitted one more truth about herself. *And I'm so very practical.*

She moved toward the bureau and pulled open the second drawer from the top. White cotton nightgowns met her eyes—some plain, some adorned with lace or embroidery. She pulled one out and inspected it. The lace around the neckline was coming away from the rest of the garment. She let out a sigh as she dropped it to the floor and picked up the next one. This one had a pale reddish stain on the sleeve, faded but still visible. Strawberry jam? Blackberry juice? A memento from one of the children, no doubt—and unacceptable.

She threw it over her shoulder, letting it land wherever it may, then reached for another. This, too, had a stain and was so old, the fabric was as sheer as gossamer. It went on the floor with the others. As did the next and the next, all discarded for one reason or another, until the drawer held no more and only the sachet in the corner remained, the muted fragrance of roses meeting her nose.

She sat heavily on the bed, one plain nightgown clutched in her hand, the only one without a rip or a stain, but still not what she was looking for. Tears misted her vision.

This is hopeless. I'm hopeless! How am I supposed to seduce a man when I don't know what to do? Or have anything enticing to wear? And how am I ever going to manage to wait until midnight without driving myself to insanity?

A heavy sigh escaped her.

I can't do this. I should just retrieve the note. He'll never have to know.

She rose from the bed, strode toward the open French doors leading out to the small balcony and froze. Jake ambled toward the bunkhouse.

Too late! It was only a matter of time before he saw her invitation. Now she had no choice but to follow through.

Slipping back into her room, her heart hammering in her chest, her mouth dry, she sank into the vanity chair and stared at her reflection in the mirror.

"Well, you certainly got yourself into a mess, didn't you?"

The image in her mirror merely stared back at her.

Jake loved it when he finished his chores early...well, at least they were done until everyone came in from the summer pasture. He had a few moments to himself and truthfully, wanted to spend them with Evie, but she hadn't been outside when he left the barn. He'd seen her earlier, when she supervised his continuing riding lessons as well as his training of Cinnamon, and then he'd seen her again when she'd been sitting with her friend Marisol, but after the woman left, Evie had disappeared into the house. He admitted enjoying watching them and hearing the occasional burst of laughter carried by the breeze. Evie's most especially.

He couldn't just go up to the door of the main house and knock, could he? Maybe invite her on a walk down to the little house to pick blackberries again. He had enjoyed that, much more than he ever thought he would. Maybe he could ask her to ride with him out to the summer pasture. Despite Clementine almost killing him, he had liked that, too, but suspected it was because he enjoyed her company more than anything else.

He couldn't quite bring himself to march across the lawn and knock on the door. She may be napping with the children. If she was, he didn't want to interrupt.

An image popped into his brain of Evie curled up on the bed, one of the children—or possibly two—sleeping against her, a sweet smile on her face as she dreamed.

The vision in his head was so clear, so vibrant, it shocked him. That's the image he wanted—no, needed—to draw of her. He headed into the bunkhouse, quiet and still at this time in the afternoon, although Grub would be returning shortly to start supper. He reached under his pillow to pull out the sketchbook. As he did so, a small envelope came with it. His name was written on the front. He looked around the empty room then ripped the envelope open.

'*Meet me at Pequeña Casa at midnight.*' It was signed with a big 'E' in light, feminine script. His heart, the one that was beating so normally in his chest just a moment before, started pounding hard, and he sank to his bunk, just staring at the words, reading them over and over.

Anticipation sang through his veins.

How was he supposed to wait until midnight when all he could imagine was Evie sprawled out on the bed, her eyes half closed in pleasure? Unless, of course, he mistook the note. What if it wasn't an invitation at all?

He read the note again to calm the doubts slamming his brain. Evie was a straight-forward woman. She didn't mince words. She didn't say one thing but mean another.

Yes, this was exactly what he thought it was. Excitement and a little anxiety rushed through him. He wanted to run out to *Pequeña Casa* right now, but he couldn't. There were still chores to be done, still so many hours until midnight. How in heaven was he supposed to wait when he felt like this? Like he could jump the moon on Clementine's back?

He tucked the note in his pocket and rose from his bunk, unsure what to do with himself.

In the end, he did what he had to do, though the anticipation was killing him. Slowly. Heartbeat by heartbeat. He performed the rest of his chores, ate supper with his bunkmates, washed up, and tried to read, though he couldn't seem to focus on the words on the page. He participated in a brief although stupid conversation regarding the merits of shaving or not shaving with Cesar, but couldn't concentrate on any of it. His mind was in a constant state of excitement—his body, too—and hope, with a little bit of anxiety thrown in for good measure, made waiting that much harder.

But wait he did...until he didn't think he could stand it any longer.

Cesar blew out the last lamp, casting the bunkhouse in darkness except for the moonlight shining in through the windows. Jake lay in his bunk and listened to the noises he'd grown used to...the snoring so loud, it could peel the paint from the walls, Grub's constant mumbling, other less savory sounds one hears when one shares close quarters, and when he couldn't wait any longer, when the prospect of holding Evie in his arms became more than he could bear, he rose from his bunk, grabbed his boots and crept out of the bunkhouse, closing the door softly behind him. He sat on the wooden stump and pulled his boots on, then looked at Flower, who had followed him outside. The cat rubbed up against his legs, her purrs seeming very loud in the silence of the night. The dog was there as well, but barely lifted his head from the rug he slept on.

"You can't come with me," he whispered to the cat, though he was certain Flower wouldn't listen. She rarely ever did. He said nothing to the dog, whose snores once again rumbled from his chest.

Surprisingly, Flower did listen this time, and stretched out on the porch in front of the door where anyone could trip over her if they weren't careful. Was she helping him? Keeping anyone who might want to follow from doing so? Or at least slowing them down because they'd tripped over her?

Jake grinned at the silly idea, then rose from the stump, and started walking. The full moon shed a bright light, much brighter than usual, to guide him on the path to the little house, but maybe it wasn't the moon at all and just his desire to be with Evie. A soft glow emanated from the little house as he drew closer, and he quickened his pace.

He stepped up on the porch and knocked lightly then opened the door slowly. It creaked on its hinges. Stopping in the doorway, he drank in the sight before his eyes, his heart thundering in his chest. Evie stood beside the table, her eyes shimmering, reflecting the light radiating from the candles scattered throughout the room, that smile he adored lifting the corners of her mouth. She looked so beautiful it took his breath away.

Her voice, when she finally spoke, shook. "I wasn't sure you'd come."

Jake stepped inside the little house and closed the door behind him. "Why wouldn't I?"

She shook her head and shrugged, the movement making the candlelight glimmer on her hair, which she left free to curl over her shoulders. She gave a rueful little laugh. "I'm not in the habit of inviting men to a…a…" Her voice was huskier than usual as she let the words die, but her stare was intense until color flooded her cheeks and she looked down at the floor. He noticed her feet were bare, her boots pushed against the wall. "I'm not even sure what I should do."

"You can start by coming a little closer."

She did as he asked and took several hesitant steps in his direction until she was standing in front of him, her eyes wide in her face as she looked up at him, her smile tremulous and unsure. He gathered her in his arms, exactly where he wanted her to be. Her entire body quivered as he tightened his embrace.

"You're shaking. Are you afraid?"

"And nervous. It's been a long time." She gave a short burst of tense laughter.

The anxiety in the depths of her eyes, the color more gray than blue now and as light as he'd ever seen them, were a reflection of her statement. "Ah, darlin', I'm nervous too," he admitted as he looked down at her, hoping to ease her fears. "We'll go as slow as you like. Or not at all. We can just hold each other."

His words had the desired effect. Some of her trembling ceased and the lightness of her eyes changed, though it was subtle. If he hadn't been standing so close, he never would have noticed.

"We can't stay long," she whispered before she rose up on her toes and pressed her lips to his. She kissed him with heat and longing, filling the empty place in his soul he never knew was there. He pulled her tighter against his body, deepening the kiss, his tongue sweeping into the warm recesses of her mouth to tangle with hers. She tasted of mint and sweetness and hope all rolled into one and he couldn't get enough. Not now. Not ever.

That she should want him as much as he wanted her thrilled him beyond belief. It was there in her kiss, in the way her fingers curled in his hair, in her indrawn breath. His heart pounded, not only in his chest, but in his ears, as his lips slid over hers, drinking in everything she offered, wanting more.

He nuzzled her neck, then licked at the spot where her pulse beat strong. Her breath quickened as she tilted her head back, allowing him greater access, and he complied, pressing tiny kisses along the long column of her throat, then coming back to the place where her pulse thumped the hardest, just beneath her ear. The subtle fragrance of roses met his nose as he burrowed his lips in her hair.

Evie tightened her embrace, her body pressing into his. "More," she murmured, her voice thick with desire and once again, he fulfilled her command, brushing his lips lightly along her jawline until he captured her mouth in a kiss that left them both gasping. Her arms tightened around his neck, as if she didn't trust herself to stay on her own two feet, her body pressing into his so tightly he could feel her breasts against his chest.

Blood surged through his veins like a fire out of control and all he wanted to do was carry her to the bed and lay her down, but he forced himself to go slow, to savor every moment, every touch, every emotion coursing through him. For the both of them.

All his good intentions fled as she pulled away slightly and looked up at him, her eyes heavy lidded but holding a mischievous gleam. A delightfully wicked smile lifted the corners of her mouth as her hands trailed over his shoulders and downward. Jake sucked in his breath, caught up in the touch of her hand and the expression on her face, forcing himself to stand still, curious to see what she planned.

Her smile widened just a bit as she fingered the buttons on his shirt, then began unfastening the garment, slowly, one button at a time. She pushed the fabric apart from his shoulders, letting it fall to the floor with a soft whoosh. Her hands splayed across his bare chest, but she never took her straight-forward gaze from him, desire smoldering in her eyes. The heat of her touch nearly singed him, and his longing for her flamed even more, if that was possible.

He growled low in his throat as he pulled her close and dipped his head, capturing her lips with his once again, wondering if he'd ever stop wanting to kiss her. No, he never would. Her mouth was made for kissing, but only by him.

He maneuvered her toward the bedroom, guiding her backward until the bed impeded any further progress. "You have too many clothes on," he murmured in her ear as he nuzzled the soft skin of her neck.

She shivered in his embrace and leaned her head back to gaze at him, her eyes wide and full of...was that daring? Confidence? Hope? "So take them off."

Her voice, so husky, struck him to the core and he eagerly complied, starting with her skirt, easily undoing the fastenings to allow the suede garment to slip to the floor.

He let out an exasperated groan as his big fingers tried to manipulate the small buttons on her sheer blouse. One more minute and he'd rip the thing from her, sending all those ivory fastenings scattering. He brought his lips to hers again, kissing her deeply, his tongue sweeping into her mouth as he tried again.

Evie rested her hands over his, stilling his movements, probably sensing his frustration, though she was as eager as he. He could feel it in the slight tremor that rippled through her. He broke the kiss and stared into her eyes, which seemed to glimmer with need.

"We have time, Jake." Though she whispered the words, there was impatience in her voice, too. He tried again, this time more slowly, his fingers a little less clumsy and much more successful. He smoothed the blouse from her shoulders, allowing it to glide to the floor.

He barely squelched the frustrated moan building in his throat. There was another blouse beneath the one he had removed. He paused for a moment then forced himself to work the buttons of that as well, this time a little more skillfully. Thankfully, she wore no corset. He was certain he would have knotted the laces instead of loosening them in his haste to feel her skin. At last, he took off her short chemise, pulling the garment over her head and tossing it in the corner. His mouth twisted into a smile as he plucked the string that held up her drawers, allowing the light garment to slip down her legs and puddle at her feet.

She didn't try to cover herself. Not at all. She stood proudly in front of him, her back straight, her head tilted to the side, her eyes flashing with desire.

He gazed at her naked form with awe, his eyes sweeping over her from head to toe and back, the candlelight reflecting on her smooth skin, creating an almost rosy glow. Years of riding had defined her muscles, but there was a softness to her, too. He inhaled deeply. She was perfect in every way—from her long muscular legs to her nipped-in waist, to her heavy breasts that seemed to beg for his touch. "Beautiful," he murmured, his voice sounding thick to his own ears.

She didn't acknowledge his statement. Instead, she pulled him closer, but there was a pinkish glow on her cheeks and a mischievous glint in her eyes as she reached for the fastening of his trousers. She, at least, didn't seem to have as much trouble, and in moments, his legs were bare, though his trousers stuck on his boots. He eased her down until she was sitting on the edge of the bed. "I should probably take off my boots."

"That would be helpful." She stared up at him, her pupils so dilated, all he could see was black with just a hint of color at the edges, and that gleam which told him how much she wanted him. The mere thought filled him with a joy he could hardly contain.

He toed off one boot, tossing it in the corner, then pulled off the other and shimmied his trousers to the floor. He turned toward her in all his glory. Her eyes widened with admiration and curiosity. He reached out and caressed her face, then cupped her chin. "You *are* beautiful."

A blush colored her cheeks as she reached for him, wrapping her arms around his neck, pulling him closer. "So are you. Kiss me again. And again, until neither of us can think."

Jake laughed softly. "Yes, ma'am." He lowered his head and took possession of her mouth, his tongue gliding between her lips to tangle with hers.

She pulled away, her fingers caressing his lips. "More," she demanded, her voice husky and almost raw with need.

He complied, his mouth on hers once again, his tongue twisting with hers, her body pressed against his so close he could feel her pounding heart beating in rhythm with his, the warmth of her body nearly burning him where they touched. He eased her down to the mattress gently, his lips never leaving hers, and followed, stretching out beside her.

She gasped, sucking in air, when he finally broke the kiss. "Touch me." Again, it was a command, one he was more than willing to obey.

"My pleasure." It *was* his pleasure. Her flesh felt like velvet beneath his fingers as he caressed her, starting with the soft skin on her face, then venturing lower, touching her throat and collarbones, then finally the crease between her full breasts. He followed each touch with his lips, kissing every inch of her, the faint scent of roses stronger now.

How many times had he dreamed of touching her this way? Of caressing her soft skin. Of lying down beside her, letting his hand roam over her taut, lean body? Too many times to count. Each time he took pencil in hand to draw her, this is what he thought about. This and so much more.

Evie let out a sigh and pulled him closer, her fingers in his hair, almost as if directing him where to kiss or lick next. He settled at her breast, lightly grazing the nipple with his teeth before licking the soft crest into a hardened peak and drawing it into his mouth, sucking lightly. Beneath him, her breath came in soft, little pants, as he left one breast and concentrated on the other.

Evie sighed, her hands skimming over his back, his shoulders, and around his neck, as if she couldn't get enough of touching him, either. Had she dreamed of this as well? Had she awakened with her body on fire, the visions in her head vibrant, only to realize she was alone?

He dismissed the thought and concentrated on loving her. He moved slightly, kissing his way back to her mouth, capturing her lips with his for a long, slow kiss before moving to her neck. Her breathing increased, coming in soft little pants as he lightly swirled his tongue against the delicate shell of her ear, drawing the lobe into his mouth, tugging gently with his teeth while his fingers grazed over her breast. Evie gave a little whimper then arched her back, pushing against his hand, showing him without words that she wanted more.

Again, he was more than happy to comply as he brushed his lips against hers, then took possession of her mouth, his tongue dancing with hers, the taste of her intoxicating, filling his head as well as his heart and soul.

Though his mouth never left hers, his hand roamed over her soft belly, edging downward until he slipped his fingers easily between the springy curls of her womanhood to find the core of her.

"Oh!" Evie gasped against his lips, followed by another intake of breath as he slowly began caressing the smoothness of her folds and the key to her release between them. He set a rhythm, slow and steady, increasing the pressure a little at a time, the moans and little cries from deep in her throat spurring him faster. He slipped a finger into her, then another, stretching her, preparing her for his entry, while pressing the palm of his hand against her in a circular motion. If it had been a long time, the last thing he wanted to do was hurt her.

Another breathy sigh met his ears and suddenly, she stiffened, her heels digging into the mattress, her hips rising off the bed, straining against his hand. She let out a surprised cry and then she laughed in that husky tone that filled his head, her hips lowering to the bed as her body shuddered around his fingers, moving once more to the rhythm he'd set.

His mouth took possession of hers. Withdrawing his fingers, he brought his hand up to caress her soft, round belly and full breasts. Taking his time, he stroked her skin, bringing her nipples to hard points again, before leaving her lips and drawing one of those nipples into his mouth, sucking lightly, swirling his tongue against the sensitive peak.

Evie squirmed beneath him as he paid attention to one breast then the other, then moved to position himself between her legs.

He felt the heat of her, scalding in its intensity, as he eased into her, slowly, inch by inch, so he wouldn't hurt her, allowing her body to become accustomed to his length and width.

Evie let out a little whimper.

He stopped, though it pained him to do so, and looked at her. "Am I hurting you?"

She shook her head on the pillow, her eyes half closed. Roses bloomed on her cheeks and a fine sheen of perspiration glowed on her face, extending down to her neck and chest, which heaved with each indrawn breath. She didn't answer in words, simply wrapped her strong legs around his thighs, pulling him in deeper, until his body pressed tightly against her.

Jake groaned. He couldn't help himself. She was so warm, so tight, so wet. He needed a moment, more than a moment, to collect himself and gain control, which was easier said than done as Evie began to move beneath him once more. She may not have done this in a long time, but her body remembered. Her urgency communicated itself to him and he found himself lifting, then plunging into her to fulfill her silent plea.

She whimpered as he glided in and out of her, holding on to his restraint for as long as he possibly could. Her nails dug into his back and her legs tightened around him even more as she moved with him, faster and faster until he thought he couldn't wait anymore, but wait he would. For her. Until she received her pleasure again, until she cried out his name. The ache of holding back, of waiting, when all he wanted to do was explode inside her, was exquisite.

"Now, Jake!" Her thighs pressed against him as her nails dug into his backside, and then her body was pulsing around him, squeezing the length of him with such power, he nearly cried out himself.

Every muscle in his body tightened as he plunged into her one last time, the force of his release making him groan. His toes curled and a shiver raced through him. At that exact moment came a sense of completeness, not for the act itself, but for how it made him feel. Inside. Deep in his heart.

He *belonged*. With her. With the entire extended family. For the first time in his life, he was part of something bigger than himself. It was a heady feeling, and a curious thought to have at this moment, but there it was, and it made him hesitant to leave Evie's heat.

He opened his eyes and gazed at her face bathed in the light of the flickering candles, her eyes still half-closed. A small, satisfied smile tilted the corners of her mouth. He dropped a kiss on each corner and slowly withdrew from her, though he was more than reluctant to do so, then gathered her close. "Evie? Are you all right?"

She snuggled up to him and let out a sigh of what sounded like contentment. "Hmmm." And then she giggled, sounding like a young girl. "Can we do that again?"

He laughed and held her tighter, letting his heartbeat return to normal, then dropped a kiss on her forehead. "Just give me a minute or two."

Candlelight flickered over Jake's face, showing the dark whiskers on his cheeks, chin, and over his upper lip as Evie cuddled a bit closer, her head resting on his shoulder, her leg thrown over his —a most unladylike position, and yet she didn't care. She wanted…no, *needed*…to feel his warmth, to feel the length of his body along hers. She laid her hand on his chest, the thick hair there tickling her palm as his arm tightened around her, supporting her back, keeping her close.

Who would have thought she'd feel like this? Like she could walk among the clouds, or that making love would make her feel so energized, but completely sated at the same time. And a bit more confident, yet still unsure. She couldn't believe how daring she'd been, demanding that he kiss her, insisting he touch her. Or how wonderful it felt to have him comply, his hands so gentle as they caressed her, smoothing over her body like he worshipped every inch of her. And still, she had wanted more, wanted to feel him inside her, his fullness stretching her, bringing her to the heights she hadn't known existed until that burst of pleasure made thinking impossible and all she could do was let herself feel.

God help her, she wanted to experience that again…and again. Did that make her wanton? She didn't care if it did. Already, her blood was rushing through her veins, just thinking about what they'd done, what he'd made her feel. She smiled as a blush heated her face, and continued her slow perusal.

His eyes were closed, his long thick lashes shadowing his cheek. A silly little grin played on his lips, and his chest rose and fell in a regular rhythm, but she didn't think he was sleeping. Was he thinking the same thing as she? Did he feel like he could walk on the clouds? Would he want to make love again? Could he?

So many questions, none that she would ever ask aloud, but there was still a way she could find out. She moved slightly, drawing closer, and planted kisses along his jawline while her fingers smoothed through the soft mat of hair on his chest, then lower to feel the hard muscles of his abdomen.

"What are you doing?"

His voice startled her, and she giggled in response. "Touching you. Is that all right?"

"More than all right." He let out a subdued chuckle but didn't move otherwise, as if giving himself over to her curiosity. "Do what you will."

Encouraged by his invitation, unsure of what she was doing, only that she'd loved the things he'd done to her, Evie lifted herself up on her elbow. She gazed into his warm amber eyes as her fingers drew lazy circles across his stomach, then upward to rake through the hair on his chest once more as she leaned over and kissed him, her tongue tracing the outline of his lips before he opened his mouth and allowed her entrance. She kissed him with all the passion and love she had for him, her mouth taking possession of his, feeling that breathlessness that accompanied the touch of his lips.

Jake sighed when she pulled away to plant soft kisses on his cheek, his forehead, the place where his skin met his hair just above his ear. Her hand slid over his nipple, amazed that it could become hard like hers had. Intrigued, she moved slightly, kissing her way down his neck, across his collarbone, and lower until she could draw that hard nipple into her mouth. She tasted salt and soap against her tongue as she swirled it around and around, just as he had done to her.

Jake whispered her name and started to caress her arms, her back, then sweep up the back of her neck to plunge his fingers into her hair, the heat of his touch searing her deep in her soul.

She glanced up at him and caught the expression on his face… it was a combination of intense pleasure and even more intense concentration. His brow was furrowed, but his eyes were wide open, watching her, the heat in their depths unmistakable.

"Has it been a minute or two?" Was that her voice, so raw, so impatient, so thick with desire? She didn't wait for him to answer as her fingers quested lower and she wrapped her hand around his hard, smooth length.

He stiffened for a moment then groaned. "I believe it has," he answered. She heard the strain in his voice as if he struggled to let her explore him.

She straddled him then, impaling herself on his erection and sat still for a moment, allowing herself to adjust to the size of him. Then she began to move, slowly at first, rising up then lowering herself, using the muscles in her legs to control her actions.

His hands were everywhere—finally released from the control he exerted—caressing her face, her throat, her shoulders, her breasts. His thumbs flicked her nipples, drawing them into hard points.

Evie moaned with pleasure as he rose up a little and his mouth replaced his hands, his tongue tenderly swirling around the crest before drawing the taut peak into his mouth and sucking gently.

Blood coursed through her veins, and her heart pounded in her ears as his mouth captured her other breast and her body began to tense, building toward that same explosion as before. And she wanted to feel that sweet ecstasy. She quickened her pace and his hands slid to her hips, guiding her, pushing the rhythm. His eyes were closed now, sweat beaded on his forehead, but that little smile played on his lips. And then his eyes flew open to stare into the depths of her very soul as his fingers found the key to her release between their bodies and pressed hard.

That look was all it took to push her over the edge. Her body tightened, spiraling almost out of control, soaring higher and higher. If heaven was just beyond the stars, she found it. Her climax hit her with such force, she cried out. And still, she kept riding him, her body pulsing around him, feeling the hard length of him inside her. She picked up the pace—faster—harder—until he, too, shouted in satisfaction and filled her with his essence. She fell on him, her mouth once more taking possession of his, her tongue tangling with his.

She sat up, still impaled on him, and gazed into his eyes, her hands resting on his chest, her fingers spread over his hard muscles. She moved slightly, rising up from him, though she didn't want to. Not really.

"No, not yet." He brought his hands to her hips and held her in place, his smile so mischievous, so full of delightfully wicked intentions that she settled herself on him once again, leaned over and kissed him. When she broke the kiss, he laughed. "That's better."

"You know I'm going to have to move…eventually."

"I know. I just don't want you to." He smoothed his hands along her thighs. "Are your legs cramping?"

She shook her head. "No, not at all, but I am a little thirsty."

He smiled up at her, mischief dancing in his eyes. "Come to think of it, I'm a bit parched myself."

"Whiskey? Bourbon?" There had to be some of each in the kitchen if *Pequeña Casa* was used as much as Marisol said. "Water?"

"Champagne? I think this night definitely calls for champagne."

"I don't think we have any, but I'll have to get up in order to look."

Jake laughed as his hands grasped her shoulders, pulled her toward him and took possession of her mouth once more. "I'll stay thirsty."

Jake looked down at Evie, asleep in his arms, the warm glow of the flickering candles casting a golden light over her. They'd made love three times, and each time it was a revelation, more glorious than the one before, but they couldn't stay here much longer. The sun would be up soon, bringing with it the inevitable chores keeping Montaña del Trueno prosperous, yet he didn't want to move, didn't want this night to come to an end.

He planted a kiss on her forehead. Evie sighed in her sleep then moved a bit closer to him, her leg thrown over his, her head resting on his shoulder. Her hand sprawled across his chest over his heart, seeping warmth into his skin. That feeling of completeness, of *belonging*, became so profound, his soul was flooded with it. He'd never felt that before. It was overwhelming and welcome...and so very scary.

Is this what I've been searching for my entire life? Is this what had been missing when I thought I had everything I ever wanted?

Startled by these waves of pure emotion crashing over him, he stiffened. Evie shifted in her sleep and mumbled something he couldn't quite catch. He held her tighter, never wanting to let go.

She was his light, his dawn of a new day filled with hope, and when he looked into her eyes, he saw a future that was different than anything he'd ever known. Or dreamed of. Or thought was even possible.

Is this love?

He'd never been in love. Ever.

How does one know one is in love if one has never experienced it? And yet, he didn't doubt his feelings for her. Not one bit. It was more than fondness and admiration for the woman she was.

No, it went much, much deeper than that. The sense of belonging stayed with him, growing, blossoming, filling the places in his soul that had never been touched.

He watched her with the children—her grandniece and -nephews. She was affectionate with them, always hugging them, kissing them on the cheek or forehead, ruffling their hair, laughing with them. He'd never experienced that as a child. Growing up at St. Anselm's hadn't provided the sort of affection she poured on the children. Yes, he'd been well cared for. His belly had never been empty. He'd had a roof over his head, and he'd been educated, but that was all. Father O'Malley and the Sisters there had a certain fondness for him, but that fondness had never been shown as openly as Evie showered on the children.

Her affection wasn't on display to just them, either. It extended to everyone in her circle—her niece and nephews, Hilde, Antonio, Charley, and Felicity. Even her friends were recipients of the love she had to give.

His gaze swept over her fine features as he held her a little tighter, his fingers caressing the soft skin of her bare shoulder. Such goodness radiated from her, even in sleep, that his heart skipped a beat, only to resume with a painful thud.

I am in love with this woman! The revelation hit him with all the subtlety of an anvil dropping on his head.

And on the heels of that epiphany, another whispered through him—he had no choice but to tell her the truth about what had brought him there. He'd put it off for too long, and the telling of it had grown more difficult, especially after what they'd shared, but she deserved to know. Not just part of it, but all of it—even at the risk of breaking her heart. And his. Dread filled him. If she asked him to leave—

He drew in his breath. The mere thought of leaving, of never seeing her again—even worse, of hurting her—made the newly found realization of loving her more urgent and painful.

She moved, snuggling into him closer, and pressed a kiss to his cheek. He hadn't realized she was awake.

"Evie?" he whispered.

"Hmmm?"

"I have something to tell you."

"What is it, Jake?" Her voice was soft and sleepy, her body, pressed against his, so warm.

"I love you, Miss Evie Miller."

She sighed and snuggled a little closer. "I love you, too, Jake."

"You love me?"

"I do. With all my heart."

Elation swept through him and just as quickly, fear that he could lose something so fragile so fast. And it was fragile, this new feeling filling him.

He rushed on before she could say anything else. "There's something I need to tell you about my past. About who I was." He spit out the words he was certain would ruin everything. "I was a gambler."

She stiffened against him, then leaned up on her elbow, and looked down at him, her face, in the light cast by the candles, clearly showing her confusion. "What?"

"A gambler. That's how I made my living these past few years. High stakes poker games where there was no limit on what you could bet. I've won and lost fortunes too many times to count."

Her brows furrowed with questions but before she could say anything, he confessed, "But I think you should know that I haven't touched a card or made a bet since I came here."

The admission didn't help. She untangled herself from his arm and sat up, pushing her hair out of her face. That face, the one he'd fallen in love with, showed the myriad of emotions running through her—confusion, betrayal, anger, love—or what he thought was love—he saw them all in the depths of her eyes and his heart went from being full to shrinking so much that it hurt.

"A gambler," she repeated, as if trying to absorb the word, then her eyes narrowed and she stared at him, as if she could see into his soul. "How does a gambler end up here, on my ranch?" She sucked in her breath as the full realization hit her. "In my bed?"

He dreaded telling her everything, but knew there was no escaping it now. If there was any hope for a future with her, a future he'd been thinking about, she had to know. "How did I end up here? In all truth, Evie, I was running."

"Running? From what?"

He hesitated, his gut tightening as the name of the man who could ruin his chances for a happy life tumbled from his mouth, though in truth he was just as guilty. He never should have lied to her. "Not what, but who. Erik King."

Her frown deepened, pulling down the corners of her mouth. "Who is Erik King?"

"A fellow gambler. Someone I should never have played against." He couldn't look at her and see what his confession was doing to her. He couldn't look away, either. "I knew of his reputation, but I didn't know him, never met him. I should have walked away from the table as soon as he introduced himself."

"But you didn't." Her voice became icy with anger, and tears shimmered in her eyes, turning them from light gray to the darker gray of storm clouds building in the distance. "And you lost."

"Actually, I won. Walked away with enough to buy this ranch twice over."

"If you won, why did you run?" She shook her head, obviously puzzled. "I don't understand."

"Beating him, winning against him was a cardinal sin. At least in his eyes. He became insistent that I play him again so he could win his money back and didn't like it when I said no, kept saying no, even though I knew the consequences of doing so. King doesn't play by the rules." Ashamed of his actions—of hurting her—he reached out to caress her face, but she pulled away. At least, she hadn't scrambled from the bed the moment he told her what he had been. Knowing how she felt about the profession maybe that meant there was a chance she would forgive him.

"Why didn't you just play him again? Or simply give him the money you'd won?"

"I offered several times to give him back his money. He refused." He'd never make her understand how utterly ruthless and unreasonable Erik King could be. "It wouldn't have made a difference anyway. I damaged his reputation when I won. Hurt his ego. The only way to remedy that, in his mind, was to play him again. I was damned lucky to walk away from him the first time. I knew I wouldn't be so lucky again. They'd find me, days later, floating in San Francisco Bay with a hole in my chest like so many others who went up against him." He let out a long sigh, already feeling the pain from the bullet that may eventually come for him. Or maybe that pain was caused by the look on her face.

"When Father O'Malley placed your advertisement beside my coffee cup that morning and told me I needed to grow up, to give up the cards and find a more respectable life, I knew he was right."

"I see." She scrambled from the bed then, pulling the quilt with her. She wrapped it around herself, hiding her soft, supple body from his eyes. "You lied to me." She flung the accusation at him, her voice choked. "And kept lying to me about who and what you were, knowing I despise gambling and those who participate in it, knowing what happened to Regina and Javier… and Tom. You lied to me about why you were here. It wasn't about wanting to marry me at all. You were just…" She heaved in her breath like it was an effort, like it hurt her to do so and then she stiffened, her eyes narrowing. "You used me. Used Montaña del Trueno." She stopped speaking. Tears sparkled in her eyes. "Was any of it real, Jake? Was it all a lie?"

Jake flinched as she listed the sins against him. He threw his legs over the side of the bed and sat up, his body tense. "What I feel for you *is* real, Evie."

"I don't believe you."

That much was obvious and he didn't know what to say to convince her, but he had to try. "When you asked me why I had replied to your—"

"Lucy's."

"Lucy's advertisement," he corrected himself, "I said I was looking for a change. And I was. That much was true. It's still true. I found that change when I came here, Evie. You and the rest of your family helped me…see what could be." He paused for a moment before admitting. "I'm still gambling, but not with cards or money. I'm gambling with my heart now."

"Why are you telling me this, Jake? Why now? After we…after I…after telling me you love me." Spots of color highlighted her cheeks as if embarrassed by the pleasure they'd found in each other's arms.

He let out a sigh of resignation. "I do love you, Evie. That's why I thought you deserved to know the truth. All of it."

She drew in her breath as if trying to gain control of herself and unclenched her fists then grabbed her chemise and drawers from the floor where they'd dropped in their urgency to touch each other. Her movements were quick and jerky. "You didn't have to tell me at all. I probably never would have known." She backed out of the doorway to the bedroom until he couldn't see her anymore. "The lie and your profession isn't all of it, is it?" Her disembodied voice came from beyond the bedroom. He could hear the quilt drop to the floor and the rustling of clothing as she donned her undergarments.

Oh, he hated hearing the hurt and anger in her husky voice, knowing he had done that. If she reacted this way to the truth, how would she react to the rest of it? He stared at the doorway, waiting for her. "No."

A moment later, she appeared, clad in her lace-edged drawers and short chemise, her hands on her hips. "What else? What aren't you telling me?"

His gaze rose to meet hers. "There is a strong possibility Erik King might find me and show up here to get back what I won from him or—"

She didn't let him finish. "What?" She trembled as she stood before him. He could see it. Hell, he could feel it even though he wasn't touching her, and his heart squeezed a little more. "This man, this Erik King, could come here—" Her mouth snapped shut as the consequences of his actions seemed to become clear to her.

He rose from the bed, wrapped the sheet around himself, and approached her warily. He wanted to touch her, draw her into his arms and hold her, but didn't dare. "I'm sorry."

"You're sorry?" she whispered, incredulity in her voice.

To his ears, it was as if she shouted. The impact to his heart was the same.

"For what? For lying to me? For making me fall in love with you? Or for bringing danger here?" She drew in her breath, her chest heaving with the effort as she stared at him, her eyes glittering with hurt and betrayal. And so much anger.

She squeezed past him and grabbed her skirt and blouses from the floor, then turned to him once more in all her righteous glory. "How could you say you love me, then tell me you may have put my whole family in jeopardy? How could you?"

He shook his head. He had no answers that would satisfy himself, much less her. Truthfully, he should never have lied to her, even if it was a lie of omission. Hell, he should never have come here, knowing what kind of man King was.

"I think you should go." She stood there, staring at him, her clothes dangling from her hands. "I think you should leave before this…this Erik King finds out where you are."

"I *am* sorry, Evie."

She glared at him for a moment longer. "You should be." She turned and strode away, grabbing her boots from the kitchen as she did.

The door to the little house slammed with a bang, the sound very much like his heart breaking.

~

I fell in love with a gambler!

She wiped the tears from her eyes and finished dressing quickly on the porch, then left *Pequeña Casa*, running back to the homestead as fast as her feet could carry her. She stopped at the gate and wiped her face again, then took several deep breaths to still her thundering heart.

She passed through the gate, closing it behind her then cautiously made her way between the barn and the bunkhouse, careful to avoid being seen by any of the ranch hands just beginning their day. When everyone had left the barnyard, she slipped into the barn and headed up the central aisle where Spitfire waited in her stall.

She didn't want to be here when Jake eventually came back. She didn't want to see him, and yet, she did. She wasn't done telling him what she thought about him. Yes, she did love him, more than she thought possible. She could have dealt with the fact he was a gambler, could have gotten over the real reason Jake came to Montaña del Trueno, but putting her family in danger… no, that was something she just couldn't accept. Or forgive.

"There's nothing worse than an old fool, Spitfire."

Spitfire nodded as she reached out to smooth her fingers over the horse's nose.

She swiped at her face one more time, then grabbed her equipment from the tack room and began to saddle her horse. Her fingers were clumsy, and tears continued to blur her vision. She hated crying, hated this feeling of weakness, of betrayal. Worse, she loathed the fact that she had allowed herself to fall for him to begin with. All these years, she'd fought to be strong, independent, and confident, and here, one man had reduced her to a blubbering idiot.

"Ah, there you are!" Teddy entered the barn and strolled down the aisle. "I've been looking all over for you." He laughed softly. "I must be losing what's left of my mind because I thought I checked in here."

Evie stiffened as she tightened the cinches on Spitfire's saddle but didn't turn around. The last person she wanted to see at this moment was Teddy. Her nephew would take one look at her and see…that she'd been a fool, perhaps the biggest fool in the history of the world. She cleared her throat and fought to fight the constriction making it difficult to draw air into her lungs. "Why were you looking for me? Are the children all right?"

"The children are fine. I was getting concerned though, especially when you didn't come down for breakfast. You're usually the first one up…well, you and Hilde." He came a little closer. "So, where were you?"

"I went for a walk." Her voice cracked. If she heard it, then most certainly he did as well.

"Before the sun came up?" He took a few more steps toward her and she turned away to avoid meeting his eyes. "Jake seems to be missing as well." He looked at her. "You were with him, weren't you?"

"That's none of your business, Teddy. My life is my life, and you have no right to interfere." She took a big gulping breath, trying so hard to keep her composure, to keep from bursting into tears, but she failed, and the sound that issued from her throat was something she'd never heard before.

"*Tia* Evie? What's wrong? Why are you crying?" The tone of his voice changed, becoming deeper, harsher, and filled with suspicion. "Did he hurt you?"

"I...I can't talk about this." With quick movements, Evie climbed into the saddle and rode from the barn.

Jake waited until the barnyard quieted, then entered the bunkhouse and stopped short, startled to see Teddy sitting at the table, his arms folded across his chest, his dark eyes glittering with suspicion, a look he was more than familiar with.

"I've been waiting for you to show up." He stood quickly, making the chair legs scrape against the floor. "What the hell did you do to my aunt?" It wasn't a question. It was an accusation.

Jake moved past him, his muscles tense, his heart beating hard, and grabbed his soft-sided suitcases from beside his trunk and tossed them on the bunk.

Teddy followed him, his gaze going from Jake to the suitcases. "She's crying," he said harshly. He shook his head, understandably angry, then glared at him. "I haven't seen her cry since I was a kid. And it's your fault, I'm sure. What the hell did you do?"

"I told her the truth," Jake admitted, though it was the last thing he wanted to do, especially to Teddy.

"And what truth is that?"

He started taking items from the trunk to stuff in the empty, soft-sided satchel, then glanced at Teddy.

"I'm a gambler, Teddy. I won a lot of money from a fellow gambler, and he is after me." He ran his fingers through his hair and took a step back, his focus on the man in front of him, waiting for the punch that would knock him on his ass. "I answered Lucy's advertisement, in part, to leave San Francisco and get away from him."

"You lied to her?"

"Yes."

The corners of his mouth tilted upward, and sympathy reflected in his eyes. "Oh, Jake, you don't know what you've done. No one lies to *Tia* Evie without paying the consequences, especially about what you were. You know how she feels about gamblers."

Jake turned away to grab more clothes from the trunk. "I'll finish packing my things and go."

"Running away again?" Teddy scoffed as he began to pace back and forth. "Isn't that what brought you here in the first place? Things get a little uncomfortable and you just take off instead of facing it?" He stopped pacing and stood in front of Jake, his eyes narrowed, his stare so intense, Jake cringed a little inside. "Is leaving really what you want to do?"

"No." Leaving Montaña del Trueno was not what he wanted to do. Not at all. He had fallen in love with Miss Evie Miller. He'd also fallen in love with the ranch and the people here, the slow rhythm of the days, the camaraderie he'd been shown by his fellow bunkmates. He'd grown particularly fond of the children—sweet Savannah, with her million-and-one questions; Miguel, with his eyes full of mischief. And Toughie. He'd never seen a more active child or one who seemed happy all the time. Even Ramón had earned his affection.

But it was Evie that held the highest place in his heart. He loved her.

And he was more certain of that now than ever before. The

old Jake, the man he had been, would have walked away without a thought.

"Look, Jake, you're not the same man who came here." Teddy drew his attention. "I didn't like you much then, and I certainly never wanted you and *Tia* Evie to get together. In fact, I warned her away from you, more than once. You're a maverick. Knew it the first time I saw you. Always doing things your own way, but I've seen how much you've changed. You've worked hard. You've learned." He shook his head, a smile playing at the corners of his mouth. "Never saw a man with as much natural ability as you when it comes to the horses. Though I hate to admit it, you might be better than me." He took a step back, but his gaze was intense and remained that way. And then something happened Jake didn't expect at all. A gentleness crept into Teddy's dark eyes. "We all make mistakes, Jake. Every single one of us. We wouldn't be human if we didn't. The important thing is that we learn from them." He glanced at the shirt in Jake's hand then back at his face, that softness still in his eyes. "Do you love her?"

"I do. I've never loved anyone more."

"Then stay and fight for her, man."

He shook his head. It was impossible. He couldn't stay because if he did, there was still the danger he could possibly bring to the family, and he never wanted to do that. "I didn't just lie to her about my past, Teddy. There's more."

The man shook his head, confusion evident on his face as his brows lowered and his eyes squinted. "More? Lying wasn't bad enough?"

"There's Erik King," he said.

"Who is Erik King?"

"He's the one I won all the money from. He isn't the kind to let that go. I'm certain he's looking for me."

"I see." Teddy shook his head. "So, your plan is…what? Find this man first? And give him his money back? Do you even still have that money?" He folded his arms across his chest and tilted his head slightly to the side, his gaze intense. "Kill him?"

Jake stiffened. The thought had run through his mind, more than once. It would solve so many of his problems if Erik King was no longer among the living, but he wasn't a violent man. He may have defended himself with his fists when the situation warranted it, but he'd never killed a man, never even held a gun in his hand. He doubted he could take someone's life.

"I'd get that thought out of your head right now, Jake," he scoffed, his tone sharp. "I don't think you have it in you to kill him. And then what? You'd be running for the rest of your life, and I don't think you want to do that, either. *Tia* Evie would *never* forgive you for that."

He was right. Evie would never forgive him, but maybe it was just as well. She had asked him to leave and that's as far as his plans went. He shoved another shirt into the suitcase, not even bothering to fold it first. "It doesn't matter. None of it does. She told me to leave so that's what I'm doing."

"You're a fool, Jake." Teddy rocked back on his heels. "Wouldn't it be better to—instead of facing this man on his terms —alone—you face him with us? We'd stand behind you if he should come here."

That statement shocked him, making his entire body stiffen as a little speck of hope raced through his mind. He stared at the man, confused and unsure, but at the same time encouraged, though he couldn't help asking why.

Teddy shrugged. "For *Tia* Evie. If she loves you like I think she does, it'll break her heart if you leave."

"But she told me to leave."

"She's upset. Understandably so. *Tia* Evie values honesty, but she has a big heart. She will forgive you." He gave a little smile. "Oh, maybe not right away, but she will. Not if you turn tail and run though. Think about it, Jake."

"Is he stayin'?" Antonio appeared in the doorway to the

bunkhouse, his big frame blocking out the sun, but only momentarily, as he stalked into the room.

Was it his imagination, or did the big man seem bigger? Yes. Yes, he did. And intimidating, so much so, that Jake took a step back, his muscles tightening, as the man approached him.

Without a word of warning, Antonio curled up his fist and let it fly, catching Jake in the face.

Jake staggered back from the force of the blow and reached for the post of the bunk so he wouldn't fall flat on his ass, but missed and fell on his ass anyway. His eyes watered from the pain. The man packed a hell of a punch.

"You deserved that." Antonio loomed over him, breathing heavily, his mustache fluttering with every breath. "I told you that if you ever hurt Miss Evie, you'd answer to me."

"You did." Jake held his hand to his nose, gingerly touching it. He wasn't sure it wasn't broken—it didn't feel the same as the last time it was broken—but it still smarted, making his eyes water. He glanced at Teddy from his position on the floor. "You want a go, too?"

"No, I don't think that's necessary." Teddy extended his hand, his smile spreading, obviously pleased seeing Jake on his ass. And who could blame him?

Jake grasped the offered hand and rose to his feet, warily watching as Antonio went to the ice box, chipped away at the block of ice that had been delivered yesterday, and wrapped the pieces in his handkerchief. He returned and held it out. "Here. Press this against your face."

Jake did as he was told. The ice felt good against his skin. Cold. Soothing. "Thank you."

The big man nodded. *"De nada."*

"So, what's it going to be, Jake?" Teddy drew his attention. "You gonna stay and fight for her? Or are you gonna turn tail and run like a coward?"

"Think carefully, son," Antonio counseled. "Evie would never give up so easily."

"No, she wouldn't," Teddy added with a wry chuckle, "but then *Tia* Evie has more plain stubbornness than anyone I've ever known. She'd dig in her heels and do what needed to be done." The man gave him a sidelong glance. "Are you staying?"

Jake didn't have to think. He already knew his answer. "I'll stay." It was the right decision. At least, it felt right in his heart, but there was still the matter of getting Evie to forgive him. That wasn't a forgone conclusion. Teddy had spoken the truth. The woman was as stubborn as a mule—maybe even more so. And then, there was Erik King. Just because he decided to stay, didn't mean that King had given up on him. "What about King?"

"What about him?" Teddy shrugged. "If he dares to shows up here, we'll take care of it."

The simple comment stunned him. No one, not in all the years he traveled this earth, stood up for him like that. He'd always fought his own battles, and here was this man telling him he wouldn't be alone. It was unexpected and humbling and maybe even made him feel like he was worthy. "Are you sure? You don't know him or what he's capable of doing."

"Doesn't matter. We Silvas don't run from a fight. Never have. Never will." Teddy grinned, closed the trunk and sat on it, then pointed to the bunk beside him while Antonio pulled up a chair and slid into it, the wood creaking just a bit. "Now, let's figure out what you're gonna do to win *Tia* Evie back. I promise, it isn't going to be easy."

Jake sank to the mattress and eyed his visitors...now apparently his co-conspirators. Was it his imagination, or did Teddy and Antonio seem to be getting blurrier? He blinked several times, which didn't help at all. In fact, it seemed to make his vision worse. He gingerly touched the skin around his eye. Yes, it was swelling up nicely, which was causing his fuzzy vision. He brought the handkerchief filled with ice up to his eye and nose and placed it gently against his skin. "Are you sure you want to help me? I seem to recall you telling me to stay away from her, so why now?"

"Let's just say I've had a change of heart. And I do want to help you." Teddy jerked his thumb toward Antonio. "He does, too. Heath and Esteban will help. Uncle Charley and Aunt Felicity as well."

"Even Hilde," Antonio added, "though I would be wary of her cast-iron skillet."

"Why?"

"Because we've never seen *Tia* Evie happier," Teddy admitted, "and I, for one, want to see that again. I think she deserves it."

"I don't know what to say except thank you."

Teddy laughed then, not a little chuckle either, but a full-blown, deep from his gut, laugh. "Oh, don't thank us yet."

*E*vie let herself into *Pequeña Casa* and closed the door behind her. She just needed a little time alone, and God knows she couldn't find that at the homestead.

Two weeks had come and gone since the morning he told her he loved her, then revealed the truth about his past and why he'd come to the ranch. Teddy had told her Jake was staying, that they couldn't afford to lose another ranch hand, and Jake had become too much a part of Montaña del Trueno.

And so everywhere she looked, *he* was there. In the riding ring, continuing his lessons though she wasn't sitting on the fence watching him; chopping wood, his muscles bulging, his bare back gleaming in the sun; pushing that damned wheelbarrow from the barn to the compost heap. Taking care of the horses, his hands smoothing over their coats with such gentleness, she ached to be touched the same.

There was no escaping the man. In fact, it seemed that he turned up everywhere she happened to be, and she didn't think it was an accident.

On the contrary, she was convinced it was a damned conspiracy, perpetrated by her family. Every single one of them.

The only way to truly avoid Jake was to stay locked in her room. She couldn't do that. She wouldn't. There was just simply too much to do for her to take to her bed and wallow in self-pity. And anger. Though if she was truthful with herself, she had to admit she wasn't nearly as angry as she had been for the truth he omitted. No, it was the other thing—the prospect of King finding him on the ranch, endangering her family, that frightened her, keeping her on edge, causing panic to grab hold of her heart.

On the other hand, Jake had been on the ranch for almost three months, and no one had come looking for him. Perhaps, King wasn't nearly as ruthless and persistent as Jake thought him to be. Perhaps, he wasn't looking for Jake at all. Perhaps Jake had done a good job of covering his trail.

She opened the windows to let in some fresh air, the slight breeze moving the lacy curtains, then strode toward the little sink and the long, skinny cabinet beside it. From the bottom shelf, she grabbed a bottle of liquor, not caring which one, and a glass, then pulled out one of the kitchen chairs and sank into it. She poured herself a glass of the fine sipping whiskey—just a little—then poured a little more, filling the glass half-way, and placed the bottle on the table within easy reach. A vase full of cheerful yellow roses sat in the center. Someone had been here since her night with Jake. One of the boys? Marisol and Sergio?

She took a sip of whiskey. The heat flowed all the way to her stomach, spreading warmth, but did nothing to dull the pain in her heart, as her gaze flew to the open bedroom doorway and the big brass bed. Memories of their night together assaulted her. She could feel the touch of his hand, the sweetness of his kiss, the pleasure that had rocked her soul.

She shouldn't have come here. Jake was here, too.

Biting her lip, she averted her gaze from the bed and brought the glass to her lips to take another swallow. A big one. The whiskey clogged her throat, making her cough, but still, she finished what was in the glass then placed it on the table and pushed it away.

Footsteps sounded on the porch a moment before she heard a decidedly feminine giggle come through the window. "Put me down, Charley. I'm too heavy and we're both too old for you to be—"

The rest of her sentence was cut off by the unmistakable sound of a kiss and then another giggle. "Oh, Charley."

Evie stiffened, her mouth dropping open in surprise. What were Charley and Felicity doing here?

A blush rose to her cheeks as she answered her own question. They were here for the same reason everyone else came here—stealing a moment alone. They were in their seventies! Or at least their late sixties. Surely, they didn't still….?

Perhaps, they did.

Charley's deeper voice floated through the open windows. "We're not too old, sweetheart. We'll never be too old. Besides, you don't weigh a pound more than you did the day we married."

Evie rose from the table and just stood there, not knowing where to go, wishing for all the world that she could fall through the floor and disappear. A moment later, the door swung open and there they were, Aunt Felicity in Uncle Charley's arms—like a bride being carried over the threshold. It took a moment for them to realize she stood there.

"Evie!" Charley exclaimed, his face flushing. Even the tips of his ears reddened. "We…I…wasn't expecting to see you here!"

"That much is obvious, Uncle Charley." She nodded toward her uninvited guests. "Aunt Felicity."

Felicity's face blossomed with color as well, and the smile faded from her lips. "Put me down, Charley."

He did as she asked, then took a few steps into the room, his hands on his hips, once again in full control of his composure. "What are *you* doing here?" He pulled a handkerchief from his pocket and held it out to her. "You look like hell."

"Charley!" Felicity admonished him, her voice filled with dismay.

Leave it to Uncle Charley to state the facts as he saw them, without sugar-coating his words. Evie couldn't refute his statement. How could she? She did look like hell. Dark circles were under her eyes from not sleeping. Unless, of course, she'd been crying, which she seemed to be doing a lot of within the last two weeks, and then her eyes were all puffy and red.

"Thank you, Uncle Charley." She took the handkerchief and swiped at her eyes, which had started watering again. "I feel like hell. And a fool."

"A fool? No, you were never a fool, Evie." Sympathy flashed in his light blue eyes. "What happened between you and Jake?"

She shook her head and sank into the chair she had recently vacated. "Teddy was right. He *is* a maverick, following his own rules." She glanced at Felicity then turned away, unable to stomach the empathy in the woman's eyes, then poured more whiskey and took a big gulp. It burned her throat, but she didn't care. "Teddy warned me that he'd break my heart. I didn't listen." She gave a rueful laugh, though it sounded more like a choked cry to her own ears. "Oh, no, I just had to be stubborn, like I always am."

Charley squeezed her shoulder, offering comfort, which only made the ache in her throat worse. "Tell me," he said, his voice soft and full of affection.

She could always count on Uncle Charley. He was level-headed and calm. He would listen without judgment. "He lied to me."

"What did he lie about?"

"Everything." She let out a huff, still reeling from the truths Jake had admitted. "His past. The reason he came here." She pulled in a deep breath, frustrated with the lump in her throat which made doing so difficult, even more annoyed with the tears that kept leaking from her eyes, no matter how many times she wiped them. "It wasn't about wanting to get married. Not at all. He was looking for a place to hide."

"I see." He took a moment before he spoke. "That may be why he came here, but it isn't why he stayed. He didn't have to tell you." His voice changed, becoming deeper and more authoritative, as if she were on trial and he needed answers. "What about you? When you found out about Lucy's plan, you were one hundred percent against marrying anyone."

"That is true. I was. I was perfectly happy, content with my life."

"Hmmm, you say that, but were you?" He pulled out a chair and gestured to his wife to sit.

"Hush, Charley. You talk too much." Felicity caressed his shoulder, then took the seat he offered. She looked up at him, her face reflecting all the love she had for him. A fresh wave of tears filled Evie's eyes just seeing that expression. "That's what made you such a great lawyer, and an even better judge, but now is not the time." Felicity turned to Evie and demanded, "Do you love him?"

"What?"

"It's a simple question, dear. Do you love him?" This time Felicity's voice was stronger as she enunciated each word. "The truth now. What's in your heart, not your head."

"I do."

"Can you live with knowing why Jake came here? Can you live with his past?"

She nodded. She could. It was the other issue, the problem that seemed to be much more difficult to reconcile. "There's more," she said. "Something you don't know." She narrowed her eyes. "Or maybe you do." Her gaze flicked to Charley. "Maybe you do as well. There isn't much that happens here that you don't know." She scrutinized his expression, but as usual, Charley's face told her nothing. Whatever he thought or knew he kept to himself. She sniffed then used the handkerchief to wipe her eyes and focused on Felicity once more. "There's a man who might be looking for Jake. According to him, this man is ruthless and isn't above killing people. If he finds Jake here, it could put all of us in danger. The children…everyone." She couldn't continue, her heart constricting with fear.

"Why is that man looking for Jake?"

"Jake won a lot of money from him playing poker, enough, he said, to buy this ranch twice over. Apparently, that was an unforgiveable sin. That man—King—wants a rematch and isn't willing to take 'no' for an answer, but even if Jake agrees, he could still end up—" she shivered, unable to finish.

Felicity shook her head. "My girl, I'm going to tell you what my mother used to tell me. Don't borrow trouble."

"What does that mean?"

"It means don't fret and worry over something that may never be." She reached for the bottle of whiskey on the table. "Charley, dear, would you get me a glass, please?"

He did as she asked, but brought two glasses to the table instead of one, and took a seat. Felicity poured a generous amount for all of them, put the bottle down and took a sip. "It's been how many months since Jake has been here?"

"A little more than three. He arrived the day Lucy and Ben married."

"And that man hasn't shown up, has he?" She didn't wait for an answer. "To my way of thinking, if that man truly wanted to find Jake, he'd have been here already. Nothing would have stopped him. He would have talked to all of Jake's friends in—where is he from?"

"San Francisco."

Felicity gave a slight nod. "That man would have frequented all the places that Jake would. He might have even hired someone like the Pinkertons, but the point is, Jake would have been found by now."

"How do you know?"

She shrugged, her eyes brightening, her smile widening. "It's what I would have done. It's what Charley would have done. In fact, he has, in the past, utilized the Pinkertons for a case." She glanced at her husband, love shining in her eyes, then turned her attention back to Evie.

"I hadn't thought of it that way. You may be right. Three months is a long time."

"Ask yourself, how you would feel if he left?" Again, she didn't leave room for Evie to respond. Instead, she reached over and grasped Evie's hand, squeezing it. "I think you should forgive him. Not for him, but for you. You deserve every bit of happiness you can find."

Evie glanced at the strong hand holding hers, then back at Felicity. "What about that man?"

Again, the woman shrugged, an elegant lifting of her shoulders, then released her hand and sat back in her seat. "Let him come."

"Let him come?" Evie jumped from the chair, nearly knocking it over, and started pacing. "Are you insane! What about the children? And the rest of you?" She couldn't believe Felicity would say such a thing.

"There isn't a person on this ranch who would let anything happen to the children, Evie. You know that. As for Jake, I don't think anyone here would hesitate to defend him—myself included, if—and I mean *if*—that man should come here. Even if he does come here, I doubt he would try to kill Jake. Or anyone else for that matter." She smiled then and her eyes sparkled with a hint of mischief. "He can't win his money back from a dead man." She rose from her seat and pushed Evie toward the door. "Now you go and think about it."

"But—" Evie sputtered, but never finished. Propelled by a strength she didn't know Felicity possessed, she tried to stop the momentum, but couldn't, not until she stood on the porch, the hands pushing her suddenly gone.

"No 'buts,' my girl. Go. Take a long walk and think about everything I've said." The door closed in her face.

Evie stood on the porch, stunned Felicity could be so forceful, and just stared at the closed door. Who knew behind the sweetness Felicity showed the world was a woman with backbone. Of strong conviction. Of uncommon strength.

Reeling from Felicity's actions, Evie reached for the doorknob. She had every intention of stalking back into the cottage, and continuing the conversation, but changed her mind when she heard Charley's voice coming through the open window. "You should have been a lawyer."

Felicity laughed before there was the unmistakable sound of a kiss being given. "I didn't spend all those years in the courtroom with you and not learn anything."

Evie hung her head for a moment, then left *Pequeña Casa*, taking the path that would lead her back to the homestead, Felicity's words echoing in her head.

Her life would never be the same if Jake weren't in it. And yet, she didn't know if she could forgive him for the lie he told—or didn't tell—or for the possibly of putting her family in peril. For the first time in a long time, she'd found love, and she didn't want to give it up, but how could she trust him again? Would she suspect every word that came out of his mouth from now on?

What if King came looking for Jake? Would he? The only person who could answer that was Jake. Her pace quickened.

She didn't see Jake in the corral, nor walking across the compound pushing the wheelbarrow. He wasn't in the barn, either. She continued to the house, passing between the rose bushes, and stopped. The table on the patio was set up with the silver coffee service reserved for company or special occasions.

Had she forgotten she had invited guests today? What was today anyway? Tuesday? Friday? She'd lost all track of time as one day seemed to flow to the next.

Savannah came out of the house, carrying a plate of Hilde's

cookies. She stopped briefly and gave Evie such a glare, Evie took a step back. Savannah laid the plate on the table and turned, her dark eyes full of reproach. She placed her hands on her hips in perfect imitation of Teddy. Savannah was definitely her father's daughter, right down to that intense stare. "Where have you been?"

Nothing like getting scolded by a six-year-old child. "I went for a walk." She glanced at the table. "Did I forget something? Did we have a date?"

The girl shook her head, making her long braids move over her shoulders.

"Then what is all this?"

Savannah huffed, like Evie was the dumbest woman alive, her hands still on her hips, that intense stare never losing focus. "It's for you and Mr. Jake. You have to talk."

"Me and Jake? Oh *carina*, it—"

The girl didn't let her finish, though she wasn't rude. "Isn't that what you make me and Miguel do? You make us talk to each other. You make us 'resolve our differences.'" She huffed again in exasperation. "Isn't that what you always say?"

"It is." Evie was a little taken aback, not only by the fact that Savannah, her sweet and inquisitive grandniece was acting like an adult, but that she'd actually been listening and learning all these years. Still, the circumstances were much different than when she and her brother were arguing, and she stated so. "This is different, *carina*."

"No, it's not." Savannah shook her head. Ah, the stubbornness of the Miller ancestry came shining through. "It's not different at all, *Tia* Evie. I like Mr. Jake. You do, too. I saw you kissing him."

Heat rushed to her face. "You did?"

The girl nodded. "A couple times."

The corners of her mouth began to lift, almost beyond her control, as her gaze swept over her grandniece. "When did you get so smart?"

The girl smiled at her finally, unable, it seemed, to keep up the glare her father was so famous for. A hint of white showed in the space where her missing tooth had been. "I'm always smart. Mama says so. *Tia* Jenny says so. You say so, too." Her smile widened. "I'm going to be a lawyer like Uncle Charley when I grow up. Or a doctor, like Uncle Ben." She pulled out a chair and ordered. "Sit. Your guest will be here any minute."

Evie did as she was told, amazed that this precious little girl had outsmarted her. She didn't doubt for one moment the girl would be anything she wanted to be—whether a doctor, a lawyer, or anything else.

As she grabbed a napkin and laid it over her lap, Evie looked around. No one was about, but she didn't doubt Hilde, and possibly, Antonio, were at the kitchen window, watching and waiting. Perhaps, her nephews' wives as well. In fact, she wouldn't be surprised if her nephews watched too, although they should be out at the summer pasture. She looked down at the table, and studied the blood-red roses in the vase, her stomach already knotting.

"Hello, Evie."

His voice, deep and rich—the one that haunted her dreams—drew her attention. Evie started, then turned her head, and just looked at him. He had changed from his work clothes into the suit she'd first seen him in, and he looked so handsome she had trouble concentrating. Right beside him was Miguel, wearing a grin that stretched from ear to ear. The boy's hand was clasped in his much larger one and that, more than anything else, melted her heart.

Jake Hannigan *was* a good man in all the ways that mattered. He'd proven that over and over again.

"Now talk to each other." Savannah ordered in such an imperious way, Evie tore her gaze from Jake and just stared at her. The girl smiled, obviously pleased with herself, then grabbed her brother by the hand. "Come on, Miguel." They went as far as the swing, settling themselves on the soft cushions. Apparently they were going to chaperone this little *tete-a-tete*, probably determined to stay until she and Jake made up.

Jake, his attention briefly on Savannah, smiled, then turned his devastating, utterly too charming grin on her. "She's quite the force to be reckoned with."

"Yes, she is. Stubborn, too."

"So is Miguel." He gestured to the chair opposite her. "May I?"

"Of course. I don't think either one of the children would forgive us if we didn't follow through on their plans."

He slid into the seat, took a deep breath, and let it out slowly. His eyes were warm and filled with regret…and something else, something she recognized when she looked in her own mirror. "I'm sorry, Evie. I should have told you everything right from the beginning."

"Yes." The anger was still there, even with his apology. "You should have told me about King. About your past. More than that, you shouldn't have lied to me. Maybe I over-reacted, but you have to understand, the last man who lied to me died. I can't forget that."

She searched his face, reminding herself that he wasn't Tom, and admitted. "I'm afraid, Jake, that you'll lie to me again and hurt me. Or end up like Tom. I don't know if I could bear that."

He reached across the table and laid his hand over hers, squeezing her fingers ever so slightly. "I promise, I'll never lie to you again, even if it's a lie of omission. I'll tell you anything you want to know." His eyes held a slight sheen of moisture. "I love you, Evie. Please say you forgive me. If you can't, I'll go, but I don't want to. I'd much rather stay and spend the rest of my life proving to you how much I love you."

Her heart hitched with longing and tears blurred her vision. He was promising forever, and he meant it. Every word. She could see it in his eyes and hear it in his voice, and the vision of them sitting together when they were old and gray, watching the sun sink into the horizon, flashed through her head. He would leave Montaña del Trueno and take that dream away if she asked him.

She couldn't do it, couldn't say the words. The simple truth was that she loved this man, loved him with all her being, faults and all, but still, there was one more thing she needed to know. "What about King? What if he should come here?"

"I would give my life before I allowed him to hurt anyone on this ranch, Evie. You have my promise."

Yes, she believed him. He'd never let any harm come to them. She twisted her hand beneath his, weaved her fingers between his strong digits, and whispered, "I want you to stay."

CHAPTER 19

"Miss Evie, you have a visitor." Ana strolled into the kitchen, a wide smile on her face. She held a dust rag in one hand. In the other was a bottle of lemon oil, and the faint aroma of citrus filled the air to mix with the chickens roasting in the oven.

Evie put the carrot and the peeler down on the butcher block table. Another of Lucy's mail-order husbands? She hoped not. "Thank you, Ana."

"Do you want coffee?"

Evie shook her head. The sooner she got rid of this visitor, the better she'd feel. It shouldn't take long, either, just long enough to tell whoever it was that he was too late. She loved Jake.

She turned to Felicity and gestured to the bowl of vegetables on the table. "Would you mind terribly finishing these?"

"Not at all. Go see to your guest."

"Thank you."

She washed and dried her hands, then untied the apron and laid it over the back of a chair. After leaving the kitchen, she stopped briefly at the mirror in the hallway to check her appearance. Staring at her reflection, a terrifying thought skipped into her head, and immediately, her stomach clenched with fear. What if her visitor wasn't another suitor at all? What if it was Erik King finally tracking Jake down? What if…she forced the thoughts away, but her stomach remained knotted. She took a calming breath, forced a smile to her lips, and stepped into the parlor but didn't move from the doorway as she sized up her visitor.

A black-suited gentleman stood in front of the table, admiring the photographs lined up there. He didn't touch them or move them around like Mr. Ambrose had. Indeed, he stood with his hands folded behind his back, leaning forward a little so he could see each one clearly. He chuckled low in his throat and nodded his head full of silver hair at a few of them, as if he could see beyond the angelic faces in the pictures. He looked harmless. Then again, what would a ruthless man look like? Still, she was prepared to deny Jake was at the ranch.

She cleared her throat. "Hello, I'm Evie Miller."

Her visitor turned around and the first thing she noticed was his kind eyes and beaming smile. The second thing she noticed was the white clerical collar at his throat. This was no gambling kingpin or a prospective husband, but a man of God.

He moved forward, his step spry and agile as he reached for her hand. She noticed right away the air of comfort surrounding him. There was something so pure, so loving, in both his countenance and demeanor that she felt instantly at ease.

"Miss Miller!" he exclaimed, the faint traces of an Irish accent complementing the comfort of his touch somehow. "It's a pleasure to finally meet you. I've heard a great deal about you."

Evie blinked as he released her hand, taking that feeling of solace with him.

"Forgive the intrusion, but I'm looking for Jake Hannigan."

Understanding dawned and she sighed with relief. "You must be Father O'Malley."

He gave her a beaming smile. "That I am."

"I've heard a great deal about you as well. Jake speaks of you often."

"Does he now?" His merry blues eyes were kind. "That maverick." He lowered his voice to a conspiratorial whisper. "I prayed harder for that boy than anyone else, but I always thought my prayers did little good. Until now. I can tell you, with the utmost authority, as a man who's known Jake most of his life, he's very happy. Finally." His rocked back on his heels, his smile widening. "God works in mysterious ways, doesn't He?"

She returned his smile. She couldn't help herself. Father O'Malley was extraordinarily charming, though she didn't doubt he could be a taskmaster when he chose to be, at least according to Jake. "Yes, He does." She tilted her head as she looked at him. "Is Jake expecting you?"

"No, he's not. I thought I'd surprise him." He smiled, and once again, that feeling of ease swept over her. No wonder Jake was fond of this man. "He doesn't know I've been transferred from St. Anselm's to St. Gideon's in Santa Fe. I didn't want to tell him until I was sure."

There was more, Evie suspected, but she didn't know what. She didn't know the man except for what Jake had told her. As she gazed at the priest, she found herself under the most intense scrutiny she'd ever received, even more intense than any look Teddy had given her. After a moment, he gave a slight nod, as if she'd passed some kind of test.

"You love him."

Heat rushed to her face. "Is it that obvious?" She laughed then admitted, "I do."

"And he loves you."

"He said as much."

Father O'Malley patted her hand. "He wouldn't say it unless he meant it, and you can trust that from someone who has known him since he was three years old."

The comment lightened her heart, but he hadn't needed to tell her Jake loved her. He showed her in so many ways. "I know Jake will be excited to see you. Let me take you to him."

"That would be lovely." He picked up a leather satchel from a chair, then joined her in the doorway. "Lead the way."

She led him through the house, stopping in the kitchen to introduce him to Hilde and Aunt Felicity, as well as to Savannah and Miguel, who were busy at the table cutting shapes in cookie dough. Ramón giggled from his highchair, completely content with his own piece of dough. Even Toughie seemed absorbed in pounding the dough on the table. Smudges of flour and bits of dough were on his face as well as in his hair.

"You have a lovely home and a beautiful family, Miss Miller," Father O'Malley said when they stepped outside to the patio, "and from what Jake wrote me, a fine ranch."

"Thank you." She smiled at him, seeing in him what Jake must have seen—a kind, gentle soul. A genuinely good man in all the ways that mattered. "And it's Evie, please."

She led him to the riding ring and stopped at the fence. Flower, the other two cats, and the dog were there as well, watching Jake who was in the middle of the ring. He was on Cinnamon's back, gently tugging on the reins and squeezing his thighs against her sides as he put the horse through her paces. There was more Cinnamon had to learn. Jake, too, for that matter, but they were learning together and doing well.

Father O'Malley laughed as he dropped the satchel beside the fence and just stood there, his hands on his hips. "Well now, will you look at that? I never thought I'd see Jake Hannigan working with horses. He always had a healthy fear of them."

"He's not afraid of them anymore. In fact, he's developed quite a fondness for them." She watched man and beast in the middle of the ring and her heart swelled. "As you can see, they respond to him very well, especially Cinnamon. It's a gift when one can communicate so well with an animal and Jake has that gift." She gestured to the cats and dog. "With them, too, especially Flower, the orange one."

"Jake always liked cats." The priest agreed as he rested his arms on the fence. "I remember the one who used to sneak into the home every night. More than once, I found that stray cat asleep on Jake's cot." A knowing look settled on his face as he turned toward her, and his voice lowered, as if imparting a secret. "The boys didn't think I knew about it, but I did."

He turned back to Jake in the ring and a satisfied sigh escaped him. "Never thought I'd see the day when that maverick would become respectable either. I never approved of his gambling."

Pride filled her, making her heart sing. "He hasn't touched a card or made a bet since he came here."

His gaze swept over her and once again, Evie felt like she was being given a test, but it didn't bother her, especially when he gave her a benevolent smile. "Perhaps he's understood something clearly at last. I think that may be because of you, but whatever the reason, I'm glad."

Her cheeks grew warm from the compliment. *If* she was the reason Jake never picked up a card again, she'd take it. She forced her gaze away from the priest, called Jake's name, and waved at him.

Jake turned in their direction and his smile, the one she loved to see, froze for a moment before it grew wider. He directed Cinnamon to the fence, slipped from the saddle, and crawled between the slats.

"Father! What are you doing here?"

The old priest opened his arms for a hug. "I came to see you, boyo. I have something to tell you." He laughed. "Actually, I have two things to tell you."

Evie's eyes instantly misted as the two men drew each other into a bear hug that would have broken the ribs of any other person. There was plenty of backslapping, too.

"I'm so happy to see you. It's been too long!"

"Yes, it has." The priest took a step back and blurted out, "First, the good news. You'll be seeing more of me. I've been transferred to the boys' home in Santa Fe."

Shock at the news made Jake's mouth fall open. He recovered quickly, but there was still surprise in his voice. "You've left St. Anselm's?"

"I have. After thirty-five years, I was asked to run St. Gideon's here in Santa Fe. It's a feather in my cap, to be sure." The man's expression was pure pleasure mixed with not a little pride. "I arrived only yesterday and my first thought was to see you."

"Congratulations are in order then. I'm pleased for you. The boys at St. Gideon are about to have their lives changed for the better." Jake shoved his hands in his pockets. "What's the other news? Is it just as good?"

Father O'Malley instantly sobered as sadness flitted into his bright blue eyes. "I'm afraid not, boyo."

Jake stiffened, his smile fading as a slew of emotions passed over his face. Whatever joy he'd found in Father O'Malley's visit disappeared in an instant and his face drained of color.

The priest hesitated, his eyes darting from Jake to her then back to Jake, and that feeling of dread she'd experienced earlier intensified. It could only mean one thing, but she hoped it didn't.

"It's all right, Father. Evie knows everything."

Evie moved a step closer and slipped her hand into his. She squeezed a little and gazed deeply into his eyes, but she addressed her statement to Father O'Malley, even as her stomach knotted and her mouth went dry. "And whatever it is, Jake and I will face it together."

Jake gave a slight nod then squeezed back. He took a deep breath and let it out slowly, struggling for calm, though Evie could clearly feel the tension in the hand holding hers. Indeed, it looked like every muscle in his body was as taut as the strings of a violin. "It's about King, isn't it? Is he on his way here now?"

"He might be. Or he might be here already. I don't know." He looked away then turned his attention back to them, as if he didn't like what he needed to say. "He came to see me."

The panic that flashed in Jake's eyes was undeniable and he squeezed her hand a little tighter. "How did he know about you? I've kept that part of my life hidden. No one knew about the boys' home. I thought I made sure of that." He drew in a shaky breath, then let loose with rapid-fire questions, his voice as tense as his body. "What happened? How did you know it was him? Did he threaten you? Did he try to hurt you? What did you tell him?"

"He didn't threaten me at all and I didn't tell him anything."

The tension in the air was so oppressive that even Cinnamon nickered and stomped her hoof against the dirt. "So how do you know he's coming here?"

"Are you going to let me tell you or are you going to keep interrupting me?" Father O'Malley huffed, his face turning slightly red, impatience flashing in his eyes.

Jake quickly apologized, though Evie could tell how anxious he was for answers. It was there in his expression.

"About a week ago, I was upstairs in my room packing for my move here, when Sister Agnes fetched me. She said I had a visitor and that he was waiting in my study. When I went downstairs, he was sitting in that old wing-back chair—you know the one—and looking as innocent as a newborn babe." His body trembled slightly with what Evie assumed was anger and disappointment in himself.

"He introduced himself as bold as you please. Said he was wanting to make a donation to the home. If I hadn't heard his name before or knew what I did about him, I never would have suspected him of being anything other than a distinguished, wealthy gentleman. He gave me an envelope filled with cash—to my utter disgrace, I accepted it—and then he left. It wasn't until after his carriage pulled away that I realized he saw your last letter to me. It was sitting on my desk along with the money you sent, but it wasn't in the same place as I'd left it. I know he read it though I have no proof." Tears of regret and shame clogged the man's voice. "I'm sorry, boyo. He knows where you are because I was careless. It's my fault."

Sympathy for the older man flashed through her. She could see it was the same for Jake as he reached out and laid his hand on the man's shoulder. "No, Father, it's mine. I…I should never have put you in that position to begin with." He let out a long sigh. "I'm just glad he didn't hurt you. He would have, regardless of the fact that you're a priest. I know you wouldn't have told him anything."

"And I'm sure if I hadn't come down from my room when I did, I would have found my study ransacked." He reached down and grabbed the handles of valise and lifted it, a frown drawing down his bushy white eyebrows. "I thought you might need this. Now that he knows where you are, I have no doubt he'll insist on another chance to win back what he lost."

Evie studied the valise as Father O'Malley handed it to Jake. She noticed how soft the leather seemed to be, as well as the initials emblazoned on it. She also became aware of how heavy it appeared. "What's in there?"

"It's the money I won from King. Every cent of it." He accepted the bag, then glanced at her. She couldn't read the expression on his face. There was love there, certainly, but there was also dread and sadness.

"What are you going to do?" she asked, even though she was afraid of the answer.

He didn't respond, but he did look at her. Tears stung her eyes and a lump lodged in her throat. He'd leave…to protect her and the family. He'd face King, knowing that he might not survive the encounter, and she'd lose another person she loved to a gambler. Well, she wasn't going to stand for it.

"You're not leaving," she said, her voice filled with conviction. "Don't even think about it, Jake. Whatever happens, we will face it together." She looked at him, her gaze roaming over his face. "I will not lose another person I love." She held up her hand, even though he had yet to say a word. "Don't even try to argue with me."

"We'll talk about it later."

She shook her head, adamant. "No, we won't." Despite the bitter ache in her throat, she turned to Father O'Malley, forcing a smile to her lips. "Please stay for dinner, Father."

"I'm afraid I can't, my dear, but thank you for the invitation. I really need to get back to the boys' home."

"At least stay for coffee or a glass of lemonade before you go."

He accepted her invitation with a request. "Lemonade, please, if you don't mind. I really can't stay long."

"If you'll excuse me then?" She walked away, anxiety, fear, and heartbreak making each step agony.

"Extraordinary," she heard Father O'Malley exclaim.

"Yes, she is," came Jake's quick response.

Jake watched her walk away, admiring the grace of her stride he always did. His heart swelled with the love he had for her even as it broke, shattering into a million pieces. It amazed him how fast he could go from being happy to being filled with dread. How quickly his dreams of the future—with her—could die.

"What are you going to do, Jake?"

Unable to speak for a moment, he simply shook his head. "I was going to ask her to marry me."

"And now?" Father O'Malley asked, the concern in his voice nearly Jake's undoing.

Again, Jake shook his head. "I can't."

"You love her."

"I do. So much so that I can't do this to her." His attention flew to Evie as she brought a tray with a pitcher of lemonade and glasses to the table, then disappeared back inside the house, her steps slow as if a heavy weight had settled on her shoulders. She was scared, he knew—he'd felt the trembling in her hand when she held his—knowing that King might be here, knowing what that meant. Guilt and anger raged through him. He had done that to her and it wasn't right.

"I am sorry, boyo."

"It's not your fault. It's mine. All mine. And I accept responsibility. I should never have gambled with King. I knew better. I knew his reputation, knew what he was a capable of." He clenched his hands into fists, his short nails digging into the soft flesh of his palms. "I should never have fallen in love with her either."

"I don't see how you could have helped yourself. She's a lovely woman…and probably much stronger than you give her credit for."

He had no doubts about that. Evie was strong…look at all that she had accomplished, but this…this was different. She'd never dealt with a ruthless, relentless man before, one who didn't take no for an answer, one who wouldn't hesitate to kill.

The sound of horse's hooves pounding into the barnyard startled him. Already the threat of King was having an effect on him. Would he jump at every shadow now? Every noise? He relaxed, the tension seeping out of him, when he saw that it was Teddy— not King—riding into the yard, leading a young pitch-black colt behind him. "If you'll excuse me, Father."

Father O'Malley followed his line of sight. "Of course. Who is that young man?"

"Evie's nephew. Teddy. I have to tell him what you've told me. About King."

"He's the angry one you mentioned in your letters, correct?" The priest's eyes radiated sympathy. So did the expression on his face. "I understand. Do you want me to come with you?"

Jake shook his head, already feeling the tension rising up in him again. "Thank you, Father, but this is something I need to do myself. I won't be surprised if I find myself knocked on my a—behind."

"As you wish, son." Father O'Malley nodded toward the patio, where Evie was settling into her seat at the little table. "I'll just be getting to know your Miss Evie a little better. I think I'll enjoy that. She *is* an extraordinary woman."

He watched the priest stroll toward the patio and take the seat on the other side of the table, across from Evie. The smile on her face, though warm and inviting for Father O'Malley, was just a façade, and she would keep it up until they could have a moment alone together. He dreaded that conversation almost as much as he dreaded the one he had to have with Teddy.

Jake turned his attention to Evie's nephew. Already the pain in his chest, around his heart, made breathing in and out more difficult, but he couldn't put it off. Waiting wouldn't change anything. King was here—or soon to be. The summons to sit across the poker table from him so he could win back his money was inevitable. So was the bullet meant for his heart.

Jake put one foot in front of the other and headed toward the man who'd become a friend, though he doubted that budding friendship would survive this.

Teddy grinned at him. "Afternoon, Jake." He gestured toward the colt. "Meet your next project. What do you think?"

"He's magnificent. What's his name?"

Teddy shrugged. "I haven't named him yet."

Jake smoothed his hand over the colt's nose and looked deeply into the horse's eyes. "If you're taking suggestions, I think Midnight would suit him."

"Excellent choice." He handed Jake the rope. "Midnight it is." He moved toward one of the smaller paddocks, tied Soldier Boy's reins to the fence, then opened the gate. Jake led Midnight into the corral, and removed the rope from around his neck, allowing the colt to run free within the enclosure. He joined

Teddy at the gate and leaned his arms on the fence, his gaze on Midnight.

"Look at the way he runs." Once again, his jaw clenched as an overwhelming sadness filled him. It would have been a pleasure to train this colt.

"That's why I chose him. He's got heart."

After a moment, Jake cleared his throat and glanced at Teddy. "I need to talk to you."

Before Jake could utter a word, voices drifted to them from the patio. Both men turned at the same time.

"Who's that man with *Tia* Evie?"

Jake focused on the patio where Evie sat with Father O'Malley, his eyes misting just a bit to see the woman he loved with the man who held such affection in his heart. "That's Father O'Malley."

Teddy turned toward him, surprise making his eyes widen. "Your Father O'Malley?"

"Yes."

"What's he doing here?" On the heels of the question, suspicion lowered his brows in an instant and pulled down the corners of his mouth. "Is it that King person you told me about? Is he coming here?"

"Unfortunately, yes. He might be in Serenity already."

Teddy's stare was as intense as Jake had ever seen it. "What are you going to do?"

Jake couldn't get the words to come.

"You're leaving. Because of King."

Jake nodded though it broke his heart. He didn't want to leave—he loved the ranch—more importantly, he loved Evie, but he didn't have very many choices. King would come for him. Or summon him for the opportunity to win his money back. It wouldn't be a friendly invitation. The odds Jake would walk away from the encounter unscathed didn't seem likely.

"What about *Tia* Evie? She loves you. She'll be devastated if you leave."

"She could be hurt if I stay. Any of you could. It's too dangerous for me to stay here." He couldn't bring himself to utter the word 'die,' though he was well aware that was a very distinct possibility. "—if King holds true to form."

"So you think he'll just ride out to the ranch and shoot you?"

"That isn't King's way. No, he'll demand that we meet and play cards so he can win his money back, but even once he wins...that's when he'd shoot me."

"Do you still have the money you won from him?"

"I do." He pointed to the black valise leaning against a fence post, the one he should have put away as soon as Father O'Malley handed it to him.

Teddy glanced at the bag then back at him and shrugged. "Then just give it to him."

"I tried that, too." Jake's body stiffened, every muscle taut. "Several times. He refused my offers and started harassing my housekeeper so badly, she quit. Left 'invitations' on the table inside my entry hall so I'd know he was there in my house. When that didn't work, he resorted to burning my house to the ground." He shook his head. "It's King's ego. He *has* to win."

"So you're going to leave, going to allow him to win, whether you play cards or not."

"I don't see where I have very many choices."

Teddy shook his head, then stared so fiercely at him, Jake felt the intensity of it all the way to the pit of his stomach. "I thought I told you once before that Silvas don't run from trouble, that we'd stand beside you."

Gratitude made his throat close. That Teddy, and the rest of the family, would stand up for him, help him, overwhelmed him. "You did. And I appreciate that, but..."

"But what?"

Jake shook his head. He wasn't going to win this argument.

He knew it. Teddy knew it, too. "So what am I supposed to do? Just wait for King to make his move? To force my hand?"

"In a word, yes, but until he does, we'll have time to figure something out." Teddy smiled suddenly, which was unusual considering the circumstances. "*Tia* Evie always taught us that there was a solution to every problem. I'm sure there is for this one, too. Tonight, after Heath and Esteban come in from the summer pasture, we'll all sit down and discuss it. Antonio and Uncle Charley, too. Hell, we'll call a family meeting after the children are asleep and we'll come up with a plan."

Emotion choked him, so much so that he could hardly speak. "I don't know what to say."

Teddy clapped him on the back. "*Thank you* will suffice."

She liked Father O'Malley. She really did. He seemed like a kind and gentle soul, but she wished he'd never come to Montaña del Trueno…especially not with the news he delivered. King was here or soon to be, and she knew exactly what that meant. Jake would leave, whether she wanted him to or not, either to avoid him or to confront him, and possibly lose his life. Neither option was acceptable.

She stared at Father O'Malley's departing back until the dust of his passage settled back to earth. Unshed tears stung her eyes and she drew in a shuddering breath. She raised her eyes to the heavens. "I will not lose another person I love to a damned gambler."

Jake was seated in one of the patio chairs when she approached him. He tried to look relaxed, as if neither one of them had received devastating news, but it was all an act. She could see how tense he was, his muscles taut, and though he smiled at her, it wasn't the same charming grin she'd come to know.

"You're leaving," she stated without any preamble, though the words had to be forced from her throat. "Whether I want you to or not."

He shook his head as he stood. "No, I'm not, but I will answer King's call when it comes. I won't have a choice. I'd rather meet him somewhere away from here than have him come to the ranch."

Her heart was so heavy in her chest it seemed as if it was hardly beating at all. Her voice came out barely above a whisper. "He'll kill you."

Jake opened his arms.

She stepped into his warm embrace and rested her head against his chest. His heart beat strong, a steady rhythm that was somehow comforting. His voice rumbled from deep in his chest when he finally spoke. "I won't let that happen, Evie." She found solace in his embrace for the moment, but she knew it wouldn't last.

"We'll figure a way out of this, Evie. Teddy's calling a family meeting tonight." He dropped a kiss to the top of her head. "It'll be all right."

Even as he said the words, she knew they were untrue. She lifted her head from his chest and stared deeply into his eyes. He wore that charming smile she fell in love with, but behind it, she clearly saw his worry, like he didn't believe the words he said either. She said nothing, though her heart ached, determined to keep the illusion alive...for a little while at least...and simply held him tighter.

Jake removed the rope from around Midnight's neck and gave the horse an affectionate pat on his rump. The horse wasted no time racing toward the opposite side of the training ring, as far away from Jake as he could get. Teddy had been correct. Midnight had heart, but he also had an abundance of stubbornness and a reluctance to learn. He fought…everything. All he wanted to do was run.

He took off his hat, wiped the sweat from his brow, placed it firmly back on his head, and headed toward the fence where Evie, Teddy, and Antonio watched his training progress…or lack thereof, exhaustion and lack of faith in the job he was trying to do dogging his steps. It didn't help that he could think of nothing but King since Father O'Malley's visit. The threat of him colored everything he did. And maybe that was Midnight's issue. The horse obviously felt the tension within him. It was almost impossible not to.

"If he hates the rope this much, imagine how much he'll hate the reins and the saddle," he announced as he approached them.

"Some horses take longer to train, Jake. You're doing fine." Teddy offered. "He'll be magnificent when his training is done."

"If you say so." He flexed his hand and wiggled the fingers on both hands, trying to get rid of the cramping, then climbed through the railings of the fence. "Cinnamon was much easier."

"That's because she liked you." Evie said, as she laid her hand against his cheek. "Midnight hasn't made up his mind yet."

"Don't let him see how frustrated you're becoming," Antonio said. "That'll make—"

The man's comment was cut off by the sound of thundering hooves as a horse and rider raced into the barnyard. "Who is that? And why is he riding hell-bent for leather?"

"It's Ben." Teddy started away from the fence at a run, followed closely by Antonio.

"What's Ben doing here?" Evie asked aloud, as the horse and rider drew closer, close enough to see the sweat on the horse's flesh…and the terror on Ben's face. "Something's wrong. Something's happened to Lucy." Her face lost all color as they ran forward.

Ben sawed on the reins then jumped from the saddle before the horse even came to a halt. Antonio caught the reins, easing the mare to a stop. Breathless, sweating profusely, Ben had a cut on his lip and his eye was red and swelling, almost completely closed. "Eric King has Lucy!"

Jake knew this day would come—hell, the eventuality had been hanging over him for months, like a hangman's noose hovering over his head—he just never expected King would stoop so low as to involve an innocent like Lucy.

"What happened?" Teddy demanded, his face reddening, anger making his voice tight.

Ben shook his head, his eyes shiny with unshed tears. "King and his men…just barged into the house…as I was leaving to see a patient who couldn't make it to town." He wiped the blood still trickling from his mouth, gasping so hard, he could hardly speak. "I wasn't expecting them. I'm embarrassed to admit it only took one punch to bring me to my knees."

Jake stiffened, guilt for the situation he'd put Lucy in—put them all in— overwhelming him. His heart hammered in his chest as his gaze shot to Evie. She hadn't said a word, but she didn't have to. Fear was there on her pale face. "Did they hurt her?"

"Slapped her once or twice. She fought them like a wildcat though." His voice was tight. "I've never seen her so angry. She throws a mean left hook and got one of King's men in the jaw. Scratched him, too. It didn't stop him from overpowering her."

"How do you know it was King?" Jake asked, though he had no doubt in his mind. Who else would hold Lucy hostage? The Silvas had no enemies. Only he did. And he brought this on them.

"Cocky son of a bitch introduced himself as proud as you please. Said he knew who we were, knew where you were, said he was going to win his money back no matter what it took."

Evie finally spoke though her voice quivered. "And they just let you go?"

"I was to deliver a message." Ben nodded, then directed his statement to Jake. "He said to meet him at the Silver Spur Saloon at noon and he'll let Lucy go."

He didn't have a choice and he knew it. King had made sure of that. He held all the cards.

He reached for Evie's hand, threading her fingers between his. "I'm sorry, Evie."

She glanced at his hand then up at his face, her eyes as dark as storm clouds on the horizon. "You're going to meet him."

"I have to. He won't let Lucy go if I don't."

Her gaze roamed his face as a single tear rolled down her cheek. "He'll kill you."

He gently wiped the wetness away with his thumb.

"King isn't going to kill anyone," Teddy stated. "We'll make sure of it. It'll be just like we planned at our family meeting, only with a few changes, the most important one is that we save Lucy first." He turned toward Antonio. "Ride out to the summer pasture for Heath and Esteban. Tell them what happened and get back here as quickly as you can. We're heading into town."

Evie peeked inside through the kitchen window of Lucy's house, her heart in her throat, hoping that King's men hadn't moved her to another location after they sent Ben to the ranch with King's message. Conflicted and nervous, part of her wanted to save Lucy, the other wanted to be with Jake, though she was supposed to be comforted knowing Esteban would make sure no harm would come to him. Still, all that did was make her worry about the both of them. She had lost too many people she loved to men like King and his thugs. It didn't ease her terror.

Perspiration from the ride into town made her skin clammy but it was fear that made her hands shake and bile rise to her throat.

The plan, quickly revised from the original, was to ride into town and split into groups. Evie, Uncle Charley, Heath, Ben, and Teddy would free Lucy while Jake and Esteban met with King, and Antonio went to report the situation to the Marshal.

It hadn't been a plan she liked—none of them did—but it would have to work. If nothing else, they had the element of surprise, though she was certain King's men were alert to the possibility someone would try to rescue Lucy. Her hope was they could get her out of the house before King's men even knew she was gone, then let the Marshal and his deputies take the men into custody.

That's what she wanted to happen. Whether it did or not remained to be seen, but there was one thing she knew for certain—she wasn't about to lose either Lucy or Jake without a fight.

"Do you see her?" Uncle Charley whispered as he crept up beside her, startling her. Before she could respond or stop the thunderous pounding of her heart, her attention was drawn to Heath and Ben climbing the stairs to the second-floor veranda, their footsteps barely making any sound on the wooden risers. Teddy was at the front of the house, also looking in windows, trying to locate where King's men were keeping Lucy. She hoped Antonio, as well as the Marshal and his deputies, were on their way.

"No, she must be somewhere else," she whispered finally. But where? In the parlor? One of the upstairs bedrooms? The dining room? It was a big house, with part of the first floor set aside for Ben's office, the room where he saw his patients, and a small sitting room where other patients waited for their turn to see him.

Lucy could be anywhere.

Evie moved from the window to the back door, Charley following closely. She had no gun, no knife, nothing to protect herself with except her wits. She heard footsteps above and hoped that it was Heath and Ben letting themselves into the house and not one of King's men coming out to the veranda to look around. She listened closely, but heard nothing else...no screams of surprise, no thumps and thuds of a scuffle. "Are you ready?"

Uncle Charley gave a slight nod as she reached for the doorknob, twisted it slowly and eased the door open, thankful the hinges didn't squeal. She took several steps into the kitchen and froze, her heart nearly stopping as conversation drew her attention from the dining room just beyond. She clearly heard Lucy's voice and that of a man, but there was no yelling, no threats being issued. Surprisingly, they were discussing—of all things—photography.

Smart girl. Only Lucy could draw someone, even her abductor, into a polite conversation about her favorite hobby.

She advanced into the hallway, keeping her back against the wall. The staircase leading to the second floor was on her right and she glanced up, almost expecting someone to be standing there, keeping watch. Her heart in her throat, she crept further along the wall.

The pocket doors to the dining room were wide open. She peeked around the corner and caught sight of Lucy tied to one of cushioned chairs at the dining table. Her hands were tied as well, but they were in front of her so she could sip at the cup of coffee placed before her. She didn't appear hurt, other than a reddened spot on her cheek that resembled a handprint. There was a man in the room with her—big, broad of shoulder, well-dressed, his dark hair curling at the nape of his neck, but his back was to the doorway. He held up one of Lucy's cameras, turning it this way and that, inspecting it, clearly curious, before placing it on the table.

Catching Lucy's attention, she held her finger to her lips, warning her to be quiet then mouthed, *How many?*

Lucy, her eyes wide, tapped her finger against the teacup clutched in her hands once, then raised her gaze toward the ceiling.

"Are the ropes too tight?" the man asked suddenly, his voice seemingly full of regret. Perhaps, he didn't want to be holding Lucy hostage. Perhaps, he could be reasoned with. Hope flared in her heart.

"A little. I have pins and needles in my hands."

"If I loosen the ropes, will you promise not to try anything?"

Lucy's mouth spread into a charming smile, one meant to disarm. She nodded, her glance taking on that innocent gleam Evie knew so well. "I promise. I could even show you how to take photographs if you free me."

Uncle Charley nudged her shoulder. She turned her head around to see Charley point toward Teddy coming out of the little room where Ben saw his patients, his guns drawn. He wasn't a crack shot like Esteban, but he was good enough. She waved a little, drawing his attention, then pointed into the dining room and held up two fingers. *Lucy*, she mouthed, *one other*. She raised her gaze toward the ceiling as Lucy had done and raised a finger, letting him know there was one more person upstairs, though she had no doubt Heath and Ben had or would take care of him. There was no noise from the upper floor, not even footsteps.

Teddy moved toward her on feet as silent as a puma, anger tightening his lips. He entered the dining room just as Lucy's captor rose to his feet and moved toward her, Evie hoped with the intention of removing the ropes around her hands.

"I wouldn't move if I were you," Teddy warned as he pressed the bore of the gun into the man's back, the fabric of his suit jacket puckering against the metal.

"Shit!" the man exclaimed but didn't move. "Don't shoot me. I didn't hurt her."

"Then who put that red mark on her cheek? Looks like somebody slapped her." Teddy asked in response to his statement, his tone deep and angry.

The man shook his head. "That was Ballard, not me. I'd never hurt a woman."

"Are you all right?" Evie rushed into the room and quickly untied Lucy's hands and removed the rope holding her to the chair. She drew her niece into her arms and held her tight, the relief rushing through her making her knees weak and her throat constrict with gratitude.

Lucy nodded as she withdrew from the hug and rubbed at her wrists. "I'm fine. Angry, but fine. I knew you'd come." She paused for a moment to gain her balance, then bombarded them with questions. "How's Ben? Is he all right? What's happening with Jake? Did he win?"

"Ben is fine. He's upstairs with Heath," she said, as she tossed the ropes to Charley and nodded toward the man Teddy held at gunpoint. "Tie him up."

Lucy approached her jailer and, incredibly, smiled at him as

Charley tied his hands behind his back. "You know, Harris, I think you're in the wrong business. You seem to be a nice man, despite holding me against my will. At least you were kind, unlike your partner." She smoothed her fingers against her cheek, the one that still held the imprint of a hand. "My advice? Get as far away from Erik King as you possibly can. He'll lead you to nothing but trouble."

"Yes, ma'am." Harris had the good graces to hang his head in shame. "I am sorry, Miss Lucy."

A startled shout came from upstairs then utter silence, causing all of them to look up toward the ceiling, each one of them holding their breaths, waiting, wondering who had yelled. Lucy grabbed her hand, squeezing it tight. She didn't say a word, but she didn't need to—fear drained the color from her face, leaving the handprint on her cheek to stand out in stark relief. "Ben," she whispered, and rushed into the hallway, pulling Evie along with her. Charley followed, as did Teddy and the man Lucy had called Harris.

A few minutes later, though it seemed like an eternity, Ben and Heath led the other man downstairs, his hands held straight up, the risers creaking under the weight of the three of them. There were scratches on the man's face, four of them, like someone had raked their fingernails against the skin. They no longer oozed, but still looked raw and painful. Below the scratches, a bruise was starting to form.

Evie turned toward Lucy. Pride made tears spring to her eyes, knowing her niece had defended herself, proving she was no helpless miss. She'd learned well, growing up with three brothers.

Lucy grabbed the second rope from Charley's hand and moved toward the man. She handed the rope to Ben as soon as the trio left the staircase. "Tie him up. Let's see how he likes it."

Ben made quick work of tying the man's hands behind his back, as Heath holstered his gun. Lucy stared at the man, her anger seeming to stifle the air around them. "I told you your plan wouldn't work. I warned you what would happen." Then, without another word, she slapped the man across the face, the sound like a crack of thunder as hand connected with flesh. The man staggered from the force of the blow and growled low in his throat but didn't say a word.

Evie watched the tableau before her still watering eyes, surprised their haphazard plan had worked so well. On the heels of that thought, she yelled, "Jake!"

"Go!" Teddy told her. "We'll meet you at the saloon. Don't go in. Don't distract him in any way."

"I'll go with you, *Tia* Evie." Heath offered, as he patted the gun in its holster.

Teddy nodded. "That's a better idea."

Evie didn't wait for Heath, she simply strode toward the front door, her heart hammering in her chest, and flung it open. Antonio, the Marshal, and his deputies stood on the front porch, ready, it seemed to enter the house. She jerked her thumb toward the interior of the house then took off at a run, praying Jake was still alive.

Jake pushed open the batwing doors just as the clock at the Town Hall struck noon, and entered the Silver Spur Saloon. Every muscle in his body thrummed with anxiety. He glanced around, the hair on the back on his neck standing up straight. Aside from King, who sat at one of the felt-covered tables in the middle of the room, a bottle of whiskey and two shot glasses in front of him, the place was empty. Not even the bartender was in sight, but that didn't mean one of King's henchmen wasn't waiting in the shadows. King never went anywhere without his 'protection.'

Dread made his stomach twist, and he tightened the grip on the valise he carried as he took another step into the room, allowing the doors to swing closed behind him. "King."

The man had changed since the last time Jake saw him—older, grayer, thinner. The only thing that hadn't changed was the look in his eyes and the arrogant expression on his face. He shuffled the cards in his hand one more time, then laid them on the table, but his intense stare was on Jake. "Did you really think I would let you walk away without giving me the chance to win my money back?" He gestured to the valise. "Is that my money?"

"Every last cent."

"You ready to lose it?" His chilling smile widened just a bit.

Jake didn't answer the question but advanced into the room and dropped the valise on the table. He saw movement to his left and his suspicion was confirmed. King wasn't alone, but it wasn't one of his henchmen moving out of the shadows. It was Oscar, wearing that same arrogant smirk he always did. Jake stiffened, every muscle in his body taut, and he clenched his hands into fists, wanting to wipe the sneer from his face.

"Surprised to see me, *bastardo?*" Oscar gloated as he approached the table, then stopped to King's right. His chest puffed out, as if proud of himself.

Jake said nothing. His jaw clenched tight though he tried not to let Oscar—or King—see how rattled the man's presence made him. It didn't stop the questions from colliding in his head though, questions he barely had time to answer. Had they known each other before, or had they just met and decided to both exact revenge at the same time? It didn't matter. The odds of him walking away, win or lose, decreased dramatically. If King didn't kill him, Oscar might.

King laughed without humor, and the chilling smile that intimidated more than one man across the poker table appeared on his face. "I see you already know my associate. Oscar here was instrumental in telling me so many things about your new life."

"I owe you for my broken nose—" Oscar stepped closer, close enough for Jake to smell the pomade he used on his mustache. "And for stealing my woman." His dark eyes seemed to snap with delight at the prospect of revenge for wrongs real or imagined, but his hand trembled as it rested on the handle of the Colt holstered in the gun belt around his waist.

He hadn't known Oscar could shoot. The question remained —would he? He glared at the man and answered his own question. Yes, Oscar would shoot him, without giving it a second thought. He'd probably enjoy it—that is, if Jake gave him the chance. He wouldn't.

Dismissing Oscar, Jake faced King once more, eyeing the man he'd come to loathe.

Movement from the corner of his eye caught his attention. He saw Esteban come in from the back of the saloon and stand silently next to the long mahogany bar, his hands hanging loosely by his sides, his stance relaxed, but his eyes were alert, encompassing the whole room. He, too, wore a gun belt, the leather worn and supple, the pearl handles reflecting the lamplight. Some of Jake's anxiety eased. Esteban would have his back though it surprised him that Esteban even had a gun belt. Surprised him even more to learn the man was a crack shot.

King noticed his entrance as well and leaned back in his chair, eyeing him. "Who's that?"

"A friend."

"Hmmm, I'm surprised you have any friends, Hannigan."

Jake didn't respond to the insult. He pulled out a chair opposite King but didn't sit. "The terms," he stated, his voice surprisingly calm though he felt anything but, "I play this one game, all or nothing, for exactly the amount you lost and I never want to see or hear from you again."

He then focused on Oscar. "As for you—" He didn't finish the sentence, but he didn't have to. The threat was quite clear, and the man backed up a step before he stopped himself. Fear passed over Oscar's face, but it was fleeting, replaced quickly by an expression of derision.

Jake returned his attention to King. "One game and one game only. Win or lose, Lucy goes free."

The gambler committed to nothing. Jake didn't think he would, given the man's outsized ego. But the game hadn't been played, and he still had a card or two up his sleeve. If he remembered correctly, King wasn't given to physical pursuits—he preferred to let others do his dirty work. Jake could take him out with one well-placed punch to the face. Oscar, too, if need be. He just had to be patient, though he didn't feel as if he had an ounce of patience in him.

"Sit. Deal the cards."

"Not until you agree."

King's dark eyes swept over him as he reached into the pocket of his suit jacket.

Jake stiffened, ready to defend himself if King was reaching for the little derringer he carried. He let out his breath in a rush when he saw it wasn't a pistol, but a cigar.

King took his time lighting it. A stall tactic? Or one meant to ratchet up the tension? Definitely the latter, just one more trick in King's arsenal of intimidation.

"Fine. One game and Lucy goes free," he said finally, and gestured to the chair with the cigar. "Now sit. Cut the cards." He drew in on the cigar and blew out a stream of smoke. "You better not lose on purpose, Hannigan."

Jake said nothing as he slid into his seat and reached for the deck of cards on the table. He cut them like he was told then pushed the deck toward King. "You deal."

King shuffled the cards one more time then quickly dealt them, a smug smile parting his lips around the cigar.

Jake picked up the cards one at a time and stifled the groan building in his throat. Perspiration made his shirt stick to his back, and he felt the tickle of sweat as it rolled down his face. At any other time, he would have rejoiced at the cards in his hand, but not now. What were the odds that he would be holding a

Royal Flush again, all hearts, the same hand as he had when he won from King the first time? It defied logic and surely meant his death. King wouldn't hesitate to claim he cheated. Hell, King wouldn't hesitate to kill him, and if he didn't, Oscar might.

He glanced across the table and studied King's face, which seemed a little red as he looked at the cards in his hand. If his expression was any indication, he wasn't happy with what he held. He moved the cigar from one side of his mouth to the other and stared at Jake with an intensity worthy of Teddy. "Place your bet."

Jake pushed the valise toward the middle of the table. "All or nothing."

King shook his head. "That's not how it's done, Hannigan."

"It is this time. You agreed. One game and Lucy goes free."

The man took a deep drag on his cigar, then blew out a plume of smoke. He wasn't happy, but that was all right. Jake wasn't here to make him happy. He was here to free Lucy and get out of this alive.

"Show me your cards," King ordered after a moment.

Jake held the cards to his chest then slowly laid the cards on the table and spread them out. The Queen of Hearts seemed to stare right at him.

"You son of a bitch!" King spit out as he looked at the cards, the cigar falling from his mouth to land on the table. If possible, his face turned even redder and his eyes opened wider. "How the hell did you do that?" He jumped up from his seat and reached into his suit jacket pocket, withdrawing the little derringer he always carried. "You...you cheated," he stammered. "There's no way in hell you could have won again with the same damned hand!"

There were two guns pointed at him now—King's little derringer and Oscar's Colt.

"Stand up!" King ordered. "I warned you against cheating."

Jake rose from his seat slowly, his hands hanging down by his side, eyeing his opponent and the gun in his hand. He'd get out of this situation. He had to. For Evie. And the future he wanted. *That* was worth fighting for. *She* was worth fighting for.

His mind worked quickly, planning his strategy, waiting for the opportunity to disarm King. All it would take is one well-aimed punch. Just one and he could walk away.

Or should he take down Oscar first? The man was sweating, his dark eyes darting back and forth, the hand holding the gun shaking. "How could I cheat? *You* dealt the cards."

"No one beats Erik King like that. No one!" Spittle sprayed from King's lips and the little gun in his hand wavered as he gestured.

Jake stood absolutely still, though it took every ounce of his determination. One false move and King could shoot before he had a chance to knock the man on his ass.

"Who are you anyway? A nobody!" Beads of sweat rolled down King's face and his eyes narrowed. "A fucking orphan! No one will miss you when you're gone." He gasped for air and seemed to struggle doing so.

Maybe King would give himself a heart attack. He certainly appeared to be working up toward one.

"No one will care whether you live or die!" The derringer shook in the man's hand as it wavered toward him once again. "I am Erik King!" he all but screamed, then got control of his weapon and pointed it straight at Jake's. "No one does this to Erik King and lives to tell the tale! No one!"

The loud report of the gunshot followed closely by another echoed in the room, making Jake jump. He felt no pain, which was odd. He glanced down at his chest, but no blood blossomed on his shirt. Stunned and confused, he looked up. Neither King nor Oscar were standing. Both were sprawled on the floor. King had a perfect round hole in his forehead and the blood Jake had expected to flow from his own chest flowed from Oscar's instead.

He turned quickly as Esteban joined him, smoke still coming from the barrels of the guns in his hands.

"What did you do?"

Esteban shrugged as he holstered his guns. "He talked too much. I had enough." He inspected his handiwork. "I don't enjoy killing, Jake. It's not something I go out of my way to do, but in this case, they both had it coming. Besides, King wasn't going to let you walk out of here. Saw that much for myself. Neither was Oscar. One of these days, you'll have to tell me what happened between you and him."

Stunned, not only by the amount of words Esteban issued at one time, but by the fact he killed both King and Oscar, Jake could do nothing but stare at him. Relief rushed through him, so swift, so hard, his knees grew weak. That feeling didn't last long. "We need to get Lucy...."

"Lucy is fine." Esteban gestured toward the batwing doors.

A crowd of people stood in the entrance to the saloon, holding the doors open. No, not a crowd. *His family*. Lucy, flanked by her brothers, her hand in Ben's, stood in the doorway. She didn't look worse for wear. Yes, tears had stained her cheeks, and she had an ugly mark on her face, but she was alive and well, and apparently very angry. Gratitude that she had been found, unharmed, constricted his throat as his gaze drifted to Teddy, who gave him a slight nod, then to Heath, who flashed a triumphant grin. Antonio looked satisfied, his arm around Charley. The Marshal was there as well, the shiny star pinned to his vest winking in the sunlight. He didn't see King's henchmen. He assumed they were in jail, exactly where they belonged.

His gaze scanned the crowd, looking for Evie. And then he saw her as she moved into his sight. His Evie. There were tears on her face too, but her smile was warm and encouraging. And appeared to be only for him. Love swelled his heart, making it beat a little faster. He started walking toward her, toward his future.

"Don't forget your money," Esteban said, as he jerked his thumb to the valise on the table.

Jake backed up a step, grabbed the valise by the handles, and headed toward the door once more. As soon as he stepped through, he dropped the valise on the wooden sidewalk and pulled Evie into his arms. "It's over," he murmured, still astonished that he hadn't died facing King.

Evie gazed into his face, her eyes seeming to drink in the sight of him as her hands splayed across his chest. "Are you all right?"

"I am now." He dropped a kiss to her lips, regardless of everyone watching, then blurted out, "Marry me." There were audible gasps from those around them, but he ignored the sound, his focus solely on Evie. A myriad of emotions played across her beautiful face, surprise being the most noticeable.

"Yes, I'll marry you." Tears sprang to her eyes and her smile widened.

True happiness surged through him, truer than anything he'd ever felt before, and love? That was there as well, filling his heart, making it pound harder in his chest. "When?"

She laughed as her arms tightened around him. "I don't know. Planning a wedding takes time, Jake."

His gaze settled on her as his hand gently caressed her cheek, then cupped her chin. "Now."

Evie's eyes widened. "Right now?"

"Yes, why not?" He smiled. "I don't want to waste another minute. I want everyone to know how much I love you."

She laughed in that deep way she had, and it reverberated in his heart. He wanted to hear that sound for the rest of his life. "Everyone already knows, Jake."

"Good, so you'll marry me right here, right now. We're all here. I can't think of a better time."

She shook her head, instantly sobering. "But we're not all here. Hilde, Felicity, and Marisol would be very angry with me if they weren't involved in the planning. They've been waiting for this day as long as I have." Her smile was full of promise, her eyes begging him to understand, and his heart melted. He could deny her nothing. "And I couldn't imagine getting married without the boys' wives. Or the children." She caressed his cheek, her hand warm on his skin. "Don't you want Father O'Malley there as well?"

"I do." Jake agreed, then dropped another kiss to her lips as he tightened his arms around her, determined never to let go, not today, not tomorrow, not ever. "You tell me when."

"Two weeks?"

"I can live with that." He smiled as he as he took a step away from Evie, though he didn't let go of her hand, then looked at those around him, so grateful he had responded to Lucy's advertisement in the first place. "We're getting married."

Lucy let out an excited squeal then grabbed Evie in a bone-crushing hug, while Charley was the first to extend his hand to him, followed by Heath. "Congratulations, Jake."

"If you ever make her unhappy," Esteban warned as he patted the handles of the guns in their holsters, "You know I know how to use these."

Despite the implied threat, Jake didn't take offense, though he was surprised it was Esteban who issued the warning and not Teddy. "I won't make her unhappy. You have my word."

"That goes for me as well, Jake." Teddy said, as he grabbed his hand and shook. "I may not shoot you, but I can certainly knock you on your ass."

Jake wasn't too sure about that, but there would never be a need to find out, so he just laughed.

Antonio was the last, clasping his hand in a tight grip. "Welcome to the family, son." He grinned, his bushy mustache lifting. "Are you sure you want this?" He gestured to everyone gathered around them, all talking at once, giving and receiving hugs and heartfelt tidings of good wishes. "We all come with her."

"I've always wanted to be part of a family." His throat constricted with emotion. "This one will definitely do."

EPILOGUE

Jake stood in front of the rose arbor, the white banner threaded through the slats fluttering in the breeze, the smell of roses permeating the air. He looked out at the guests assembled in front of him and felt a surge of love so profound, it made his heart skip a beat. It was a small group, mostly Evie's family, soon to be his family, too. A few friends, again, all Evie's, though they had accepted him into their fold. He was both honored and humbled for that privilege. His fellow bunkmates were there as well, men he'd come to admire and formed a kinship with in the past few months.

Father O'Malley stood beneath the framework of intertwined roses, the well-worn Bible Jake remembered from long ago open in his hand. He smiled briefly before he turned serious.

Dressed in his best suit, a blood-red rose pinned to his lapel, Teddy beamed in his position of best man. Who would have thought the person who objected the most to him courting Evie would become his staunchest ally?

Teddy cleared his throat. "Are you ready?"

Jake's heart thumped steadily in his chest, filled beyond

comprehension with indescribable joy, something he never thought he'd have. "More than you'll ever know."

He stopped speaking as the first strains of a violin filled the air. A silence descended over the crowd as the guests rose and turned toward the back of the house. The door opened and Savannah stepped through, dressed in pale yellow, carrying a basket full of yellow roses. It was obvious she took this honor to heart as her expression ran the gamut from somber to animated within seconds.

Lucy followed, also in yellow, though the bouquet in her hands contained roses of white, pink, and coral, all gathered from the bushes around the garden. A few moments later, Evie appeared in the doorway, Antonio and Charley beside her, linking their arms through hers.

Jake held his breath as she slowly walked toward him, the small bouquet of ivory roses in her hand matching her dress. She was a vision of beauty, an angel on earth who helped him see what he could be.

Pride made his chest swell, and love filled his heart to bursting that this strong, intelligent, compassionate woman would be his. Antonio kissed her cheek when they brought her to a stop in front of him. Charley did the same then placed her hand into his. Evie squeezed his fingers as she gazed into his eyes. Her thick, dark lashes were spiky with wetness, but the confident smile on her face and the warm glow in her gray-blue eyes let him know she'd shed happy tears.

"Dearly beloved," Father O'Malley began, his accent seeming to be more pronounced.

It was over in moments, the words the good Father intoned striking deep within his heart, a commitment he would spend the rest of his life trying to uphold.

"You may kiss the bride."

Jake didn't move, too caught up in drinking in Evie's beauty, seeing the love she had for him shining so clearly in her eyes.

"Kiss the bride, *boyo*," the priest repeated, his voice laced with humor as he nudged him a bit.

Startled, Jake laughed then lowered his head, and brushed his lips against hers, the taste of her mouth sweet with the promise of forever. "I love you, Mrs. Hannigan," he murmured, his voice tight with all the emotion of this moment.

"I love you, too, Mr. Hannigan." She sighed as she repeated her new name. "Mrs. Hannigan." She smiled up at him, despite the tears spiking her lashes. "I like the sound of that, though it might take me a little time to get used to it."

"Take all the time you need." He reached out and wiped the wetness from her cheek with his thumb, reveling in the softness of her skin. "We have the rest of our lives."

"Yes, we do." She gazed at him, her eyes so warm, her smile so beautiful, it made his heart beat faster.

He laughed, unable to help himself, as they stepped away from the rose arbor. He escorted Evie down the aisle between the rows of chairs, nodding to those who had witnessed their vows, shaking the hands of those who extended them, while Evie accepted warm hugs and kisses to her cheeks even as lively music began to play, and the guests meandered toward the makeshift dance floor. "Dance with me."

Her eyes opened wide in surprise as a blush blossomed on her cheeks. "We've never danced before. I didn't think you knew how."

"Of course I do." He grinned, so damned happy he could hardly believe it. This couldn't be happening, could it? Was it a dream? An elaborate fantasy? If so, he hoped no one would pinch him and wake him from it. "Let me show you." He took her hand and led her to the dance floor, then pulled her close, his heart thumping hard in his chest.

They'd barely made a full rotation around the dance floor when Jake felt a tap on his back.

"May I cut in?" He turned, Evie in his arms, to see Teddy.

"Of course." Though reluctant, he relinquished Evie into her nephew's arms and left the dance area, though he didn't go far, just to the end of the first table that surrounded the space. His gaze followed her every graceful step as she went from each one of her nephews to Charley then finally to Antonio. Her face glowed, her smile wide with all the love she had, and it struck him, like a mule's kick to the chest.

How did I get so lucky?

He felt a presence beside him and glanced to his left. He didn't recognize the man. He wasn't one of Evie's friends or an acquaintance of the family. "Hello. May I help you?"

"Forgive the intrusion. I seem to have come at the most inopportune time, but I'm looking for Miss Everleigh Miller."

Jake pointed to his wife, swirling around the dance floor, once more in Teddy's arms, her laughter filling his heart. "That's her." He tore his gaze away from Evie and glanced at the man, whose focus was on Evie. "Seeing that she's a little busy at the moment, is there something I can help you with? Are you interested in one of the horses for sale?"

The stranger didn't answer the question, simply stared at Evie, his expression holding not only disappointment, but embarrassment as well. A flush colored his cheeks when he turned toward Jake. "Again, I ask for your apologies, but I seemed to have intruded upon a wedding."

"You have."

His gaze settled on Evie. "And is she the bride?"

Jake smiled, his heart bursting with pride. "She is."

"I see." The man gave a small sigh as regret filled his pale green eyes. "I'm Henri Robicheaux. I received a letter from Miss Miller, asking to meet, but I see I am too late."

"Ah, I understand."

"I should have…never mind. I've never been a man who lived with regret." Henri let out another sigh as his gaze shifted back to the dance floor. "Who's the lucky man?"

Jake's smile widened. "That would be me."

Once more, Henri ripped his focus away from Evie and settled it on Jake. "Well then, I won't interrupt. I wish you both well."

"No, please stay and enjoy the party. Help yourself to a cup of coffee and piece of cake." He leaned forward a little, lowered his voice and gestured to Marisol's oldest daughter, who'd been widowed a little more than a year ago, sitting alone at one of the tables, her head bobbing to the music. He'd been told she had recently enlisted Lucy's help in finding a husband. "If you're looking for a wife, I'm told Aricely over there might be agreeable to getting to know you. If you'd like, I could introduce you. At the very least you could ask her to dance. I'm sure she would enjoy that."

The man brightened, the flush disappearing from his cheeks. "I think I will. Ask her to dance that is. Thank you."

"Not at all." Jake grinned, wondering if his future included matchmaking, as Henri moved toward the table where Aricely sat.

After a moment, he strode toward the makeshift dance floor and tapped Heath on the shoulder. "May I cut in?"

Heath relinquished his hold on Evie and took a step back. "Of course."

Jake took her hand and smiled, then whirled her around. "Hello again, Mrs. Hannigan."

"Hello, Mr. Hannigan." Evie laughed, her eyes glowing before they turned serious. "Who were you talking to?"

"Oh, just another one of your mail-order husbands."

"Really?" Color blossomed on her cheeks.

Jake nodded.

"Did you tell him he was too late?"

"I did. I also told him how lucky I am."

"Lucky?"

"Yes, ma'am." He kissed her lightly on the lips, then smiled as he whirled her faster. "So incredibly lucky to have found such an enchanting woman with such a beautiful heart." He glanced toward the horizon and caught the sun beginning to set in the distance. Already, the sky was turning pale pink with just a hint of magenta.

"You know what I want to do right now?"

Evie wiggled her eyebrows at him, mischief dancing in the bright glow of her eyes. "I think I know."

Jake burst out laughing. She'd never ever done that before and he loved it. "Yes, that, too." He drew her closer, so close he could feel her heart beating in rhythm with his. "But right now, I want to sit on the porch with you, hold your hand, and watch the sky turn colors as the sun sets. That's what I want—today, tomorrow, and every day after that." He smiled down at her, anticipation coursing through his veins. "What do you say?"

Tears of happiness shimmered in her eyes. "I say yes."

The Beginning

ACKNOWLEDGMENTS

While writing is a solitary pursuit, no writer truly does it alone so….

To Lexi Post, for always holding my feet to the fire;

To Jan Walkosz and Paige Wood, the very best beta readers a writer could ever have;

To my son and his wife, who continually show me what love is all about;

To my editor, Jill, who showed me so many things I didn't know I didn't know;

And finally, to my husband, who has supported this passion of mine from the beginning. Forty-three years and still going strong!

Thank you all!

ABOUT THE AUTHOR

Marie Patrick has always had a love affair with words and books but it wasn't until a trip to Arizona, where she now makes her home with her husband, that she became inspired to write about the sometimes desolate, yet beautiful west. Her inspiration doesn't just come from the Wild West though. It comes from history itself. She is fascinated with pirates and men in uniform and lawmen with shiny badges. When not writing or researching her favorite topics, she can usually be found curled up with a good book. Marie loves to hear from her readers. Drop her a note at Akamariep@aol.com or visit her website at www.mariepatrick.com.

www.ingramcontent.com/pod-product-compliance
Lightning Source LLC
Chambersburg PA
CBHW050529110726
47899CB00005B/1646